THE SKYDUST DUKE

SKYDUST KINGDOMS #1

TL SHREFFLER

Cover, editing and interior design created by the professional team at *The Runaway Pen.* For rights inquiries, contact therunawaypen@gmail.com.

Contents

Dresengard
Bratzia
The Grapevine Mountains
Gravenmere
The Greater Rog Mountains
Windhaven Ranch
The Abyss
Forsynthia
Astravelle
Illysea
Sera'naya

The Agrarian Calendar of Forsynthia

"Each season is touched by Valestra's wand: rain and flower, wind and song."

~Ancient Forsynthian Proverb

Vimspring

Season of Thaw & Renewal

Events: Planting

Brightspell
Days 65-96

Budreach
Days 97-129

Greencall
Days 130-161

Ardoursol

Season of Light & Growth

Events: Midsummer

Sungilt
Days 162-192

Solmere
Days 193-223

Amberfen
Days 224-255

Hallowsin

Season of Mist & Reflection

Events: Harvest

Duskwane
Days 256-287

Fallowmere
Days 288-319

Hearthbrim
Days 320-351

Brumadir

Season of Frost & Prophecy

Events: **New Year

Stargrave
Days 352-384

Frostfall
***Days 1-32*

Thawmere
Days 33-64

384 Days

From the Desk of Old Lord Cornelius Blackwood

A kindly reminder to our new steward from Bratzia, in reference to the names of the Forsynthian seasons. Please mark the day of the agricultural quarter in addition to the solar year on all of your missives.

384 Days in a Year and **96 Days** in an Agricultural Quarter (Season.) A solar year is divided into four seasons.

The Four Seasons

Vimspring - season of thaw and renewal. Planting season. *Months: Brightspell, Budreach, Greencall*

Ardoursol - season of light and growth. Tending the fields. *Months: Sungilt, Solmere, Amberfen*

Hallowsin - season of mist and reflection. Harvest. *Months: Duskwane, Fallowmere, Hearthbrim.*

Brumadir - season of frost and prophecy. The new year begins. *Months: Stargrave, Frostreed, Thawmere*

THE FORSYNTHIAN SEASONS

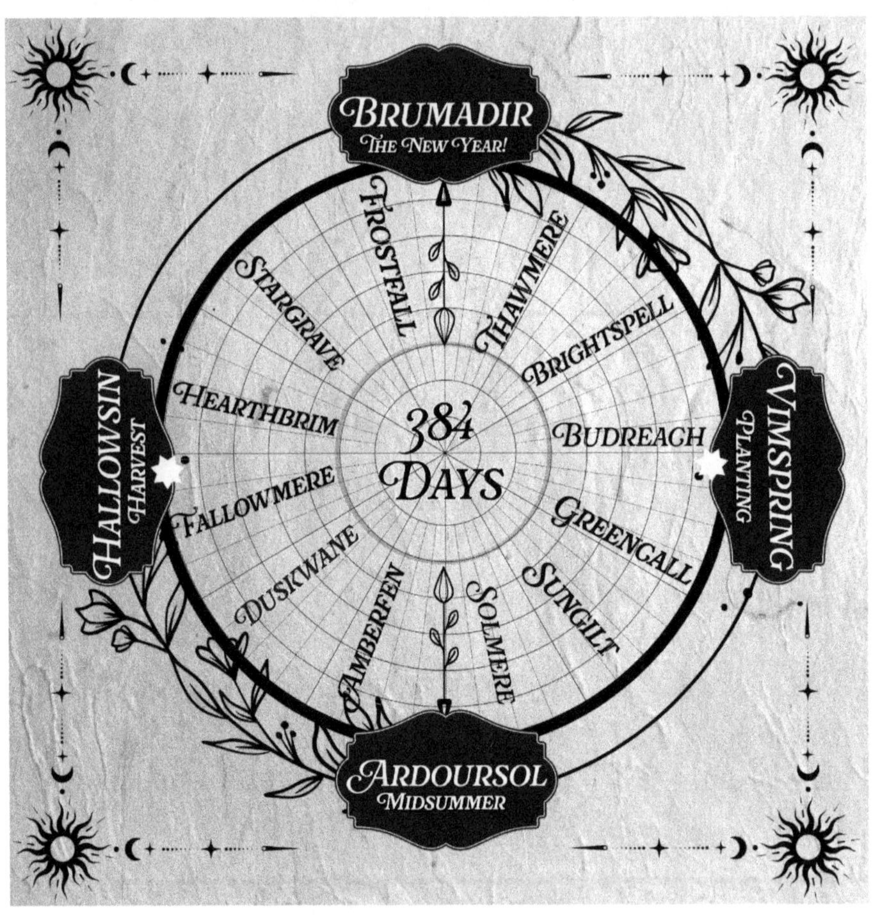

The Origin of the Daemon King

An excerpt from "A Brief History of Nilos" by Forsynthian historian Argile Cartwright.

When the meteor hit the continent of Agea ten thousand years ago, the Kingdom of Forsynthia was in its infancy.

Prior to the meteor's arrival, Nilos was an insignificant blue speck of a planet in the Twin Rings galaxy. Its flora and fauna followed the natural evolution of bacteria into plants and aquatic life, then into warm-blooded mammals, then primates, then mankind. Ten thousand years ago, the meteor entered the atmosphere at terrifying speeds, creating an arc of fire across the sky, visible from pole to pole. Most of the meteor dissolved into rubble and sand. But a large molten chunk landed at the southern tip of the continent, opening an abyss over a hundred miles long. Although never confirmed by living eyes, its depths were rumored to reach the center of the planet.

Fed by Nilos' rich atmosphere and native resources, specks of life lying dormant upon the meteor began their own, mutilated form of evolution. These parasites grew and evolved within the Abyss, undisturbed for thousands of years until, without warning, the Daemon King appeared. A black, abhorrent beast of tremendous size, whether the creature was plant or mammal or insect or "other," remained unknown. Its body a writhing mass of tentacles, with poison-tipped claws and acidic maw, the Daemon King began spawning monsters into the Abyss.

At this time, as though orchestrated by a hand much greater than mere evolution, the Luminous emerged, humans of immense power and talent rising up from among the normal population. Whether gained from meteoric dust or by destiny or fate, the ability to channel a mysterious power called *mana* manifested among certain people of Nilos. Due to their glowing hands while channeling, the term “Luminary” or “Luminous” was adopted, and later, the name “Skytouched” was coined by the common people. The most powerful channelers formed families, then allegiances, establishing the ruling class of the Kingdom of Forsynthia. The same pattern repeated in the neighboring kingdoms of Bratzia, Dresengard, Illysea, and Sera’naya. Day-to-day life changed forever, as generations of Luminous soldiers went into the Abyss to fight off the monsters and preserve Nilos’s blooming civilization.

Technology evolved, moving through the Bronze Age into the Iron Age. Then, with the advent of combustion engines, the world entered into a brand new era of industrial revolution.

Guns were provided to the armies of Forsynthia to fight back the daemonic horde, but bullets proved ineffective against the monsters’ alien powers. The Skytouched remained the most efficient means of combating the creatures. Gunpowder proved only somewhat effective against the Daemon King’s regenerative body. Despite technology’s progress, it seemed only Luminary soldiers were capable of restraining the horrors of the Abyss. And so the Luminous remained the sole protectors of the kingdom. Year after year, special units of Daemonguard were trained by the military to protect the kingdom against the nightmares of the Abyss.

Many exceptional heroes rose up through the ranks of Skytouched to defeat the Daemon King. Over and over, the war was won, and the enemy was declared “dead.” But it seemed that, no matter how many times the Daemon King was killed, the heart of it remained buried somewhere deep within the core of the planet. Like a tenacious weed, the creature would lie dormant for a period of time before spawning again.

Sometimes, the monster's dormancy lasted several generations, allowing the Kingdom of Forsynthia a chance to rebuild and their people to thrive. Sometimes, its dormancy lasted only a decade or so before the creatures of the Abyss surged again.

And so the tides of war and peace, of chaos and security, came and went for the people of Nilos.

Many stories have been written about warfare and battle—fewer have been written about the aftermath. Our tale begins shortly after the Daemon King's defeat, at the end of a grueling ten-year siege in the Abyss, with the Kingdom of Forsynthia returning to a period of uncertain peace on the cusp of industrial revolution.

Chapter 1
The Invitation

CELISE STOOD ON THE front steps of Gravenmere Castle, her calico skirt clutched in hand.

She rested her parasol against her shoulder and stood still for a moment, listening to a bird trill from a drooping cherry tree next to the front drive. Behind the castle stretched the rambling Grapevine Mountains, their purple peaks contrasted by a crystal blue sky. A hedged lawn of sculpted shrubbery, walkable garden rooms, and glowing marble fountains sprawled within the castle's monolithic walls.

She tugged at the high, itchy collar of her dress, borrowed from her younger sister's closet.

I am not good enough to stand here, she thought.

She could leave. She had traveled a full day and night by train to reach the estate of the Blackwood family. A hundred times over, she had thought of changing tickets in Castleberry City. It would make more sense. She could find work and a little room to rent, though she wasn't very good at anything. Still, she could clean, and she knew a lot about horses.

She braced herself and rang the bell that hung beside the front door. The hollow brass sound startled a robin from a nearby tree. She watched the bird fly away.

That should be me, she thought.

Her invitation to the duke's castle was a mistake.

Celise remembered the day she and her sisters were summoned to the Great Hall by her father, Lord Sebastian Dhastel. She was brushing down a horse when the summons came. A serving girl, her hair tied in two buns on either side of her head, popped around the corner of a stall and said, with a touch of concern, "The Master wants you, miss."

"Oh?" Celise murmured, as drowsy in the afternoon heat as the sleepy bay mare she was brushing. "I will come immediately."

The Dhastel estate was an equestrian ranch with a sprawling mansion house, several guest pavilions, and stables to house more than five hundred horses. It was midday, and the estate was bustling with activity. Horse trainers, wranglers and ranch hands ran back and forth, pulling along a plethora of horses on leads. Dhastel stallions and draft horses were in high demand across the Kingdom of Forsynthia. Their family was known for their specialty breeds: lady's walkers, load-bearing draft horses and hearty standardbreds. Ten years ago, her father was commissioned by King Valienthe to breed a special warhorse for the Daemonguard. Dhastel "Hellions" were too temperamental for common jobs, but the fearless beasts were highly prized among soldiers and huntsmen alike.

The county fair was at the end of the month, and the Dhastel family's newest stock always made an appearance.

As Celise followed the maid back to the manor, she passed by the farm manager, Mr. Talisworth, who gave her a slight nod. Mr. Talisworth was a very tall man, with light blond hair and a jutting brow, characteristic of the northern people of Dresengard, the land of his birth. It wasn't common to encounter his people this far south, but Celise had known the horsemaster all her life. Behind Talisworth, a young farrier laden with tools followed at his heels. They headed to a row of tethered horses in need of shoeing.

The manor house was a good hike from the stables, and by the time she reached the back entrance, Celise was sweating in the late summer heat.

Alert yet quiet, Celise took off her boots and exchanged them for slippers to enter the house. Not much to be done about the dust on her tunic shirt or the bits of straw that clung to her pants. She walked into the house with a cold pit in her stomach.

What did her father want?

Probably nothing good.

She went to the Great Hall, a large central room in the Dhastel manor where her father spent his days entertaining guests, or relaxing with his hounds before the hearth. After a riding accident two years ago, during a particularly rainy autumn season, Lord Sebastian Dhastel had lost much of the mobility in his right leg. He walked with a crutch, and his riding days were well over.

The Great Hall was the largest room on the ground floor of the manor, fit for a banquet of a hundred people. The wattle and daub interior was immaculately kept. When Celise was younger, she used to imagine herself walking through the ribcage of a giant horse whenever she entered the room. Thick, black beams of stout oak gave the Great Hall a strong sense of presence and prestige. Between the vertical beams, the whitewashed walls were polished with fine clay and limestone. Wooden studs and rails created a geometric, almost celestial pattern of hexagons and half-stars across the vaulted ceiling. The wood displayed galloping horses, mountains and scrollwork, a treat for the eyes should anyone find themselves gazing upward. The Great Hall was symbolic of the Dhastel family's wealth, and their ties to the kingdom as one of Forsynthia's noble houses.

The Great Hall's floor was covered in a single rug that spanned the entire chamber. Celise tread softly over the blue and tan geometric patterns. The banquet tables were pushed neatly to either side of the room, not currently in use. A half-circle of overstuffed leather couches and armchairs filled the space before the empty hearth.

There, her father sat next to his wife, Lady Marcella Dhastel.

Her father was drinking a mug of beer. The foam stained his beard. His skin was bronze from working outdoors most of his life on the ranch, and his wiry hair was gray with age, but his beard still held a dark brown hue.

"Ah, here at last," Marcella said with a soft sneer.

Celise's two younger stepsisters were present as well. They sat upright on a chaise lounge like two little dolls before their parents.

Heather, the youngest at sixteen years old, had sunny yellow hair and a wide forehead.

Katrina, the older of the two at eighteen, was dressed in her fencing regalia: a white padded jacket, knee-length breeches, calf-high socks and thick leather gloves. Her dark violet eyes flashed to Celise, then away, her chin tilted upward. A servant stood nearby holding her mask and foil. Her long black hair was tied back in a braid, with loose tendrils falling about her face.

Celise paused before her father and bowed low, until her forehead almost touched her knees. Then she quietly moved to an empty chair, where she sat adjacent to her sisters, her eyes lowered. She avoided the sharp gaze of her stepmother.

"Now that we are all here, my daughters, I have important news to share with you. An invitation has arrived in the mail." Lord Sebastian Dhastel's grumbling voice effortlessly carried through the Great Hall.

Celise folded her hands in her lap and kept her eyes focused on the flagstone. Her raspberry-colored locks fell across her face in a wild tangle. She felt numb as Lord Dhastel opened a sealed envelope in his lap. He slid out a square of heavy cardstock and held it up to the afternoon light. Then he read the letter aloud to his daughters in a round, booming voice:

The Duchy of Gravenmere
Blackwood Hall
Year of the Restless Moon
Season of Ardoursol
Month of Amberfen, Day 26

To the Esteemed Lord and Lady Dhastel of Windhaven Estate,

It is with the highest regard that I extend to you and your household a formal invitation to attend a gala hosted at Gravenmere Castle on the evening of the 10th day of Duskwane. The gala is in celebration of the thirty-second birthday of my son and heir, Elias Blackwood, Lord High Commander of Firehelm Fortress and the Duke Apparent of Gravenmere.

It is my sincere hope that you will attend, accompanied by your daughters: the ladies Heather, Katrina and Celise. Their grace and upbringing shall lend great charm to the evening's festivities. Many notable members of the military and court will also be present. We anticipate an evening full of merriment and esteem.

The gala shall include a banquet, formal dancing and a concert by the Plum Dahlia Quartet, an award-winning ensemble out of Castleberry City. At the end of the evening, we ask that all guests plan to stay for a special announcement.

Kindly send word of your acceptance by courier no later than the first of Duskwane, that we may make accommodations for your household.

We wait in anticipation of your reply.

Signed,

Bernard Friza

Penned on behalf of His Grace,

The Duke of Gravenmere
Lord Cornelius Blackwood

Her father finished reading and silence fell upon the hall. Then Katrina and Heather burst out talking.

"A ball at the Blackwood estate?"

"The Blackwoods are very rich, aren't they, father?"

"Did His Grace write the letter personally?"

"What did he mean by 'a special announcement?'"

Lord Dhastel held up a strong hand, silencing his two younger daughters. "Blackwood's clerk wrote it," Dhastel explained with a chuckle. "It's a standard invitation. I expect many noble families received a similar letter. This will be a large event, the largest you've attended yet. I don't know what manner of announcement Old Blackwood refers to. I suppose that's what makes it 'special.'"

"I have my thoughts on that," Marcella said. She plucked the letter out of her husband's hand and scanned over it, her lips pursed. The lady's black hair was braided on top of her head, held in place with two gold hairpins. Her skin was white as cream, just like her two daughters. Marcella was many years younger than her husband, and it showed. "He names our daughters specifically. It's been two years since the war ended. I think Blackwood is looking for a match for his eldest son."

Katrina wrinkled her nose. "The Mad Dog duke? But he's already been engaged *seven* times!"

"Hush, Katrina," Marcella snapped. "Can you imagine what life would be like as a duchess? Either of you girls would be lucky to wed a Blackwood. *A duke is still a duke.*"

The room fell silent as Marcella read over the invitation, her brow arched and a scheming glint in her eye.

"Why do they call him the Mad Dog?" Heather chanced a question.

"Because he's utterly *mental*," Katrina giggled.

Marcella hushed her daughters with a firm stare, then went back to inspecting the letter, as though it held some sort of secret code.

Celise cleared her throat. "Am I to attend the ball as well?"

"Don't get ahead of yourself, girl," Marcella snarled before Lord Dhastel could reply. "By some wretched twist of fate, it appears Blackwood's steward dug up your name from the Dhastel family's records. It's a fluke. *Of course* the invitation isn't *meant* for you."

"Now now, Marcella, this is a happy occasion," Lord Dhastel murmured with a gentle frown. "Let us not risk offending His Grace. Celise was named in the letter, so she should attend the ball. Just . . ." he waved his hand in the air. "Make sure she has something appropriate to wear."

"Something not stained with horse drool," Heather whispered to Katrina, and the two girls sniggered.

Marcella looked furious at her husband's request. A tantrum flitted across her face like a silent black cloud. Then she composed herself. She sat back in her chair and regarded Celise with a scrutinizing eye. A smirk perched upon her pointed, hawklike face.

"I suppose we can dig up a dress from last season's closet. You may attend, Celise, if only to hold Katrina's drink while she dances with the duke."

"Yes, my lady," Celise murmured, feeling numb.

Her stepmother continued, "Be grateful, child. You'll be in the company of war heroes and the Forsynthian elite. This party is far above the grasp of an ignorant, *dimlit* girl like yourself."

Lord Dhastel didn't seem bothered by his wife's snide remarks. He reached down to scratch his favorite wolfhound behind the ears. The dog sighed and leaned against his leg. Celise watched through a tangle of raspberry hair.

Her father continued in his stately manner, "I shall post our reply today. It's been some time since I visited the Blackwood estate. This is a good business opportunity. Old Blackwood has ties to the military. He might be interested in our latest stock of Hellions. I'll have to bring a catalogue. This last generation has a more natural amble—much easier to ride."

"You always think of your horses first," Marcella said with a coy smile. "I will ask after Blackwood's wife, Estoria, and the reason behind this ball. I want to know what Her Grace plans for her eldest son. If this is about finding a bride, we must be prepared. I wonder if Lady Verabon has any tidbits to share—she and Her Grace are close." She placed an elegant hand against her chin in thought. "Our book club meets tomorrow. I'm sure the ball will be *a popular* topic of conversation." Then, with a rustle of skirts, Marcella leaned forward and smiled at Heather and Katrina. "Now, girls, the most exciting part—it's time to order new dresses!"

Katrina squealed, while Heather clapped her hands.

Lord Dhastel winced. A bit gruff, he said, "Within reason, my dear."

"For this event, we must spare no expense, *my love,*" Marcella gushed, as though her husband were a naive lad. "Our daughters *must* be dressed in the latest fashion! It will make all the difference. If Katrina is to become a duchess, she must look the part. I wonder if the duchess Estoria has a favorite color. I would guess *emerald green,* but that's the Blackwood's house color and a bit too on the nose. Come, girls, let's retire to the sitting room, and we'll review my latest copy of *The Modern Lady's Wishlist.*"

Katrina and Heather leapt to their feet, bowed to their father, then skipped from the room hand-in-hand, chatting excitedly all the way. Celise thought they looked like a pair of prancing show ponies, ready for their big debut at the circus.

A bit slower and much quieter, she rose to her feet and began to follow her stepsisters out of the Great Hall. She kept her shoulders hunched. She hoped, if she left quickly enough, her stepmother would forget about her. But Marcella wasn't finished.

With a drawling tone, the lady called, "Don't wander off, Celise. I will send the maids to your quarters this evening to take your measurements. A few of Katrina's dresses from last season should suit you. But first, immediately, I insist you take a bath. If we use enough soap, we should get the horse smell off of you."

Celise stumbled, turned and bowed to her stepmother, then to her father, even though he wasn't looking at her. Then she left the Great Hall.

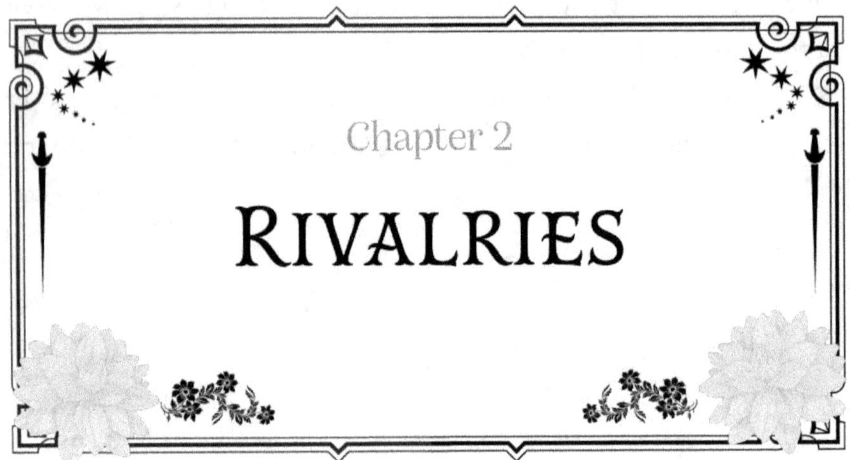

Chapter 2

RIVALRIES

THE SOLID OAK DOORS of the Great Hall shut with a resounding *boom!*

Celise likened it to the closing of a coffin lid.

She pressed a hand over the hard knot in her stomach. Standing in the empty corridor beyond the Great Hall, she gazed sightlessly at the floral wallpaper. She felt utterly blindsided.

Attend a gala? she thought. *Has my lord father lost his mind?*

Celise didn't consider herself truly part of the Dhastel family. She didn't often think about her noble blood. She lived in a room meant for a farmhand above the stables, and indeed, she felt more like a hired hand than a nobleman's daughter.

The Blackwoods, on the other hand, were the *elite*. She was unfit to stand in the presence of such a high-status family. She had no interest in dancing with the young duke or finding a husband of any kind. She was happily committed to her life as a spinster, and she expected to die an old maid.

This is a mistake, she thought again.

"Hello *Sluggy*," a voice interrupted her thoughts.

Celise whirled around. Katrina emerged from the shadows next to the staircase. She carried her fencing foil in one hand and her leather gloves tucked under one arm. The buttons of her white jacket were popped open around her neck, revealing a cotton undershirt and a glimpse of her graceful collarbone.

Katrina had obviously been waiting to catch Celise in the hallway before she could escape the house. A gleeful, malicious look sparkled in Katrina's eyes. Naturally a dark violet color, they glowed with a luminous light. *Mana.*

Celise shuddered—she felt a terrible sense of foreboding.

"It's a shame you were accidentally named on the invitation. You're going to cause Mother so much needless worry," Katrina sneered. "If you must attend, I promise I'll select my very best dresses for you. *Only* my favorites."

Celise felt a burning sensation deep in her gut—a distant flare of anger. As a young girl, she had once sported a fiery temper, but years of Marcella's beatings and Katrina's bullying had taught her to hold her tongue at all costs.

Still, that fire simmered deep down like hot coals in a forgotten hearth.

She quickly pulled the wool over her feelings, tightening down on that burning core.

"That's very considerate of you, my lady," Celise murmured, carefully pronouncing her words. The best way to put off Katrina's games was not to play at all.

"Don't you care about what you wear to the ball?" Katrina mocked her.

"I have no desire to attend the ball, my lady," Celise whispered. "I shall only go if our father insists."

Katrina's face contorted at those words. "*Our* father? You don't resemble our family in the slightest. That bitch who birthed you was a whore and your real father was a farmer. That's what Mother believes. You're just a lousy, *dimlit* commoner."

The burning coals in Celise's gut grew a few degrees hotter. Katrina noticed. Her smile curled a bit wider. "Don't think the duke's invitation makes you *one of us*. You should *make yourself scarce* before the ball. Perhaps you should fall off a horse so you can stay behind."

Celise's shoulders went stiff, but she didn't dare reply.

Katrina sneered. "I can help you. I'll make it look like an accident. There are many ways to *fall down*." Katrina's left hand was glowing with mana. She gripped her foil by the hilt. A silver-white sparkle trickled down the length of the thin blade.

Quick as a whip, Katrina flicked up the foil and touched it against Celise's shoulder.

Snap!

A sharp *zap* of mana struck Celise through the blade. The impact threw her backward. Celise was not very tall or heavy, and she slammed against the wood-paneled wall with a soft, *"Ah!"*

"Point!" Katrina cawed.

Celise bit her lip, already feeling the bruise spreading across her shoulder through her tunic shirt.

"A few more of those, and you'll be in no shape to attend the ball," Katrina pouted with fake sympathy. "Consider this a warning. If you attend this ball, I'm going to torture you every step of the way."

Celise felt her control slip. "Perhaps I'll attend just to spite you," she said, her words pathetically soft, her throat stiff with fear and anger.

"What did you say?" Katrina snapped.

Damnable dust, now she'd done it.

Flushing bright red, Celise straightened up and ran down the hallway. She moved at a fast trot like an anxious horse. She didn't want to trigger Katrina's predatory instincts by acting like prey—but it was probably too late for that.

Why did I do that? Why did I talk back?

She didn't like turning her back on Katrina, not when her bullish stepsister was in a bad mood. The muscles along her back remained tense, expecting one last blow.

Celise didn't have long to wait.

A gust of wind brushed her shoulder, spinning her around. *Mana.* The force of the *push* almost made her trip. She stumbled a few steps before catching her balance on a low wooden table at the side of the hallway. It was startling, but Katrina could do a lot worse.

On top of the wooden table, a vase began to glow with a faint bluish light. The vase seemed to move by itself. Before Celise's eyes, the priceless object wobbled, unbalanced itself and fell to the ground.

No!

With a quick dive, Celise caught the priceless heirloom before it shattered on the floor. *Oof!* She fell, landing clumsily on her bruised shoulder, her arms wrapped around the heavy vase. She winced in pain, but the vase was saved.

Celise remained on the ground for a moment, her heart racing. If the vase had shattered, Katrina would have told Marcella, and Celise would have been whipped.

Cunning Katrina almost pulled it off.

At that moment, light footsteps echoed from the top of the stairs, and Heather's voice called down to them, "Katrina? Do you have Mother's copy of *The Modern Lady's Wishlist?* I can't seem to find it."

Katrina glared at Celise, a look that promised more pain to come, then she stepped back. She tucked her foil under her arm and straightened her crooked collar. Then Katrina ran lightly up the stairs. "I'm coming, Heather! Just a moment! I was just dealing with *the staff.*"

Celise climbed to her feet and carefully set the vase back on the small table. By the time she looked back at the staircase, Katrina was gone.

She glared at the empty landing at the top of the stairs.

The Dhastel family was Luminous, boasting several generations of mana channelers. Unfortunately, Celise was a *dunslug*. She didn't have any evidence of the Dhastel gift, which made her *common*—unfit for the ruling Luminous class—and less useful than half of the kingdom's skilled workers.

Without fail, all of the Forsynthian aristocracy were Luminous, born with the ability to channel *mana*, a mysterious *power* stored within their physical bodies. It seemed that humans were either born with mana or not; it didn't develop later in life, but appeared at birth. The trait was passed down through bloodlines, but it sometimes spontaneously emerged among the working class. Some commoners were born Sky-touched, and it was considered an immense blessing from the celestial goddess, Valestra. Either they enrolled in the military academy as soon as they turned sixteen, or they attended special schools to apply their mana to a trade. Some became exceptional musicians, seamstresses, bricklayers or other artisans.

But not Celise. Hers was a normal, ungifted life.

Her mother died in childbirth, and a midwife identified Celise as a *dunslug* shortly after she was born. Many times, Celise had tried to prove the midwife wrong. Young children often got flickers of mana in their hands before they learned how to regulate it. On rare occasions when her temper flared, she imagined a sense of power gathering in her palms.

Just like she felt now.

With a bit of force, Celise thrust out her left hand as though shooting a blast of energy out of her palm, straight at the top of the stairs where Katrina had disappeared. She clenched her jaw and held her arm stiffly before her.

Nothing happened.

Nothing *ever* happened.

A few seconds passed. Then, with a sigh, Celise abandoned her ridiculous pose.

She continued on her way to the kitchen at the back of the house.

As Celise approached the door to the kitchen, a maid with a tray full of biscuits rushed past her.

"Out of the way!" the maid barked, almost slamming into Celise, who shrank back, pressing her slight form against the wallpaper.

Just inside the kitchen, a bell rang incessantly. There, a wood panel displayed almost thirty different bells. Each one was numbered. Each one was *shined.*

This bell belonged to Marcella's room.

The mistress of the house had some meager channeling ability, though not as powerful as her daughter, Katrina. Marcella couldn't do anything truly impressive, but her powers were strong enough to frighten the staff. A plate exploding in the middle of a tantrum wasn't unheard of. Once, the butler had fallen down the stairs under suspicious circumstances and fractured his wrist. Lord Dhastel had given his wife a firm lecture behind closed doors. Laws protected commoners against that kind of thing—if Marcella were caught.

She was never caught.

Celise watched the panicked maid flee down the hallway with her tray. She imagined Marcella seated in her private rooms with her two daughters, the latest edition of *The Modern Lady's Wishlist* in her lap, picking the most popular designs for their new dresses.

They'll cost a galleon apiece, no doubt.

Celise detached herself from the wall and slipped through the kitchen doors. Hot steam filled the air. By the mouthwatering scent, Chef Beechwin was making onion soup and pork roast for dinner. The Dhastel manor's kitchen sported no less than four clay ovens. A butcher block countertop with eight cooking stations spanned the length of the room. The magnificent, country-style kitchen suited the grand old house. Generations of Dhastel servants had used it to prepare the family's meals.

"What is it, child?" the chef roared when he saw her. He took a second look, then yelled to his wife, "Lilibeth, see to the girl's needs. She looks ready to fall into a pot."

Lilibeth was up to her elbows in a sink full of dirty dishes with a scullery maid on either side. As the chef's wife, she oversaw the desserts and breakfast menu for the household. She wore a dress of light blue livery and a long apron. She looked up, a lock of frazzled gray hair falling across her round face. "My goodness, girl, you look like you've eaten a spoiled pepper. Come, sit down out of the way. Chef's busy. You know how he gets 'round a roast."

In the heat of the kitchens, Celise was beginning to feel more and more lightheaded.

"There is a . . ." she mumbled. "There's *a ball* at Gravenmere Castle. It's a birthday party for the . . . the Mad Dog?"

"Oops, easy does it! Don't lose your feet!" Lilibeth took her by the elbow and guided her to the corner of the kitchen. Celise found herself sitting on a wooden stool with a biscuit in hand. Lilibeth patted Celise's sweaty face with the corner of her apron.

"Now what's this about a birthday party for a dog?" she asked.

"She means the Mad Dog duke!" one of the scullery maids laughed. "Don't you read *The Lady's Letter*?"

"I didn't know *you* could read, Ivy."

"I can't, but Dasha can! She keeps us all updated on the latest news. Everyone is calling Lord Elias Blackwood the 'Mad Dog' duke!"

"Blackwood? You mean the Hero of the Realm? The man who defeated the Daemon King?"

"The very same!"

"I went to a parade in his honor after he returned from the war." Lilibeth shook her head. "Oh, well, I can't be bothered with that now. Celise is in a state!"

Celise spoke up, still lightheaded, "Marcella told me to bathe . . . to get the horse smell off . . . before the dress fitting . . . for the gala . . . ."

Ivy laughed. "Lady Marcella said that? She would rather lick a toad than let you attend a ball!"

"Shut your trap, Miss Ivy!" Lilibeth snapped, glaring at the outspoken maid. "Don't forget Celise isn't like us. She's Lord Dhastel's eldest. If Marcella requires her to bathe, then we shall see to it! Now start heating water for the soaking tub in the cellar and bring the Castile soap. We must assist the child."

"Right away, ma'am!" Ivy called. She pulled her hands out of a dirty sink, dried them off on her apron, and started hauling a big pot toward the ovens.

Chapter 3

THE DRESS FITTING

After her bath, Celise returned to her lofted bedroom above the stables. The gentle rustle of horses drifted up through the floorboards. A clay bowl of birdseed rested on her windowsill, where a yellow finch twittered merrily as he ate his dinner. She sat at the edge of her bed and watched the little bird as she unwrapped a towel from her hair. A soft wool robe covered her slight, waiflike form.

Celise lived in a modest room above the stables. Her belongings fit into a single weathered chest at the foot of her bed—she didn't own very much. The rest of the room's furniture was rescued by helpful servants from Marcella's donation piles. Her iron bed frame was sturdy, if a bit scuffed. Straw and flock filled her secondhand mattress. Burlap curtains framed the windows, embroidered with little yellow buttercups. On the wall hung four small paintings of the famous Grapevine Mountains. One of the paintings was stained by water damage.

A single square window looked down over a fenced dirt corral, which connected to a grassy paddock, which opened into an expansive pastureland behind the Dhastel estate. Beyond acres of grazing horses, a dirt country road wandered past the pasture's fieldstone walls.

Suddenly, Celise heard a ruckus of stomping boots on the staircase up to her loft. She heard Mordwen's familiar voice drift up the stairwell:

"*Curse these damnable steps, why are they so uneven? Crow's rot, this entire barn is about to fall over!*"

"Watch your step, Mordwen!" sang out the young maid, Dasha.

Celise's room didn't have a proper door, so she hung a linen curtain across the entrance. Throwing the curtain aside, three servants entered her bedroom: Steffie, Dasha and Mordwen. Steffie and Dasha did most of the tailoring for the household, from refitting uniforms for the stable-hands to mending Lord Dhastel's wardrobe. Their arms were laden with colorful dresses from Katrina's closet.

Mordwen entered the room after them with a moody scowl. A hard-bitten widow, the Head Housekeeper had worked for the Dhastel family since Celise's father was a boy, more than forty years now. She was the only servant immune to Marcella's tantrums, since Lord Dhastel had a soft spot for her.

Technically, Mordwen didn't need to be in the room for the dress fitting, but Celise considered her a great aunt of sorts, and the old bitty went about the grounds as she liked. By the look on Mordwen's face, it seemed that word of Celise's predicament had reached her already.

"Now, my girl, no need to explain; I've heard everything. My only question is, how did your name end up on this *devastating* invitation?"

Celise found herself smiling at Mordwen—her first smile of the day. She shrugged her fragile shoulders. "The Blackwoods must have a very thorough clerk."

"Right," Mordwen said. "*Very* thorough . . . but I think we best consult the cards for this. It all seems too auspicious!"

"The cards!" Steffie cheered.

Mordwen reached into her housecoat and pulled out a stack of thick, dusty purple cards. They were bigger than playing cards by a good inch, almost too large for the old woman's hands. The backs were decorated with geometric patterns printed in bright goldenrod, visible against the purple cardstock.

"Ooh, a fortune telling?" Steffie gasped. She dumped her armful of dresses down on the bed, swept her blond hair out of her face, and moved to sit down near Celise.

"Oh no, you don't! You and Dasha get the room set up. What are you lazing about for?"

Mordwen snapped her fingers at the maid. Steffie pouted and stood up again, then went to help Dasha lift a heavy mirror up the staircase. In the meantime, Mordwen shuffled her cards. Celise felt hypnotized by the geometric patterns sliding back and forth in the master's hands. Mordwen never explained why or how she shuffled, but she used various techniques, her lips screwed into a frown, her eyes focused on a distant spot on the wall.

"Oh Mother of Dust and Moon, She who governs the fates of Her children," Mordwen muttered. "Why has Celise been summoned to this ball? What glory or tragedy awaits her at Gravenmere Castle?"

Celise was mesmerized. She felt a little chill run down the back of her neck. She wondered what the cards might reveal.

Mordwen withdrew a card. She glanced at it. Grunted in satisfaction.

"What is it?" Celise couldn't help but ask.

The old woman revealed the card with a bit of flair. Celise's eyes fixated upon the painting of a pale hand holding a glowing wand. Steffie let out a loud gasp from across the room.

"You drew Valestra's hand! That's so rare!" Steffie said.

"Oh, yes! *My suspicions were correct,"* Mordwen crowed. "This is more than just a chance invitation. This card reveals that Valestra's wand is stirring the pot. Your invitation to the ball is no mere coincidence, Celise. This, my dear, is *fate.*"

"Fate?" Celise whispered.

"Watch the mirror!" Dasha shouted when Steffie almost dropped it. Together, the two maids wrestled the heavy mirror into the bedroom, then placed it against the wall next to Celise's bed.

Mordwen pulled out another card from the deck. This time, the card was painted with a shooting star falling into the ocean. "This card depicts the meteor that struck Nilos so many eons ago. It means a *significant change* in your destiny," the crone declared. "Coupled with Valestra's wand, this is *very* auspicious! It seems that fate is guiding a catastrophic change in your life, my girl. Whatever happens at Gravenmere Castle will *change the course of history*—perhaps for the entire Kingdom! It's the will of the Goddess Valestra." Mordwen fixed Celise with a stern gaze. "What do you think of that?"

Celise gulped. "I don't know."

"I think it's rubbish!" Dasha called across the room. "Put the cards away. You're scaring the girl!"

"It's not rubbish," Mordwen said with a snort of indignation. "I'll prove it. The next card I pull will be Celise's birthflower. I trust the Goddess will give it to us as a sign. Once I draw her birthflower—which is—"

"The Starlight Dahlia," Celise supplied.

"Lovely. Once I draw the Starlight Dahlia from the deck, her fate shall be sealed!"

Mordwen began shuffling again, muttering under her breath and closing her eyes, her wrinkled face tilted toward the ceiling. The theatrics were quite impressive. Dasha stopped her work to watch. Steffie abandoned the heavy mirror and ran to Celise's side, where she placed her hands on her shoulders. Celise couldn't help but feel a bit excited.

"Ah-hah!" Mordwen yelped as she pulled a card from the deck and thrust it under Celise's nose. "Here it is!"

"The Abyssal Rose!" Steffie declared.

"Oh." Celise's shoulders slumped. "It's not for me." She didn't know who the rose belonged to, but it wasn't her zodiac's birthflower. She was born in the cold season of Brumadir, in the month of Stargrave, with the Star as her zodiac sign and the Starlight Dahlia as her flower of birth.

"Who does the Abyssal Rose belong to? Anyone in the room?" Steffie asked.

Celise and Dasha both shook their heads, "no."

"Let me pull again," Mordwen blustered. "It wasn't the first card I touched; there was another one at the front of the deck. I had a misgiving. . . ."

"Put the cards away, Mord!" Dasha rolled her eyes. "You're disturbing Celise! Just look at how pale she is! No more talk of destiny or fate. No *catastrophe* is going to happen at Gravenmere Castle that will *change the fate of the kingdom.*"

"The cards don't lie!" Mordwen spat.

"Balderdash and nonsense!" Dasha snapped. "Celise was invited *by accident* to the ball by an overzealous steward, and there's nothing more to it than that."

Steffie patted Celise's arm apologetically. Celise gave her a wan smile. Then the maids went back to work clearing space for the dress fitting in the small room.

Celise sighed and gazed out the window again. She wasn't surprised. *The Abyssal Rose.* Of course Mordwen's reading would be for someone else and not for her. What interest did the Goddess Valestra have in her fate?

Mordwen quietly slithered up to her side and thrust the cards into Celise's hands: Valestra's wand and the falling meteor. "Remember these," she cautioned. Then she stacked up the rest of her card deck and slipped them back into her pocket. Celise fumbled with the two cards for a moment, admiring their detailed artwork. Then she placed them on the windowsill, standing them upright so she could see them from her seat.

Meanwhile, the maids began laying out dresses on the bed.

"Most of these styles are from at least three years ago," Dasha lamented. "I'm surprised Katrina's kept them this long."

"We can't send Celise off to a ball wearing *that*," Steffie muttered. "She should at least look like she belongs!"

"She belongs, no matter what she wears!" Mordwen scoffed.

"But she doesn't, ma'am, not really," Dasha insisted. "I mean no disrespect, but we all know Celise wasn't raised right by His Lordship. She doesn't know the first thing about a lady's etiquette; none of us do, and she doesn't have any of those flashy powers." Dasha brushed off a sprigged cotton dress—an off-yellow color dotted with tiny, nondescript flowers—and handed it to Steffie. "Put this one in the 'maybe' pile."

"Our Celise is just as worthy of becoming a duchess as any of Marcella's brood," Mordwen said. "Celise is every inch a noblewoman by birth. Perhaps this will be her chance to take back her birthright!"

"Even without mana?" Steffie glanced sadly at Celise.

Mordwen harrumphed. "She's heir to Windhaven Estate by blood and birth order. What should it matter?"

Celise stirred. "You know as well as I do that it does," she pointed out. "I'm a *dunslug* and I have no intention of challenging Marcella's daughters for the estate. I know my place. I'm happy working in the stables."

"I would say you've *settled* for the stables, my girl, but I'm not sure you know what happiness is."

Celise sighed and returned her gaze to the window, her thoughts wandering far out past the purple mountains. She was secretly grateful for Dasha's honesty. No, "his Lordship" hadn't raised her at all to be like a proper lady. She had lived in the stables since a young girl, and she had never gone to etiquette school like Heather or Katrina. Although she seldom interacted with her noble family, she didn't quite belong among the servants, either. As a lord's daughter, an invisible barrier existed between herself and the staff. Even if she worked alongside the servants, she wasn't really part of their world. She fell solidly between the cracks: not quite a servant, not quite a lady. For that reason, her romantic prospects had always suffered around the Dhastel ranch. Although a few stable-hands or wranglers had taken an interest in her over the years, they were always warned off.

Too pureblooded to marry a servant—yet unfit for a gentleman.

She didn't truly belong anywhere.

Life had always been this way for Celise. Lord Dhastel had lost all interest in his eldest daughter after she was identified as a dunslug. Then he remarried Marcella, who was every inch a spoiled heiress. Celise was discarded the moment Marcella became pregnant with Katrina.

The servants had disliked their new mistress instantly. The lord's new wife had feigned a "horse allergy" her first day in the manor house. Using her allergy as an excuse, she kept the servants cleaning all day and night, trying to chase away every last speck of horsehair or dander that might touch the floors. The torture never stopped. Marcella kept a mental list of slights she perceived from the unlucky staff. Her sneezing fits always arrived when she wanted to punish someone. Feigning innocence, she would force anyone who offended her to clean the house from top to bottom, even if the floors were spotless. The whole house walked on eggshells around her. Celise had witnessed her stepmother's pettiness firsthand many times over.

One harsh winter, when she was ten years old, Marcella had locked Celise out of the house in the middle of the night, hoping the child would freeze to death in a snowstorm. Celise didn't remember the incident, but as Mordwen told it, young Celise had found her way through the storm to the stables, where she had wandered into the stall of the most fearsome stallion in the herd. A stable-hand had found her cuddled up to the giant horse the next day.

None of the servants wanted to admit openly what their mistress had done, but after that, Celise's room was moved out to the stables. The horsemaster, Mr. Talisworth, put little Celise to work mucking stalls. Marcella seemed to forget about the girl's existence, except to sneer in her direction when their paths crossed.

Because of her stepmother's hatred, Celise wasn't brought up like her two younger half-sisters. She barely knew how to read simple letters, and she couldn't write in Forsynthian high script. She might have noble blood, but she knew absolutely nothing about being a lady. The only times she encountered her younger sisters were to remove the tack from their horses.

The gala would be her first foray into polite society.

It was overwhelming.

Interrupting her thoughts, Steffie pulled Celise up to her feet and tugged her over to a stepping stool in the middle of the floor. "Come over here, my lady. Let's get started. It won't take but an hour, and we'll go quick. I'm already behind on this afternoon's mending."

Steffie boosted Celise up onto the stool, where she reluctantly gazed at her own reflection. A mousy girl stared back at her in the mirror: gaunt-faced, undersized, thin as a pine shaving, and bronzed by the sun, with raspberry locks that had no business being so dense or frizzy. Celise's wide eyes dominated her face. She thought she looked like a goblin child wearing a clump of vines on her head.

Dasha brought over the first of the dresses: a soft pink gown with little roses sewn into the sleeves and bordering the skirt. Simple and pleasant, it was best suited for daywear. Together, Dasha and Steffie pulled the dress over Celise's head and tugged the skirt down over her small frame. Then they stood back, surveying their new project.

Celise stood with her spindly arms spread out like a scarecrow. The oversized dress drooped toward the floor.

"This is going to take a lot of pins," Steffie said.

Celise felt embarrassed. She was turning twenty-four that coming Brumadir season, but she looked as young as her half-sisters due to her small size. Katrina's dress was cut for a figure much more curvaceous and womanly than her own.

Celise knew she had a boyish figure. If she wore a bulky jacket and tied her hair up under a cap, she could pass herself off as a boy, which was how she dressed around the stables. Even on a renowned ranch like the Dhastel estate, it wasn't safe for young women to work alone. Her father employed dozens of stable-hands and farriers, and the workforce changed season to season, as part-timers left during the winter months and new ones were hired each spring. She had learned to hide her femininity as much as possible.

As the maids tucked and pinned Celise's new dress, Dasha commented, "In all honesty, perhaps it's best if Celise doesn't stand out at the ball."

"Mm-hmm," Steffie agreed around a mouthful of pins.

"Elias Blackwood has a *sinister* reputation," Dasha continued. "He's been engaged seven times since returning from the war. All of his fiancées flee from him."

"I meant to ask you about that," Celise ventured. "Is that why *The Lady's Letter* calls him the Mad Dog?"

"Yes," Dasha confirmed. "*The Letter* ran an article about him a few months ago. They dubbed him the 'Mad Dog' because he chased Lady Raelia Riverton out of his house with a sword. He was *frothing* at the mouth. Haven't you heard?"

"Of course she hasn't heard," Mordwen said with a sarcastic bite. "Our Celise doesn't read that brain-rot rubbish. *The Lady's Letter* is nothing more than a gossip column."

"He carries horrific scars from the battle," Steffie chimed in, ignoring the grouchy old crone. "His arms and face are mutilated by fire! He walks with a limp and he drools continuously. His teeth are all broken! He mashes up his food and drinks it through a straw. He's cruel, eccentric and unfit to wed anyone."

"How ridiculous, to say that about a war hero!" Mordwen huffed.

But Dasha agreed. "They say the military altered his mind with all sorts of strange spells and hexes when he fought in the Abyss. They say the war drove him insane."

"Perhaps he's a bit eccentric?" Mordwen grumbled.

"He's *horrible*," Dasha repeated. "I've already asked around. You know how servants talk."

A brief silence fell on the room.

Is any of it true? Celise wondered, a new sense of dread coloring her thoughts. Only two years ago, the soldiers had returned home with the Daemon King vanquished. The siege in the Abyss had lasted ten years. She didn't know if Lord Elias had spent an entire decade fighting monsters underground. Surely, that would make anyone lose their mind?

Of course, *The Lady's Letter* was sensationalized to entertain its readership. The popular magazine was based out of Castleberry City. It published all sorts of gossip about the nobility: important parties, latest trends, new engagements, and profiles of the most eligible bachelors or bachelorettes. It wasn't "real" news, but . . . if Lord Elias was crippled and scarred, that explained why he couldn't find a bride. It also explained why Old Blackwood would use his son's birthday as an excuse to throw a "matchmaking" soiree.

"The Blackwoods are practically royals," Celise pointed out, her voice low and thoughtful. "So, if they're going to such lengths to see him settled, then the gossip must be particularly bad."

Dasha and Steffie exchanged a meaningful look that Celise couldn't read. She wondered how many young ladies would attend the gala hoping to become the next duchess. Wouldn't they be put off by the Mad Dog's reputation?

Then she thought of Marcella's words: *"A duke is still a duke!"*

Continuing in her soft voice, Celise mused, "Do you really think Marcella would marry off Katrina or Heather to the Mad Dog?"

"I think that woman would do anything for power," Mordwen said darkly.

Dasha nodded. Steffie looked pale.

Good riddance, Celise thought. *If Katrina marries the duke, then she'll leave the Dhastel household to go live at Gravenmere Castle. Maybe then I'll have some peace.*

Celise wished her little sister the best of luck.

The following day, Celise's father summoned her into the dining hall just after the dinner hour. Celise didn't have any time to change out of her work clothes but found herself running into the manor house with muddy boots and a stomach full of dread.

Once again, Celise entered her family's presence wearing dusty overalls and a tweed cap over her braided, pinned-up hair.

She hovered just inside the doorway of the small, informal dining room. Heather was seated at a harp in the corner. The harp sparkled with each stroke of her fingers as an entrancing melody filled the dining chamber. Heather's mana channeled through the shined instrument, illuminating the strings of the harp in a pale blue glow. Her mana allowed Heather to loop the melody so that she could play her own accompaniment to the song. From the hallway, it sounded as though two or three harpists sat in the room and not just a soloist.

Celise was enchanted by the sound, though she tried not to show it. She hovered in the doorway. Her presence went unacknowledged. She didn't want to interrupt Heather's performance.

Finally, Heather finished her song and stood up. She bowed to Lord and Lady Dhastel.

"I hope it pleases you, Mother," she said.

"It's much better than it was last week," Marcella allowed, which was high praise. "Not yet worthy of a blue ribbon, however. Keep practicing."

"I thought it was lovely," Lord Dhastel said to his youngest daughter.

Heather beamed at their father, then she took her seat at the end of the table next to Katrina.

Only then did Lord Dhastel seem to notice Celise's presence. He glanced at her just long enough to take in her soiled clothes. Then he averted his eyes, as he always did when she stood before him, as though he couldn't bear the sight of her for more than a minute at a time.

"Marcella and I have been discussing the coming ball and banquet at length. We've decided you should eat with us in the main house until the gala so you can learn proper table manners."

Lord Dhastel motioned to an empty chair near the end of the table, close to her sisters. As Celise walked down the length of the table, he began reading over his steward's reports.

Before Celise could sit down, Marcella waved to one of the servants attending the table. "Place a towel down on the seat," she said. "I won't have the girl staining the chairs with her filthy clothes."

Celise felt a twinge of humiliation as the servant placed a white towel down on the chair across from her stepmother. Then she sat down. Across from her, Marcella perched as stiff as a stuffed eagle, her eyes focused on Celise's every move, a sneer hovering about her lips.

"Tomorrow and from now on, I expect you to *bathe* before entering the house," she snipped. "I don't want you to embarrass us at the banquet. Many important people from around the kingdom will be there. At the very least, you shall learn to sit properly and conduct yourself."

Celise bobbed her head, keeping her eyes focused on her plate.

The dinner hour passed with agonizing slowness. It seemed Marcella was more interested in humiliating Celise than instructing her. At first, the rot-queen criticized Celise's slouched posture. "Sit with your back straight, so you don't spill soup down your bodice!" Then came a million other rules she would have to remember at the banquet.

Celise dropped her utensils several times, overwhelmed by paralyzing anxiety.

Katrina sniggered at her clumsiness while Heather averted her eyes.

Celise had to endure a barrage of criticisms until the grandfather clock struck eight in the evening. Lord Dhastel put down his fork. With a groan, he stood up and gathered his papers, then he walked down the length of the table.

"You're retiring early?" Marcella asked.

"I have to review our accounts before the fair next month," Lord Dhastel murmured. Celise wondered if she imagined the slight downturn of Marcella's lips. He dropped a brief kiss on the top of his wife's head as he strolled past. He didn't look at Celise as he walked through the doorway and turned down the hall toward his study, carrying a stack of papers in hand.

Celise waited until Lord Dhastel left the dining room. Then she shot up to her feet. She bowed to her stepmother and turned toward the door, eager to run back to the stables where she belonged.

But Marcella wasn't finished with her yet. "Girl, I wish to speak to you for a moment."

Celise felt a shiver run down her spine. She stepped aside as Katrina and Heather both exited the room. Then she turned to face her stepmother. Marcella didn't rise immediately from her place at the table but took a moment to pat dry her lips. Then she folded her napkin and set it down next to her plate.

She held out a hand to Celise. "Come here, let me look at you."

With a lump of fear in her throat, Celise crossed the room to stand before her stepmother. Marcella stood up from her chair. She was almost a half-foot taller than Celise, a woman of striking beauty with strong shoulders, a wide bust, sloping neck and a proud jaw. Celise remembered being in awe of Marcella's dark, dramatic beauty when she first wed her father almost eighteen years ago. That's when Celise had tentatively thought of Marcella as her new mother. However, that role didn't last very long.

As Celise grew into a young woman herself, her awe of Marcella's beauty gradually diminished. Now, nearing the age of forty, Marcella's jaw was a bit more heavy, her eyes a bit less bright, and an extra thirty pounds clung to her tall frame. Still, with her luscious black hair and wide, dark eyes, Marcella turned heads wherever she went.

The gorgeous matron looked over Celise like a master appraising a horse. Her hand went to Celise's jaw, lifting her chin slightly to study her features. Celise kept her eyes downcast, wondering if her stepmother would strike her. With Marcella, one could never tell.

But her stepmother only smiled—a cold, calculating look.

"Such an unusual hair color," she mused. "A pity, truly, that such a rare quality is wasted on a giftless child. I assume you take after your mother because you look nothing like your father. I doubt anyone would believe you're my daughter at the gala."

Celise cleared her throat. "If it pleases you, ma'am, I can accompany you as a servant alongside Dasha . . . ."

"Unfortunately, no. The old lord, Cornelius Blackwood, named you in his invitation, so you must appear among the nobility, no matter how unsuitable I find you. Your name will be on the guest list, so you will be announced alongside Katrina and Heather."

"I see."

"I don't expect you'll have any luck with the duke, unless the Mad Dog has a taste for urchins."

"I would never presume to dance with the duke," Celise said.

"Of course you wouldn't, and I forbid it!"

Celise's eyelids fluttered. She glanced up and met Marcella's gaze, then looked away. Marcella spoke softly, but her words were laced with ice. Celise knew what the threat meant. She bore several scars along her back from Marcella's punishments. The rot-queen never wielded the cane herself but enlisted her loyal staff to do it. The carriage driver, the gardener and Lord Dhastel's footman were all in her pocket, and many of the ranch hands as well, who were still taken with her beauty.

"Was that a defiant look?" Marcella sneered.

"No, ma'am," Celise whispered.

"Don't cross me," Marcella snapped. Celise flinched, expecting a strike that didn't come. "Now you listen to me, girl: you are only attending the dance to support your sisters. Don't you dare do anything to embarrass *my* family. If you put so much as a foot on the dance floor—or cause any kind of scandal—you will rue the day you were born. Your father might be against sending you to a convent, but there are *other places for unwanted women.*"

Celise didn't react to her stepmother's threat but did her best to pretend to be deaf and dumb.

Marcella released Celise's jaw, her hand falling back to her side. "For the next two weeks, you shall meet with me for an hour each morning until we leave for Gravenmere. I will do my best to make you presentable for the gala, although I feel my efforts will be wasted. Do not make me regret this."

"Yes, ma'am. I will do whatever you ask."

"Good. Now, when we meet tomorrow morning, you must wear a skirt and slippers, *not* men's clothing, and nothing smelly or covered in hay . . . ."

As the long list of requirements spilled from Marcella's lips, Celise found herself hunching lower and lower. *Maybe I should fall off a horse to avoid the ball,* she thought. It sounded a lot more pleasant than enduring the next two weeks of torture.

"I will see you in the morning in the Great Hall. Don't be late."

Marcella dismissed her with a wave of her pale hand. Celise bowed deeply and left the room. As soon as she entered the hallway, she started to run, unable to restrain herself any longer. Her boots pounded on the floor as she darted down the length of the dark manor, passing by dim wall sconces and charging down wood-paneled hallways. She flew out the back door and across the wide lawn, barreling toward the stables like a galloping horse.

It was hard to breathe in the house, but out under the stars, she felt much better. Her claustrophobia faded. She ran until she was covered in sweat, her legs aching, her lungs heaving. Then she threw herself down upon the cool grass.

I can't do this, she thought. *It's too much. I'm not like them. I'm not meant to be in high society.*

The gala was going to be a disaster.

Two weeks wasn't enough time to learn lady's etiquette—Katrina and Heather had both attended school for two years for proper training. What if she brought shame to the Dhastel name? What if she let slip that she worked in the stables? What if she accidentally spoke and behaved like a common laborer?

How much longer would her stepmother tolerate her?

Celise's eyes traveled to the barn at the side of the field, where she saw one of the upper windows aglow with lantern light. It looked like Mr. Talisworth was still in his office. She gazed at that warm window for a long moment. Should she go to him? Tell him her fears? Ask him to help her with some scheme to avoid the ball.

He would help her, but . . . .

Was there truly any escape?

Could anyone protect her from Marcella?

It all seemed out of her hands.

Celise sighed, her eyes returning to the two moons above her. One was high in the sky, a pure silver color, called the Kinder Moon for its gentle light. The other was close to the horizon, a pale orange like a copper coin, which they called the Maddening Moon. Only one day a year was the Maddening Moon alone in the sky, and that was Darkwell, the last night of Hallowsin, which heralded the end of harvest season. Darkwell was a holy night when ghosts and daemons were thought to walk the land.

The celestial goddess Valestra governed over the two moons, and it seemed they were dancing early this year. The Kinder moon usually didn't appear in the sky until after midnight during the summer months of Ardoursol.

Mordwen would say it was a sign.

A sign of what?

Destiny? Fate?

She thought of Mordwen's oracle cards and her unfinished fortune. *Valestra's wand. The meteor.* A significant change in her destiny.

As her panic faded and her heart calmed, Celise's thoughts turned inward. Did she want her life to change? This was a much bigger question than simply pondering the moons. As overwhelmed as she felt, some part of her was also curious about the ball. How had her name come to be on the invitation? Was it truly by chance—a diligent clerk too thorough at his job—or was some greater force at work? Some higher will?

Perhaps Valestra's wand was at play.

Don't be silly, she chided herself. *You were invited to the ball by mistake. It's best to keep your head down and stay invisible.*

But, maybe some small part of her didn't want to hide. Maybe she was tired of feeling out of place no matter where she went. Tired of Marcella's threats. Tired of Katrina's bullying. Wouldn't it feel good to transform into someone else, if only for a few days?

What awaited her at Gravenmere Castle?

A bit of warmth awakened in her breast. Celise felt an unfamiliar fire—long ago stifled, all but smothered—stir in her heart.

Was it courage? No, not entirely. But maybe it would *become* courage someday.

The next two weeks were spent in a whirlwind of activity, preparing Celise for her introduction to high society. Marcella's hurried lessons in etiquette were confusing at best. Celise didn't remember any of it, and her stepmother gave up by the end, leaving Celise with a long list of rules to memorize.

Marcella forbade her from doing anything at all at the gala: no eating, dancing, speaking or sitting. She could stand prettily in her dress and smile, curtsy but not too deeply, and if she must sit, do so with poise, as though sitting on a pin. She must follow Katrina and Heather everywhere and not wander off. She mustn't be out of their sight for even a minute. *And no horses.*

Now, standing on the front steps of Gravenmere Castle, Celise wondered once again why she had come so far to attend a party she wasn't truly invited to. Her fragile self-assurance had dissipated with the morning dew. Every small sign seemed like a bad omen.

A gust of wind rustled through the hedges. The front drive seemed overly long, solitary and winding. Beneath the midmorning sun, she felt a shiver of foreboding. She pulled in a steadying breath, trying to ease the knot of apprehension in her stomach.

She reached up and rang the bell.

Chapter 4

A Clandestine Event

THE ECHO OF THE brass bell faded into silence.

Celise shrank away from the castle's heavy doors, pulling her silk shawl a bit closer about her small form.

Now what?

Behind her, she heard Marcella, Katrina and Heather stumbling out of their carriage, dresses rustling and shoes clip-clopping on the cobbles.

Their arrival was almost a day later than expected. A fallen tree on the rails had delayed their train overnight. So instead of arriving the previous evening, they were reaching the castle by midmorning the next day. Celise didn't see any other carriages waiting along the front drive.

Marcella was furious, of course.

Perched on a green bluff overlooking a dark pinewood forest, Gravenmere Castle was built in a "T" formation, with wings on three sides. The gabled roof of the great hall could be seen for miles around. Pointed, spearlike towers pierced the sky. A broad curtain wall encircled the castle's rambling grounds, which encompassed more than a hundred acres of gardens, pavilions and outbuildings.

Celise had never seen such a mammoth-sized estate.

Centuries ago, Gravenmere Province was its own sovereign land, and the Blackwood family was its royal bloodline. But Gravenmere had been absorbed into the Kingdom of Forsynthia during a previous spawning of the Daemon King. Now, the province made up almost a quarter of the kingdom and was the largest duchy, or "dukedom," in the realm. Gravenmere Castle stood at the center of the province and served as the Blackwood family's seat of power. Their wealth funded much of the Forsynthian military, and their bloodline was a close contender for the Forsynthian throne.

As their carriage driver began unloading their bags, Celise hovered on the wide doorstep before a pair of sturdy double doors, unsure of what to do next. Should she ring the bell again? Or did she wait? How long did a *proper lady* wait at the door?

Just as Marcella reached the top of the front steps with a scowl on her face, the knob turned, the door creaked open, and a butler in smart green livery appeared. The stiff mustache on his upper lip made his speech seem stilted and formal.

"How do you do?" The butler's eyes, fixed with a permanent look of bored disdain, swept over Celise's plain dress, then past her to focus on Katrina and Heather, who were just climbing the stairs.

Her younger sisters looked stunning in the latest fashion from *The Modern Lady's Wishlist*. Their long pagoda sleeves trailed past their elbows, falling in wide, bell-like shapes. Lace-trimmed undersleeves gathered at their wrists with tiny ribbons. A modest crinoline added structure to their long blue skirts, though as daywear, the dresses were not nearly as wide as formal gowns. With matching ribbons in their hair, the two ladies looked youthful and elegant.

Celise's dress was plain in comparison. Steffie had done her best, but not much could liven up the simple calico cotton that buttoned up to her jaw. The print was of tiny, nondescript flowers spattered across a faded yellow base. The hems of her sleeves were not the popular pagoda style but were cut straight and narrow and buttoned at her wrists. The double-layered fabric and high neckline made the dress itchy and hot.

It was not fashionable in the least. Beneath the stifling dress, she wasn't used to wearing such a tight corset, and walking in a bustle felt like being hitched to a wagon.

"Lady Dhastel and her two—pardon, *three*—daughters: Katrina, Heather and Celise," Marcella declared, pushing past Celise and the butler into the house. "My husband shall arrive shortly with our maid. Our train was delayed. You'll find our names on the guest list."

"Of course, my lady. Welcome to Gravenmere Castle."

The butler moved aside with a gracious bow, and the ladies all filed into the ancient stone building through the open front door. Sunlight flooded the foyer through a star-shaped skylight far overhead. The entryway was wide and drafty, but every detail was exquisite, from the polished wooden floor to the crown molding to the vivid oil paintings and green damask wallpaper that decorated the anteroom. Celise was surprised. By the outward appearance of the castle, she had expected a cold, dreary fortress of gray stone, but the main areas of the castle had been refurbished into comfortable living quarters. It certainly outshone the Dhastel mansion, which, although majestic in its own way, carried an aged ranch-house feeling.

"Excuse me, ladies," the butler suddenly drew her attention. He indicated a leather-bound guestbook resting on a low table. "Please, if you will sign next to your names," he said, and offered Marcella a fountain pen.

Celise gulped.

Her stepmother and two half-sisters all signed the guestbook with quick, flourishing gestures. Celise hesitated, fumbling a bit to hold the pen. She had never learned Forsynthian high script or practiced a signature. After studying the other looping letters and little squiggles in the book, she invented one on the spot. She whipped down a few loops and swirls and something that looked like a "C" and a "D." She was proud of her creativity, but the butler didn't seem to care.

The butler took their coats and Celise's parasol, with a promise to deliver the items to their rooms. Two more servants arrived to carry their bags and trunks. Soon they were alone in the anteroom, waiting for *something*, but Celise wasn't sure what.

Or whom?

Suddenly, a bit of movement caught Celise's eye. A narrow hallway led away from the foyer, running parallel to the front of the house. It was a servants' passage, not one the guests would use. As she turned to look, she caught a glimpse of a dark shadow sweeping down the corridor.

As curious as a cat, Celise leaned a bit to gaze down the narrow passage. She caught another glimpse of the shadow—it was rather tall. She saw the slope of broad shoulders, a dark jacket and a wave of black hair.

The man turned to the side. For a moment, she saw a tantalizing outline of a masculine jaw.

Then he opened a door at the end of the hallway, slipped through and was gone.

Celise's fingers clutched at the rough fabric of her skirt. The man didn't strike her as a servant. His posture was very straight. Even at a glimpse, his wide shoulders and tilted head held an air of authority.

A strange sense of intrigue stirred within her, very unlike her usual self.

Who was that? she wondered.

She wanted to follow after him, if only to escape the awkward silence of the foyer.

A very slow minute stretched as the three women stood in the anteroom. Marcella was obviously waiting for someone other than the butler to come and greet them. Celise found herself turning away from the servants' passage and stifling a yawn in her sleeve. She tried to hide it from Marcella—she was pretty sure "yawning" was on the list of things a lady couldn't do.

Then Katrina said in hushed awe, "Look! It's all *shined!*"

She pointed to an entryway table along the left wall. A handful of bright enamel urns and ceramic vases filled with flowers covered the table. A portrait of the Blackwood family hung above it. Celise's eyes combed over the portrait, wondering which child was the Mad Dog. She counted two brothers and a sister dressed in formal attire: the girl wore a white chiffon dress, while the boys wore little green waistcoats. None of the children were smiling.

"Have you ever seen so many shined objects, Mother? They must cost a fortune," Katrina whispered, approaching the table curiously.

"Mind your gifts," her mother said with a strained voice and a bright smile. "Just because they're shined doesn't mean they're for your use."

"This is just like the Skydust Museum in Astravelle," Heather whispered, awed. "I think that mirror is shined as well!"

Celise's eyes traveled to the opposite wall, where a gilt mirror inlaid with roses and curling leaf motifs hung next to a doorway.

"Unfortunately, the mirror is *just* solid gold, not *shined* or *enhanced* in any way," a booming voice reached them. "Allow me to welcome you personally to Gravenmere Castle, Lady Marcella Dhastel."

Celise stiffened. Her stepsisters whirled about. Katrina and Heather quickly dipped into graceful curtsies, their skirts lifting gently as they bowed. Celise dipped as well, though more like a bird pecking at a worm in the grass.

Lord Cornelius Blackwood descended the staircase at a stately pace, his steward following on his coattails. Celise recognized the bristly man from the oil portrait. Stout, bow-legged, with gray mutton chops and a dignified cane, something about the old duke reminded her of a bulldog. Celise couldn't help but notice the gold buttons on his black coat and cuffs. Beneath his velvet coat, he wore a green brocade vest and a starched white shirt. His clothing was as rich as the house's decor.

This would be the Mad Dog's father.

His steward caught her attention as well, who followed the old duke down the staircase. The fellow wore a suit of dark green livery and a top hat, but his wavy hair held a subtle lavender color, like the wisteria in the front drive, and his skin was a rich brown tone, warm and smooth. His eyes were hazel. Celise blinked twice. Although the Kingdoms of Bratzia and Forsynthia were staunch allies, she hadn't seen a Bratzian man for many years. The minerals in their mountain kingdom gave their people's hair an unusual silver-lavender color. She glanced away before the Bratzian steward noticed her stare.

Old Blackwood swept up to Lady Marcella and took her hand. He placed a kiss on her knuckles. "Hello, *hello*, my dear Lady Dhastel. I trust your journey from Windhaven was uneventful? No trouble on the road? We were concerned by your absence last evening."

"A tree fell across the train tracks. A minor inconvenience, but besides that, our journey was safe and uneventful." Marcella swept into a deep curtsy. "You honor us with your presence, Your Grace. Our kingdom is at peace now because of your son."

"The kingdom might be at peace, but one can never be too cautious." Old Blackwood cleared his throat. "Is your husband in attendance, by any chance? I was hoping to have a quick word with him."

"He is arriving soon, Your Grace. He took a separate carriage."

"I see." Old Blackwood looked disappointed. "I was hoping to catch him before the hour grew later, but I am heading into an important meeting. *Do* have him send for my steward when he arrives. He mentioned you have some excess stock. My steward will be able to discuss an arrangement with him and handle any contracts. The military is always in need of good horses."

The Bratzian man standing behind Old Blackwood bowed low.

Marcella smiled widely. "Of course, Your Grace. I will certainly pass along your message to Lord Dhastel. Before you go, please allow me to introduce you to my daughters: Heather and Katrina."

"A pleasure," Old Blackwood nodded to them. His gaze lingered on Katrina. Then his eyes flicked over to Celise. "And this would be your third daughter, correct?"

"Yes, ah . . . she is . . . *simple,* my lord."

Simple? Celise was appalled but didn't say anything. She ducked into a curtsy again, but Blackwood barely nodded to her. Instead, he made a grand gesture, his arm encompassing the room: its vases, the portraits, the gilded mirror and all the rest.

"Welcome, dear ladies, to Gravenmere Castle. I expect tomorrow's gala to be a *clandestine* event, with a special surprise at the end of the night. I hope you won't retire early. There will be fireworks to celebrate." The lord's eyes returned to Katrina. "I think you and your sister will enjoy the surprise a lot."

Katrina blushed and dropped her eyes demurely.

"How splendid!" Marcella gasped. "Is Lord Elias about the grounds, by any chance? We were hoping to wish him a happy birthday."

"Unfortunately, you just missed him. We are heading into a meeting, and he's a few steps ahead of me. As Lord High Commander, his work at Firehelm Fortress keeps him quite busy. I must apologize for his absence, but he will be available tomorrow for the ball."

"I see." Lady Marcella raised a delicate eyebrow. She took a step closer to the duke's elbow. In a softer voice, she murmured, "My daughter is most eager to meet your son. Merely a small request, Your Grace—perhaps your Elias might dance with my Katrina tomorrow night? She's quite charming. I'm sure he will enjoy her company."

"Oh ho!" the old lord laughed. "She certainly has her charms!"

Marcella looked pleased. Encouraged by Old Blackwood's response, she added, "Katrina has heard a lot about your son. She's quite taken with him, but you know how girls can be—brimming with hope, yet painfully shy behind the lace."

Katrina's cheeks turned a bit pink. Celise thought she was doing a wonderful impression of a sweet, shy girl.

"Hm," Blackwood grunted, his chops quivering. "I would love to oblige the young lady, but Elias isn't one to dance unless pressed. He'd sooner spar in the training yard or ride off on that hellhorse he brought back from the Abyss than waltz in a ballroom."

"Surely, you jest!" Marcella laughed into her wrist. "Such good humor, Your Grace. Perhaps a gentle press from you might encourage him? For one set, no more. Katrina would be most honored."

Old Blackwood chortled and hooked his thumbs into his jacket pockets. "My, my, but you'd make a fine diplomat, Marcella."

"I'm flattered, Your Grace, but I am simply a mother who cares only for her daughter's happiness."

The old lord released a sigh. "I can relate, more than you know. Very well. I'll nudge the boy. But I'll not guarantee his dancing will be graceful. The last time he waltzed, he nearly trampled a lady's lapdog."

Heather squeaked. Then she clapped a hand over her mouth, stifling a giggle.

"Perhaps Katrina will teach him how to tread more lightly," Marcella said with a polite smile.

Blackwood smirked. "Let us hope."

At that moment, the steward stepped forward to whisper something into Blackwood's ear before backing quickly away.

The duke nodded to Marcella. "Lady Dhastel, I must leave you now in the capable hands of my staff. Please relax and feel free to explore the castle. My wife, Estoria, has planned a tea party in the gardens this afternoon. You'll find schedules written up and posted around the grounds. Do keep an eye on the time—I forget exactly when it starts."

"We are honored." Marcella curtsied, and her daughters followed her example like little bobbing chicks. Celise hunched down and up, the awkward stork of the lot.

After Old Blackwood left the foyer with his steward in tow, Marcella's smile lost some of its charm. Her lips became tight. "I *do* hope Lord Elias shows up to his own ball."

Katrina's eyes widened. "Why wouldn't he?"

Marcella didn't answer, but her lips remained pursed. She took a moment to adjust her lace gloves.

At that moment, a servant emerged from the hallway to their left. He was a young man dressed in emerald green livery. With a sharp bow, he said, "My lady, may I show your family to your rooms? We have you in the Moongazer Tower across the courtyard. It faces southeast. I hope you find it to your liking."

"The Moongazer Tower?" Lady Marcella preened. "I've heard it has a wonderful view of the Blush River."

"Yes, ma'am, and the Grapevine Mountains are lovely at dawn."

With a nod, the servant led them deeper into the castle.

Celise followed her stepsisters and stepmother through the manor's extensive hallways. As they walked, she thought of Marcella's comment. Why would Elias Blackwood not attend his own ball? Perhaps the rumors about his temperament were true. She wondered at the length of the guest list she had spied in the ledger. Hundreds of names were listed, and most of them had signatures.

Despite the size of the list, it sounded like the Mad Dog wasn't much of a social butterfly.

". . . he's a few steps ahead of me," Old Blackwood said. Celise nibbled at her bottom lip. Could the man she had espied in the servants' hall possibly be . . . ? No, a famous figure like Elias Blackwood wouldn't use the staff's corridor. Perhaps it was his footman she had seen.

The manservant escorted the four women under a sweeping staircase, through a vaulted library filled wall-to-wall with books and comfortable armchairs, then out across the grounds. A central courtyard stood at the heart of Gravenmere Castle. Celise was surprised to see several different pavilions, each with their own little manors in miniature, located off the courtyard. Delicate metal signs hung above blooming trellises at the head of each path, denoting which walkway led to which pavilion. A large chalk sign in the center of the courtyard contained a detailed schedule for all the events that afternoon and the next day.

Marcella stopped to read it, obviously memorizing the times.

Katrina gasped. "The tea party will start in an hour! We should hurry and get changed. I don't want to greet the other ladies in a stained dress."

Katrina's daygown was far from stained. Celise thought it looked very clean after traveling in it for two days. But yes, a change was probably necessary.

"They're holding the tea party in the famous Zodiac Gardens," Marcella said. "This should be a treat for us all."

"What are the Zodiac Gardens?" Heather asked as they walked.

"It's a special park on the Gravenmere grounds with all the birthflowers of the Forsynthian Zodiac," Marcella explained.

Katrina cut in with an air of knowing, "The gardens are described in *A Tour of Forsynthia*, a book in Father's library. It lists all of the most famous locations in the kingdom. Gravenmere's Zodiac Gardens ranks number thirty-six on the list."

"Is that so? I didn't realize!" Heather said, her eyes bright with awe. She clapped her hands. "This is ever so exciting!"

"Now girls, try not to act *too* excited; it's unladylike," Marcella cautioned.

Celise sighed inwardly.

A tea party?

Just another opportunity to embarrass herself.

The ball wouldn't take place until *tomorrow* evening. She still had a full weekend to endure before they returned home to Windhaven Ranch. She tried to think of a convenient excuse to stay in the guest tower, but she didn't want to try Marcella's patience so soon, not after their train had arrived so late.

The Moongazer Tower was, as described, to the southeast. They followed the flagstone path through the grounds to a round stone building abutting a grand curtain wall that encircled the castle. By the slitted windows and heavy sandstone blocks, Celise guessed the tower was originally built to withstand a siege, but the Blackwood family had extensively re-outfitted the tower as a guesthouse. The walls were whitewashed and the roof shingled, which softened the tower's appearance, transforming it from a lonely outpost to a fairytale setting. The window frames were painted deep evergreen, the Blackwood family's color, and a beautiful garden surrounded the tower's base, rich with purple clematis vines, pink hydrangea beds and rows of proud hollyhock.

Marcella and Heather chatted excitedly about the garden, pointing to little stone statues and features hidden among the beds. The servant unlocked the tower's door and opened it. Then he carried their bags inside.

Celise followed her family into the tower. The eccentric round guesthouse was three stories high. The ground floor housed a comfortable entertaining area with a wood-burning stove, soft lounges, a wine bar and tables. The floor above that was a master bedroom, and above that, a smaller bedroom and bathing chamber with two twin beds. Finally, the top floor housed two little rooms separated by a narrow hallway, presumably meant for traveling servants.

Their luggage had already been delivered and was waiting inside the doorway. At Marcella's direction, the manservant began carrying various bags and chests to different rooms. She didn't seem to notice how the servant struggled to lift their heavy trunks up the stairs. Celise found herself lending a hand without thinking. The servant seemed surprised but didn't refuse her.

Katrina and Heather claimed the twin beds on the second floor. A gift basket from the Blackwood family sat on a table at the corner of the room, next to a door that led to a bathing chamber. The basket was filled with soaps, scented oils and candles. The two young ladies immediately began unwrapping it and trying the different perfumes.

Celise followed the Blackwood servant upstairs onto the highest floor: the attic. The ceiling was low and slanted so that the manservant had to duck around the rafters. There, two doors faced each other across a narrow hallway. Dasha would take the second bedroom when she arrived.

The servant unlocked the east-facing bedroom and led Celise inside. It had a latched double-paned window that opened outward onto the roof. The servant left her suitcase and garment bag at the foot of her bed, then swiftly retreated back down the stairs, where Marcella was already calling.

Celise was amazed. Did she get a whole bedroom to herself?

A plush green rug covered the hardwood plank flooring, and a four-poster bed—large enough for two people to sleep side by side—took up most of the room. A vanity with a humble mirror and a storage chest occupied the other half. Squeezed into the corner was a copper tub large enough for one person to sit.

It was perfect for a traveling servant. Perfect for *her*, who didn't require much at all.

Celise went to the window and looked outside. To her surprise and delight, she discovered that the window opened out onto the roof, and if she was careful, she could climb down the wooden shingles onto the curtain wall.

Suddenly, she was excited.

She wondered what the stars would look like from the curtain wall at night. It would be a lovely place to watch the sunrise in the morning.

Then she quickly shut and latched the window as though hiding a secret. If Marcella found out how easy it would be for Celise to slip away, she would ask for her room to be moved.

Instead, Celise went about putting her one nice gown away, trying not to wrinkle the layers of tulle and silk as she hung it in the wardrobe. Steffie had spent hours finishing the ballgown over the past two weeks. She had encountered considerable difficulty cutting all the excess material to fit Celise's tiny frame. Then she had stitched up the bodice into a fashionable shape. The soft gray silk glinted like moonlight. Celise didn't let herself enjoy the fabric. She knew her stepmother would take it away as soon as the gala was over.

Suddenly, Katrina's voice drifted up the spiral staircase, echoing throughout the stone tower.

"Celise! *Dear Sluggy,* come here! I need help with my dress." Then, exasperated, "Where has she run off to? We only have an hour before tea time! I don't want to miss it. Anyone who's *anyone* will be there!"

Celise groaned quietly to herself—she had been waiting for this moment. Of course Katrina would treat her like a handmaid. She hoped Dasha would arrive soon with Lord Dhastel.

Closing her suitcase, Celise slid her luggage under the bed, and then she walked down the stairs to her sisters' room, prepared to help Katrina and Heather bathe and dress for afternoon tea.

Chapter 5

The Zodiac Gardens

Exactly one hour later, a manservant dressed in dark green livery arrived at the Moongazer Tower to escort the ladies to tea.

Katrina and Heather dashed excitedly down the spiral staircase to the ground floor, their faces washed, their hair brushed out and rebraided, and their dresses refreshed.

By the front door, Marcella waited in a white lace dress, her skirts boosted up with a stiff bustle, her parasol in hand, and a familiar scowl on her face. She glanced over Katrina and Heather, then gave them both a nod of approval. She barely looked at Celise, who still wore her calico dress from the train ride. Celise hadn't found the time to change; she was too busy helping Heather and Katrina with their stays. But she wetted her hair to tame the frizzy bits, and she managed a spritz of perfume from Heather's gift basket when her half-sister wasn't looking.

Lord Dhastel was just arriving with Dasha in tow. The maid looked tired from a long day of traveling as she carried Lord Dhastel's trunks into the cozy tower. Celise felt more at ease seeing her friend arrive, but she barely had time to smile at Dasha before she was rushed out the door by her stepmother.

"Don't forget to call for Old Blackwood's steward!" Marcella said to her husband as she headed out. "He wishes to discuss an important matter with you. It's about your horses."

Lord Dhastel nodded and waved them off.

Like a group of sparkling peacocks, the four ladies walked across the castle grounds led by a footman in green livery. The midafternoon sun filtered through a thin layer of wispy clouds overhead. Duskwane was the first month of Hallowsin, when harvest began. The days were cool and breezy before the leaves changed color and the storms swept in from the Grapevine Mountains. Still, Celise was clammy in her dress.

She tugged at her uncomfortable collar as the servant led them across the Gravenmere grounds. They crossed the central courtyard, following a large sign that read, "To the Zodiac Gardens." She had to admit she was a bit curious. The Forsynthian zodiac was well studied, especially among new brides and expectant mothers. Shrine maidens, who lived as paupers and dedicated their lives to the Celestial Goddess Valestra, the Mother of Dust and Moon, created special charts for each newborn that went on for pages and pages. They believed a person's character and destiny correlated to the season and month of their birth. Their largest temple stood in the royal city of Astravelle, where the queen consulted the high priestess each New Year about the kingdom's fortune.

Celise didn't know if she truly believed in birthflowers, zodiac signs or fortune telling. She thought of Mordwen's prophecy from the day of her dress fitting. Although Mordwen's cards weren't always accurate, they appeared to predict some sort of *catastrophe* at the gala. Of course, she hadn't seen any evidence of an impending disaster, but the weekend wasn't over yet.

Celise nibbled on her bottom lip.

Could the ball truly be *a clandestine event?*

Would it shape the future of the kingdom?

It's useless to think about these things. She supposed it didn't matter one way or another. According to Mordwen's cards, whoever was fated to become the Duchess of Gravenmere *wasn't her*. It was someone with the birthflower of the Abyssal Rose.

Celise's eyes were drawn to the path ahead. The castle grounds were full of brightly dressed ladies. Who could it be? Surely, more than one woman at the gala had the birthflower of the Abyssal Rose?

After passing through a corridor of flowering hedges, the Dhastel ladies reached the gated entrance to the famed Zodiac Gardens. Standing next to the gate, an elderly man in green livery with a top hat was handing out little pieces of paper.

"Name, my lady?" he asked Marcella, who stood at the front of their group.

"Dhastel," she said.

The servant referenced his ledger, which rested on the wooden podium beside him. He flipped through the names with a white-gloved hand. Then he murmured in satisfaction.

"Ah, yes, we have you at the Blue Rose table with Lady Estoria Blackwood, and your daughters will be seated at the Silver Thistle. Please take these vouchers in case you get lost; our staff can direct you."

"Thank you," Marcella said, and took the small squares of paper. She handed one out to Katrina, Heather and Celise. Each ticket was stamped with gold foil, with their names and table and seat numbers written in elegant black calligraphy.

"Lady Estoria hasn't overlooked a single detail organizing this event," Marcella said with a sigh of satisfaction. "Even the seating arrangements have been planned down to the letter. How lovely to have all the work done for us! Come along, girls."

With a rustle of skirts, they passed under the iron archway into the Zodiac Gardens.

Immediately Celise's eyes were met by a wall of bristling white roses, bobbing globe thistle, curling moonflowers, and dancing yellow daffodils. Each flower was immaculately shaped: no moldy stems, brown petals or nibbled leaves. The blooms sparkled with health and vitality.

Katrina and Heather gaped openly at the vibrant garden.

Beyond the wide bed of globe thistle and vining moonflowers, the path widened into a circular courtyard. Butterflies and hummingbirds darted between the shrubs. The garden beds were arranged in a circular formation like the spokes of a great wheel, with flagstone paths weaving throughout. Each bed was planted in celestial order according to the Forsynthian zodiac.

A marble fountain stood at the center of the wheel, creating an axis point around which the whole garden turned. A statue of Valestra, the Mother of Dust and Moon, towered above the fountain. In one hand, she held the Wand of Power, while the other hand clutched her book of knowledge. Her divine wand was said to conduct the movement of the stars, and her book of knowledge held the fate of every last man, woman or child born upon the planet Nilos.

At the foot of the Mother was an astrolith, an ancient stone dial covered in planetary runes that aligned with the heavens during solstice. It was a whimsical addition to the garden, though Celise had no idea how to read it.

As she turned in a slow circle, surveying the mounds of dense flowers, she saw zodiac-themed statues hidden among the beds. There were twelve zodiac constellations in all: The Fawn, The River, The Eagle, The Wolf, The Hourglass, The Twin Otters, The Raven, The Lantern, The Veil, The Phoenix, The Guardian, and The Star. The statues were elegantly carved from limestone with a master's touch. The Eagle sat proudly upon a weathered tree stump, its noble head raised high. The Twin Otters lounged on their backs, their paws intertwined in friendship. The Lantern hung from the hand of a mysterious cloaked figure, guiding the hunched wise man forward. The Star was designed like a swirling flame with a torch at its center. It burned an ethereal blue color, and beneath it hung a scroll of prophecy.

Celise hardly knew what all the zodiac signs all meant. She was mostly familiar with her own zodiac, the Star, and she knew a bit about the Hourglass, which belonged to Mordwen. She thought Dasha might be an Otter, but she wasn't sure.

Lady Marcella floated past her daughters, motioning to them with a flourish of her hand. "Come along, ladies. Let's not block the entrance. More guests are arriving behind us."

Celise trailed along after Katrina and Heather like a horse on a lead.

Ahead of them, a female attendant in green livery was giving a tour of the garden. A group of ladies gathered before the guide. Celise found herself joining the group like a piece of driftwood getting caught up on a sandbank. She craned her neck to see around a forest of ribboned hats, while Katrina grabbed Heather's hand and elbowed her way to the front.

The attendant held a little pamphlet in hand as she enthusiastically described the flowers at her feet: *"This flower is named 'Glowbell.' It aligns with the season of Vimspring. It's the birthflower for all children born in the month of Brightspell under the constellation of The Fawn."*

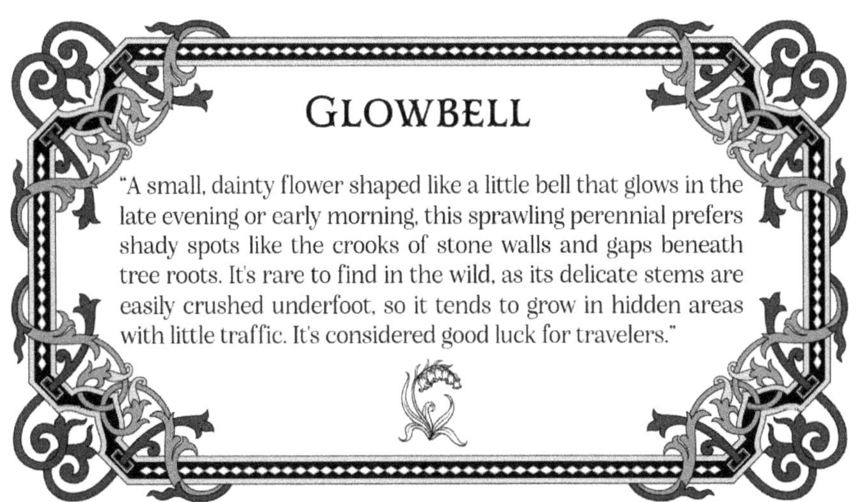

GLOWBELL

"A small, dainty flower shaped like a little bell that glows in the late evening or early morning, this sprawling perennial prefers shady spots like the crooks of stone walls and gaps beneath tree roots. It's rare to find in the wild, as its delicate stems are easily crushed underfoot, so it tends to grow in hidden areas with little traffic. It's considered good luck for travelers."

The gathered ladies bent forward to inspect the little clusters of blue flowers on the ground. Celise heard Heather gasp with joy from the front of the group. “Oh! That’s *my* birthflower. I was born in Brightspell, and I know all about glowbells! You can dry them and grind them into tea. It helps balance your mana channels.”

The ladies all murmured in appreciation.

Celise wondered if she would be able to find her birthflower in the overcrowded gardens: the Starlight Dahlia.

The guide seemed eager to continue the tour. “Now, if you’ll follow me, we’ll head to the next area of the garden, which includes three constellations for the season of Hallowsin: The Lantern, The Veil and The Guardian.”

“Are those for the months of Duskwane, Fallowmere and Hearthbrim?” one of the ladies in the front asked. Her voice carried a husky, rich accent, totally new to Celise’s ears.

“Yes,” the guide said without hesitation. “Those would be the correct months.”

A few of the women in the back tittered behind gloved hands. “Does she not know the months of the season?”

“I think she is from Bratzia,” another girl whispered.

“What is a Bratzian doing here, of all places, on all days?”

“Did the duke send invitations to other kingdoms?”

“Yes, my sister and I are from Bratzia!” the bold girl said from the front row, raising her voice to a very unladylike level. “In Bratzia, we have *birthstones* instead of birthflowers, and we count the months differently. We go by the lunar calendar, and we have thirteen months in our lunar year, not twelve.”

“Oh! I see!” one of the ladies responded, embarrassed. “Thank you for telling us! My friend and I didn’t realize . . . .”

“What a *delight,*” another girl drawled.

The ladies stirred around her. Curious, Celise craned her neck, but she couldn't catch a glimpse of the Bratzian girl who had spoken.

The attendant continued her tour. She led the group of women under a trellis covered in vining lumenbloom. In a cheerful voice, she read off her pamphlet:

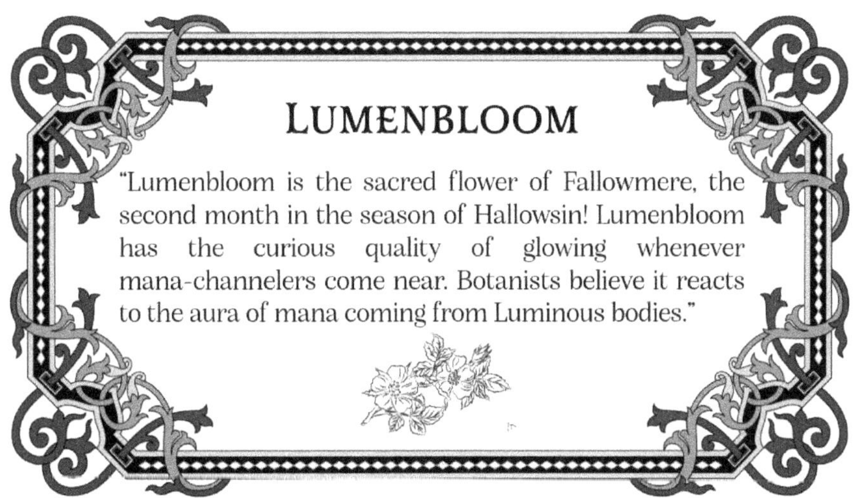

LUMENBLOOM

"Lumenbloom is the sacred flower of Fallowmere, the second month in the season of Hallowsin! Lumenbloom has the curious quality of glowing whenever mana-channelers come near. Botanists believe it reacts to the aura of mana coming from Luminous bodies."

"How is that possible?" a lady asked.

"We don't entirely know," the guide explained with a practiced voice, as though she had prepared for the question. "The meteor that created the Abyss changed many things about our planet. Not only did it trigger the evolution of mana channelers and daemons, but its alien dust changed the flora and fauna as well."

"Oh, how marvelous!" another girl exclaimed. "I want to plant some in my garden back home!"

As the ladies passed under the trellis, the trumpet-shaped flowers pulsed with a strong light, similar to flickering candles. Celise watched the flowers glow—she had seen lumenbloom before on a trellis near the market in Sultan, a small village on Dhastel lands. As far as Celise knew, all of the Forsynthian elite were Skytouched to some degree. These lumenblooms were very bright, their glow visible even in full daylight, with so many gifted noblewomen in the gardens.

She was the last one to pass under the trellis. When she brushed her fingers across their soft petals, the flowers dimmed. It was very obvious. The blooms seemed to curl inward and shrink away.

Celise sucked in a quick breath. She pulled back her hand as though stung.

Just another reminder of what she lacked.

Feeling self-conscious, she quickly passed under the trellis. She glanced around, hoping no one had noticed, but the group of ladies was already far ahead. She hurried to rejoin them.

Next, the guide led them to a bed of Ashfeather Bloom. This flower was much taller than the glowbells. Its fluffy, golden leaves glimmered like embers, and lacy white blossoms floated at the ends of long, delicate stalks.

The attendant continued to read from her pamphlet: *"Ashfeather Bloom is associated with the month of Duskwane, the first month of Hallowsin: the season of harvest, mist and reflection. Today just so happens to be the tenth day of Duskwane and Lord Elias Blackwood's birthday. So this would be his birthflower."*

The ladies all pressed forward, eager to learn more about the duke.

Katrina's voice carried from the front of the crowd: "If His Grace was born in Duskwane, does that mean he is the Lantern zodiac?"

"Yes, that is correct!" the servant said with a big smile. "His Grace is, indeed, the Lantern."

"What does The Lantern characterize?" another lady asked.

"Giftedness. Someone who is very talented," the guide said, but the ladies were not satisfied.

"It also means wisdom and insight," another girl added.

"Wasn't that the Veil, not the Lantern? The Veil zodiac is all about looking inward, while the Lantern is about *seeing beyond. . .*"

"It means someone who prefers the nighttime hours. A night owl!" Heather chimed in. The rest of the ladies dissolved into speculation. High-pitched voices filled the air.

The servant spoke a bit louder, trying to be heard above the chattering crowd:

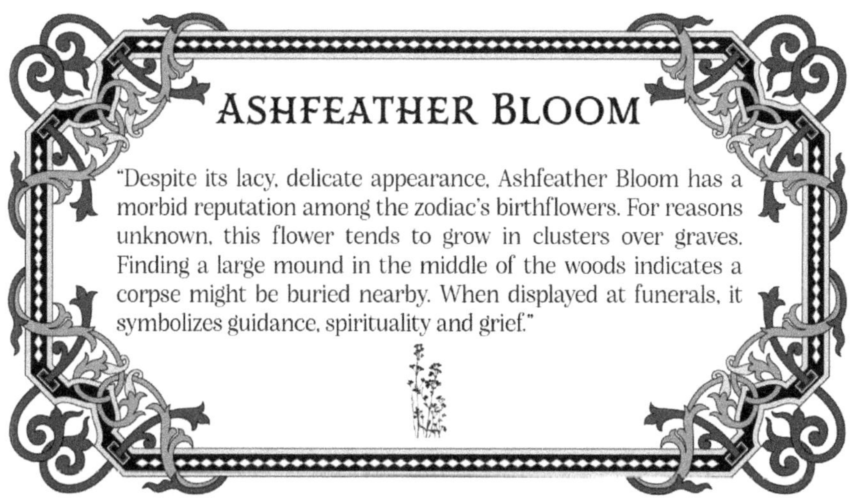

ASHFEATHER BLOOM

"Despite its lacy, delicate appearance, Ashfeather Bloom has a morbid reputation among the zodiac's birthflowers. For reasons unknown, this flower tends to grow in clusters over graves. Finding a large mound in the middle of the woods indicates a corpse might be buried nearby. When displayed at funerals, it symbolizes guidance, spirituality and grief."

"Well, that's unpleasant," Celise said under her breath. Her eyes traveled over the garden bed. Was a body buried under all of those morbid flowers? Perhaps the zodiac gardens were not as innocent and lovely as they appeared.

She smirked privately at her own dark humor.

Then, as the group huddled closer to the Ashfeather Bloom, a strange sight caught her eye.

A garden gate, very old and rusty, was half-buried under a towering camellia bush.

Celise wasn't sure why her eyes were drawn to the odd gate. It lurked in the shade of a black maple tree, perhaps a dozen yards from their small group. It seemed suspicious.

Celise extracted herself from the flock of ladies and walked into the shade of a black maple. She frowned as she approached the gate. It didn't fit the garden's immaculate design at all. In comparison to the pristine Zodiac Gardens, this corner seemed spitefully ignored, as though whatever lay beyond the weathered gate was meant to remain hidden and forgotten.

Celise felt an unexpected yearning nip at her heels. She wanted to explore. She found herself creeping through the mountainous camellia bush, her curiosity piqued.

The gate's iron bars were bound shut with a heavy chain. A wooden sign, faded and decayed, hung from the stone archway above the gate. It read, *"No Trespassing."* Still, she peered through the bars. A dreary shroud of mist covered the world beyond. How mist could gather beyond the wall on a sunny day was a mystery. Celise sensed a peculiar chill in the air, more than just the shade of the maple tree.

"Celise!" a voice called from behind her, startling her.

She turned. "*Oh!*"

Heather approached down the moss-covered path. Celise quickly abandoned the mysterious gate, feeling guilty.

"Stay close to us! Don't forget what Mother said," Heather warned her. "You're not to wander off!"

"I wasn't," Celise said, her hands gripping her skirt.

Her half-sister nodded and looked at her apprehensively. Celise didn't know what to expect from the youngest Dhastel daughter. Heather was quieter than Katrina and less abrasive, though she seemed inseparable from her older sister.

"What's your birthflower?" Heather asked.

Celise was surprised by the question.

At her startled look, Heather shrugged. "I've read a lot of zodiac books. I was just wondering."

"I was born in Stargrave," Celise said. "So my zodiac is The Star."

"That's the last month of the year. That means your flower is the Starlight Dahlia," Heather said helpfully. "I haven't seen any in the gardens yet. We probably won't be able to recognize one. The Starlight

Dahlia only blooms under a clear night sky with plenty of starlight. That's how it got its name."

"Aren't children born in Stargrave considered bad luck?" Katrina pointed out, walking across the courtyard to join them. Apparently she had grown tired of the Ashfeather Blooms and Elias Blackwood's zodiac sign. "That's so predictable. Everything about you is a bad omen."

"That's not true." Trying to be factual, Celise pointed out, "Because Stargrave is the coldest and most isolating month of the year, it has the highest infant mortality rates. But that doesn't mean I have any particular bad luck."

Katrina snorted. "I think you're *rife* with it." Then, with a raised chin, the young heiress declared, "I was born in the month of Sungilt at the beginning of Ardoursol, so that makes me a Wolf." By her stance, she obviously felt her constellation was the best of all. "The Wolf's character is one of grace and power, and my flower is the Abyssal Rose."

Celise felt suddenly ill.

The Abyssal Rose?

Like Mordwen's fortune?

"It's the *most* beautiful flower," Katrina bragged. "Look, there's a bed over there!"

Celise's eyes followed her half-sister's hand to a bushel of red blooms further up the path. Heather rushed ahead, coming to pause in front of a sprawling mound of roses. The blooms were about the size of teacups, the petals darker close to the stem, with varying shades of black and violet opening outward into bright crimson tips. The flower was both wicked and stunning, not unlike a poisonous snake.

"The Abyssal Rose," Celise echoed under her breath. "*Lovely.*"

"It's superior to the other flowers," Katrina said, tossing her long black hair over her shoulder. Then she read off the sign at the foot of the garden bed:

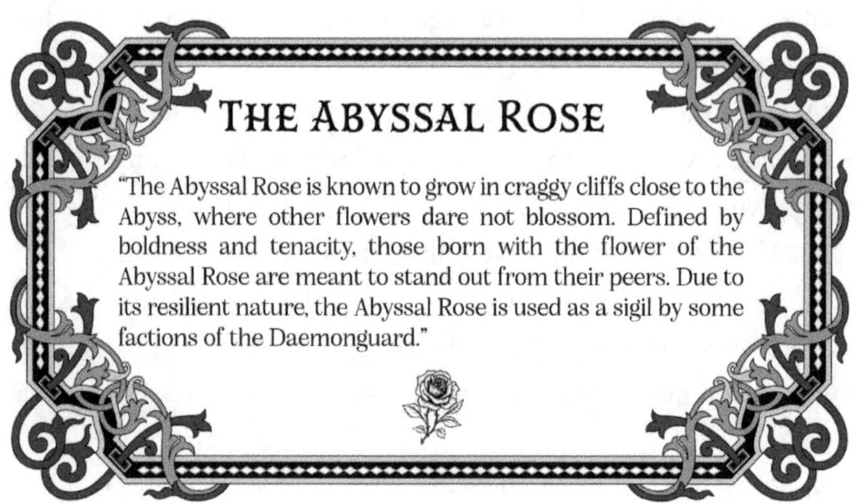

THE ABYSSAL ROSE

"The Abyssal Rose is known to grow in craggy cliffs close to the Abyss, where other flowers dare not blossom. Defined by boldness and tenacity, those born with the flower of the Abyssal Rose are meant to stand out from their peers. Due to its resilient nature, the Abyssal Rose is used as a sigil by some factions of the Daemonguard."

Katrina gloated, "I'm definitely resilient—I have the gold medals to prove it!"

Celise remained quiet. She studied the rose thoughtfully. She thought the plant looked rather threatening, its blossoms tipped with bloody crimson, its thorns long and curved. Sharp and beautiful all at once. Just like Katrina.

Unable to help herself, Celise wondered if Katrina might be the girl to change the fate of the kingdom. Was she destined to become the duchess of Gravenmere?

Perhaps Mordwen's prophecy would come true.

Celise felt sick to her stomach again. Not that she envied her sister—the Mad Dog duke sounded like a turbulent fellow—but she worried the kingdom's fate was about to take a bad turn.

Heather pointed out, "It says the Abyssal Rose is a sigil of the Daemonguard, so it must be a sign, Katrina! You're meant to catch Lord Elias's eye at the ball!"

Katrina smirked. "I certainly plan to."

She looked as confident and self-assured as the roses.

Chapter 6

The Tea Tournament

Interrupting Katrina's bragging, a servant approached the three ladies down the garden path. The maid wore a green dress with belled sleeves, a white apron and a little white bonnet upon her head, fastened under her chin by a length of lace.

The young woman called to them in a cheery voice, "May I show you to your table, my ladies?"

Celise would have liked to explore the gardens a little more—she had yet to encounter a Starlight Dahlia—but it seemed like Katrina was satisfied after finding her own flower.

"Yes, let's sit down for tea. I want to see who else is assigned to our table," Katrina said.

One by one, the servant inspected each of their tickets. Then the young woman led them down a flagstone path to their right, which wandered away from the Zodiac Gardens, under an arched trellis, and toward their next destination.

Celise, Heather and Katrina followed.

Before long, the flagstone path opened into a tea garden filled with chairs and tables. The towers of Gravenmere Castle created a bold backdrop beyond the walled garden. Wispy white clouds trailed across a cool azure sky, framing the castle's peaked roof and pointed spires.

A trellis of climbing lumenblooms divided the tea garden into two halves. The older wives and matrons were seated on one side of the trellis, screened from the younger, unmarried ladies. Celise caught sight of Marcella, already seated at a table, deep in conversation with two other noblewomen of similar age. Celise didn't know what the highborn mothers spoke about, but they looked thoroughly engrossed in the topic.

Heather suddenly grabbed Katrina's arm and pointed. "Katrina, look!" she gasped. "Isn't that Ambrosia Verabon, your rival from the Luminous Lady's Fencing League?"

"Oh," Katrina stiffened, looking toward the far end of the pavilion. "I wouldn't call her a *rival*."

"But last season she almost won your gold medal. . . ."

"*Almost?* My parry was *much* faster than hers. The referee called the point, and there's nothing more to say."

Heather fell silent.

Celise remembered the incident earlier in Vimspring when Katrina had competed for the Forsynthian Royal Cup. A lot of contention had surrounded the gold medal. Some of the papers implied that Katrina might have been favored unfairly. Celise wouldn't have thought twice about it, except that Katrina had been particularly cruel to her after the match. She had bullied Celise relentlessly around the stables until Mr. Talisworth complained to Lord Dhastel.

Ambrosia Verabon—the lady in question—was seated under a shady gazebo with twelve other girls. She was very beautiful, with luxurious indigo-colored hair and bright green eyes that dominated her pointed face. She wore a lacy white hat upon her head and a bright magenta dress with a swooping neckline.

With a sinking feeling, Celise noticed that the servant was leading them directly to Ambrosia's table.

Oh no.

Her palms began to sweat.

Celise tried not to feel like a total imposter as she approached the group at the Silver Thistle table. Her stepmother's words rang out in her head: "*Stand straight; your posture is crooked. Pronounce your words; don't mumble. You're walking too loudly; lean forward on your toes. Don't touch your face when addressing a lord or lady. You're standing incorrectly. My, my, but you're a hopeless case, aren't you?*"

Katrina reached the head of the table with Heather by her side. Celise guessed that Katrina knew some of the ladies from the fencing league.

"Who's this?" One of the ladies asked, giving Celise a curious look.

"This is my sister, Celise," Katrina said quickly.

"I didn't know you had another sister."

"She's . . . um, well, she's not really . . . ."

"Well. She's not *well.* She's often ill," Heather suggested.

The young woman glanced at Celise, noting her petite frame and slightly hunched posture. "I'm glad you were feeling well enough to attend the ball."

"I wouldn't miss it," Celise managed.

Then she swept up her skirts and sat down, trying to remember her stepmother's whirlwind lessons on table manners. Her two younger half-sisters perched in their seats like birds alighting on a branch. She couldn't capture their grace if she tried.

After all of the ladies were seated, a servant made introductions in a stiff, formal tone: "This is Lavender Dupont, Margaret Thelise, Felicia Credence, Bernadette Goodweather and Ambrosia Verabon. . . ."

At the name *Ambrosia,* Celise sensed Katrina stiffen. A scowl flitted across her face but quickly disappeared.

Two of the young ladies at the table were from Bratzia, with their soft lavender hair and light brown complexions. On closer inspection, they looked like twins. Celise assumed they were the same outspoken girls from the garden tour.

"You two know each other, don't you?" Bernadette Goodweather asked, a blond girl wearing a pale blue dress with puffed sleeves. She looked between Katrina and Ambrosia. "You were both contenders for the gold medal, weren't you?"

"I'd hardly call Ambrosia a contender," Katrina snarked.

The indigo-haired heiress simply smiled into her cup, but her sharp eyes spoke differently. "We were tied until the last second. Katrina scored the winning point. Some of the spectators didn't agree with the referee."

"Didn't a fight break out in the stands?" Bernadette Goodweather asked.

"My fans were upset," Ambrosia shrugged.

"Fans? *As if,*" Katrina muttered, her cheeks flushing bright pink.

Ambrosia flashed her another haughty smile. Celise noticed her teacup beginning to glow a dark blue color. *Mana.*

Katrina picked up her own cup and ignited the shined porcelain. Her own mana glowed crimson red.

It was a small but significant flex of their power. Celise sensed something threatening about the tension between the two ladies.

Then the other girls at the table began picking up their shined teacups. One by one, the cups began to glow with different light—pink, blue, purple, and green—as the noblewomen channeled their mana through their hands. The water inside the cup heated, allowing their tea to steep.

After some hesitation, Celise lifted her cup to her lips and pretended it was warm.

The conversation flowed from there. Soon, the soft clink of china and feminine voices filled the shade beneath the rose-laden trellises. The table was artfully arranged with a display of bright pink cupcakes at its center. More plates full of cucumber sandwiches, sugared peaches and lemon wedges, honey-glazed shortbread and chocolate-dipped strawberries filled the table. Two female servants in Blackwood livery stood in the shade nearby, ready to refill a cup at a moment's notice. The young ladies seemed as poised and practiced as their mothers at this sort of socializing. Shined teacups glinted. Long skirts rustled. The variety of gowns created a rainbow of refinement. It was all very lovely. Picturesque. Perfect.

Celise's bright blue eyes drifted upward as beams of sunlight trickled through the wisteria vines. She found herself wondering what it must be like to live in this world, where every occasion was like an oil painting staged to perfection. *Nothing* could be unpretty. *Nothing* could be unclean, imperfect, cheap or common. She missed the simplicity of the stables, of her lunches spent with Mr. Talisworth or by herself in the fields with the horses. She didn't know how to be herself in this kind of company. She wondered if the other ladies knew how to *be themselves* at all, or if their entire world was a mask.

Did they ever take the mask off?

She watched her stepsister, Katrina, out of the corner of her eye. A little scowl alighted on Katrina's lips; she looked just like her mother. Her eyes darted around the table at the other ladies. Her evaluation of their clothes and appearance was obvious to Celise, though well guarded. Katrina was stacking up chips, as it were, comparing her own charms to theirs. Celise thought all of the women looked excruciatingly beautiful. She felt like a little mouse compared to a flock of exotic birds.

True to her zodiac sign, Katrina wasn't content to sit quietly at the table for long. She leaned forward, loud and outspoken, regaling the other ladies with stories from Windhaven Ranch. Most of the young women owned Dhastel horses. Celise wasn't surprised. Dhastel walkers, only thirteen to fourteen hands high in white or cream colors, with gaits as smooth as silk, were bred for fine ladies.

"Do all three of you live at Windhaven?" One of the Bratzian twins asked, nodding to Heather and Celise. Celise recognized the rich accent from their earlier walk through the gardens.

Heather answered, "Yes, we do."

"That must be lovely, living around so many horses," the twin said.

"Celise spends the most time with the horses," Katrina said behind her teacup. She cast a sideways glance at Heather, who barely held back a giggle.

The second Bratzian twin said to Celise in broken Forsynthian, "Your hair is . . . a very nice color. Like . . . a flower." She pointed.

Her sister helpfully translated, "She means your hair looks like the flowers behind you. It has a bright berry undertone. I have to agree; it is very unusual. Eye-catching."

"Oh . . . thank you," Celise murmured and fell silent. Her coloring was uncommon in Forsynthia. Her features were more like her mother's, or so she had been told.

The ladies all watched her expectantly, as though Celise were supposed to carry on the conversation, but she didn't know what to say.

"I must apologize for my sister; she's a bit shy," Katrina jumped in, then jabbed Celise with her elbow. "You're terribly rude when you sit there and stare at people. It's off-putting!"

"Sorry, um," Celise murmured in a soft voice. "Thank you. I think everyone at the table looks very beautiful."

The Bratzian twins smiled at her. Celise smiled back, a bit timid. A beat of painful silence followed.

Then the light-haired Bernadette Goodweather said to no one in particular, "I'm sure you've all heard the rumors. Do you think it's true? Old Blackwood intends to find a match for his son by tomorrow night?"

The unmarried ladies shifted about and flitted their fans, listening.

"I heard the Mad Dog duke is going to announce a bride at the ball," Ambrosia Verabon offered.

"Is that true?" Katrina asked. "How do you know for certain?"

"My mother is close friends with Lady Estoria Blackwood," Ambrosia explained. "The Blackwoods are eager to see their son wed. They've tasked him with selecting a bride from his dance partners. That's why there are so many young ladies in attendance."

"I heard the new engagement is supposed to be announced at midnight," Bernadette agreed.

"Then it all comes down to the ball," Katrina said, before shutting her mouth, as though she had admitted too much.

So that's what Old Blackwood meant by a "clandestine" event, Celise thought to herself. *No wonder he asked Katrina and Heather not to retire early.* He must have said the same thing to all the families in attendance.

All of the young women seemed to realize the same thing at once. They glanced around the table at each other uneasily, some apprehensive, some smiling, all sizing up the competition. Celise glanced down at her folded hands. She didn't consider herself in the running for a duke, of course. But she wasn't at all above the gossip. She, too, wondered which lucky lady would be selected as the young duke's betrothed.

Or . . . *unlucky* lady?

"Have you read *The Lady's Letter*?" one of the girls dropped her voice low. "Do you really want to dance with the Mad Dog duke? He's a bit frightening, isn't he?"

"Maybe he's just misunderstood," another young lady said. "*The Lady's Letter* exaggerates things sometimes. They named him the Hero of the Realm when he returned from the Abyss, because he killed the Daemon King."

"He's not the only hero," the second Bratzian twin muttered into her teacup.

Yes, she had a point. As Celise recalled, five Luminous warriors had faced the Daemon King in the final battle, one from each of the Five Kingdoms.

"I know Raelia Riverton personally," Ambrosia Verabon said, her nose tilted upward. "I recall when she broke off her engagement to the duke. She would never lie about such a thing. Elias is horrifically scarred, with a brutal temper. He's *crackpots* mad." She snapped shut her fan and tapped it on the table, as though to emphasize her point. “Crackpots! I’ll dance with him for a round, but not for two.”

The girl next to her laughed. "Oh, come off it, Ambrosia! You wouldn’t turn down *a duke* for a second dance. He might be ugly, but he’s still a Blackwood. I heard Lord Elias broke off the engagement with Lady Riverton. He spurned her, so she retaliated.”

Mutters broke out around the table behind twirling fans.

“Nonsense . . . .”

“Ridiculous!”

“Could it be true?”

“I wonder if his scars are really that grotesque?” Heather asked, and the other girls paused to listen. “Has anyone seen him? Does anyone know?”

Celise felt a stab of anxiety at the sudden tension. It seemed all of the young women were a bit apprehensive—and intrigued—by the Mad Dog duke. One by one, they all shook their heads.

“Lady Riverton told me he’s a recluse,” Ambrosia continued, a little smirk on her lips. “He’s exiled himself to the Blackwood’s hunting lodge at Summervale Cottage, far out in the countryside. He’s rarely seen around the city, and when he makes an appearance, he wears a mask.”

“A mask?” Katrina laughed. “That’s all a bit *theatric*.”

“Well, it’s the truth. No one has seen his face since he returned from the war, except for Lady Riverton. You can’t trust a man who wears a mask.”

“He was rumored to be quite handsome in his youth,” one of the girls said.

“After ten years at war? Who’s to say?” Ambrosia raised an eyebrow and sipped her tea.

The group fell silent. The women glanced at each other behind their fans.

“Well, I’d dance with him if he asked,” one of the twins said.

“So would I,” a blond girl sitting next to Ambrosia agreed.

It seemed the ladies were feeling competitive again, and a simmering tension fell over the table. Celise glanced down at her untouched teacup. She wondered—did Elias Blackwood really wear a mask? It made the figure of the Mad Dog even more mysterious.

"I don't understand the urgency," one of the ladies said, breaking the brief silence. "Why must the duke choose a bride tonight?"

Ambrosia arched a knowing eyebrow. She looked pleased to share the latest gossip. "It's all a bit scandalous. High King Valienthe is pressuring the Blackwood family to see the duke settled and *out of the way*." Her voice lowered even further. "To put it delicately, the Princess of Illysea spoke too highly of him."

The ladies all leaned forward with interest.

Ambrosia continued, "The princess publicly defended Elias's reputation to *The Lady's Letter*. Now people are speculating—why? Does she harbor hidden feelings for the Hero of the Realm?"

Her friend, Bernadette Goodweather, interjected, "Nonsense, the princess has been engaged to the crown prince since childhood! Their wedding is in six months' time!"

"Exactly my point." Ambrosia tapped her fan again. "Maybe she's getting cold feet? In either case, after she publicly defended Elias's reputation, Prince Alric Valienthe became jealous and complained to his father, so now the king wants Lord Elias to wed posthaste."

"Can the king do that?" one of the girls asked. "Force the Mad Dog to wed?"

"A king's suggestion carries a lot of weight," Ambrosia shrugged.

"I find it hard to believe the royal family would be worried about the Mad Dog stealing away a princess," Katrina sneered. "How absurd."

"I suppose that's royalty for you," Ambrosia said with a knowing sigh, as though she were personal friends with the king himself.

Celise listened with interest. So, the future Queen of Forsynthia had defended Elias Blackwood's reputation, which caused a schism of jealousy between the prince and the duke. It sounded like two stallions butting heads over a mare.

But what had caused the Princess of Illysea to get involved in the first place? Did she know the Mad Dog? Why would she cause such a scandal?

"Do you think Elias and the princess are secret lovers?" One of the ladies asked the question on Celise's mind.

Ambrosia smiled gleefully. "My point exactly! It seems suspicious. I think they must have some sort of connection."

As the ladies began chatting animatedly over this new gossip, Celise remained quiet and listened. She sensed there was more to the story, but no one else at the table seemed to have further details to share. The ladies all gave their various opinions, then the conversation turned away from the Mad Dog to the royal wedding and other affairs. They discussed the different popular waltzes that might be performed at the gala. Some steps were more trendy this year than last year, though Celise knew nothing about dancing.

"Are you feeling up for the ball, Katrina?" Ambrosia Verabon asked suddenly, her eyebrow raised. "Your feet are so slow, I'm surprised you know how to waltz."

Katrina's brow darkened—prettily. "I can waltz just as well as you, Ambrosia. I believe *your* clumsy footwork is to thank for my gold medal."

"My *feet* are faster than yours—and my hand. The referee made a mistake. The winning point should have been mine!"

Katrina and Ambrosia glared at one another.

The ladies turned to watch the argument. One of them interrupted, "Let it rest, Ambrosia. Your fans complained enough about this after the championship. . . ."

"It was *my* gold medal!" Ambrosia sneered, then thrust her chin at Katrina in a rather unladylike way. "*This one* cheated. The referee favored her from the beginning. She batted her eyes at him several times."

"That's not true!" Katrina gasped. "I'm the fastest foil in the junior league."

"Then prove it!"

"How are we supposed to do that?" Katrina mocked. "Shall we duel each other with our teaspoons?"

"What's all this?" a voice sang upon the perfumed air. Celise looked up, dismayed, as their argument drew a group of older women to the Silver Thistle table. At the forefront was none other than Lady Estoria Blackwood. Although well-along in years, the silver-haired duchess walked with a sprightly step. Immediately behind her came Lady Marcella Dhastel and Lady Delaney Verabon.

"What is all this fuss about the gold medal?" Lady Verabon asked.

"Katrina, you know it's unladylike to brag," Marcella snapped.

"I wasn't bragging, Mother. Ambrosia mocked me. She said I cheated!"

"What utter nonsense!" Marcella gasped.

Delaney Verabon tilted her chin and didn't look at either of the Dhastel women. "However the final match turned out, it's in the past," she said.

"What do you mean, 'However it turned out?'" Marcella demanded. "It turned out *very* clearly. Katrina won!"

Lady Verabon went to stand behind her daughter and placed her hands on Ambrosia's shoulders. "Well, there was a dispute among the judges."

"Among the *fans,* perhaps. The judges were *in agreement*," Marcella glared.

"If the winner of the Junior Cup is still in dispute, we can settle the matter here and now," Estoria said with a regal tone.

"Whatever do you mean? You don't suggest a fencing match at a tea party!" Marcella laughed nervously, exchanging a glance with Katrina, who was still glowering at Ambrosia across the table.

Estoria laughed. "Of course I do! Why not? We have plenty of room on the grounds, and the afternoon is still early. I'll have my servants bring the foils and jackets out of storage. We can proceed within the hour!"

Marcella looked shocked.

Lady Verabon cooed to her daughter in a soothing voice, "Ambrosia, my sweet, I know you had strong feelings about the gold medal, but perhaps you should apologize to Katrina—"

"Mother—"

"Where's the fun in that!" Estoria interrupted. "Let's settle this once and for all with an impromptu fencing tournament here in the gardens. I love spontaneity!" She clapped her hands. "Clear the tables! I'll have my servants bring out the fencing gear. Of course, it won't be for a *real* gold medal . . . but perhaps the winner can have some other prize? A shined cup from my personal set?"

"A 'Teacup Tournament'?" one of the girls cried. "I love that idea!"

"This is very exciting!" a Bratzian twin agreed.

"Perhaps it will become a new trend!" Heather added.

"If it pleases Your Grace . . . ." Lady Marcella began, looking strained. "The girls are off-season . . . and their dresses are so pretty . . . I can't imagine they would agree to a match."

"Of course I would!" Katrina stood up from the table, her stiff skirts pushing back her chair. "I'll be happy to remind Ambrosia why she lost the gold."

"If that's the case, then I'm sure Ambrosia would like to prove the referee wrong!" Lady Verabon scoffed, defending her daughter.

Ambrosia remained silent, a haughty arch to her eyebrows.

The Duchess Estoria clapped her hands. "Wonderful. This will certainly spice up the afternoon! Now, if you'll follow me, I know just the place where we can hold a match. Roffolo, will you inform my husband about our change of plans? I don't think he'll want to miss this."

A manservant in green livery bowed from the edge of the gazebo. Then he hurried off down one of the garden paths.

Heather stood up and linked arms with Katrina. They went to stand near Marcella at the end of the table.

The other young ladies didn't move until Ambrosia Verabon set down her teacup. She smiled at Katrina. Celise didn't think it was a friendly look, but amongst ladies, it was hard to tell.

"All in the spirit of good sportsmanship," she said, as though the idea were hers all along. "Let us prepare for the match!"

Then all the young women set down their teacups and stood up from their chairs, chatting in excited voices and moving gracefully in their fine dresses. The Blackwood staff came to clear the table. The group began to separate as Ambrosia and her mother went to change into their fencing garb. A few of Ambrosia's closest friends left with her, but most of the ladies followed Her Grace Estoria Blackwood across the gardens to the new location for the Teacup Tournament.

A servant approached Marcella and Katrina and bowed low. "Please, if you will come with me, I will have you fitted for your fencing jacket and helm in our recreation hall. There will be servants to help you dress and prepare for the match."

With a regal tilt to her head, Marcella blew past the servant like a flagship. Katrina and Heather were like two fishing boats in her wake.

Celise watched them walk away. She felt like the events of the afternoon were quickly spiraling out of control. She climbed to her feet and swayed for a moment, hovering at the edge of the empty table, unsure of what to do with herself.

No one looked back.

No one called for her.

She hesitated, wondering if Marcella would notice when she didn't follow after them, but her stepmother did not turn back. It seemed she was . . . *forgotten.*

Celise waited in the shade of the gazebo, invisible, as her stepmother disappeared from sight. She wondered if Marcella would remember her and send for her, but after several minutes, the table was cleared and she was left alone in the pavilion. The servants filled up their trays and carts with used cups and empty dishes, then disappeared. No one asked after her. No one glanced twice in her direction.

Somehow, she wasn't surprised.

Celise took a breath of perfumed air and clutched her calico skirt in hand.

Should she join Lady Estoria and her entourage?

She didn't have a desire to watch Katrina's tournament. She had been on the receiving end of her sister's foil several times. She would much rather explore the Gravenmere grounds.

Marcella had told her *no wandering off.*

Yet . . . her stepmother would be busy for the next hour or two with the Teacup Tournament. Would she notice if Celise took a little tour of Gravenmere by herself?

To her right, in the opposite direction of the tea tournament, a brick path led through a tangled cottage garden full of pink poppies, bachelor buttons and sunflowers. Celise didn't see anyone walking there. No ladies, gardeners or hired hands. Solitude at last.

It probably loops around to the Moongazer Tower, she reasoned. She could rejoin Dasha back at the tower after she stretched her legs.

Celise stepped out from between the white marble pillars of the gazebo. Like a little ghost, she started down the garden path, her slippers crunching softly on the packed dirt. With each step, the tension eased from her shoulders.

Finally, she could breathe.

Chapter 7

The Ghost Swords

Celise lost track of her direction.

Gazing about the luscious scenery, she followed the brick path through the cottage garden, down a slight hill, and then into an orchard of espaliered apple trees. She passed by several pavilions with little cottages where other guests were housed, and then more gardens, until somehow she arrived at the north wing of Gravenmere Castle.

She hadn't seen this side of the castle before. A wide stone staircase led up to an extravagant pair of double doors, propped open. Inside, the manor's staff swarmed about like excited bees. Celise caught a strong whiff of onions and rosemary. This must be the kitchens.

She felt bolder and more comfortable around the servants than the aristocracy. Curious, she wandered up to the open entryway. No one stopped her. The castle's staff dashed back and forth, arms laden with towels, blankets, refreshments and everything in between. It felt like she had walked into a busy hotel.

Celise didn't mean to trespass, but she wasn't eager to return to the Moongazer Tower just yet. While she was free and unescorted, she might as well see what she could of the castle.

She walked through the north wing's busy ground floor. She saw a great hubbub at the end of the corridor and a cloud of steam—she assumed that was the entrance to the kitchens. If she wandered in that direction, she would definitely be noticed. So she headed for a quiet staircase instead. She climbed up to the second floor, which was less busy.

Actually, the second floor appeared to be deserted.

Celise reached the landing at the top of the stairs. She hesitated for a moment before continuing down the second floor's hallway. The corridor was wide enough for four people to pass comfortably side by side, which made its emptiness even more apparent. Compared to the ground floor, it was totally silent. Rich green rugs trailed the length of the hall. Standing vases, taller and broader than herself, shined with all sorts of colorful enamels, lined the hallway. She had never seen such expensive, immaculate decor. She imagined a whole army of servants spent their days cleaning Gravenmere Castle. The place was so large that as soon as they were finished, they likely had to start over from the top. She kept her gloved hands buried in her sprigged cotton skirts and tried not to touch anything.

Treading softly, Celise passed by the long line of giant vases and locked doors. It was a bit eerie and more than a little disappointing. There wasn't much to see, and now she definitely felt like she was trespassing.

Finally, at the end of the corridor, she saw a sign of life. There, a manservant dressed in brown livery was hovering about a pair of heavy wooden doors. He seemed to be having difficulty with the knob. His key was stuck, and he rattled the brass knob in his hand with an air of frustration. As Celise watched, the servant finally got one of the doors open and let himself inside. He left the door cracked.

Celise glanced around the hallway, but she didn't see any other servants or attendants nearby. Then she turned back to the door, wondering about what she had just seen. The man wasn't dressed in green livery like the rest of the Blackwood staff. Something about his behavior seemed . . . odd.

She felt the desire to investigate.

Her conscience reminded her that she shouldn't be wandering about Gravenmere Castle unescorted. She didn't truly belong there, and the second floor was otherwise empty. The room beyond the cracked door was probably out of bounds. But . . . why not take a quick look? She was used to passing unnoticed around the Dhastel estate like a little ghost. She likely wouldn't be noticed if she explored a bit more.

As she approached the door, a glimmer of mysterious light caught her eye.

More curious than concerned, she peeked inside.

The soft, flickering light of gas lamps illuminated the room beyond the cracked door. She saw unfamiliar metal objects glittering on the walls. She pushed the door open with a cautious nudge.

She stared.

Gas lamp chandeliers illuminated a long chamber with golden light. The room wasn't quite as large as the Dhastel Great Hall, but close to it. Only two of the chandeliers were lit, casting the room in a sparkling half-shadow. Her eyes traveled to the wall closest to her, where rows of metal rods coated with bright enamels were mounted on metal hooks. The rods sported hilts and pommels, as though designed for combat.

She gasped softly.

They were *ghost swords*.

She recognized the hilts from drawings and illustrations she had read. Ghost swords were the weapons of the Daemonguard. Luminaries channeled their mana into the shined rods, which focused their power and projected a slightly transparent "ghost" blade. The "blades" appeared like vapor or mist emitting from the rod, which was how they got their name.

Celise took another step forward, gazing around the wide, half-lit chamber. The room held quite a collection of "blades," though without any mana channeling through them, they looked more like grounding rods. From one to two inches in diameter, the rods varied in size and shape. Some were almost as long as she was tall; others were very short, perhaps the length of her forearm. The enamels were a plethora of colors and patterns. Some looked like rods dipped in spilled acrylics, with patterns of marbled purple, silver, green and gold. Others were shined scarlet red or matte black. Still others were checkered blue and yellow. One had vining bands of pink and orange. The weapons had a deadly reputation, yet up on the wall, they hung like bright and colorful wands. They almost looked like children's toys.

She wandered deeper inside, her mouth slightly agape. The room didn't look like a soldier's armory—more like a collection of family heirlooms. She passed by a glass case that ran the length of the room, filled with military medals. The plaques and nameplates beside the medals detailed the history of the Blackwood Luminaries that had served in the Forsynthian military. Despite the oil portraits and nameplates, Celise couldn't begin to unravel the rich heritage of the Blackwood house. Their bloodline seemed to go back to the founding of the kingdom, perhaps even before. She didn't know what the medals meant, but they were polished and well kept.

Her sense of inferiority grew.

The opposite wall from the ghost swords held a variety of shined shields and helms and a full suit of armor from the Iron Age. She saw the Blackwood family crest centered on the wall: a green dragonfly on a black diamond. It seemed she had stumbled into the Blackwood family's trophy room.

She started to get a bit nervous. She really shouldn't be there.

Then a door slammed shut across the room, making her jump. Her heart leapt into her throat. Her eyes flew to the opposite end of the chamber, where a mysterious pocket door was hidden in the shadows beyond the gas lamp chandeliers. It probably led to a servants' passage.

The servant in brown livery must have left the trophy room. She didn't see anyone else in attendance. Except for a wide variety of interesting artifacts, the room was empty. Whoever the intruder had been, he had slipped away while she was distracted.

Perhaps he was a ghost?

She smiled at the thought. She wasn't opposed to the idea. But she wasn't about to go chasing after a ghost around the castle—she had explored quite enough of Gravenmere for one day.

Now what?

Celise sensed her little adventure was already drawing to a close. She should leave the room and return to the Moongazer Tower . . . but she found herself lingering. She glanced through the tall glass windows on her left. From this height, she could see a checker-patterned pavilion just outside the north wing of the castle. Sprawled under the pale Hallowsin sky, a tiled pavilion of black granite and white quartz was visible from the trophy room. It wasn't immediately next to the castle, but slightly removed at the center of a trim, green lawn, framed on three sides by boxwood hedges.

A group of ladies gathered there.

Ah. The Teacup Tournament.

She had a clear vantage point, though the figures looked rather small. Celise thought she recognized Lady Estoria Blackwood in her emerald green gown among the gathering of pastel and lace dresses. The ladies stood in a loose circle around the checkered pavilion, where two figures in white fencing jackets faced off against each other. That would be Ambrosia and Katrina, no doubt. From this distance, they looked like toy figurines dancing about on strings.

A spark of mana drew her eye. Ambrosia was on the defensive. The fencing match had begun.

Celise watched with mild interest. Fencing was a sport, not *real* swordplay like how the Daemonguard trained to fight monsters in the Abyss. Ambrosia and Katrina's foils couldn't compare to the ghost swords hanging from the treasury's walls. A flash of mana sparked whenever the tip of a foil touched a jacket. That's how points were scored—by mere touches. But that was all the power required to join the Luminous Lady's Fencing League. She didn't think Katrina or Ambrosia had enough mana ability to ignite a ghost sword.

Then again, what did she know about such things?

A whistle blew. It seemed Estoria Blackwood herself was refereeing the match. The silver-haired matron raised a little colored flag. Had Katrina scored the first point? Or was it Ambrosia? For a flicker of a moment, Celise wished she was just a little closer so she could see the action.

Suddenly, she heard the thunder of pounding footsteps from the hallway. It sounded like a large group of people was approaching. The footsteps were joined by a hubbub of deep voices. She heard the unmistakable baritone of old Cornelius Blackwood booming down the hall.

Celise froze. Her heart leapt into her throat. The voices were just outside the door! She looked around the trophy room, panicking. There weren't many places to hide among the trophies, and her dress made it doubly hard to maneuver.

Finally, she dragged open a heavy wardrobe that stood against the wall. She pushed aside a rack of antique Daemonguard uniforms and flung herself inside. No sooner had she pulled the door shut, leaving just a crack to see by, than three men entered the room.

Her heart pounded.

She felt a bit faint.

Oh no! she thought. *Now I've done it.*

"That's strange; I thought I ordered all the doors to be locked on the second floor," Old Blackwood blustered. Then he continued, "To conclude our tour of Gravenmere Castle, Meister Barbaros, I wanted to show you our family's treasury. We hold the finest collection of ghost swords and shined armor outside of the Royal Skydust Museum. *Better* than the museum, if you ask me, but I might be biased." Blackwood chortled at his own joke.

"Your collection is impressive," Barbaros agreed.

Meister Barbaros had a Bratzian accent, his vowels clipped and his "T's" very pronounced. Celise thought of the twins she had met in the rose garden. Was a Bratzian guildmaster attending the gala? It sounded like Meister Barbaros had some important business with the Blackwoods.

"We have a similar room like this one in our guildhall," Barbaros said. "You come from a warrior's bloodline, I see."

"Yes, *yes*. I never served on the Daemonguard myself; I was born into an era of peace, before the last spawning. My son, however, has quite the military career."

"Who hasn't heard of the Hero of the Realm?" Barbaros grinned.

Through the crack in the wardrobe's doors, Celise noticed a third figure—very tall, wearing a dark coat—standing next to Barbaros. The tall man did not respond to the compliment.

Was this . . . the Mad Dog?

Trying to calm her racing heart, Celise breathed deep and slow as she watched the men move deeper into the room.

"Did you bring the prototype?" the tall man asked.

"I did, Lord High Commander." With some shuffling, Meister Barbaros withdrew a long wooden box from his jacket. A smaller box followed the first. They looked like a matching set.

Lord High Commander? Celise leaned forward, her slight form pressed carefully against the wardrobe door, her ears perked. Wasn't that the military title for Elias Blackwood? Was the Mad Dog standing just a few feet away from her? Maybe she could catch a glimpse of his face? She wondered if she should throw open the wardrobe and reveal herself, just to get a clear view of him. She would be the first lady at the gala to see the Mad Dog in person.

Surely, he wouldn't be wearing a mask in a meeting with a Bratzian guildmaster.

Then again, what did she know?

Celise squinted through the cracked door. Not far from the wardrobe, a full set of shined armor stood at the center of the room, a stunning example of Iron Age craftsmanship. Three men came to stand before the armor. Unfortunately, due to the angle, she couldn't see their features clearly. Meister Barbaros was the most visible. She caught the outline of his lavender-pale hair. It was very curly. The top of his head was bald and shiny. She thought he might be wearing a monocle.

Celise watched the tall figure of the High Commander unlock one of the boxes with his gloved hands.

Odd that he's wearing gloves indoors, she thought. She wondered again about his mask, but he was standing slightly behind the set of archaic armor. All she could see was his dark hair, which looked shiny and slicked back with oils.

She squinted until her eyes were watering, trying to see what the box contained. Then the duke plucked a lump of gold out of the case.

It was . . . a *bullet.*

"These slugs are quite large," the Mad Dog mused.

"Necessary to shoot down daemons," Barbaros assured him.

"I can think of three ways to shave down the size. It would save on the cost of materials and shipment," Elias said.

Barbaros winced and exchanged a look with Old Blackwood. "I am glad to hear it," he said. "The larger box contains our new anti-mana pistol. Please test it at your earliest convenience, Lord High Commander. We welcome any notes you might have for the design. We've named the prototype the 'Starcaster Cannon.'"

Celise listened with increasing interest. Were they talking about a shined gun? Guns weren't used by the Daemonguard, everyone knew that.

"Why call it a cannon when it's a pistol?" the commander asked in his brusque Forsynthian accent.

"Once you see the design, you'll understand," Barbaros said with a hint of humor.

"What is an anti-mana pistol?" Old Blackwood asked. "I thought you were designing a gun that could *channel* mana. . . ."

"That's exactly what this gun does," Barbaros explained. "A shined gun is easy to make for any half-skilled artificer. However, most shined guns overheat and blow up under the force of a Luminary's natural power. That's why mana-infused firearms aren't used by the Daemonguard. Too many missing hands."

Old Blackwood snorted. "True."

"Our new *anti*-mana gun incorporates a secondary chamber for the purpose of *defusing* excess mana. The trigger must be pulled twice to get off a shot, but that's to help moderate the output of mana and prevent the gun from exploding. In short, it means soldiers can use the weapon safely without the risk of losing a limb."

"It sounds promising," Elias allowed.

Barbaros jumped at the compliment. "It packs quite a kick. The new hazard for soldiers will be avoiding a broken shoulder. The bullet passes from the first chamber into the second chamber, where it's coated in a special mineral oil to reduce the risk of instant combustion. When the trigger is pulled the second time, the mana burst discharges the bullet through the barrel."

"I take it this mineral oil is infused with skydust of some kind?" the High Commander asked.

"A special recipe, Your Grace." Barbaros tapped his nose. "Trade secret."

"A gun safe for Luminaries to use? That's a wonder of the modern era," Old Blackwood said.

"We hope to begin production as soon as the factory is built," Barbaros agreed, his voice laced with implication.

Old Blackwood clasped his hands behind his back and cleared his throat. "Right, yes, the factory. Allow me to allay your concerns, Meister Barbaros. The project is fully funded, as promised. We began construction of the kilns five months ago. The opening ceremony should be in eight weeks' time. You can begin transporting the dust the week before the factory opens."

"Is there any way to offload our supply now? We have twenty thousand pounds waiting in our warehouses for mixing and glazing. Dust #210 Bloodglass is highly unstable if stored more than six months—"

"How unstable? Is it explosive?" the Mad Dog snapped.

"Hard to say."

A beat of silence passed between the three men. Undeterred, Meister Barbaros continued, "By *unstable*, we also mean *unpredictable.* The dust can react with any number of things it comes into contact with. Depending on what it reacts with, one batch firing might lose power, another might catch fire, and another might become acidic, poisonous, or any of that."

Celise was fascinated.

The deep rasp of the High Commander's voice came again, "Are all the different mixtures of skydust this unstable?"

"No, I am only speaking of Dust #210 Bloodglass," Meister Barbaros explained. "We can attempt to refresh the batch, but the final product might not be as potent after firing."

"I'm not sure I follow. What do you mean by 'firing'?" Old Blackwood grumbled.

"He's referring to the factory's function," Elias said.

The guildmaster continued, "Allow me to explain, Your Grace. Perhaps a century ago, at the bloom of the industrial age, large deposits of skydust were found in the Rog Mountains of Bratzia. As you are well aware, skydust is a unique, alien mineral from the meteor that struck Nilos thousands of years ago."

"Who isn't aware of that?" Old Blackwood scoffed.

With a slight bow, Barbaros continued his long-winded explanation, "To create a shined sword, or a shined object of any kind, we must first coat the blade with a specific kind of enamel glaze. We use skydust—or just *dust*—as the base for these glazes. Just like a baker uses different recipes for different kinds of bread, or a potter uses different kinds of frit to achieve a specific color or texture for his pottery, our kingdom's artificers have developed mixtures of skydust for different qualities of shined weapons. A specific 'dust' gives a shined weapon its traits.

"During our guild's application for this military contract, we provided your son, Lord Elias, with an extensive tour of our guildhall in Gigas. Artificing is an art form to our people. Boys and girls who show aptitude enter the guilds as young as thirteen years old. We have many different thousands of varieties of dust—but #210 Bloodglass was chartered by your military specifically for combat. It will give the Daemonguard an unprecedented advantage if the Daemon King were to rise again."

"And what makes Bloodglass so special?"

"It crystallizes a daemon's flesh, slowing their movements considerably during battle," Elias explained. "It would be extremely effective as a bullet or other ranged weapon, but it has yet to be tested in a practical setting." In a darker tone, he added, "If the batch is degrading as you say, Meister Barbaros, then I imagine it's hard to predict what it might do."

"Which is why we want to transport it as soon as possible," the guildmaster agreed. "The final step of our production process, after glazing, is *'firing'* the coated objects in the massive kilns constructed in your factory. Under such intense heat, we're concerned the dust might react poorly, as it's been sitting and degrading for so long."

"If the dust becomes unstable, we can't use it," Elias pointed out. "We might need to amend the contract. Perhaps we can test a small batch to see if it's still viable."

"*Testing?*" Meister Barbaros stammered.

"To ensure quality. We can't proceed with a bad mix."

"You promised your military contracts were secure."

"They *are* secure," the commander growled—a spark of temper. "But we can't work with defective dust, and I won't be pressured into storing twenty thousand pounds of worthless material. We should test each batch before you transport it."

"Testing each batch will waste time and product!" the meister groaned.

"We need assurance! Otherwise we'd be throwing away goldlarks by the bin!"

"It's not our fault your construction took so long," the guildmaster complained, his voice rising in anger. "We were promised a fully functional factory in Vimspring! We met our deadline; you blew past yours like a runaway train!"

"We ran into delays getting permits for the factories," Old Blackwood said. "King Valienthe didn't want the new industrial kilns built so close to the Bratzian border. There were security issues, but we appealed *thirteen* times to get our plans approved—"

Abruptly someone tapped on the door. Celise started, her elbow bumping into the back of the wardrobe. Lucky for her, the sound was swallowed by the servant's footsteps, who entered the room.

"Your Grace?"

"What is it, Roffolo?" Old Blackwood called.

"Her Grace Estoria Blackwood has requested Lord Elias's presence at the checkered pavilion. There is an impromptu fencing match underway, and she wants her son to award the winner. She wishes him to greet his guests."

A beat of silence passed. Elias said nothing.

"A fencing match? What is this nonsense?" Old Blackwood grumbled.

"You can see them out the window, Your Grace."

Old Blackwood turned about and crossed to the row of tall windows. Master Barbaros followed him. The two men left Celise's line of sight, but she could easily imagine their view of the checkered courtyard, visible from the castle's second floor.

"A fencing match? *Now?*" Blackwood blustered again.

"Ah, it looks like my daughters are in attendance," Meister Barbaros crooned. "Perhaps we should continue this discussion later tonight over dinner. Lord High Commander, you are welcome to test the anti-mana pistol at your leisure. Please, take the gun and the casings with you. Consider it a birthday gift."

Elias closed the box of bullets with a firm snap. Then he tucked the wooden case into his jacket and left the room, his boots slamming on the wooden floor. Celise felt his energy pass by the wardrobe like a crackling thundercloud. She shuddered. The Mad Dog did not seem like the friendly or diplomatic sort. Not at all.

After a pause, Meister Barbaros said in a soft voice, "Is he always like this?"

"Temperamental to a fault, no respect for decorum . . . . I truly don't know where my son has gone, Meister Barbaros. A man came back from the Abyss, but he is not the boy I raised."

The Meister made a sympathetic grunt in his throat.

"Oh well," Blackwood recovered himself. "Let us get on with this award ceremony. Trust my wife to instigate a fencing tournament in the middle of a tea party. If it were up to her, she'd put a sword in the hand of every lady in the kingdom!" Blackwood laughed. "Let's go downstairs."

As the two left the room, Celise overheard Meister Barbaros's retreating voice: "My daughters are enjoying their stay in Castleberry City . . . very kind of you to offer up your townhome. . . ."

Celise held her breath until the two men left the room. Then she spilled out of the wardrobe with a flurry of sneezes. Her heart raced in her chest, and her cheeks were flushed with unfamiliar excitement.

The Mad Dog seemed as intense and ill-humored as the rumors described.

She had almost seen his face!

She worried at her bottom lip, thinking over everything she had just heard. How much of the Blackwood's meeting was top secret information? She had just learned of a brand new military weapon—a gun that could channel mana—and dust-shined bullets. She didn't think the papers or science journals had announced anything like that yet. Ghost swords were still the preferred weapon of the Daemonguard. That much was common knowledge.

Had she just witnessed a revolutionary new weapon?

She really needed to get out of this room.

Shaking the dust off her skirts, Celise ran as fast as she could to the door. She paused before rushing through it. She listened to make sure the hallway outside was empty. She could hear an echo of retreating footsteps as Old Blackwood and Meister Barbaros walked down the hall. She held her breath and waited a few more seconds before easing outside into the corridor.

The heavy wooden door slammed shut behind her, carried by its own weight.

Celise jumped. She whirled around. It almost felt like someone had slammed the door from the other side. How ominous! She stared at the door suspiciously, then buried her hands in her skirts, clutching the fabric anxiously. She needed to leave the north wing of the castle and return to the Moongazer Tower. If the fencing match was already finished, then Marcella would be looking for her soon.

Then, abruptly, a gloved hand grabbed her upper arm. "Caught you."

Celise gasped. She instantly recognized the gruff, masculine voice beside her. She went stiff—then a strong hand wrenched her around.

Celise gazed, terrified, into the face of the Mad Dog duke.

At first she flinched back, wincing as though struck, expecting a horrific sight to meet her eyes that would haunt her nightmares for years to come. But there really wasn't much to see. True to the rumors, the duke wore a black mask that covered half of his face. It startled her. But that was all. His scars were hidden behind a plain and unremarkable piece of lightweight metal, perhaps copper, coated with black enamel paint. The glossy black mask covered part of his forehead, his nose and his left eye down to just below his left cheekbone. Most of the left side of his face was hidden.

The right side of his face was not scarred, and a piercing gray eye framed by dark lashes met her terrified gaze. The duke's sleek black eyebrow was lowered in anger, his wide lips turned down into a decided scowl. A shadow of stubble framed his jutting, arrogant jaw.

Celise couldn't hold his gaze—her eyes kept traveling downward.

A white starched collar hid most of the duke's neck, bound with a black cravat. He wore a vest of stormy silver brocade under a black frock coat. Very somber. It struck her as funeral attire, far from the punchy colors suitable for a party.

"What are you doing here?" that harsh, raspy voice demanded.

"I . . . I . . ."

“You were in the treasury. Don’t lie to me, girl. I watched you leave right after my father. This floor is off limits.” His eyes flitted to her bright hair. “We don’t have any guests from Sera’naya. What is your business here?”

Celise’s mouth went dry. The Mad Dog’s anger washed over her like a physical force. Her throat wouldn’t allow her to speak. To suddenly find herself face-to-face with a man like Elias Blackwood—after all of the rumors, gossip and anticipation—left her stricken with terror.

“Are you a spy?" he snarled. His grip tightened on her arm. His one visible eye searched her own—piercing, hardened, gray as ice.

"No . . . I was just . . . looking around . . . ." Celise realized how absurd that sounded. Her heart raced too fast for her to think straight. She couldn't seem to catch her breath. For a horrible moment, she began to swoon. Her vision swam. Little white spots danced in the corner of her eye.

Mother of dust, was she going to faint?

Then a strange sound reached her ears. An uproar at the end of the hallway interrupted their standoff. The roar grew in Celise's hearing like an ocean wave, rising in volume and intensity. She finally pried her eyes away from the duke's burning stare and looked up the corridor. Her gaze traveled past the long row of standing vases and beyond the tall windows dressed with green brocade drapery.

She gasped. "Oh!"

At her slight sound, Elias looked up as well.

A small horde of servants was charging at them down the hallway. Three notable figures were in the lead: a woman wearing a white chef's hat, a stout man with a black scowl on his face, and a lavender-haired Bratzian who was unmistakably the Blackwood's steward.

"There! The young master can settle this," Celise overheard the steward say. "Since Her Grace is indisposed at the Teacup Tournament, our *wayward star* can make a few choices for *his own* birthday banquet. Lord Elias, your timing is excellent! I'm so glad we found you. We have several urgent matters to discuss concerning the ball—"

"Your Grace, the merchant delivering the pork this morning never arrived!" the cook burst out in a high, frantic voice. "We are now eight hours behind schedule, and we *must* move forward with a different option. We have enough venison on hand, but venison *is a much different beast* than pork. Changing the main dish requires a revised twelve-course menu for tomorrow's banquet!"

"The feast took months to plan!" the chef's assistant wailed.

Several more assistants sang out, "We're behind on preparing the meat! It must be tenderized!"

"And marinated overnight!"

The cook continued, "All of the side dishes were planned for honey-glazed pork. Venison is much more savory. Now, I've already designed a menu to compliment the venison, but Mr. Friza insisted we get your approval—"

Celise braced herself as the rush of servants collided with them. She found herself taking an unexpected step toward the duke, seeking shelter in his powerful shoulder. In the sudden crush of people, she found her nose suddenly pressed against the velvet lapel of the duke's jacket.

"While I have you," the steward said, coming right up to Elias and ignoring Celise completely, "I have two documents here that need signing. The decorator for the ballroom has yet to be paid. If you could sign right here at the bottom, I'll see to the rest. This next contract is for a delivery of rugs your mother arranged—"

Elias's grip loosened on Celise's upper arm as the servants continued to swarm them. Instead, his arm shifted to her waist. With a slight turn, he placed his body more fully between her and the crush of servants, instinctively using his size as a shield.

Celise's mouth gaped open. The roar of the crowd suddenly dimmed.

Tha-thump.

She gazed up at the duke, now standing behind him with a clear view of his slick oiled hair. His strong shoulder blocked the majority of the servants from seeing her or touching her. She found herself staring at the nape of his neck with a certain amount of awe. In her small world, few people had ever physically shielded her from harm. She couldn't remember a single instance. Too often, she felt the sting of a riding crop or a cane along her back. Not even Mr. Talisworth could intervene once Marcella or Katrina targeted her.

Yet Elias had placed his body between hers and the mob of servants.

A sense of warmth rushed through her, of a kind she had never experienced before.

A blush rose in her cheeks.

As Celise gazed at the duke's strong back, another man pushed his way to the front of the group. By his green overalls, Celise wondered if he worked in the Blackwood stables. He was holding a round tweed cap in his big hands. "Beg pardon, my lord, but a pipe burst in the Sungilt Cottage. I have a plumber on the way, but which room shall we reassign to the Goodweather family?"

The steward rushed to add, "I have several options selected, young master, but your mother is very picky about where to house the guests. It can be a delicate affair. Do you have any insight into her preferences?"

"Mr. Friza," Elias finally snarled, "Do you lack the capacity to do your job? None of these decisions require my input in the slightest. My father pays you a small fortune to manage the staff. Why is a groundskeeper and half the kitchen up here?"

The rotund man wearing green overalls paled. "I apologize profusely, my lord—"

But Mr. Friza didn't seem deterred. With a practiced smile, he bowed and repeated himself, "I understand your concern, my lord, but this *is* an emergency. Perhaps not the kind you oversee at Firehelm Fortress, but we can't proceed without some direction—"

"Venison is fine. What else?" Elias snapped.

"Oh, thank you! *Thank you!*" The cook gasped. She looked liable to faint from relief. Her assistant grabbed her arm as her knees shook.

"Your signature, my lord," the steward repeated, and held out one of his papers along with a shined pen.

Celise took advantage of the drama and the duke's distraction and quietly made her escape. She ducked behind the groundskeeper and swam through the crowd of eager servants, holding her breath like a diver. Luckily, she had a special knack for slipping away unnoticed, having honed her skills over a lifetime of avoiding Marcella's temper. Although part of her yearned to remain by the duke's side and witness the full scene, she sensed her window of opportunity closing. It was time to exit stage left.

She finally broke free of the crowd, hiked up her skirts, and hurried down the hallway, her ill-fitting shoes sliding on the polished floor.

"Wait!" The duke's harsh, commanding voice echoed behind her with military precision. "Stop her! Stop that girl immediately!"

"Who?" one of the servants called. "Which girl?"

"Do you mean *me*, my lord?" a maid called from the back of the crowd. "How can I be of service?"

"We have one more matter to settle, my lord," Mr. Friza said, placing himself before the duke. "About your mother's delivery, where shall we have the rugs stored? We don't want to disturb the guests—"

Elias called after her again—"*Damnable dust, seize that woman!*"—but Celise didn't look back. She hustled down the stairs to the first floor, hunching forward to remain out of sight. She didn't hear anyone coming after her; the servants were all too focused on the duke.

Celise reached the landing on the first floor and turned left, sprinting away from the kitchens to the wide-open doors that led out onto the castle grounds. Once she was outside, she paid no heed to her direction. She selected the first path she saw that led away from the castle and ran down it. She didn't stop running for quite a ways until she was absolutely certain no one had followed her.

She found herself at the side of a pond where a little bench looked over the water. She collapsed in the shade of a drooping satinwood tree. The pale, feathery leaves fluttered in the cool Hallowsin breeze.

Sweat pouring from her brow, her breath tight in her lungs, Celise took several minutes to calm her racing heart.

By the Maddening Moon—did she really just *hug* the Mad Dog duke?

The smell of his cologne was still rich in her nose. When she turned her head, she caught a whiff of that cinnamon-pepper scent. Zesty, sharp, with a hint of something richer like cream . . . vanilla? By its complexity, she had no doubt the cologne was very expensive, perhaps even a Blackwood exclusive.

She closed her eyes for a moment as the smell summoned a tickling sensation to her stomach. The Mad Dog's slick, oiled hair and broad shoulders remained in her vision. She felt the sensation of his arm sliding around her waist. She recalled how he had placed his body between hers and the staff. How he prevented her from being knocked over.

It was a small thing, and yet . . .

It didn't fit at all with his cruel reputation.

She gnawed on her lip, gazing into the green waters of the pond, turning the encounter over and over in her mind. His mask. His intense gaze. His energy, like a winter storm washing over her.

The Lady's Letter was not exaggerating, she decided. She could see how a highborn lady could detest the duke's temper—perhaps even fear him. But she didn't see him that way. In her world, he seemed more like a hero than a villain.

Despite this, she hoped she never encountered him again.

A patter of footsteps and a humming voice interrupted Celise's thoughts. She looked up as a female servant in green livery came trotting down the path around the pond. The young woman looked like she was headed back to the castle. She held a little yellow flower in one hand and was humming away, not paying attention.

Celise stood up from the bench. "Excuse me?" she called.

The maid looked up with a start. She quickly shoved the wildflower in her apron pocket. "My lady!" she said and dipped into a quick curtsy.

Celise still wasn't used to the title and felt like an imposter. She bobbed her head in return. She had forgotten if it was customary for ladies to acknowledge servants in such a way. She didn't think so.

She must keep up her charade.

"Hello," Celise said. "I went on a walk, and I fear I've become lost. Can you help me?"

“Oh, of course! Don't worry, my lady; it’s easy to get lost on such a large estate. May I escort you back to your quarters? Where are you staying?"

"The Moongazer Tower.”

“My, but you’ve wandered quite far!” The maid gave her a polite, if perplexed, smile. “Please come this way.”

Celise followed the maid down the path in comfortable silence, preoccupied with thoughts of ghost swords, shined bullets and the masked duke.

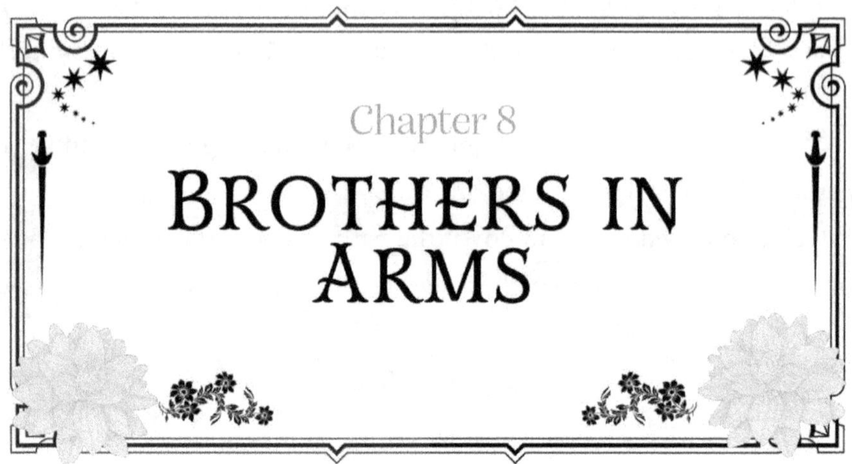

Chapter 8

Brothers in Arms

By the time High Commander Elias Blackwood signed all of the steward's contracts and reviewed the banquet's menu, the girl was gone.

She had slipped off as quickly and mysteriously as she had appeared.

It was . . . irritating. He was used to dealing with military men—soldiers of the Daemonguard who obeyed his every order without question. If he were at Firehelm Fortress, where he spent most of his time, a dozen men would have jumped at his command—"*Seize her!*"

But the servants at Gravenmere were an unpolished lot.

Walking at a fast pace, his black coat swirling about his boots, Elias blew into his study and slammed the door behind him. Despite being heavily used, the room held a distinct air of abandonment. A layer of dust covered the unused chairs and settee that filled the center of the room. Along the walls, the ghostly, pale impressions of missing portraits were visible against the dark damask wallpaper. A conspicuously large spot on the wall behind his desk was empty. Three mirrors, two for decoration and one for dressing, were each covered by a heavy muslin cloth.

Dreary shadows obscured the rest of the room, hiding the cluttered bookshelves, the vases of dead and dried flowers, the soot-stained gas lamps and the broken grandfather clock that stood in the corner. Elias didn't allow the maids into his private study, and he didn't mind the gloominess of the room. He had spent years fighting abhorrent monsters in the twilight conditions of the Abyss. The sun at high noon bothered his eyes far more than a shuttered window.

Elias crossed to the claw-footed executive desk at the end of the room—a behemoth of black walnut and ebony inlays that could have doubled as a dining table. It was swimming in stacks of unsorted papers, opened letters, writing tools and inkwells. As the upcoming head of the Blackwood family, his tasks were without end. He had already taken over much of his father's work. Magistrates from across Gravenmere's domain sent him difficult queries. Truly, the life of a future duke was one of making decisions. The townships on his father's land always needed him to sign a document, allocate funds, or approve an addendum. And he was happy to do so.

Until he lost his patience.

Hands shaking, he set down the wooden box containing Meister Barbaros's shined bullets and his new anti-mana pistol—the Starcaster. Then he hunched over the desk, gripping the edge of the wood, his pulse throbbing in his temples, his shoulders stiff with tension.

Searing pain lanced across his forehead.

The ground tilted. He gripped the wood.

He struggled not to lose consciousness.

Dark drapes covered the west-facing windows. Still, the sunset found a way to pierce the curtains and stab his eyes. A tick began in his clenched jaw as bolts of shooting pain traveled from his shoulders up his neck to the base of his skull. With a grunt of frustration, he swept his arm across the top of the desk, smashing a collection of glass bottles and vials to the ground. Expensive oils and tinctures soaked into the green carpet. The potent scent of laudanum assaulted his nose.

He waited for the migraine to pass.

It would eventually.

Two years ago, the final Battle of the Abyss against the daemons was won. But at a high cost. His entire unit perished in the hellfire that sprung from the Daemon King's maw. The most elite Luminaries of the five kingdoms had turned out for the fight. Without their Skytouched powers, the Daemon King would have broken loose from its underground realm and flooded the world with violent, bloodthirsty monsters. Elias was one of five soldiers at ground zero whose mana talent finally subdued the beast.

He still bore the scars from that battle. The marks on his neck and left side were just part of the damage.

For six months after the Daemon King's defeat, he had remained in a military hospital, sucking down gruel through a straw, surrounded by Luminous medics and doctors. They brought him back from the brink of death, though for what purpose, he couldn't divine. His family had paid the king exorbitant amounts of goldlarks to save his life. Then he was discharged, deemed unfit for service due to his disfigurements, adorned with no less than twelve medals, and given a cushy job as a paper pusher at a military training academy.

His days were filled with meetings, budget concerns, lesson plans and deadlines. It was far from the life he was used to, but the war was won, and the kingdom was at peace. He grimaced at that thought. What did soldiers do during a time of peace? He didn't know. For the last ten years, his mind had been trained upon one simple, clear, unnegotiable goal: kill the Daemon King. Kill it by any means necessary. *Do what needs to be done.*

He had never imagined what would happen after the Daemon King was defeated.

His life had taken on a slow, methodical, almost plodding pace. Repetitive. Quaint, really. It should have been *nice*—but he hadn't expected the stark, gaping hole of irrelevancy that yawned within him. When the emptiness became too brutal, he buried himself in paperwork.

A lot of paperwork.

There was plenty of work to keep himself busy around Firehelm Fortress. Testing was underway, and next year's Luminous recruits for the Daemonguard were about to be selected. Really, he had no time for a gala, courtship, high society or anything else.

The migraine surged again.

Elias held onto the desk like a drowning man clinging to a boat at sea. He had only slept a few hours the night before. After three years of training and seven years in the Abyss, he was used to patrols that sometimes lasted five to ten days straight. It wasn't good for the body, but old habits were hard to break. His sleep schedule was one of many things still adjusting to life after the war.

At least the migraines were brief.

True to Dr. Shelley's promise, the headaches were less frequent now than when he had first returned from the Abyss. But they still occurred weekly. It had taken a small battalion of genius-level medics to heal him after his battle with the Daemon King. He didn't like probing too deeply into their methods. Doctor Maeve Shelley had assured him he would live with functional mana, his head and heart intact as they should be. All of the important bits worked as they should—he would live a full life, just like any other man. Shelley had performed a miracle. He shouldn't be ungrateful.

But some days, he was *truly, unabashedly ungrateful.*

Another burst of pain shot behind his eyes. *Starfire,* it blinded him.

He gritted his teeth as the tension increased along his forehead.

Between jagged bolts of pain, an image danced before his eyes: the bright sheen of the girl's berry-colored hair. Why it came to mind at that moment, he couldn't say. He hadn't seen that color of hair in many years. It was a striking feature of the Sera'nayan people. During his time in the Abyss, he fought alongside many of their warriors. He didn't think his father had included any Sera'nayan families on the guest list. Not for lack of an alliance—the desert kingdom was on friendly terms with Forsynthia—but it was too far away for convenient travel.

Who was she, and which family did she belong to?

More importantly, why was she in the treasury?

Breathe.

Not many people understood the powers he wielded as the strongest mana-channeler in the realm. He didn't need to hear the girl rummaging around in the wardrobe to know she was there. He had sensed her vital spark the moment he had entered the room, as natural as a draft from an unlatched window. At first, he suspected a wayward servant hiding away. But when the girl appeared, she was dressed like a lady of means.

She was . . . unexpected.

"You dusty bastard, pull it together," he snarled. The pain was beginning to recede now. He sucked in another breath, forcing the red-hot daggers to sheathe themselves.

Just like a summer storm, the migraine passed as quickly as it arrived. It left him winded, wrung out, exhausted, and furious at his body's betrayal.

But it wasn't really *his* body anymore, was it?

He hushed the thought.

His mind returned to the girl. Whether by accident or intent, she had overheard his conversation with Meister Barbaros, which was classified information concerning the Daemonguard, the anti-mana pistol and the kingdom's new factories.

Whoever this girl was, she might pose a risk to the kingdom's security.

But . . . she seemed too clumsy and timid to be a spy.

How bothersome.

As the tension released in Elias's neck, he felt the icy heat of his migraine pass from his body. His cramped muscles eased. He took a breath and stretched out his left arm, which always bothered him, then straightened his cravat.

He opened the lid of the wooden box and took out the Starcaster.

He immediately understood why Meister Barbaros had called it a *cannon* and not a pistol. The design was unlike any firearm he had seen before. The barrel was thicker and longer than the average pistol. The length of the weapon spanned his forearm from elbow to wrist—heavy and unwieldy for one-handed shooting.

His eyes sharpened as he inspected the prototype from nose to grip. The dual-chamber action resembled something like an infinity symbol. Five bullets to a round—not much. But with Dust #210 Bloodglass, only one bullet should be enough to stop a daemon in its tracks.

It would not be an easy weapon to conceal—but that wouldn't be a concern in the Abyss. He imagined the roar of the shot, the recoil that would jolt through his arm, and the unmistakable impact of its shined ammunition.

Would it stop a daemon at twenty paces? Fifty paces? A hundred?

He needed to test it, but how?

Suddenly, the door opened behind him.

"Elias! There you are, you stormy stag! Why are you lurking about in the dark on this happy day?"

"Kiran," Elias grunted, glancing up from the gun.

First Officer Kiran Kindale strolled into the dark room with a familiar pep in his step. He wore a white jacket and trousers with a dark indigo vest underneath, a stunning ensemble that perfectly complemented his warm brown skin tone. His hair, styled in a mop of careless curls, was dark brown at the roots and faded into a blondish-gold color at the ends. His eyes were a stunning reddish amber. Kiran's family hailed from the island kingdom of Illysea, where his rank was similar to a baron. Illysea's princess was engaged to Forsynthia's crown prince, so the island's food and clothing were very trendy at the moment. Kiran's breezy accent, curly hair and brown skin were almost a fad.

Elias raised an ironic eyebrow at his old friend. His father had taken on Kiran as a ward when he was still a boy, so Kiran and Elias grew up like brothers. Both Luminaries enlisted in the army together when the Daemon King spawned a decade ago. Still, the two noble sons were like night and day. Kiran was shorter and outgoing, with a puckish nose and a jester's grin. Elias was taller, paler, quieter, and more withdrawn.

With a tap of his fingers, Kiran activated the shined sconces on either side of the door. Red flames flickered to life, casting an ethereal glow about the study.

"Red?" Kiran muttered. "Why did you change them?"

"The blue light bothers my eyes."

"Is that why you're hiding in here? The daylight? If I didn't know any better, I'd say you were turning into a daemon."

"Let's not jest," Elias said in a low voice.

"Your mother is looking for you, you know. She was awfully upset that you didn't show up to the Teacup Tournament. She's trying to draw you out."

"I have no interest in fencing."

"Why not? You spend all day overseeing new recruits at Firehelm Fortress. I thought a little swordplay would *rouse* your passions. Two gold medalists competed for your hand, and you weren't even there! It was absolutely delightful. Your mother was *fuming*."

"I was dealing with party business, if you must know. *Her* party business."

"I don't believe it. That's why your father hired a steward."

"That's what I thought, too." After a pause, Elias asked, "Do we have any guests from Sera'naya attending the ball?"

"How should I know? I haven't seen any." Kiran strolled across the room and flopped down on the high-backed chair behind the desk. He kicked his boots up onto the walnut wood tabletop and put his arms behind his head. "I hate to side with your mother on this, but it's *your* birthday party. You should at least greet your guests!"

"A party I didn't want on a day I care nothing for," Elias grumbled. "I have more pressing concerns to deal with."

"Like what?" Kiran gave him a reproachful look.

"Like this." Elias held up the gun. Kiran's face instantly changed.

"What's *that?*" Kiran gasped.

"The guildmaster from Gigas calls it an anti-mana pistol."

As Elias described the Starcaster's dual-chamber action, Kiran leaned forward across the desk, a manic light entering his amber eyes as he gazed at the new weapon. He pushed an unruly lock of blondish-brown curls from his face.

"Posh," Kiran murmured in admiration. "Will these become standard issue for the Daemonguard?"

"As soon as they're proven safe . . . yes." Elias raised a dark eyebrow in thought. "On that note, how is your new hand?"

"Thank you for asking." Kiran lifted up his right hand, displaying a shiny gold prosthetic with five moving fingers and a detachable wrist-watch. "Flexible."

"I see you haven't blown it off yet."

"Third time's the charm," Kiran winked. "These flimsy prosthetics were designed for old diabetics in mind, not S-rank soldiers. But Dr. Shelley tells me this one should be more resilient. I take it as a challenge. We'll see if I can't blow it off by Brumadir."

Elias smirked. His right hand twitched. He glanced down at it, then away.

Kiran noticed. His face fell slightly. "You can laugh, you know. I do. I don't regret it at all. After what you did, the whole kingdom owes you their right hand."

"I know."

His oldest friend cleared his throat and forced a jovial smile. "Now, do I get to play with your new toy, or are you keeping it all to yourself?"

"It's not loaded," Elias said, passing the new weapon to his second in command.

Kiran spun the gun about in his shined hand as though he was born with a Starcaster in his grip. He made the weapon's clunky size look sleek and lightweight. The gun's shined plating caught the solitary beam of light from the window, casting a mesmerizing glimmer across the polished wood floor. Kiran marveled at the intricate craftsmanship, his fingers tracing the smooth slide. Barbaros's artificers had made it beautiful, with filigree engraved on the interlocking gold and silver components.

"Well, this is a mighty fine piece of ingenuity," Kiran finally said and placed the gun back down on the desk. He climbed to his feet. "I wanted to check on you, but I see you're just as moody and sullen as I expected. Your mother sent me with a message—she has invited you to dinner with Meister Barbaros. They'll be in the dinette just off the library this evening. His daughters will be joining him." Kiran waggled his eyebrows. "They're twins, you know. They're quite lovely. And they're dying to meet the *Mad Dog duke*."

"I'll take my dinner alone in my office, Kiran," Elias said dismissively.

"Are you patrolling again tonight?"

"Do I have a choice?"

Kiran's eyes flickered again to the mess of spilled bottles seeping into the rug. "Those tinctures are expensive, you know, and Doctor Shelley gave them to you for a reason. You need to sleep, Elias. You can't stay awake for days on end like we did in the Abyss."

"I sleep just fine," Elias snapped.

"Prove it. Go to bed right now."

Elias rolled his eyes. "You sound like a nursemaid."

Kiran's voice turned chiding. "Don't do this, Elias. It's your birthday. You have other soldiers you can post on patrol. I brought four members of the Daemonguard from Firehelm, just like you asked. They're in the servant quarters having an absolute *ball,* I might add. Let them work. You should enjoy yourself." He sighed. "I can go to the infirmary to request more laudanum for you, but how am I going to explain this to Forrest? The man will want to know if you're relapsing—"

"No, Kiran." Elias glanced up and caught Kiran's eye, fixing him with a deadpan stare. "I don't need laudanum. I sleep soundly. I'm patrolling tonight because it is my *duty.* The men should enjoy themselves unless there is a true emergency. Allow me this one pleasure—to roam my father's grounds without a crowd of servants and houseguests staring at my back."

Kiran tried to return Elias's formidable gaze, but it wasn't in his nature to look so stern. The solemn expression quickly faded from his amber eyes, to be replaced by a terrible look of pity, which made Elias uncomfortable. Then his old friend gave an exasperated shrug. He adjusted the cuff of his jacket to better cover the shined prosthetic on his right arm. Then abruptly, Kiran climbed back to his feet. "You know where to find me if you want some company."

"Have a good evening, Kiran."

"You too, brother."

His right-hand man left the office as quickly as he had come in. Kiran shut the door behind him with a softness that belied his earlier humor.

Elias rubbed a hand over his eyes. He looked around his chambers, surrounded by books, atlases, shadows and shined instruments, relieved to be alone.

Her hair was the color of raspberries. She slipped away quick as a whisper, like someone used to being unseen.

He really shouldn't be thinking about that girl. He doubted he would encounter her again.

Elias stood up. He walked around his desk, where he took hold of the heavy drapes and pulled them closed.

Chapter 9

Under the Maddening Moon

THE SUN WAS SETTING and the sky filled with orange light as the maid escorted Celise back to the Moongazer Tower. She saw the checkered pavilion in the distance, empty, and the tournament ended. Fencing was a fast sport; matches didn't last longer than ten minutes, and it was growing close to the dinner hour. It seemed Estoria Blackwood and the other ladies had all dispersed.

It filled her with a sense of dread.

By now, she was most certainly *missed.*

Celise followed the maid back to the southeast tower across the Gravenmere grounds. Her calico skirts, damp at the hem from the dew-laced grass, whispered as she walked. The sun was low in the sky, minutes before sunset, when they reached the walkway that led to the door of the Moongazer Tower. Dusky shadows cast the garden in a purple shroud. Long stalks of foxglove and hollyhock wavered in the breeze. Celise felt a bit fragile herself. As she followed the maid silently, a cold knot tightened in her stomach.

They reached the porch. Before the maid could lift the knocker, the knob turned and the green door opened. Lady Marcella's puffed sleeves filled the doorway, a frigid smile plastered on her pale features.

"Celise," she said, looking past the maid, "I am so relieved to see you've safely returned. Please, come in."

Celise shared a glance with the maid, who looked startled by Marcella's appearance. The maid bowed swiftly and retreated without a word. Celise watched her swift departure with slight yearning, wishing she could run away from the tower as well. But it was time to accept her fate. She turned back to the tower door and quietly passed over the threshold, a little chill running down her arms as she stepped past Marcella.

The door snapped shut behind her.

Celise entered the dark, shadowy foyer just inside the tower's door. Through a second archway, she glimpsed Heather, Katrina and Lord Dhastel all supping at a long oak table. Warm lamps illuminated the room. The smell of meat pies, roasted onions, and creamy sauces tempted Celise's nose. A shined golden teacup, very fine and delicate, was placed at the center of the table on a little wooden stand. It looked like Katrina had won the match against Ambrosia Verabon. Still, her little sister didn't seem pleased. She couldn't hide the scowl from her face as she picked at her plate.

Lord Elias didn't come to watch the match, Celise realized. It seemed like Katrina's bid to catch the duke's attention had failed.

Then Katrina called across the tower, "Is she back, Mother? I told you they mistook her for the staff!"

"I took a walk," Celise murmured, her voice so soft she could barely hear herself. Her stomach growled. She hadn't eaten all day—she was very hungry. But first, she needed to explain herself.

She turned to face her stepmother—*crack!*

The blow blindsided her.

Marcella's open palm struck the side of Celise's face, a bit of raw mana charging the blow. Celise stumbled and fell to the ground as her vision flashed to white. Her head spun. She bit her lip, her ears ringing. Lying on the cold floor, she refused to make a sound.

Lady Marcella towered over her, her hands clenched tight with restrained fury.

"How dare you!" Marcella's voice was icy sharp. "Wandering off like a wayward dog! The young ladies were all worried about you. They notified the staff. Your sister was beside herself with embarrassment. You are here to support Katrina and Heather, not cause a scandal!"

Celise remained on the ground, her eyes lowered.

"Don't look so pathetic; I barely tapped you," Marcella snarled. Then she reached down and grabbed Celise's hair with a cruel hand. Her long nails digging into her scalp, she dragged her up to her feet. A shriek escaped Celise's throat. She clutched her stepmother's wrist, fearful that Marcella would rip out her hair.

With mana-infused strength, Marcella dragged Celise across the cold floor and proceeded up the tower's flagstone steps, her fist tight on Celise's scalp. The roughhewn stone scraped against Celise's arms as she tried to keep Marcella from yanking out her hair. When they reached the top floor of the tower, Marcella threw Celise inside the small attic room. Strands of raspberry-colored hair fell to the ground, pulled out by the woman's fierce grip.

"I'm locking the door!" Marcella snapped, withdrawing a ring of iron keys from her skirts. "This proves I can't trust you to obey my rules! I have *tried* with you, Celise. I have tried and tried! But you insist on defying me at every turn! You are a *parasite* clinging on to this family. I will not allow you to sully our reputation in front of the Blackwoods!"

Celise stared at her stepmother. A hollow, gaping hole stretched inside of her, swallowing her feelings.

Marcella looked even more furious at Celise's vacant expression. The barrage of insults continued: *"Useless chit . . . like a needle under my fingernail . . . should have sent you to an orphanage . . . meek, pathetic . . . illiterate . . . ."*

Her tirade went on and on until Marcella finally paused to catch her breath. She brushed a lock of dark hair from her brow. She looked winded. She placed a hand over her torso as though to steady herself. Then she sneered, “Your days at the Dhastel house are numbered.”

The heavy wooden door slammed shut behind Celise, and the iron bolt slid into place. She listened to the jingle of keys as her stepmother secured the lock. The sharp tap of heeled slippers on flagstone faded down the hallway as she marched away.

A wave of ice washed over Celise.

“Your days at the Dhastel house are numbered.”

She sat down on the edge of her soft bed, shaking, her cheek throbbing from her stepmother’s brutal hand. Marcella’s mana made her blow twice as strong, and Celise was helpless to defend herself. The mirror across the room showed her a bee-stung, swollen cheek. A dark bruise was quickly forming along the side of her jaw.

“I have tried with you, Celise. I have tried and tried!”

Since when had Marcella ever *tried* to be a mother to her?

Unless by "mother," she meant *"master."*

Celise’s hands remained firmly clenched in her lap. Her shoulders shook. Her scalp ached. A cold tear slid down her cheek. She didn’t know her own emotions. Was she angry? Was she hurt? She couldn’t name the silent ocean that surged within her. She didn’t understand her fate in life, why she was born into a family where she was treated with such contempt, and whether or not she had been cursed at birth. It was beyond her understanding.

Marcella hated her. Katrina tortured her. Her own father pretended to turn a blind eye, too busy to notice.

She was invisible.

If not for the servants, she would be truly lost.

If not for Mordwen, Talisworth, Lilibeth, Dasha and the rest, she might have given up by now. Either Marcella’s hatred would have killed her, or perhaps she would have done the unthinkable and ended her poor existence by her own hand.

She rebuked that dark thought with a firm shake of her head.

Celise found herself rising to her feet. She kicked off her ill-fitting shoes. Then she began undoing the ties of her dress. She pulled the stiff material up over her head. Then she unlaced her corset. The heavy cloth was suffocating. She felt a sudden need to free herself. A need to breathe. She missed her usual overalls and her tweed cap. She felt safer as a boy. But her usual clothing was neatly folded and put away in a room above the stables. All she had brought with her to wear at the castle was a shift or another stifling gown.

I don't belong in this dress, she thought, flinging the material down on the floor.

She was not a warrior. She wasn't born with indomitable charisma like her half-sister, Katrina. Girls like her didn't have special destinies. Even her birthflower was elusive—it only bloomed under starlight. She had no great ambitions, no notable powers. No way of defending herself against her Luminous family. She could only endure. She had learned to live in silence, making herself as small and unobtrusive as possible to avoid her family's wrath, but even that wasn't good enough.

Marcella wouldn't be pleased until she stamped out every last trace of Celise from the Dhastel family. Her stepmother had already tried to end her life as a child. If she meant to cast her out or sell her off, it would likely happen soon.

By coming to Gravenmere, she had hoped to become someone new, at least for a few days. Yet her hope was misplaced. She would never fit in among the highborn ladies. She would never be accepted as a Dhastel daughter.

She would never become a duchess.

She was not the Abyssal Rose of Mordwen's fortune.

Celise's eyes turned to the window, where the constellation of Valestra, the Lady of Dust and Moon, hovered in the indigo-dark sky. A rim of purple light crowned the horizon—the residue of skydust that still lingered in Nilos's atmosphere. The Maddening Moon of Hallowsin was rising, casting an ominous orange glow across the sky, while the silver Kinder Moon hung low above the mountains. The twin moons seemed to echo her mood.

She finally took a breath.

No, she was not the Abyssal Rose. She didn't grow like a tenacious weed along the cliffs of the Abyss. She wasn't stubborn, bold, or meant to stand out from her peers.

She was the Starlight Dahlia. A symbol of fate and fortune.

She only bloomed beneath the stars.

A clear night, full of starlight, waited for her outside the tower window. It occurred to her that, on a night such as this, the dahlias would be blooming in the Zodiac Gardens.

She sucked in a quick breath.

If she went now, she would be able to find her birthflower.

She felt a sudden yearning to go.

Why not?

It was impossible to appease Marcella. Celise would gain nothing by remaining in the tower. It was too late for her to feign obedience to Marcella's demands.

Celise only hesitated for a moment more, as a shadow of fear flitted through her thoughts. What if she left the tower, and Marcella or Katrina came to check on her? Then she shook her head. No. Her family wouldn't spare a second thought for her well-being, not tonight. No one would bring her food or drink, not while Marcella was punishing her.

She would never get another chance like this one.

Perhaps it was time to change her fate.

At last, she rose.

Celise opened the window, wincing at the creak of old hinges, and looked down. The curtain wall stretched below, a spine of sandstone blocks that followed the border of the Gravenmere estate. The wind kissed her cheek as she climbed onto the windowsill in her bare feet, her toes gripping at the wooden frame.

Dressed only in a cotton shift that fell to her ankles, Celise stepped out onto the shingled roof, clutching the window frame for balance. Then she gently navigated the ten or twelve feet down to the lip of the roof. The curtain wall was a step down from there. She lightly hopped from the shingled roof onto the stone walkway.

Feeling both daring and defiant, Celise walked along the top of the curtain wall, headed away from the tower. Her eyes scanned the grounds of Gravenmere Castle. She could see for quite a ways under the light of the twin moons. Like a miracle, she saw the distant glowing statue of Valestra barely visible within a grove of black maple trees.

The Zodiac Gardens.

A tall trellis, covered in climbing clematis, was attached to the side of the tower. Celise studied it cautiously. The trellis was very tall, and the ground was far below her, almost a thirty-foot drop if she lost her grip.

Was she really going to . . . ?

Yes.

Wearing nothing but a cotton shift, she took hold of the trellis and began climbing downward, crushing purple clematis blooms as she went. She apologized under her breath to the sad flowers. *"Sorry . . . sorry! Sorry . . . ."*

She hopped the last few feet to the ground. Her eyes traveled to the Moongazer Tower's front door, but it was firmly closed, and the hour was so late, she didn't see a single glowing candle in any of the windows. If her father were awake, then he would be deep in his cups. Marcella had likely gone to bed.

Was she really going to do this?

A bit of fear mingled with excitement made her heart quicken.

Yes. Yes. Yes.

Remembering the view from the top of the curtain wall, she mapped a route across the grounds toward the statue of Valestra. Feeling only the slightest sense of uncertainty, she started following the flagstone path toward the Zodiac Gardens. Celise's feet were toughened from a life spent outdoors on the ranch. She barely felt the flagstone walkway as she crossed the grounds.

Above her, the stars seemed to flow from horizon to horizon in two big rivers of light, illuminating the sky as though it were day. Forsynthian astronomers said their planet, Nilos, was located in the Twin Rings galaxy, which had two bands of stars, as she understood it. She didn't know where she had learned such things. She thought the horsemaster, Mr. Talisworth, might have told her.

The twin rivers above her seemed endless—the stars unfettered and free. It was hard to imagine how many worlds might exist out there beyond her own. As she made her way across the shadowy grounds, she felt some of the tension ease from her shoulders. Beneath the stars, she felt no judgment. She wasn't a servant or a lady. Here, she could be herself.

Just Celise.

The residue of skydust glowed above the Grapevine Mountains, sparkling like a distant aurora. The mysterious dust still permeated the atmosphere from the meteor's impact long ago. She rarely pondered its glittering residue in the sky. All of Forsynthia worked under it, breathed it, ate it, drank it. Skydust was just another part of life on Nilos. But it held many secrets.

She thought of the conversation she had overheard between the Mad Dog duke, Old Blackwood and the Bratzian diplomat.

The mystery of Elias Blackwood stayed on her mind.

With a slight shiver, she recalled his low, raspy voice. She saw the cut of his broad shoulders and his long black coat. His proud jaw. The wave of his dark hair and his glinting silver eye.

She felt a strange flutter in her stomach.

She was the only lady at the gala who had come so close to seeing the duke's face. He had touched her arm—not romantically at all—yet the power of his presence remained with her.

For a moment, she tried to imagine the mind of such a man: a war hero with enough power to defeat the Daemon King, now forced to entertain a flock of frivolous courtiers and power-hungry diplomats at a birthday party.

She couldn't begin to fathom his world.

She really shouldn't try.

She shouldn't attempt to empathize with someone so vastly different from herself . . . someone she would never know in person. Lord Elias Blackwood wasn't a victim in his life. He was the Hero of the Realm. Whether celebrated or abhorred, he was untouchable. He wasn't anything like herself: vulnerable, unwanted, and totally useless.

Eventually, Celise found the gates to the Zodiac Gardens. The entrance was marked by an iron archway; she remembered it from that morning, when the attendant had passed out tickets with their seat numbers. The gates stood wide open. They were not locked, which she hadn't considered until that moment.

Beyond the gates, the garden looked deserted.

Little pale lights illuminated the winding pathways through the garden beds. Clusters of glowbells shimmered between the roots of the maple trees. Baskets of glowstones hung periodically along the walkways, pale blue light emanating from their cores like hot coals. Each zodiac statue was illuminated by its own lantern. It seemed that even at night, the gardens were prepared to receive visitors.

She would have to be cautious not to encounter a guard.

Surely, Old Blackwood employed someone to patrol the grounds at night?

Celise wandered about the gardens, trying to remember which section belonged to which season. She couldn't read the signs along the path very well. They were written in Forsynthian high script, a special lettering learned by the nobility, very different from the simple letters Mordwen had taught her on the ranch. She picked out a word here and there, but for the most part, it all looked like wavy loops and squiggles.

Her ears strained for any sound of footsteps, but she heard and saw no one.

She passed under the trellis of lumenblooms, now closed and dark with no mana-channelers nearby. Then she found the bed of Ashfeather Bloom. Deeper in the garden, she discovered the Gilded Lupin: giant stalks of coned flowers towering almost six feet tall. Then she passed by the iridescent Solaris Lily, its petals as shiny as peacock feathers. It was a symbol of grace and balance.

Finally, she found the constellation of The Star placed far back behind the statue of Valestra, which governed her birth month of Stargrave. She found the section of the garden reserved for Brumadir, the cold, dark end of the year.

The Starlight Dahlia should be close by. Why couldn't she seem to find it?

Celise was beginning to grow impatient. She stepped off the path and began exploring the different garden beds, crushing moss and wet mulch under her bare feet. She bent almost double to inspect each flower. Coming to the gardens in secret had taken every last scrap of courage she possessed. It was a quiet rebellion against Marcella—perhaps the first of many. It marked a new era in the life of Celise. And she couldn't even find her birthflower!

Useless, she thought. *This night is an utter failure.*

Perhaps it was a sign. Perhaps she would never be able to change her fate.

A wave of utter despair arose with that thought.

Don't be silly. It has to be here somewhere, she told herself. She straightened up. Suddenly, her eyes landed on the trunk of a black maple tree that she remembered. Beyond that maple tree, hidden by deep shadows, was a towering camellia bush.

She saw a glimmer of iron bars.

The secret gate.

She bit her bottom lip as she pondered its existence. The land beyond that gate was out of bounds. The sign over it read, *"No Trespassing."*

Why? Where did it lead?

Perhaps the Starlight Dahlia was hidden beyond that old stone wall.

Dare she go that far?

Her foot slid toward the locked gate on its own volition. Curiosity warred with instinctive caution. Perhaps with a bit of leverage, she could climb the gate.

Bang! Bing-ing-ing!

Celise jumped. Interrupting her desperate thoughts and perhaps saving her from making a horrific mistake, the sound of a metal object clattering on the flagstone drew her attention.

"Crow's rot!" A muffled voice cursed.

With a gasp, Celise threw herself behind the statue of The Star. She trampled a bed of violets and glowbells and ducked behind the white marble icon. Her heart raced in her chest, threatening to choke her.

With a ragged gasp, Celise peered out from behind the statue. She watched two shadowy shapes emerge at the side of the garden. It looked like one fellow was carrying a heavy burlap bag. But the bag had developed a hole, through which a mysterious length of metal had fallen onto the ground.

As she watched, the luckless thief stooped down to pick up the dropped object, only to have a second length of metal slip out of his sack.

Clang! Clankity-clank!

The second rod skidded across the flagstone courtyard. It bounced and clanked across the slick stones until it came to rest at the foot of the Star statue, not five feet from Celise's hiding spot. She cursed silently in her head. What were the odds?

"Leave it, Corwin!" another man snapped from the shadows. "We're almost to the curtain wall. Hurry! Before someone comes."

"Just a minute now, Farvi," the first fellow grumbled. "No one's seen us yet. These things are worth a fortune. Here, see? I got it . . . ."

As the first man, Corwin, stooped to pick up the metal rod, he kicked it again, and it clattered into the garden bed to land on Celise's bare foot.

She yelped.

"Who's there?" Corwin snapped.

"Oi, it's a girl!" Farvi snarled.

A sharp snapping sound—then a burst of golden light. Farvi struck a match and held the flame high. Celise stared at the two men, who gazed back at her with equal shock. Farvi was tall, and Corwin was short. They wore identical suits of brown livery and flat caps pulled low over their faces. At first she thought they were employed by a noble house, but she didn't see any badges or sigils on their uniforms belonging to a highborn family. They weren't servants, despite how they appeared at a glance.

One had a gruesome scar down his cheek. The other had a gaunt, sunken face. Both looked like they had lived a hard life under the sun.

Celise stooped down and picked up the rod at her feet. In an instant, she knew what it was.

A ghost sword.

"You're . . . you're thieves!" she exclaimed.

"Aye, that's right, little mouse," Farvi growled. "*Thieves.* And you're holding one of our trophies."

Celise glanced down at the ghost sword in her hands. Then back to the brigands. Then to the iron archway that marked the exit to the Zodiac Gardens. It was shining under the moonlight perhaps thirty paces to her left. She could make it.

"Sorry," she muttered uselessly. Then she took off at a full sprint.

The two men shouted behind her. Corwin lunged after her, but Farvi grabbed his friend by the shoulder.

"Stop, you *dullspark!* Let her go. We're almost to the wall and then to freedom. Don't forget our merry band is waiting in the woods."

"They can wait a bit longer!"

"Why risk it? We've come this far. Let's make ourselves scarce before she alerts the guards."

"Rot and ruin!" Corwin cursed.

The two thieves bolted into the darkness.

Celise didn't stop running. She sprinted through the garden's archway and continued down the flagstone path to Gravenmere Castle. She passed through the midnight courtyard where she had drunk cold tea with Katrina and Ambrosia that afternoon. Her hands clutched the metal rod. Burning with determination, she thought of the Blackwood trophy room on the second floor of the castle's north wing. Should she take the rod back to the treasury? Would that be suspicious? She had already been called a spy by Lord Elias . . . what if she was accused of being a thief as well?

Celise paused to catch her breath and regain her bearings. She could see the spires of Gravenmere Castle in the near distance. Not far now. And she didn't think she was being pursued by the thieves. The cowards had fled to the curtain wall, probably looking for an unmanned gate into the wilderness that surrounded the estate.

She inspected the metal rod in her hands. She studied the blue and gold checkered design. It looked familiar. She thought she recognized it from the Blackwood treasury. A priceless heirloom with a legacy far more important than her own.

Now what?

If she had an ounce of proper sense, she would abandon the ghost blade, run back to the Moongazer Tower, climb back up the trellis, and return to her bedroom. There, she would banish all thoughts of fate and destiny. She would dutifully wrap her hair under a nightcap, slide under her cotton sheets, and dream of all the ways she might mend bridges with her horrid stepmother.

But . . . wasn't it such a strange coincidence to find herself in the Zodiac Gardens at the same time as the thieves?

She thought of Valestra's devious wand. The goddess seemed to have a sense of humor.

She knew what Mordwen would say. *There is no such thing as coincidence. Everything is connected by Her will.*

Celise took a deep breath. Alright. Perhaps the ghost sword was a sign. Then what should she do?

What would a *courageous* person do?

She didn't have an immediate answer.

I should return the ghost sword to the castle, she decided at last. She would accept the consequences, come what may. She would at least report what she had seen to someone in authority.

Not the Mad Dog himself, of course, but . . . *someone.*

A patrol must be present somewhere on Gravenmere grounds. The thieves seemed to think so. Perhaps she would find more soldiers at the front gates of the castle?

With a firm nod to herself, Celise continued down the flagstone path at a less frantic pace. She held the ghost sword in one hand, gripping the enameled rod by its bell-shaped hilt. She felt safer holding the weapon, even though it was far too long for her, and she couldn't make it work without mana. She resisted the urge to swish it around like a swashbuckling pirate. She gave it a few swipes. It was surprisingly heavy.

Celise found a bronze sign pointing to Gravenmere Castle and followed it. The twin moons lit her path. She kept an eye out for any soldiers, but the grounds were silent. It was almost eerie, seeing the sprawling lawns empty and abandoned like a graveyard.

Finally, the winding path led Celise to the front of the castle. As she emerged from around a screen of manicured hedges, she noted the curved trajectory of the front drive and a row of white marble fountains. It looked familiar. Her eyes skated over to the castle's front steps. She recalled the pair of grand double doors, where her stepmother and half-sisters had arrived that morning at the estate.

With a sigh of relief, Celise went up to the giant doors and tried to pull one open. Locked.

Well, it was past midnight. Did she really expect a butler to answer the door?

With a grunt of frustration, Celise leaned against one of the heavy wood panels, trying to think of what to do. She recalled seeing a guardhouse near the front gates of the castle, but that was a long walk down the winding front drive and an even longer trek back.

She squinted, but she didn't see any telltale lights down at the end of the winding drive. The guardhouse might be empty.

Now what?

She sighed. She was really making a mess of things. This whole "changing her fate" business seemed like a mistake. She had only meant to find her birthflower in the Zodiac Gardens under a clear sky full of stars. What was she supposed to do about a stolen ghost sword?

Suddenly, Celise heard the familiar clop of hooves on cobblestone. She looked up. A black horse of gigantic proportions was trotting down the castle's front drive at a fast clip. On the horse's back, a man dressed in a dark military jacket and a forage cap sat high in the saddle. The moonlight glinted off a silver star pinned to the front of his cap, just above the short brim. Celise didn't know what the star meant, but it looked official. He looked like he was patrolling the grounds on horseback.

Finally, a guard!

"Excuse me!" Celise called. She darted out into the driveway, waving her free hand back and forth. "Excuse me! I need help!"

The man pressed his horse. With a snort, the beast charged toward her, but Celise didn't flinch. She wasn't afraid of large horses—Dhastel draft horses were almost twenty hands high. This horse was no more than seventeen hands. Still, its powerful gait drew her eye. As the stallion came to a fuming stop nearby, she peered up at it.

A Dhastel Hellion, she realized.

The Hellion's coat shimmered like polished obsidian, with light dun markings on his flanks, and his eyes burned with a wild, untamed fire.

The breed was immediately obvious to her trained eye, even under the moonlight. Its thick neck and barrel chest resembled a draft horse, yet it was sleeker and less daunting in size than the horses used for pulling wagons and ploughs. It was larger and bulkier than an average quarter horse, more heavyset than a standardbred, and most definitely not a pony.

Dhastel Hellions were specially bred for the Daemonguard. It seemed a bit overkill for an average soldier, but if he was employed by the Blackwoods, perhaps it was a show of their military strength.

"What's the problem?" the rider demanded in a harsh voice. "Are you injured?"

"No," Celise stuttered. "I . . . well . . . ."

"Speak so I can hear you. Raise your chin and look me in the eye."

His voice rang with authority. With a bit of courage, she raised the shined rod in her hand.

"I saw two men fleeing through the gardens. They stole this from the Blackwood treasury. It's a ghost sword."

"Where did you see them?"

"That way. They were headed toward the wall." She pointed.

The man's eyes followed her pointing hand. Then he reached down. "Give me the blade."

"Alright," she mumbled, then handed the man the shined weapon.

The man's gloved hand gripped the pommel of the weapon. The rod made a soft whispering sound as he swung it in a half-circle, as though flicking water from its tip. With a crackle of power, purple light ignited down the length of the rod. The purple, misty light broadened into the shape of a saber, flaring out toward the end and curving into a trailing point. The beam of light was steady. It didn't fade but emitted from the rod like an unwavering, physical force.

Celise stared at the ghost sword in wonder.

The blade's purple light illuminated the driveway, dancing off the cobblestones. It flashed in the man's eyes as they gazed at each other.

She had never seen anything like it.

"Stand back!" he shouted, then nudged his horse. Celise stumbled back as the giant Hellion leapt into a gallop, charging down the garden path back the way she had come.

Celise gazed after the horse in wonder, admiring its powerful gait and the sleek way its muscles rippled under its black coat as it charged across the grounds.

Then a thought flashed through Celise's mind.

"Wait!" she called after the soldier, already knowing it was too late. "The thieves are meeting another group outside the castle. They mentioned a band of others . . . !"

The soldier didn't hear her.

Celise hesitated, unsure of what to do. Then, possessed by some strange force, she found her legs propelling her forward. She launched into a sprint after the horse. She knew she couldn't overtake the steed on foot, but she had to warn the soldier of the threat somehow. How could she not give chase? Her arms pumped at her sides. Her breath heaved in her lungs.

I have to tell him . . . I have to warn him . . . she thought. *Have I lost my mind?* Then, with gritted teeth, *I will do what a courageous person would do.*

I will change my fate.

Chapter 10

The Hellion

Celise followed the horse to a small iron gate in the curtain wall. If the soldier hadn't led her there directly, she never would have found it. It was only about twice the size of a standard door—not very large for a castle's entrance. The gate stood ajar. It looked like someone had passed this way not long ago.

The black Hellion charged through the doorway without breaking pace. The woodland on the other side was dense with ferns and towering trees. A forest of ancient pine and manawood crowded the south side of the castle. The soldier dismounted in one smooth movement and threw the horse's reins over a swinging pine bough. Then he dashed off into the woods.

"Wait!" Celise called as she darted across the pine needles. She struggled to catch her breath. She was too far away—the man didn't hear her. "Wait, there are others!"

She reached the side of the horse, her lungs burning. Sweat poured from her brow. She almost collapsed.

She placed her hand on the steed's neck. "Whoa now," she gasped. "Give me some of your stamina, *hm,* boy?"

The horse regarded her with a suspicious eye. Then he snorted.

Celise paused for a moment to gaze into the depths of the woods, stunned by their soft beauty. The violet glow of the ghost blade was visible through a maze of mossy tree trunks. The white bark of the manawood trees pulsed gently under the starlit night. A canopy of cerulean leaves rustled above her, casting an ethereal glow across the forest floor. Black pine trees interrupted the mystical sight.

Manawood was plentiful in the kingdom of Forsynthia, but this ancient grove was older than anything on the Dhastel estate. The air around the trees was charged with a palpable energy. She could feel it, a gentle tingling on her skin, a warmth that seemed to seep into her very bones.

Courage, she thought.

She patted the Hellion's strong withers, sucked in a deep breath, and continued into the woods. She didn't dare wander too far from Gravenmere—she didn't want to get lost outside the grounds. But she could see the ghost sword's soft amethyst light ahead of her, and she wanted to see it in action.

Now she truly had to wonder—*what am I doing?* But it was too late for that.

A cry in the darkness led her to the soldier.

He stood between two towering manawood trees, their white blossoms glowing faintly like stars in the darkness. Celise hung back, gazing onward with wide eyes.

Illuminated by the ghost sword's purple glow, the soldier stood over one of the thieves. The man cowered on the ground in his threadbare jacket, his fake livery torn and spattered with mud. She thought she remembered the thief's name—Corwin. The bag of stolen weapons was split open, its contents scattered through the undergrowth. It looked like the bag had ripped by accident while the thief was leaving the castle, and he had been frantically trying to pick up his fallen loot when the soldier arrived.

Now the thief cowered on the ground with the soldier hovering over him, the purple ghost sword raised high.

"Caught you, you nasty *hookleech*," the soldier cursed. "Thought you'd make off with half my treasury, hm? Not tonight."

"Please, sir, it wasn't me—I was paid to do it!"

"By whom?"

"I . . . I can't . . . he'll *kill me* . . . ."

"No matter. I'm sure you'll tell me everything as I remove each finger from your thieving hand."

"N-n-no! Wait!"

Celise turned away from the confrontation, horrified. Was the thief about to lose a finger? Obviously, her presence was not needed. The soldier seemed to have the situation well *in hand*.

Her moment of courage had been foolish indeed.

Now, how did she get back to the castle?

"Got you!" a voice grunted. A bulky shadow loomed out from behind a tree trunk. Without warning, a hand clamped over her mouth.

She tasted dirt. *Ugh!*

"Do you remember me, sweetheart?"

Celise gasped, but the man's fat palm was suffocating. Yes, she remembered him, though it took her a moment to recall his name from their brief encounter in the gardens. Farvi?

After years of enduring her stepmother's abuse, her body didn't know how to react. Her arms stiffened up as her legs went watery. Unable to fight or flee, she went still as a corpse. *I am not brave,* she thought, disappointed in herself. Her body went cold with terror, and her courage vanished like smoke on the wind.

Then the forest started moving. Shadows shifted back and forth against the grove of glowing manawood. At an unknown signal, a band of men emerged from the ferns and swaying pine branches to encircle the soldier.

The soldier looked up. He stiffened. He must have seen her—the woods were lit by a soft glow from the mana trees. But he didn't acknowledge her. He turned in a slow circle, his sword held out before him like a blazing torch, observing the bandits that surrounded him. He was greatly outnumbered, at least a dozen to one.

Celise trembled. She couldn't move. Could hardly breathe.

Farvi called to the soldier, "Oi, *dustlicker!* Let go of me mate!"

"And why should I do that?" the soldier said, kicking the man to the ground.

Farvi carried her forward. She sensed the strength in his big arms. He could snap her neck without trying, she had no doubt.

"Everything you do to him, we'll do to her!" Farvi threatened in a guttural tone. "Now let him go!"

A slight whimper escaped Celise's lips.

The soldier reassessed the situation and finally kicked the sad man toward his fellows. Corwin groaned pitifully as he staggered to his feet. Two other bandits came to his side to drag him up from the ground. They gathered the shined ghost swords and ran off into the woods.

"Release the girl," the soldier called in a dark, raspy voice.

"Not in a star's breath!" Farvi guffawed. "The girl comes with me. If you want us to spare her life, do the lass a favor and don't follow us."

Then Farvi flipped Celise over his shoulder as easily as lifting a sack of potatoes. She shrieked, her mouth finally freed of his grimy hand.

"Help!" she tried to scream, though her throat was frozen with fear. The words came out in a hoarse whisper. "Please, help!"

Farvi followed the group of bandits through the grove of manawood trees. His grip was tight and unyielding around her waist as he took off into the woods. Celise was horrified. Paralyzing fear overcame her. She wanted to kick and scream, but she couldn't draw breath. What did these men intend to do to her? Would they abduct her? Or kill her?

"Let me go!" she demanded, but her words were barely a gasp in her throat. Her fear had stolen her voice. She felt utterly useless. *I am a coward,* she thought. She was completely overwhelmed—and she hated herself for it.

She looked for the soldier with the ghost sword, but she didn't see any purple light behind her. She heard no thunder of hooves or distant jingle of a harness. No sign that he was in pursuit.

Of course he wouldn't chase after me, she thought. Who was she to anyone? He was probably returning to the castle for reinforcements.

Why had she followed him outside the castle walls?

She was foolish beyond belief!

A hot tear slipped down her cheek. Celise tried not to cry.

Dead leaves and twigs crunched under the men's feet. They left the manawood grove behind and climbed down a steep hill into a gully, where a narrow brook wended its way through the wilderness. Rocky hills covered in ferns and old bramble enclosed them on all sides. The men barely uttered a handful of words between their heavy, panting breaths. They seemed eager to put as much distance between themselves and the castle as they could.

In the near total darkness, Celise recalled the terrain around Gravenmere with some vague detail. The road leading to Gravenmere's front gates, which cut through miles of empty, spacious fields, would be located somewhere behind them. The thieves seemed to be headed deeper into the woods, which meant they were traveling farther into the mountains beyond the castle.

Farther into the rugged wilderness, where she would never be found.

Farvi's hands around her waist were cruel and strong.

His grip brought back terrible memories.

Like the sting of Marcella's rod on her back, too many times to count. The suffocating darkness of the root cellar when Marcella had locked her away for days as a young girl. She would starve, trapped underground, until the staff found her.

Then the snowstorm. The stables. She didn't remember that night Marcella locked her out of the house, but Mr. Talisworth and Mordwen spoke of it often. They had found her in the morning, sleeping next to the fiercest stallion in the herd. After that, she went mute. Talisworth put her to work mucking stalls, but she wouldn't say a word. She had spent the next two years completely silent. Celise didn't recall those years at all. Mordwen had brewed all sorts of concoctions trying to cure her mutism, but nothing worked. She thought of those as her ghost years, lost to time and memory.

The horses had brought her back to herself.

She remembered the first time Mr. Talisworth had put her on the back of an old mare when she was thirteen years old. She remembered the laugh that had fought its way up her throat like a mountain spring bubbling up from the earth. She remembered the freedom she had felt. She couldn't often feel her own emotions—but she could feel them with the horses.

She thought of that laughter now, of the pure bliss of riding bareback across the Dhastel estate, the sun on her hair and an unbroken gelding beneath her.

Stay strong, Celise, she thought, returning to this new nightmare.

She couldn't lose herself to her fear. She needed her wits about her.

The thieves followed the tumbling stream for a little while. Moonlight sparkled off the dark water, and Celise saw clusters of glowbells hidden between the rocks along the banks. She tried to calm down and recover some control over her body.

Finally, the men stopped running.

"This is the place," Corwin said, dropping his heavy bag of swords on the ground. "We're supposed to meet the Dread Jackal here."

Who is the Dread Jackal? Celise wondered.

She found herself dropped ungraciously to the ground. She wasn't expecting the sudden fall. She landed clumsily on her side, the wind knocked out of her.

When she looked up, she saw Farvi standing over her in his stained brown coat with his tweed flat cap pulled low over his head. She recognized the big scar on his square cheek and his mean, beady eyes.

As she blinked and squinted through the darkness, more and more of her surroundings came into focus.

They had arrived at a stone quarry that lay deep in the midnight woods, illuminated by the light of the twin moons. Surrounding the quarry, a forest of towering pine trees swayed in the wind, their gnarled branches reaching out like skeletal fingers, casting eerie shadows that danced in the moonlight.

The quarry itself was a vast, open wound in the earth, its walls a patchwork of moss-covered stones and crumbling ledges. A stagnant pool of water at the bottom of the pit reflected the starlit sky above like a mirror. It was a haunting place, full of shadows and strange echoes. Celise sensed the movement of small rodents between the rocks. An owl hooted nearby, and farther off, a disparaging cry that might have been a griffin.

She didn't want to encounter one of those giant beasts.

Beyond Farvi, about a dozen other thieves milled about the quarry, resting on large rocks or pacing over dead leaves. One by one, they piled the shined ghost swords on the ground next to the pond. Metal clinked against metal as they examined their prizes. The hilts and pommels glinted ominously in the moonlight.

"This looks like a good haul. Did we get the whole list?" one of the bandits asked.

"I checked off every last blade," Corwin said with a touch of pride. "Had to drag that bag halfway across the castle! Thought my arms would fall off."

"What about the soldier who found us?" another man asked. "Do you think he'll follow us out here?"

"I think we lost him," Corwin said.

One of the men, no more than a lumbering black shadow, pointed in Celise's direction. "Then what are we going to do about her?"

"Who says we have to do anything?" Corwin hedged, a touch of reluctance in his tone. It surprised her. She wasn't expecting any mercy from this group of thieves.

"She's seen us. She's a witness. I say we slit her throat," Farvi growled.

A beat of silence. The men seemed to consider this suggestion seriously.

Celise wondered if it was a good time to make a run for it.

Then, suddenly, she felt a vibration through the earth.

Was she imagining it?

Her fingers sank into the soft dirt. She felt the thunder of hooves through the ground. A few rocks rattled at the edge of the quarry. A pebble fell down, shaken loose from a pile of gravel and shale.

The Hellion!

A black warhorse burst through the trees. It charged down the rocky hill in two leaps, practically flying to the bottom of the quarry. The thieves whirled about.

"He followed us!"

"That damned horse!"

"Grab the ghost swords!"

The Hellion charged down the group of men, trampling them with its sharp hooves. The fearless beast reared up on its hind legs and whinnied into the night. It resembled a lion's roar more than a sound a horse should make.

The thieves scattered.

"Not so fast!" the soldier yelled from atop his giant horse. He reached into his saddlebag and flung a net through the air. The rope shimmered with mana. It entangled several of the thieves, who fell to the ground as though trapped under a giant rock.

"I can't breathe!" one of the men screamed.

Another one tried to cut his way free of the net with a knife, but the blade was useless against the silver strands. Celise saw the net sparkle under the moonlight, as though the cloth were interwoven with metal. Skydust—or shined wires of some kind?

"We call that 'daemon thread,'" the soldier said as he leapt from the saddle and approached the thieves. "You'll have a hard time breaking it. Not even a crimson cleaver can untangle itself from that."

He secured the net, binding the men fast together. The rest of the bandits hung back along the fringe of the forest, warily watching the soldier and his aggressive horse. The air was thick with tension. Celise felt as though she were surrounded by hungry wolves. How the soldier could act so cool and collected under such an immediate threat astounded her.

Then Farvi reached under his coat and drew a pistol from his belt.

"Rally, boys!" Farvi bellowed. "The Dread Jackal is counting on us! Just think of all the goldlarks waiting for you. We've come this far. Get those swords!"

He raised his pistol at the soldier.

"Watch out!" Celise screamed. She acted without thinking. Shocking herself, she tackled Farvi from the side. She wasn't very large or heavy, but with a grunt, the man's arm jerked up. The gun misfired. *Crack!*

The bullet went wild. It missed the soldier's head by a few inches and grazed the flank of the Hellion. The black horse reared up on its hind legs, screamed in pain, and took off into the woods at a mad gallop.

"You lightless little whore!" Farvi yowled and flung her down to the ground.

Celise yipped as she hit the dirt.

Before Farvi could raise his gun again, the soldier threw his ghost sword with a powerful arm. The blade's purple light flickered out like a candle the moment it left his grasp. The shined rod flew through the air, straight and true. With a loud, fleshy *thud,* the rod's tip skewered the man's arm and pinned him to a tree trunk.

Farvi screamed.

The bloodcurdling sound made Celise's hair stand on end.

Emboldened, the rest of the bandits charged at the soldier, eager to pummel him into the ground and retrieve their stolen goods. Celise sat in the dirt, her shift pushed up around her knees, her hair a mess, and her heart hammering in her throat. She wanted to help the soldier, but she wasn't a fighter. What could she do?

The horse.

Her heart twisted.

She wasn't skilled enough to aid the soldier in combat—but she could find his lost stallion. A large beast like a Hellion could trip and break a leg in the darkness. A lame horse was a dead horse. She couldn't let that happen.

And, although she hated to admit it, she felt a lot better *running away* from the battle than towards it.

On shaking legs, Celise climbed to her feet. Then she ran after the rabid horse. The Hellion's trail led her up the side of the quarry and through the dense woods. Its chaotic path was easy to see in the light of the twin moons. A corridor of broken branches, trampled lichen, and upturned earth led her through the wilderness. She could read the Hellion's power in the damage it wrought upon the forest. The warhorse was not a delicate animal—yet a bullet to the buttock would spook the heartiest steed.

Celise followed the Hellion's trail with dogged determination at a full sprint, her breath laboring in her lungs and sweat pouring from her brow.

Then, with little warning, she emerged from the trees.

A cliff.

"Oh!" she yelped. Her feet found purchase on a bed of thick moss and densely woven roots. She stopped herself from barreling over the edge of the precipice.

The beast was pacing the edge of a cliff. The sudden drop ended at a river far below. The roar of rushing water hinted at a deep, swift current. Celise saw long trenches in the ground leading up to the edge of the cliff, where the Hellion had skidded to a halt with its sharp hooves.

When the angry horse saw Celise, it reared up on its hind legs, screaming its fury into the night.

Celise took a moment to catch her breath. Somewhere in her exhausted gasps was a sigh of relief.

"Here, boy," she whispered, and clicked under her tongue to the horse. "Easy now. Come here. Don't go . . . a step farther . . . ."

The stallion was still rearing up on its hind legs at the edge of the cliff, not quite finished with its tantrum. With a burst of strength, Celise caught the horse's reins with one hand and dragged the Hellion's head around. She yanked down hard on the horse's head and stared into its fierce black eyes.

The beast's neck was powerful enough to drag her through the air. It could have easily thrown her off—but it calmed the moment their eyes locked.

Celise had always had this ability with horses.

She didn't question it.

Keeping one hand firm on the reins, she ran her other hand down the horse's velveteen nose. The beast whuffed at her reproachfully, and she hushed it.

"Easy," she repeated. "There you go. Quiet, now. I'm not so bad, hm?"

Standing at the edge of the cliff, Celise's heart pounded in her chest as she stroked the nose of the black Hellion. The magnificent beast trembled beneath her touch, its eyes wide with fear and pain. Blood matted its sleek coat where the bullet had torn across its flanks, and the stallion's breath came in short grunts. She whispered soothing words, her voice steady and calm, as she tried to keep the wary animal from bolting over the precipice.

The wind gusted around them. For a moment, the night was peaceful.

Then a commotion echoed through the trees.

Celise's head snapped up, her senses on high alert. The stallion whinnied nervously, its muscles tensing beneath her hands. She gripped the reins, her knuckles white with effort, as she struggled to keep the animal under control.

From the shadows of the woods, a lumbering brute emerged—Farvi.

Celise went cold.

The thief's square face was covered in dripping blood from a nasty head wound. One arm hung limp at his side where the ghost sword had shattered his humerus. His lips contorted in a snarl of fury when he saw her. He raised his good arm, his pistol clutched in a shaking fist. He pointed it directly at her head.

"You!" he growled. "You ruined everything, you little whore!"

Celise's breath caught in her throat, and she froze, her eyes locked onto the black muzzle of the gun. Time seemed to slow as she braced herself for the inevitable.

Then a second man burst from the woods.

The soldier appeared, his purple ghost sword held ready at his side. Silent and efficient, he charged at the bandit, his blade flashing in the moonlight.

The soldier's sword clashed against the bandit's gun just as Farvi pulled the trigger. *Cr-crack!* The bullet struck the earth and rebounded off a rock. The sword sent the gun flying—and the bandit's arm went with it.

Celise gasped. Farvi screamed. Blood sprayed the air.

The pistol and the thief's arm went flying over the side of the cliff.

Then the soldier was on him. With a mighty kick, he sent the bandit stumbling backward.

Farvi teetered close to the side of the cliff. For a moment, it seemed as if he might regain his balance, but the ground was too treacherous. With a final, desperate cry, he tumbled over the edge, his body disappearing into the darkness below.

Celise was too shocked to utter a sound. A dull rushing noise filled her ears, and her vision swam. With an unexpected moan, she swooned. She tried to catch her balance against the horse's neck, but she found herself sinking down onto her knees.

She heard a distant splash as the thief's body landed in the river.

Celise remained on her knees, kneeling in the dirt, her eyes closed, shaking from the adrenaline of the night.

Then she heard the sound of heavy boots crunching on leaves.

When next she looked up, the soldier stood on the opposite side of the Hellion, his forage cap slightly crooked, strands of dark hair falling wildly across his face. He caught the Hellion's reins in one hand so it didn't step on her. Celise squinted up at him. In the darkness, she couldn't quite make him out. He was tall, based on how he towered next to the horse, and his boots were spattered with mud.

Blood, too. She didn't want to think about that.

Far from gallant, the man roared at her, "Damnable dust, you reckless girl! What were you thinking? Why did you follow me?"

"I . . . I . . . ."

"You put yourself at risk for no reason. You . . . you *lightless dullspark!*"

Lightless? It was as good as calling her a dunslug, the official term for commoners without mana. Reeling from his reprimand, Celise stared up at the soldier, her mouth agape.

"Are you injured?" he snapped.

"N-no."

"What about your face?"

It took Celise a moment to remember Marcella's hard slap.

"Oh, no," she mumbled, pressing the back of her hand against the tender spot along her jaw. "Just clumsy."

The soldier shook his head again and grumbled, *"Foolish."* Then he reached down. Celise stared at his gloved hand stupidly, frozen in shock.

"Come on, girl, make haste! More bandits might be in these woods."

Without waiting, he grabbed her wrist and yanked her up to her feet.

Celise swayed as the blood rushed to her head. She swooned again, and the soldier reached out to grab her elbow. He missed, or perhaps she twisted away, and she found herself gripping the horse's mane for balance. She felt instantly better once she felt the heat of the horse's strong neck under her hands. She sighed and pressed her face against the stallion's dark mane. Inhaled. The smell reminded her of the Dhastel stables. It was a small comfort.

"Tempest is a Hellion bred for battle—he's not safe for civilians. Step away at once," the man barked. He stood nearby, his hand tense on the horse's bridle. She couldn't tell if he was afraid for her safety or simply surprised his horse hadn't bitten her yet. He looked like he meant to drag the aggressive beast away from her, but Celise put a hand on his arm.

"It's alright, you don't need to worry . . . I'm good with horses."

The man shrugged her off.

"Tempest is not merely *a horse*," he grunted. Still, the soldier didn't try to drag her away from his steed again. He watched her pet the fearsome stallion as though it were a mere sheepdog. A strained silence fell between them.

Celise took advantage of the quiet moment to regain her bearings. Mud smeared her shift, and her braid was a crooked mess, with all sorts of loose strands and flyaways falling around her face. But she was alive and unharmed. The night was quiet. The threat had passed.

"So what now—?" she started to ask.

Suddenly, without warning, the soldier stepped behind her. His gloved hands gripped her around the waist. With a gasp, Celise felt her feet leave the ground. The man easily lifted her up and placed her into the saddle. She found herself gripping the saddle horn, surprised by her sudden change of position.

"What—?"

"Worse than bandits roam these woods. Griffins are ravenous this time of year," he said. "Since Tempest seems to tolerate you, this will do. Stay close to my side, little moonflower."

Moonflower?

Then the soldier started leading his horse back to the quarry.

As the Hellion walked through the woods, Celise found herself studying the man's back—his broad shoulders and black military coat. She wondered what color his hair might be under his cap. In the near darkness, it was hard to tell. She had yet to get a clear view of his face. She might have glimpsed the shape of a square jawline and a strong neck in the light of his ghost sword. The shined rod now hung through a loop in his belt in a nonchalant way, as though he swaggered about with a ghost sword at his hip all the time.

"Is that your horse's name—Tempest?" She broke the silence.

"It is."

"Hellions have stormy temperaments. It's a good name. It suits him."

The soldier paused at her words, his silence rich with unspoken thoughts. He finally asked, "Are you familiar with the breed?"

"Oh, yes."

"How would a highborn lady know about Hellions?"

Celise caught herself. In the privacy of the dark woods, she had almost started speaking about the Dhastel ranch, her father's lands, the expansive stables, and the various different horses she worked with each day. But she held her tongue. This soldier had saved her life—but if he learned about her family, would he turn her over to Marcella?

The thought was jarring.

"Well?" he prompted.

Celise finished lamely, "I-I've read some books about them." Very much a lie, as reading was hardly her strong suit.

The man grunted. She couldn't tell if he believed her.

The trees parted, and they reached the quarry. At the bottom of the rocky hollow, Celise was surprised to see several men lying on the ground under the densely woven net of daemon thread. They appeared to be unconscious. Each one was stretched flat against the ground as though crushed under a heavy weight.

The soldier led them down a slight hill to the base of the quarry, where he tossed the Hellion's reins over a fallen tree trunk.

Then he crossed to the pile of fugitives, where he knelt for a moment, tightening their bonds. He drew his sword from his belt and lifted the shined blade into the air. A pulse of purple light moved down the rod to the tip, then shot into the sky with a sizzle of power—a flare. The purple star flew up through the trees. It hovered about a hundred feet above the woods like a ghostly beacon. Celise flinched and shut her eyes against the sudden, harsh light.

"What is that?" she asked.

"A sigil. It will help my men find us. They will take the thieves into custody."

My men.

So he was an officer of some kind? He was Luminous, so he was likely highborn himself, she slowly realized.

"I've never seen anyone use a ghost sword before. I heard the Daemonguard use them to fight monsters in the Abyss. Is the blade truly powered by mana?"

"Yes," the soldier said. He continued collecting his shined weapons from around the quarry. He laid out the stolen items in a row on the ground. It seemed like he was inspecting each rod for damage. They glimmered mysteriously in the soft light of the Kinder Moon.

Surprising her, he began to speak in a low voice, "Each ghost sword is shined with a different dust. The one you handed me is called Dust #120 Diamondrun. It's not my favorite, but it was useful tonight. The pommel heats up after a while and can blister the hand. This one, however, is very rare: Dust #410 Blacklight. It's said the artificer was killed before he could write down the recipe. It's very effective against shadowhide daemons. They're nigh invisible to the naked eye, but the sword emits a strange light that can reveal them. . . ."

As the soldier talked, he collected another sword from around the gully, then another, describing the different properties of each weapon and the daemons they counteracted. He activated each one with his mana, giving it a few swipes as he tested each shined rod for damage.

Celise dismounted, swinging lightly down from Tempest's saddle. She landed on the soft earth with only the slightest sound, her feet cushioned by layers of moss and loam. Feeling a bit useless, she picked up a stick and decided to check the Hellion's hooves. She had noticed the horse walking with an uneven gait. She placed a hand on the beast's withers and ran it down over the leg—the horse picked up its front foot automatically. She found a large pebble lodged in its iron shoe and dug it out with the stick. It felt satisfying to do something so simple and familiar. Her hands worked automatically. She didn't consider whether or not she was acting *ladylike*. She had put away her father's horses thousands of times before. It was soothing, and slowly, her anxiety faded.

As she worked, she continued to wonder—why did the soldier talk so much about the ghost swords, as though he personally owned them?

"What are you doing?"

The soldier's sudden question startled her. Finished sorting through his weapons, it seemed he had finally noticed her tending his horse.

"I was just checking your horse's shoes. I didn't mean any harm."

"Tempest doesn't let anyone touch him."

For some reason, Celise felt like she was in trouble. "I've done nothing wrong."

"You've done loads wrong, my girl, just by being here tonight."

Celise frowned. What did that mean? She tossed her stick onto the ground and stepped away from the horse. The man walked past her and began tying the bundle of stolen ghost swords to his saddle with a length of rope.

"The horse's gait is uneven due to its wounded flank," she explained. "I don't want his feet bothering him, too. He probably shouldn't be carrying all of that excess weight."

"It's a mere scratch. The bullet barely nicked him. Tempest has survived a lot worse."

Celise began to feel frustrated. She glared at the soldier in the darkness. "If you keep treating him this way, he'll go lame. You should care more about the well-being of your animals, sir."

"My horse is well cared for," the man snarled.

"I *sincerely* doubt that."

"You challenge my word?"

"Yes!" Celise's outburst surprised even herself. "You are a soldier—hardly better than that brute you sent over a cliff! I don't believe you care about any animal's well-being. What would a *murderer* like you know about tending a Hellion?"

A deprecating laugh ripped from his throat. "A lot more than a spoiled heiress! A lady such as yourself wouldn't know about horses bred for blood and battle. That man was going to put a bullet between your eyes, little moonflower. I saved your life."

Celise struggled for a moment, her fists clenched at her sides. "You *took* a life."

"To protect your own. Now tell me, was my judgment in error? Would you rather I let the man shoot you?"

Celise was silent. She stared resolutely at the soldier's feet, a humiliated blush in her cheeks. "No," she admitted.

"Who are you?" the soldier barked. "What business do you have on castle grounds, dressed in your undergarments and *bare feet?* How did you come to be in the gardens with those thieves?"

"Undergarments?" She glanced down at herself, realizing how she must look. "I-I was searching for my birthflower. The Starlight Dahlia only blooms on a clear night, so I thought it would be a good time to look for it."

"How *romantic*," his voice sneered through the shadows. "But I am not convinced. A lady wouldn't leave her bed so late at night to stroll about the Zodiac Gardens. Or perhaps I am mistaken—perhaps you are not a lady but a *chamberflower* running about her midnight business. Were you heading to a lover's tryst?"

"I am not a whore!" Celise glared.

"Alright, then you're a maid. I'm sure your master would like to know why *his servant* is sneaking about the grounds. Which house do you belong to?"

Celise didn't answer.

The soldier cajoled her in a mocking tone, "Come now, my lightless girl. A highborn woman wouldn't clean a horse's hooves. Tell me the truth. You're a chamberflower . . . or perhaps you are a spy?"

Celise felt a shiver of foreboding. She flinched at the word. "A . . . a *spy?* Why would you say that?"

A dark, brief silence fell between them, charged with a tension Celise couldn't name. Yet, it was familiar. She remembered that sense of *intensity* from the Blackwood treasury.

A voice suddenly interrupted them—"Hail, fellows! Who goes there?"

Celise looked up. She saw a bobbing lantern through a fringe of pine trees at the top of the quarry. A group of soldiers was approaching.

Deftly, as an afterthought, the soldier whisked off his frock coat and handed it to her. “Put this on,” he said. “Make yourself halfway decent.”

Celise glared at him in the darkness. Still, she took the coat. She wrapped it around her small form. It almost fell to her ankles, and the sleeves were comically long. The man’s scent enveloped her—it was sharply familiar, the same pepper-vanilla cologne that had clung to her dress all afternoon.

A terrible, uneasy feeling passed through her.

She chanced a look at his face. Was he . . . ?

The soldier’s cap was pulled low, and he was turned away from her to greet the patrol coming down the hill. He wasn’t wearing a mask, so she couldn’t be sure of his identity. He had a firm jaw. A straight nose. But what about his scars? She squinted through the shadows, morbidly curious.

The patrol halted about ten feet away, a group of ten men and women in standard gray military uniforms. They wore unadorned forage caps without the silver star pinned to the front. They threw up formal salutes, and the soldier saluted back.

Celise was beginning to notice a vast difference between her soldier’s long military coat and the stiff, tailored uniforms of the foot soldiers.

In a clipped tone, he said, “I caught a group of thieves leaving the castle with a bag of ghost swords from the Blackwood treasury. They’re just behind me. I’ve secured them with daemon thread.”

“And the stolen items, sir?” one of the soldiers asked.

“I have the stolen pieces here—I’ll return them to my collection. Search the woods for any more of the bandits; I saw a large group of men, at least a dozen. They’re armed, so be ready. Leave one of your lanterns. It will be useful on the ride back.”

“Yes, sir!” The group of soldiers chorused and saluted again, then ran off into the woods. They left one of the oil lanterns on the ground. The gentle golden light cast soft shadows around the quarry.

My collection? Celise paled. Her heart began to pound at a furious pace, and she felt the urge to swoon again. Now she recognized that dark, raspy voice. Only one man at Gravenmere Castle would own a Hellion—not a mere soldier, but the *commander* of the Daemonguard.

How could she be so thick-skulled?

While the Mad Dog was distracted, Celise tried to slip away through the woods.

He noticed. He whirled around. Before she could pick a direction to run, he rounded the horse and snagged her arm. Celise started to look up at his face, but she was too frightened. She had heard too many rumors about his scars. She kept her eyes half-shut and her chin pointed at the ground, avoiding his intense stare.

"The guilty always flee once they're caught," he growled. "What are you hiding? Tell me the truth. Who are you, and why were you in the Blackwood treasury this afternoon? How did you come across those thieves in the garden? Are you a spy for Sera'naya?"

Celise stifled a gasp. He had recognized her! When? Immediately? Or later, at the edge of the cliff? Her mind reeled.

"I was exploring the castle, that's all!" Celise said as her voice threatened to vanish altogether. "It was a coincidence!"

"Why should I believe you?"

"Because . . . because I helped you! Without me, those bandits would've made off with those swords. You're *lucky* I was in the gardens! And I . . . I rescued your horse."

"I suppose you want a reward then? A few silver dhrams for your trouble? Or perhaps I should send you home with a detailed report of our new skydust factories?"

"I'm not a spy!"

"Then why were you in the treasury? Why were you on the grounds past midnight? Give me a more compelling reason."

Celise opened her mouth but caught herself once again. A flurry of words died in her throat. Her mind flashed to Marcella, the Moongazer Tower, the locked bedroom, and the thinly veiled threat of selling her off. If she revealed her identity to the Mad Dog, would he drag her back to her family? It would be the final nail in her coffin.

Who was she more afraid of, Marcella or the duke?

As she hesitated, the Mad Dog groaned.

"Never mind. Don't bother," he said. "I won't believe you, whatever lie you're concocting."

"I can assure you, I am not a spy!" she whispered, staring resolutely at the ground.

"I'll believe that when you tell me *who you are.*"

Celise remained stubbornly silent.

"Don't make me lock you up," he snarled. "The sooner you tell me which family you belong to, the sooner I can verify your identity, and we can put this sordid business behind us."

She said nothing.

"Don't stand there cowering, girl. You weren't afraid of me a minute ago. If you have nothing to hide, then raise your chin and look me in the eye."

Celise finally raised her eyes. Standing face-to-face in the lantern light, both parties were suddenly illuminated in full clarity.

She finally got a look at the infamous duke.

Beneath his cap, his sleek black hair was darker than midnight, trimmed to his jaw and slicked back from his face with oils. His sideburns were dusted with the premature gray of a stressful life. His posture was straight, his chest wide. He wore a conservative, dark blue vest under his military greatcoat. A line of brass buttons ran down his left breast.

Her eyes returned to his face. He had a strong cleft chin and a square jaw with angular cheekbones. Dark eyebrows arched over his gray eyes in a sardonic expression. His lips were wide and curved. His scars were immediately visible. Her gaze traveled to the left side of his face and neck, where a large lesion—which must have been caused by fire—warped the skin into an unnatural texture. His left ear, as well, looked misshapen, though it was hidden partly beneath his long hair. The scars spread across his left cheek almost to the corner of his lip, causing one side of his mouth to pull slightly upward in a permanent smirk. The same scar caused his left eye to appear half-closed, though by its brightness and his fierce expression, she didn't think he was blind. A small nick sliced through his left eyebrow.

Celise blinked twice, staring at his stern face, terrified.

"You . . . you're Lord Elias Blackwood," she stuttered.

"I am."

"Are you going to arrest me?"

"If I have reason to."

Oh no.

Lord Elias Blackwood, the most notorious bachelor in the kingdom, looked different than the gruesome cadaver she had imagined. Unlike the descriptions in *The Lady's Letter,* the scars did not mutilate his entire face, nor did they seem to impede his ability to speak or eat. But the left side of his body must have been badly burned at one time. As her eyes flickered over his scars, she tried to hide her horror.

Celise took a step back.

A force of habit, she found herself bowing to Lord Elias as a servant might bow to a master. Her messy braid of raspberry hair spilled over her shoulder as she ducked her head down.

"My lord, um, Your Grace, um . . . I should go," she gasped.

Then she vaulted up into the saddle.

She grabbed the Hellion's reins and kicked the beast hard. "Go!" she cried.

Go, go, go!

The horse leapt into motion.

"Wait! Stop!" Celise heard the Mad Dog shout behind her. Then she heard an actual roar of frustration rip from the man's throat. She thought he sounded just like a daemon from the Abyss. "She's getting away! *Stop that horse!*"

Mother of Dust, I am not this bold, she thought.

Then she slammed her heels into Tempest's side.

The horse leapt forward into a full gallop. Tempest didn't seem to care at all that his former master was screaming obscenities after him. Celise didn't look back to see if anyone followed her. She didn't know if any of the soldiers responded to Elias's cries. In either case, his men didn't have mounts, so they wouldn't catch up with her easily.

She couldn't allow herself to be captured.

She couldn't allow Marcella to find out about her little misadventure.

She needed to get back to the Moongazer Tower as quickly as possible.

Her hands tight on the reins, Celise leaned forward almost flat against the stallion's neck, and as one, they raced through the darkness. Through touch and breath, she controlled the horse, sensing the ground through Tempest's hooves as one body. She could feel his fire beneath her, the power of his muscles, and the raging spirit of the beast as they soared over brook and gully. She had never ridden a Hellion before, but his unbroken charge through the darkness felt like riding a stormhead. She imagined lightning flashing under his hooves and hurricane winds carrying them aloft. She felt utterly fearless. Untethered. *Free.*

She would regret leaving the stallion behind once they reached the castle.

By the slope of the mountain and the lean of the woods, it seemed they were headed in the right direction. Running at a reckless pace through the dark night, Celise eventually caught sight of a white manawood grove on the next ridge. *Good. We're close.* The trees shimmered with an ethereal light under the stars. Beyond that, she saw the shadow of Gravenmere's curtain wall towering against the night.

She relaxed as they entered the grove of silver trunks and feather-soft leaves.

Elias followed the girl up the side of the quarry but gave up when he reached the woods. Tempest was too fast to follow on foot. By the time he entered the dark tree line, horse and rider had vanished without a trace into the night.

He lowered his lantern with a groan. Any attempt at tracking them would be futile. Damn. The girl had slipped his grasp once again!

Who is she?

Spy, maid, lady or thief—he needed to know!

His mind burned with a terrible fascination. It set his teeth on edge. Was she one of the gala's guests? A servant of a noble family? Perhaps she had slipped onto the grounds with the rug delivery that afternoon? It stung his pride how she had slipped through his fingers twice. He should have tied her up the first moment he recognized her, when he saw her wide, terrified eyes from across the manawood grove. *Inexcusable.* He was the Hero of the Realm and the High Commander of Firehelm Fortress, and this little moonflower had slipped through his fingers twice!

How could he call himself a soldier if he couldn't track down one simple, dimlit girl?

With a growl of frustration, he began casting about the underbrush for any clue to her identity. He pushed aside ferns and dug through dead leaves. Her escape had been frantic, desperate; surely she had dropped something of personal value? Something to give herself away?

He cast around for several minutes until his eyes detected a small, sparkly object on the ground.

Yes.

He bent down and picked it up. It looked like a hairpin. It was decorated with a small silver horseshoe attached to one end. It must have fallen out of the girl's messy braid when she fled.

He frowned. The crystals embedded along the horseshoe were very fine. It didn't look like something a maid would wear, though he couldn't imagine a lady jumping on the back of a Hellion without a shred of hesitation.

He turned the small hairpin over in his hands, thinking over their encounter. A headache began to pulse behind his eyes, and he groaned a second time.

The little moonflower had run off with his favorite coat.

Damnable dust.

He needed to get it back.

He would not let her go this time.

Chapter II

A Masked Deception

The next day, Celise woke up to a loud banging on her bedroom door.

"Lady Celise! My lady, are you awake?"

Celise groaned. She had a throbbing headache. She was terribly dehydrated. Her back was sore, and her thighs ached from her furious escape on Tempest the night before.

She gasped and sat up in bed. *Tempest.*

She had tethered the bold black Hellion to a pine tree just outside the castle gate, confident that the Mad Dog would find him.

She clutched her quilt to her chest. *Last night . . . did I really . . . ?*

Her aching muscles were proof enough that her panicked flight through the forest hadn't been a nightmare. Even after making it back to the tower, the tall, dark figure of the Mad Dog had chased her through the corridors of her mind. No matter how far she fled, he was always right behind her.

Celise pressed a hand to her fluttering heart.

He was brash, domineering, arrogant . . . .

Heroic. Brave. Skilled.

Infuriating.

She barely remembered getting back to her bedroom. Somehow, she had found her way across Gravenmere grounds to the Moongazer Tower just as gray light began to fill the sky. She had climbed up the clematis-covered trellis to the curtain wall, ignoring the splinters that cut into her palms. Then she dragged herself through the window into the tower.

Entering her bedroom, she pulled off Elias's heavy coat—*by dust and moon, did I really steal this from the Mad Dog duke?*—and her ruined shift. She shoved them both behind the wardrobe. Then she used a towel to wipe off the dirt from her arms and legs. Finally, she had climbed into bed and thrown the covers over her, waiting for the sound of boots on the tower stairs as soldiers approached her door.

But now it was daylight, and no one had come.

Had she really escaped the Mad Dog?

Why did she feel *ever so slightly* disappointed?

Glancing in the mirror that faced the bed, she winced at the sight of a dark bruise on her cheek. Her hair was a rat's nest of tangled raspberry tresses. Twigs and leaves clung to the unruly strands. Considering her gaunt appearance, she looked like a homeless vagrant. Vivid noon light blazed through the tower window, heating the small attic room like a furnace. Celise rolled over in the lumpy bed, her muscles sore, her throat parched.

The hammering on the door came again, and Dasha's voice called out, a bit higher pitched, "*Please* answer me, Celise! Are you decent? I'm going to unlock the door and come in now."

"No! No, I'm not!" Celise cried, but her words came out in a croak.

She wrapped herself up in a quilt as an iron key jingled in the lock. The bolt turned and clicked. Then Dasha pushed her way inside the room. The look of relief on the maid's face was almost comical.

"Oh good, you're here!" Dasha gasped. Then, in a lowered voice, "The trellis along the side of the tower is all crooked and hanging. Katrina pointed it out this morning. I had the *worst* thought that you might have . . . well, I won't even speak the words out loud. Marcella is in *a mood*."

Celise sighed. When was her stepmother *not* in a mood?

Dasha shut the door behind her, locked it, then leaned up against it with a bemused smile on her face. The dark-haired maid was only a few years older than Celise and one of her closest friends. In an informal tone, Dasha said, "You look like you've had quite a night."

Celise couldn't hide the bits of leaves and pine needles stuck in her hair. A self-conscious hand went to her ragged braid. "Uh . . ." she muttered.

With a mischievous smile, Dasha lowered her voice and said, "There's a man downstairs in the parlor visiting Lord Dhastel. He's asking a lot of questions about our ranch, especially the Hellions. He wanted to meet Katrina and Heather."

Celise's eyes widened. "What man? When was this?"

"Just now. I came to check on you because Marcella *doesn't want you to leave your room.* She doesn't want the man to know there's a *third* Dhastel daughter."

Celise pulled in a slow breath. Her stomach twisted.

"Oh yes. The rot-queen strikes again," Dasha said, misreading Celise's nervous look. She folded her arms across her chest and arched a black eyebrow. "That witch is trying to erase you out of the family; she's shameless about it, too. If Mordwen were here, she would be livid!"

"But the man . . . what about him? Why did he want to meet Katrina and Heather?"

"Oh, that. He had a hairpin. He wanted to know if Heather or Katrina recognized it."

Stunned, Celise inspected her messy braid again. "A . . . a hairpin?" she squeaked.

"Yes. Marcella didn't recognize it, but *I* did. It's part of a set that Mordwen gifted you on your birthday last year. Don't worry, I didn't say anything. I didn't want to get you into worse trouble with the rot-queen. I recognized the pin because I *fixed it in your hair* before we left Windhaven on the train! That was *days* ago. How long has it been since you brushed it out?"

"About that, yes . . . ."

"My goodness, how she neglects you! That woman has no conscience."

"The soldier, Dasha, what did he want?"

Dasha shrugged. "He wanted to find the owner of the hairpin. But how did he get his hands on it? Did you lose it somewhere on the grounds yesterday? Or . . . maybe last night?" Dasha gave her a coy smile, like a playful cat. "I'm surprised by you, Celise! I thought you'd sworn off romance. Your heart was always for the horses. But perhaps I was mistaken. . . ."

"The *soldier,* Dasha—was he—did he wear a mask—"

"No mask. His name is Kiran Kinren . . . no, Kin*dale*, I believe. Does that sound familiar? Kiran Kindale? Handsome fellow from Illysea, if I had to guess. He looks a lot more well-off than an average soldier. Perhaps a baronette of some kind?"

Celise's shoulders sagged in relief. "I don't recognize the name. I wouldn't know him."

"How mysterious! It struck me as odd that he's asking after the hairpin, like you're in trouble of some kind." Dasha looked over her again. "What did you get up to last night?"

"I was here . . . sleeping," Celise lied.

"Right. And I own a townhome in Astravelle near the waterfalls." Dasha rolled her eyes. "If you want to get a good look at him, he's leaving now." She nodded to the window.

Celise wrapped the blanket securely around her, scrambled to her feet, and crossed the room in three steps. She winced—her muscles were sore and stiff. She leaned out the window, peering down at the courtyard below, just in time to see a man with blond curly hair wearing a white officer's uniform disappear down the garden path. She didn't recognize him from Elias's squadron the night before. But she had no doubt he was connected to the Mad Dog somehow.

"I don't recognize him," she repeated.

Dasha looked amused, but she pretended to believe Celise's story. "Alright, well, thankfully that's over with. Let's get you ready for the day before Marcella assigns me a million more chores. I'll pour you a bath . . . ."

Celise gazed out the window for a moment longer, admiring the view of the castle grounds. Gravenmere Castle was beautiful during the day—but even more lovely under the moonlight. She wondered why Officer Kindale was trying to find her. Was he connected to the Mad Dog duke?

Were they looking for a spy?

She hunched a bit, chilled by the thought.

Elias had threatened to arrest her last night.

She was very fortunate that only Dasha recognized the hairpin.

What have I gotten myself into?

A bit of movement down below caught her attention. She watched her father exit the tower with Marcella on his arm. They shut the door behind them and strolled across the flagstone pavilion in the same direction as Officer Kindale. Her father walked with a cane in hand and a top hat on his head, very distinguished. They wore matching powder blue outfits, the color of the Dhastel house.

"I don't think Marcella will be back for a little while," Celise said in relief. "It looks like they're going on a walk."

"Good," Dasha grunted as she prepared the tub for Celise's bath. The pipes screeched and squealed, spouting hot water into the copper basin in angry bursts. "I'll get you something from the pantry in a moment. You must be starving. But let's start your bath first. I'm sure Heather and Katrina will want me to help with their dresses as soon as they finish gossiping about the officer. The banquet is only a few hours away—we don't have that much time to get ready. Now let me find that dress Steffie altered for you . . ."

Celise couldn't keep the disappointment off her face. She didn't want to attend the ball. Dasha noticed her frown and tried to brighten her mood. "Don't look so dour! At the very least, you'll be able to watch Katrina make a fool of herself. She thinks the duke is going to propose to her."

"That's a terrible idea," Celise scoffed, surprising herself. When Dasha glanced at her curiously, she explained, "A man like Elias Blackwood won't cater to someone as entitled as Katrina—she can't tolerate the word 'no.' It would be a disaster."

Dasha gave her a bemused look. "Oh? You sound like you've met the man."

Celise blushed.

"So, who would you pick for the duke?"

Celise caught herself before answering. She shouldn't care about any of this. Her little sister could have the duke if she wanted!

"I wouldn't pick anyone for the duke," she backtracked. "But why does Katrina think Elias would propose to her? Is it because she won the Teacup Tournament?"

"It's because of Marcella. Her ladyship has been filling her daughter's ears with all sorts of fantasies about life as a duchess. And you know how Katrina copies her mother. She'll do anything to please her." Dasha looked over Celise again with a curious expression, then went back to sorting through the wardrobe and preparing her dress for the ball.

Celise watched the maid air out the layers of gray silk and fluffy chiffon. Truth be told, she was curious to see how the night turned out. Would Katrina manage to secure a dance with the duke? Would the Mad Dog even attend the ball?

What if he did—and what if Elias recognized *her?* What if he arrested Celise at the ball, thinking she was a spy?

Oh Mother of Dust, save me!

"If I must go to the ball tonight, Dasha, please make me look as *unlike* myself as possible. Please! Do anything you can. Powders, paints, rouges, dyes . . . I must look completely different. I want to be—"

"Exquisite!" Dasha agreed. "Yes! I completely agree. I'm glad you're warming up to the idea. You shouldn't be hiding among the servants, not tonight. I hope you enjoy every second of the ball. I will make you outshine every woman in that room."

Celise blushed. "I don't want to outshine anyone, necessarily. . . ."

"Then we'll give you just a little more sparkle; how's that?"

Dasha hummed happily to herself as she began unpacking Celise's bags and laying out items on the bed: toiletries, scented oils, little makeup brushes and paints. A fresh chemise and underskirt. She crossed the bedroom to the wardrobe, where Celise's ballgown was hanging.

Her dark eyes widened, and she stopped mid-stride.

"Oh? What's this?" The curious maid reached behind the bulky wooden wardrobe, where she tugged out the heavy frock coat Celise had stolen from Lord Elias.

The blood drained from Celise's face when she saw it.

"What is a man's coat doing in your room?" Dasha exclaimed.

"I . . . um," Celise muttered. She couldn't help it—she blushed bright red. She tried to think of an excuse. "It was . . . it was already here in the tower. I found it."

"Did you?" Dasha said and held up the discarded shift along with the coat. "Did you stash your undergarments back here too? I'm not going to ask why this is covered in mud, but . . . ."

Celise cleared her throat. Then she stared at Dasha, at a loss for words.

"You are the most horrible liar in the Five Kingdoms," the maid laughed.

"The coat doesn't belong to Officer Kindale, I swear. . . ."

"Oh hush, there's nothing wrong with borrowing a fellow's jacket on a late-night stroll!" Dasha said in delight. "If you intend to keep it, I shall place it far at the bottom of your traveling chest. You don't want Marcella to find it."

"I . . . I don't mean to keep it for very long."

"Who does it belong to? I'll have a servant return the coat to the gentleman." Dasha dropped her voice. "Best be quick about it while your parents are out."

Celise bit her lip. She couldn't very well tell Dasha that she had Lord Elias Blackwood's coat stowed away in her personal chamber. She didn't want to tell anyone about last night's adventure.

"Just place it in the chest, and let's not speak of it again," Celise finally whispered.

With a cheeky smile on her face, Dasha carefully folded the coat. She gave it a little sniff and raised an eyebrow. "That smells like expensive cologne." Then she swiftly packed the coat away, placing it at the bottom of Celise's trunk and closing the lid with a heavy thud.

Humming a sprightly tune, Dasha went back to the tub and finished filling the deep basin with hot water. Celise wondered how the tower's plumbing managed to pump water up to the third floor, but the Blackwood family could afford the latest innovations. The whole system was either run by some sort of shined technology—likely, although it would need constant mana channeling to work—or someone had engineered a pump system in the tower's boiler room.

Dasha laid out a soft sponge, a bar of scented castile soap, and a ladle next to the tub. Celise dropped her quilt to the ground, and Dasha helped her into the big copper basin. Celise hissed slightly as her bare feet entered the hot water. She sank down onto her knees and rested her back against the side of the tub.

Dasha clucked under her tongue and pointed at her arm. "Where did you get those bruises?"

Celise glanced over, surprised to see brown marks where the thief from the night before had thrown her to the ground.

"I don't remember," she said.

Dasha looked troubled by it. Then she reached out a hand and turned Celise's face toward the sunlight from the window. She inspected the bruise along her jaw. "I do *hate* how the rot-queen treats you! I don't know how you tolerate it. That wasn't right of her, how she struck you yesterday."

"It's far from the worst she's done," Celise pointed out.

Dasha grimaced and released her face. "Not to worry, we'll make sure you're presentable for the ball. I'll use a bit of extra powder to hide the bruise."

"I am so glad you came," Celise admitted.

Dasha winked at her and began unplaiting her hair. Then she brushed out the matted tangles. The talkative maid didn't ask any more questions about the previous night, even as she extracted broken twigs and bits of moss from Celise's unruly locks.

Celise's mind returned to Mordwen's predictions of doom and destiny. Mordwen's cards had promised a *catastrophe* that would change the fate of the kingdom. But if that prediction was meant for the stolen ghost swords, then it seemed the catastrophe had been averted.

"Do you remember Mordwen's fortune-telling?" Celise asked after a few minutes, her mind filled with thoughts of the night to come.

"Vaguely."

"Do you think there's a chance it might come true?"

"No, my lady, I don't. I've never been religious. I think Mordwen's cards are mostly self-fulfilling prophecies. I wouldn't worry too much about it."

Celise sank back into the hot water with a sigh. Perhaps Dasha was right, and she should set aside all thoughts of "fate" and "destiny." She should focus on surviving the evening with her stepmother and half-sisters. If tonight was to be a *clandestine* event, it would have to involve Katrina or someone else!

She hoped against hope she didn't come face-to-face with Elias Blackwood at the ball.

Elias spent the second half of the morning in a private meeting with his father, Lord Cornelius Blackwood, the Duke of Gravenmere. They sat in a spacious chamber on the second floor of the North Wing of the castle. Their family called it the "Day Map Room," not to be confused with the "Geography Room," which was attached to his father's study and housed an extensive brandy collection.

Morning light flowed through a row of east-facing windows. A green rug covered the polished hardwood floor, edged with cream-colored scrollwork and vining leaf patterns. Sparkling chandeliers hung from the high ceiling. A tapestry spanning the south wall of the room displayed the continent of Agea, from the northern pole of Dresengard to the southern tip of the Abyss. Colorful illustrations of castles, forests, towns and mystical creatures decorated the map, drawing attention to each kingdom's features. It was a stunning work of art, with details to entertain the eyes for hours.

Elias's gaze followed the gentle line of the Grapevine Mountains from north to south, down and down to the Abyss, symbolized by a black and red swirl of smoke. On the other side of the Abyss, connected by a narrow landmass that skirted around the ancient meteor's crater, was the desert kingdom of Sera'naya.

His gaze paused there for a moment, thinking of a girl with berry-colored hair.

Then his eyes traveled east, beyond a wall of clouds to the rugged peaks of the Greater Rog Mountains and the Kingdom of Bratzia.

"Ho ho!" Old Blackwood laughed as he fed his griffix dried dates. "He snapped that right up! Good show, Berrybean. Have another."

The little catlike creature screeched in gratitude and took the sugary candy with a taloned front paw. Berrybean was about the size of a bobcat, with tawny, swooping wings, calico fur and brown, nubby horns.

Griffix were all the rage among the nobility. Domesticated from larger griffons that dwelled in the Grapevine Mountains, griffix were smaller in size, similar to house cats, with limited flying ability. The mischievous creatures weren't good for much except destroying furniture and killing birds. A flock had been introduced to the royal palace by Queen Valienthe, and now the little monsters had taken the kingdom by storm.

Berrybean sat on the back of Old Blackwood's armchair, his wings half-spread for balance, his feline face and bright green eyes smirking at Elias, who sat across from his father on a leather chaise. He wondered at the beast's intelligence. In moments like this, it almost seemed sentient.

"Now, my boy, what is this urgent matter you wish to speak of?" Old Blackwood asked.

Elias flexed his left wrist, which was cramping again. His scars pained him after swinging a ghost sword half the night. He reached into his coat pocket and drew out a letter. He tossed the envelope onto the low mahogany table.

"Another one, received just yesterday," he said.

"Another *what*, exactly?" his father grumbled, holding a teacup to his lips.

"Another death threat," Elias replied. "Considering the number of threats I've received this year and the thieves who targeted our treasury last night, I think we should call off the ball."

Old Blackwood spit out his tea. He coughed and sputtered. A helpful servant rushed forward with a white handkerchief. Blackwood practically threw the cup at the servant as he choked and pressed the napkin to his lips. He patted dry his majestic mutton chops, then took out a tiny comb from his jacket's inner pocket and combed them straight.

"Call it off? Preposterous!" the old lord choked. After recovering himself, he reached for the letter and opened it. His eyes scanned over the typeset note. Then he said, "It's hardly a threat. More like a riddle. I don't understand what it means." He read the note aloud:

"Hidden behind the moonlit veil,
Eagle, fawn and otters dance.
Your gift awaits the midnight hour,
A dark reminder of your past.
Tonight, the scales shall be righted.
A visit of abyssal doom
to seal the grave you should have entered.
More awaits within the tomb."

Old Blackwood tossed the letter back down onto the table. He grouched, "It's nonsense, if you ask me."

"I think someone is planning to sabotage the ball tonight."

"Then we'll post extra guards. A lunatic sending you riddles can't be that dangerous." Blackwood pinned his son with a firm glare. "If this is because you don't want to dance at the ball—you won't be ducking out last minute. I forbid it!"

Elias said dryly, "My concern isn't the dance."

"Then what is it?"

"It's about the *very real* death threats I've received since the war ended, which only seem to be increasing in frequency."

"You're concerned about the riddle? Which group do you think wrote this nonsense? The Association of Abyss Survivors? I thought a hefty donation would put them off. Or is it . . . what's that new one . . . Friends of the Abyss? The Compassionate Daemon League?"

"There are dozens of them; I lose track. But they are fond of sending letters," Elias said with some irony. "This riddle, no matter how obscure, portends some sort of disaster at midnight."

"A risk we will have to take," his lord father shrugged. "As for what happened *last* night, there's been a string of robberies targeting rare, shined weapons all across the kingdom since the war ended. It was simply our turn. With all the guests staying at the castle, I'm surprised that's the worst of it."

Elias glanced skyward at the alabaster ceiling and the sixteen inches of crown molding that encircled the room. "Perhaps this *isn't* the worst of it. What if an assassination attempt follows the robbery?"

"Come now, my boy, you're a Blackwood and the named Hero of the Realm. Any position of power comes with the usual *inconveniences*."

Elias tapped his finger irritatedly on the chaise's headrest. Had his father lost his mind?

"Screee!"

Berrybean caught sight of a fly and lunged off the back of Cornelius Blackwood's chair, his silken wings fluttering and failing to lift his plump body into the air. The griffix landed with a solid thump on the low table.

"Ach, Berrybean! Damnable dust, get off!" His father cursed. He tugged at the leash in his hand, dragging the hapless beastie off the table. Berrybean screeched like a hawk, digging his talons into the polished wood, desperate to kill the fly. His claws rendered deep gouges across the beautiful hardwood table.

Teacups rattled. One cup tipped over and spilled black tea across the letter, drenching the paper in amber liquid.

"Must you entertain that miserable creature?" Elias snarled, rescuing the letter with a swipe of his hand. "He should be up on the roof catching rats."

"Nonsense, that's no life for a griffix!" his father retorted. "He's a fiery little fellow, my Berrybean. Make no mistake, he's a Blackwood through and through! Perhaps I should have named him after you."

Elias felt a headache coming on.

"About these men who stole from our treasury, have you discovered which house they belong to?" Old Blackwood asked.

"I'm beginning to think they didn't arrive with our guests."

"So they're not servants?"

"No. I believe they infiltrated Gravenmere disguised as servants, but their livery is unadorned with any house sigils. I inspected their uniforms myself. Their clothes look like standard suits anyone can rummage from a secondhand shop. Convincing at a distance, but not up close."

"Bold of them! Where are the criminals now?"

"We're holding them in the Gravenmere cellars," Elias said. "I want to question them a bit more after they've sat for a few days. I want to know who hired them and if they're working with a larger group. They might know who orchestrated the hit on the Royal Skydust Museum."

"If anyone can crack the case, it's a Blackwood," his father agreed.

Elias nodded. His title and military standing outranked the local magistrates. The thieves were unlucky to have stolen from a Blackwood. The cellars of Gravenmere were converted from a dungeon, and a cell block still resided under the south wing of the castle, where the thieves were locked away securely with guards posted. They would soon be transported to a local jail.

Elias planned to visit the men before they left. He had a few questions. The ghost swords they took were telling; it didn't seem like a random robbery. Three of the weapons were shined with Dust #410 Blacklight. Odd. It seemed only the most rare weapons were targeted, which implied the hand of a specialist behind the crime.

Old Blackwood stood up and circled around the table. He clapped a hand on Elias's shoulder.

"Enough talk about the robbery—it will all get sorted! Put all these troubles from your mind, my boy. Your thoughts should be on all the eligible young women at the castle! We'll find you a bride tonight, whether by brimstone or briar patch!"

Elias snorted. "So the luckless lady shall be burned or stung by nettles?"

"You know what I mean. You're a Blackwood. No matter how harsh the terrain or challenging the task, we shall see it done! Don't forget what tonight is really all about."

"Finding a bride?"

"Fulfilling our duty to the crown!" Blackwood blustered.

Elias sighed again, quietly, to himself.

At that moment, a knock came to the map room's door. A servant opened it, announcing, "His Lordship, Kiran Kindale."

"Ah, Kiran! Come in, come in!" Old Blackwood said happily. "It's good to see you, my boy! Are you ready for the ball tonight?"

"I was born ready," Kiran winked, a roguish smile flashing across his face. He saluted Old Blackwood smartly, his eyes glinting with humor. He entered the room with his usual vibrant energy and came to stand just behind Elias on the chaise. "Are you two still discussing business? I can return in a few minutes. . . ."

"No, no. My son was just trying to convince me to cancel the ball tonight! As though I could, with half the kingdom's aristocracy in attendance. We must proceed with the evening's festivities. Besides, you lads are of the Daemonguard—I trust my castle will be as well protected as Firehelm Fortress."

"Very true, my lord," Kiran said with a bow. "Gravenmere is the safest place in the kingdom with your son home."

Old Blackwood beamed. "Good, good. My thoughts exactly. It's going to be a madhouse leading up to the banquet. But, with your help, we might be able to restore my son's reputation tonight. I don't want you to let Elias out of your sight. You must make sure he attends the ball. If the ladies see him with you, perhaps they won't be so intimidated. Help him break the ice, hm?"

"Yes, sir! Don't worry, I won't be too likable—then the ladies might prefer me to the leading man."

"Ho-ho!" Blackwood guffawed. "Good show! It's a shame my son doesn't have half your pep, Kiran. If you were in his place, you'd be married five times over by now!"

"To five different wives!" Kiran agreed.

"Oh, yes, *good show*." Old Blackwood chuckled and wiped a tear from his red cheek. "Well, in all seriousness, we *must* secure an engagement for Elias before the end of the ball. Thanks to *The Lady's Letter* and this ongoing scandal with the princess, the king himself is eager to see our Hero of the Realm settled and wed. I have three reporters from major papers attending the gala, all to lay to rest this nonsense about a 'Mad Dog duke' . . . . Ho! *Oh-ho!*"

Despite his father's best efforts, Old Blackwood began chortling at the name, big chuckles heaving through his squat body until he was jiggling with mirth. Berrybean purred at his side, rubbing his face against the old duke's pant leg.

Elias watched his father laugh, nonplussed.

"I'm glad my reputation amuses you," Elias said dryly.

"Only because it's so fitting!" Old Blackwood chuckled and snorted. "A mad dog . . . well, you certainly have bitten a few hands . . . *oh-ho!*" He laughed again.

Elias shared a pained glance with Kiran. "This is why my father brought me back from the dead—to amuse himself and retire early."

A frown flickered across Kiran's kindly face. "Come now, Elias, it's good to laugh. You're the hero who killed the Daemon King, and *The Lady's Letter* has doused you in tar and feathers! The absurdity is mind-numbing. I think it's high time we put a stop to it."

"Is killing the Daemon King not enough?" Elias snapped. "I could care less about the opinion of some *penny dreadful* magazine. People will talk until they tire of the 'Mad Dog,' then they'll move on to the next scandal."

His father sobered a bit. "Careful, Elias. You might be untouchable on the battlefield, but this is a different kind of war. The king is concerned about the princess's reputation since she spoke out on your behalf. The courtiers are wondering about your connection to her. They fear a scandal might interrupt the royal wedding."

"We have no connection. I met her once when she was twelve," Elias quipped.

"She's my cousin," Kiran pointed out, "and I'm sure she meant well, defending you to *The Lady's Letter*. It's all gone a bit sideways."

Old Blackwood continued, "Her reasons aren't important. As Hero of the Realm and the future Duke of Gravenmere, you're in the public eye. Your mother is tired of defending her son at her socials, and your last *seven fiancées* are telling. We would both like to see you married and settled, and sooner rather than later." On a more dour note, he added, "Just so you're both aware, King Valienthe has threatened to seize Gravenmere Castle if Elias doesn't marry and produce an heir within a year. So we must secure a bride by midnight, no matter the cost!"

"Ah . . ." Kiran's eyes slid to Elias with a mildly shocked expression. "That's a lot of pressure."

Elias returned Kiran's look with a somber frown. This was not news to him; he had overheard his parents arguing about it when they thought he wasn't in earshot. It had been discussed many times at the dinner table. As much as his father looked down his nose at the royal family, Old Blackwood wouldn't risk their title and lands.

A moment of silence settled upon the room as the gravity of the evening took hold. Kiran adjusted the cuffs on his jacket. Elias picked at the leather covering of the chaise. Then he forced his hand to be still. He climbed to his feet and straightened his jacket.

"Come along, Kiran. We have some business to discuss." He was tired of this nonsense about a ball and a bride. With a nod to his father, he turned and headed for the door. Kiran followed at his heels with a fluid grace that seemed to embody all the people of Illysea.

"The banquet is only a few hours away!" his father called after them. "If you fail to show up, Elias, I will personally ensure you marry a mule out of my own stables."

The Mad Dog raised a gloved hand as he exited the room.

"What was that all about?" Kiran asked as they started down the long corridor toward Elias's study. "Don't you want to find a bride, Elias?"

"There are more pressing matters at hand—like the safety of the castle." Elias reached into his coat pocket and passed Kiran the sopping wet letter. Kiran's eyes scanned over it as they walked. He snorted in mild amusement.

"Well, someone has a flair for drama," he said.

"I think it's from *him*."

"I doubt that, Elias. Ghosts can't write letters, and our old friend is definitely dead."

"I have my suspicions. The thieves last night targeted rare, shined weapons from our treasury. Only a specialist would know their value. Someone who's fought in the Abyss—who knows what the blades can do."

"Do you think it's a conspiracy, then? Our old friend survived the battle and is now stealing weapons for some nefarious purpose?"

Elias's face hardened, but he said nothing.

"You're sounding a bit paranoid, old boy," Kiran said in a softer tone.

Elias brushed his hair back from his face and picked up the pace, his boots slamming against the polished wood floors of Gravenmere Castle. Paranoia, moodiness, headaches, obsessions—all symptoms of an unnamed condition his doctors were eager to treat with all sorts of experimental potions. For the last two years, he had felt more like a lab rat than a soldier.

But he didn't think he was wrong about this.

Five elite Luminaries had entered the heart of the Abyss to fight the Daemon King in the final battle. Three had died. Well, *four* had died, technically. Some miracle or mistake of medical science had resurrected him.

Lysander of Dresengard, the Hero of the North, had disappeared. His whereabouts were unknown.

Something about the letter—its poetry and the personal nature of its contents—reminded him of his old comrade-in-arms.

Or perhaps he was truly fighting a ghost.

"How did your investigation go? Did you find her?" Elias asked, changing the subject.

"*Her?* I found many 'hers,'" Kiran quipped.

"Did you check the Dhastel family?"

"They were the first family on your *extensive* list. But yes, I checked with them before coming to report. You can't imagine their reactions, Elias, when I showed them the hairpin. You'd think I was asking them to identify an obscure mineral. Everything from confusion to excitement to concern. I couldn't tell them *why* I was asking about it, of course, so most of our conversation turned to the ball—"

"Did the hairpin belong to one of their daughters?"

"No, it didn't."

Elias paused. He gave Kiran a piercing look. His old friend shrugged. "Their daughters didn't fit the description you gave me. Neither had Sera'nayan blood nor a bruise along her jaw."

"I see."

His mind returned to the mysterious girl he had encountered in the woods.

Actually, she had been on his mind all day.

Furiously, obsessively on his mind.

He hadn't mentioned the odd little moonflower to his father. He felt protective of her, though he couldn't say why.

Who is she?

Soft-spoken, gentle and unassuming. A wallflower. Slight and small, somehow invisible. The perfect spy, if she was from Sera'naya.

She knew her way around Hellions, which was unusual for a highborn woman.

Tempest liked her, which was rare.

Not only did his horse like her—Tempest *obeyed* her, which was unheard of.

Not even the Blackwood servants approached his horse. Elias was the only man who could tend to the stormy stallion. Tempest was kept in a solitary stall reinforced with iron bars and fed through a slat in the wall. Yet this girl cleaned his hooves like he was a mild old mare!

Elias was a master at sizing up personalities—he had honed the skill over years of selecting soldiers for missions in the Abyss. He knew a coward when he saw one, and this girl was no coward. Even if she seemed meek at first, she had shown herself to be headstrong and bold.

Yet she kept herself small.

Another contradiction.

He thought of the bruise on her face. Troubling.

He lingered on that. Someone had struck her, but who? Not the thieves; she had denied it. *Clumsy,* she had said. He doubted that very much after seeing her vault onto the back of his horse. It only fueled the fire of fascination in his mind. He regretted not pressing her harder for her name.

They reached the doors of his private study. Elias removed one of his black gloves and touched the shined lock. With a brush of his fingers, a tendril of mana ran from his hand through the study's locked doors. He heard a series of turning gears and shifting pins as the door unlocked.

Then he turned the knob and thrust it open. The two men entered the study.

His office was as gloomy and cluttered as the day before. Heavy, dark curtains blocked out the light from the windows. The sharp scent of old tinctures lay heavy in the air. The broken bottles lay next to his desk, untouched.

Elias barely saw them. His gaze remained focused blindly on the desk, immersed in thoughts of *the girl.* He still hadn't puzzled out why she was dressed in her nightshift. That, and she had made off with his favorite coat. He could afford any number of jackets, but that particular frock coat had survived several campaigns in the Abyss. He considered it good luck.

He wanted it back.

Elias released a dusty, weatherworn sound from deep in his chest, thinking of his favorite jacket.

Behind him, Kiran touched the shined wall sconces to either side of the door to shed a little light in the room.

"This place really does feel like the Abyss," he mentioned.

Elias didn't respond but crossed the wide chamber to his cluttered desk, which was covered in boxes of folders and sealed envelopes.

"Mother of Dust, Elias, what in the five kingdoms . . ." Kiran muttered when he saw the desk. "What is all this?"

"Records of every family attending the ball tonight."

Kiran's eyes cast distastefully over the desk again, sizing up the stacks of folders, his eyebrows raised. "*Every* family? Why?" At Elias's silence, Kiran tutted under his breath. "I daresay this is the most interest you've ever shown a woman. By your measure, I'd call it *romantic.*"

Elias ignored his friend's teasing and began rearranging the stacks of folders. He had brought them up from his father's archives early that morning, just as the light of dawn broke across the sky. He hadn't slept at all since his encounter with the girl. If Kiran hadn't stopped him that morning, he would have been walking around the castle with his hair mussed and pine needles clinging to his jacket.

After returning to the castle last night, he had found Tempest tethered to a pine tree just outside the gate in the south wall. The girl had returned by the same way she had come. He wasn't surprised. But when he entered the grounds, he saw no sign of her, except for a telltale strand of raspberry hair clinging to a shrub near the gatehouse.

The *unmanned* gatehouse.

The guards were with him, of course.

Hellfire heathens, he was growing tired of this wild goose chase, and it had only just begun!

"Give me the hairpin," he snapped and held out his hand.

Kiran passed it over to him. "Pretty little bauble," he offered, "but the crystals are not rare. If it belongs to a highborn lass, I can't imagine she's very rich."

Elias rolled the hairpin around in his hand as he sorted through the open file on his desk.

Kiran peeked curiously over his shoulder. "And this record belongs to . . . ?"

"The Dhastel family."

"Ah."

The newly minted contract signed by Lord Dhastel of Windhaven Ranch sat on top of the pile: a hundred new horses—Hellions mixed with standardbreds—purchased for Firehelm Fortress. It was a good price. The fortress's stables were mostly empty, and they needed the stock for new recruits. He flipped the contract over and continued to shuffle through the scattered papers. He found birth records of three daughters: Celise, Katrina and Heather. Pictures of the latter two were pinned to the front of a family's summary, though the filmy black-and-white photos were hard to discern. Elias squinted at them, then set them aside. The rest of the folder's contents weren't very interesting. Various business correspondence dated back several decades between the two families. Mentions of a marriage to Ms. Marcella Bowren, a merchant's daughter who was born Luminous, who managed to climb her way into the nobility. More military contracts for Hellion stock, dating back to the beginning of the war.

"You said they only had two daughters present?" Elias asked.

"Yes, Heather and Katrina."

He frowned again. "No third daughter?"

"None at the tower. I asked about it, but Lady Dhastel denied having a third daughter. It must be a mistake in the records, or perhaps she died." Kiran gave him a searching glance. "Why?"

Elias spun the hairpin around in his fingers. "She knew a lot about Hellions."

"Who did?"

"The girl."

A glint entered Kiran's eye. "Ah. I see. She liked your horse, did she?"

"Rather, Tempest liked *her*."

Kiran was quiet, watching his old friend with a bemused smile hovering about his lips.

"What?" Elias snapped.

Kiran shrugged. "Nothing, I just think it's very interesting how hard you're trying to find this girl. No stone unturned. Has she done anything illegal?"

"No. Not exactly."

"Been on your mind, has she?"

Elias nodded absently, once again scanning over the documents.

Kiran watched him with an infuriating smile on his face. "If you're so interested in her, perhaps you should attend the ball tonight."

"That won't be possible," Elias growled and slammed the file shut. "I'm not concerned. She's just a girl." If he attended the ball that evening, it would only be to suss her out, but he didn't plan to. He turned to face his right-hand man, doing his best to hide the burning curiosity that absorbed his thoughts. “Let’s discuss our strategy for this evening.”

“Right. Your *exit* strategy.” Kiran mock-saluted him, grinning wide enough for his dimples to show. “Now the real mission begins. You know, your father will have our heads if he finds out. If I may remind you, he expects us at the ball *together.*”

“I’ll be there,” Elias emphasized. “*You* won’t be. You’ll be patrolling the grounds for any untimely threats. I think he’ll mind that a lot less.”

Kiran grinned even wider. “Oh, I do love a bit of mischief.”

Elias unlocked the bottom drawer of his desk and took out a wooden box. “Now, let me show you the mask.”

Kiran came to stand close by his side, leaning over his shoulder to take a look. The enameled metal half-mask rested on a velvet cloth inside the box. Its smooth surface was shined to perfection and glinted in the midmorning light from the window. The black piece would cover Kiran’s nose to his hairline, and a black ribbon would fasten it in place behind his head.

Elias explained, “The shined piece was specially crafted by Meister Barbaros’s artificers in Gigas.”

“The same guild that designed the Starcaster?”

“The very same. I commissioned it privately, but I haven’t tested it yet. The mask should be a perfect disguise. We will become twins in all but height.” He gave Kiran a meaningful look. “You know my mannerisms well, which makes you the perfect choice for tonight’s deception.”

“Fascinating,” Kiran said with another catlike grin. “I can think of several uses for this.”

Elias’s mouth turned downward. “No shenanigans. I’ll be expecting the mask in my hands first thing in the morning.”

“How nice of you to loan it for the full night,” Kiran mused, turning the mask over in his hands. “I suppose I will be the man to choose your future bride. I’ll make sure she’s a decent dancer, at least.”

Elias ignored Kiran's sarcasm. "Now, my father has already told me about the ladies he has lined up for me. Lady Marcella Dhastel wants me to dance with her daughter, Katrina. It's part of the contract my father signed for the horses—I believe it's the reason why Lord Dhastel gave us such a generous price."

"Ah, so the young lady is an admirer." Kiran looked intrigued. "You know, she's a gold medalist in fencing. I saw her yesterday—she's good with a foil, and it seems she has strong mana control. She won the Teacup Tournament. Your mother, Estoria, was quite impressed."

"I don't care," Elias cut him off. "My father arranged it, so dance with her first. That's all I ask."

"And if I think she's a good fit for you?"

"Then propose."

Kiran's eyebrows shot up. He looked a bit uncertain for a moment. "This is your future wife, Elias. You should at least meet her before you have a stranger propose to her. Don't you think this is all a bit . . . harsh?"

"How so?"

"Well, the lady will feel hurt if she ever found out—"

"No one will find out. I don't care about wooing a bride, Kiran. My work at Firehelm Fortress keeps me busy enough, and as my father said, my last seven fiancées are telling. At this point, I will wed whomever I must to get this matter over with. I shall perform my duty and produce an heir for Gravenmere, the king will be satisfied, and that's that."

Kiran looked sad. He turned the mask over in his hands in silent contemplation. His somber thoughts, so unlike his usual self, weighed heavy on the room.

"Are you sure this is the right thing to do?" he asked softly. "Don't you want someone to *choose* you, Elias? The *real* you? Don't you want to fall in love?"

The Mad Dog stiffened. His right fist clenched beneath the desk. Choose him? The question summoned a seething mess of ill-tempered emotions within him.

In a low tone, he explained, "I haven't danced since before the war, and I know nothing of courtship, Kiran. It's better for you to entertain my guests. I would probably chase off the young ladies like some monster from the Abyss. Besides, you know me better than anyone, and I know you will choose for me a suitable mate." With a self-deprecating tone, Elias added, "I wouldn't know how to choose one for myself."

Kiran searched his commander's eyes for a moment. Then he perked up a bit. "You're right. You would be utterly lost in a ballroom. I will do my very best to find you a lady of strength and grace who will make a good mother for your children. Someone beautiful and charming who can manage Gravenmere by your side."

"Thank you."

The two brothers looked at each other. In that look, the memories of all the losses they had endured in the war seemed to pass between them, unspoken, more than words could ever say.

Then Kiran lifted the mask to his face.

The moment it touched his skin, a slight shimmer engulfed his body. A spark of mana crackled in the air. Then Elias found himself staring at his own reflection. He took half a step back, startled. His eyes swept over Kiran's disguise. He had commissioned the mask—he knew what it was supposed to do—but seeing it in action was a shock.

"So? How is it?" Kiran asked in Elias's dark, raspy voice. He looked around the room, then winced. "Right. You covered all the mirrors." He swept a hand through a head of slick black hair. Then he held up his arms and did a little one-two step, as though he were dancing at the ball. He spun around. "Well?"

Elias indicated his right hand, and Kiran lifted the shined appendage before his face. He flexed his gold fingers. "Ah. I see it doesn't hide my prosthetic. I shall have to wear gloves, I suppose."

"Besides that small detail, it's a perfect disguise," Elias mused. "You look exactly like the Mad Dog duke. We're a few inches different in height, but only our mothers would notice that."

"*Your* mother, maybe," Kiran snarked.

"How does it feel?"

"The mask tingles a bit around my nose, but nothing I can't tolerate for a few hours. You know, items like this are typically registered with the Committee of Deviant Artifacts. I bet Barbaros hasn't filed any paperwork."

"He didn't mention it," Elias hedged. "I might file something later. I don't know."

"Ah." Kiran tapped his masked nose. "Don't worry, your secret is safe with me." Then, with a flourish, he removed the mask and slipped it into his coat. With a shimmer of light, Kiran returned to his blond-haired, brown-toned self. "Let the evening commence!"

"Indeed." Elias turned back to his desk. "Now, if you will excuse me, I have a meeting in half an hour with Meister Barbaros that I need to prepare for. We still have to settle the matter of an unstable batch of Dust he's trying to pawn off on us."

"So you plan to work through your entire birthday?" Kiran grumbled. "If I didn't know you so well, Elias, I would think you're a right arse."

"Polite society is no place for a Mad Dog. The name suits me well."

Kiran glowered at him. Then he threw up an ironic salute. Elias saluted in return.

First Officer Kiran Kindale turned on his heel and left the room.

Alone in his office, Elias removed his gloves and stretched out his fingers, which were cramping. Unsightly scars covered his palm where his sword had melted in the Daemon King's hellfire. His right hand was a few shades darker than the left with a wider palm. Was it strange, using a hand that once belonged to his best friend?

No stranger than being alive at all, he supposed.

So my father thinks I will have an engagement to announce by the end of the night, he thought with an ironic twist to his lips. Kiran could make the announcement for him. In the meantime, Elias would spend the evening patrolling the grounds and protecting the castle, as the commander of the Daemonguard was meant to do.

His mind traveled to the mysterious girl again.

She had emerged from the hedgerows of the garden onto the castle's front drive, wearing only a cotton shift under the moon, her raspberry-colored hair a tousled mess. A small slip of a thing, she had struggled to walk in her long white chemise. He had never seen such a tiny woman.

Her eyes had whispered to him of a strange sadness.

He wondered if she would attend the dance.

He almost regretted his plan to skip the evening.

Chapter 12
The Bratzian Twins

Dressed in the finest gown she had ever worn, Celise accompanied the rest of the Dhastel family from the Moongazer Tower to the banquet hall. The sun was just beginning its descent across the horizon. Golden light filled the Hallowsin sky as breezy pink clouds trailed behind the mountains.

Celise's heart fluttered in her chest like a bird trapped in a cage. Her corset was laced tight, and her small breasts hiked up to an unimaginable height. She could barely breathe through the stays that held the whole ensemble together. A crinoline cage boosted up her skirts into a majestic bell shape. The evening gown cascaded to the ground in a sweep of dove-gray silk. Her waist looked sleek and narrow. A low, square neckline trimmed with white lace framed her décolletage. Around her neck, she wore a simple black velvet choker, unadorned with any jewels or pendants. Even without the glamorous tiaras, bejeweled necklaces and brooches worn by the other women, she felt like a glowing diamond.

Celise found herself staggering into a corridor of mirrors, a preamble to Gravenmere's banquet hall. Gold-framed mirrors of different shapes and sizes, each one polished to perfection, lined the hallway leading to the feast. She caught sight of her reflection. Gone were her dusty coveralls, her tweed cap, her messy hair and twiggy frame. She didn't recognize the girl who gazed back at her. She didn't look like a boy at all. In the mirror's reflection, a dainty doll with piles of raspberry-colored tresses stood with her hands bunched in her gray skirts, looking uncertain of herself. She clutched the silk folds tightly. Dasha's makeup had transformed her face from a plain oval to an angular beauty with high cheekbones and a pointed chin. Her eyebrows were carefully sculpted, her lips painted a deep red, and her skin glassy smooth from layers of powder.

The transformation seemed like a miracle.

"Come along, girls," Marcella snipped, floating past the wall of mirrors on the arm of Lord Dhastel. Marcella's cold, dark eyes drifted above Celise's reflection without looking directly at her. Still, Celise knew the reprimand was meant for her. "It's *unladylike* to gaze at yourself in public. You'll look vain and stupid. Keep walking, *please*."

Katrina and Heather passed by Celise with their arms locked together, their heads leaned close, giggling over some private joke. Katrina wore a ruby red dress of shocking jewel tones, while Heather wore a soft teal green ensemble. Neither had spoken to Celise since seeing her emerge from the Moongazer Tower. The sight of her gray dress and simple velvet choker seemed to offend them, though Celise wasn't sure why.

"It's because you look so lovely," Dasha had reassured her with a wink. *"Keep your chin up. Go enjoy the ball!"* Then the helpful maid had pushed Celise out the door, into the cool evening air.

With Dasha's words still at the front of her mind, Celise picked up her skirts and hurried after her two half-sisters, staggering only slightly under the weight of the crinoline. With labored breath, she followed the Dhastel family through the open doors into the banquet hall. Their names were announced by a servant as they entered the room.

The long chamber was already filled to the brim with hungry guests. Hit with a wave of anxiety, Celise paused to take in the sight. Thick wooden beams bolstered the high ceiling of the cavernous room. Portraits of the Blackwood family dotted the emerald green wallpaper that covered the walls. A gleaming shield hung above a roaring stone fireplace with the Blackwood coat-of-arms prominently displayed: a green dragonfly floating on a field of black.

Dozens of round tables, each seating about ten guests, were laid throughout the room. At the very front of the room was a long rectangular table where the Blackwood family sat with a few close acquaintances. Celise's eyes, which were used to counting horses on the range, quickly estimated about three hundred guests in attendance. The rich smell of roasted venison stew and spices filled the room to the rafters. Servants walked around with trays full of cured meats, fruits and cheeses. Others carted around vats of rich creamy soup and baskets of fluffy bread, roasted vegetables, and delicate greens. A servant with a cart full of meat pies skirted around their party, heading for the tables, and Celise's mouth began to water. She had never seen such a gourmet affair in her life! She hadn't eaten since the day before, and her stomach was groaning.

Then her eyes returned to the front of the room, where the Blackwood family sat at a long, rectangular table. Her hands became clammy and moist inside her white silk gloves. She saw the grayish-lavender hair of Meister Barbaros, and seated between the Bratzian guildmaster and Lady Estoria Blackwood was a man wearing a black mask. A knot of cold dread tightened in her stomach.

As she watched, the Mad Dog took a pitcher of wine from a passing servant and insisted on filling his mother's glass. Estoria looked pleased. It was hard to imagine a grumpy military man like Elias Blackwood filling his mother's chalice with wine.

Oh well. What did she know about the ways of a duke?

At that moment, two female servants approached the Dhastel family. With a bow, the first one asked, "Will the lord and lady follow me? We have your seats assigned."

"I'll escort the young ladies to their table," the second servant offered.

"Lovely!" Katrina gushed, gripping Heather's hand in excitement.

Marcella nodded her approval.

As the servant led the three young women away through the crowded room, Celise was a bit surprised. It seemed the tables were arranged by age and rank. She supposed it made sense. That way, the young adults could socialize while their parents engaged in less riveting talk about matters of the kingdom. She was relieved that she wouldn't be seated under Marcella's judgmental eye. She still didn't know which fork to use for her salad.

Then her heart sank.

The servant was leading them to the front of the room—toward the duke's table.

Oh no.

Celise followed behind her two half-sisters with her shoulders slightly hunched. Would Elias recognize her in a fine dress with so much make-up?

It seemed their table was just next to the Blackwood table—not close enough for conversation, but close enough for Elias to get an eyeful of his potential brides. Celise recognized the same group of young ladies from the tea party: Bernadette Goodweather, the Bratzian twins and . . . Ambrosia Verabon. She groaned inwardly. Why would Estoria Blackwood seat Katrina and Ambrosia next to each other? Katrina was already bristling. She hoped another fencing match didn't break out in the middle of the banquet.

"Stop slinking about like a hungry dog, Celise," Katrina scowled at her as they approached the ladies' table. "Don't forget to apologize for your rudeness yesterday. You caused quite a stir, wandering off like you did."

"Yes, I will apologize," Celise said softly, ducking her head like a servant. She winced and caught herself. She felt like she was talking to Marcella in miniature.

The servant helped the three ladies into their chairs and filled their chalices with wine. Ambrosia Verabon, dressed in a stunning violet evening gown with lavender and blue accents, sat across from Katrina at the table. A towering bouquet of flowers blocked them from a clear view of each other—thankfully.

The Bratzian twins were seated on Celise's right, and beyond them, she saw Bernadette Goodweather and a row of other faces she partially recognized. The young ladies all nodded to Katrina and Heather as they sat down.

"I see you are doing well," one of the Bratzian twins said to Celise in a thick accent. "You disappeared yesterday before the tournament. They said you were ill. Are you feeling better?"

Celise didn't expect the kindness in the girl's voice. "I am feeling much better," she replied softly. "I went for a walk and got lost. I didn't mean to worry everyone."

"The grounds are expansive. It would be easy to get lost!" Bernadette Goodweather agreed.

"I'm afraid to walk through the gardens without an escort," another girl chimed in. Was her name Lavender Dupont? Celise couldn't remember. "It's a little scary how large this place is. Even with the signage on the garden paths, it's easy to get turned around."

The other girls all nodded, and the Bratzian twins smiled at her.

Celise smiled back.

The only girl *not* smiling was Katrina.

As Celise looked around the table, she got the distinct impression that only Katrina was upset by her behavior the day before. The other girls seemed more concerned about her well-being than offended by her absence.

Of course Katrina would *be offended,* Celise thought, *because I embarrassed her.*

But the other ladies were not like Katrina or Marcella.

Celise felt some of her tension ease. Perhaps she didn't seem as out-of-place at the table as she felt.

The servants began filling their plates with a small portion from each menu item. With a slight flush in her cheeks, Celise asked for two of the meat pies. She received a sharp look from Katrina, but the other girls didn't seem to mind. One of the Bratzian twins followed her example.

The savory pie smelled heavenly. Celise hesitated before reaching for a fork. She watched the Bratzian twins closely before choosing which utensil to use. She hoped she was doing it right. She had two forks, three spoons and four knives to choose from. At least Marcella was far away, so her stepmother couldn't scrutinize her table manners.

As she ate, she listened to the conversation.

"Is that him? Lord Elias?" one of the ladies whispered behind her fan.

"What a shame, he's wearing a mask! Just like Ambrosia said!"

"I wonder if he'll take it off for the ball?"

"Do you think he's handsome underneath it?"

"Why would he wear a mask if he wasn't *terrifying* to look at?"

"I think his chin is quite lovely. I think he has a dimple just here." One of the girls pointed to the center of her chin, and the rest tittered behind their wine glasses, stealing glances at the young duke.

With a shiver of apprehension, Celise glanced at the Blackwood table. She found herself slouching a bit, though with the giant vase of flowers standing between them, the duke probably couldn't see her.

If he did, would he recognize her?

The ladies all agonized over what Elias might look like. Despite his mask, the duke's square-cut jaw looked firm and pronounced above his white collar, and his lips were curved into a tantalizing bow shape. These features were indisputably handsome. The barest shadow of scruff darkened his cleft chin. His shoulders were straight and broad, and he carried himself with the air of a man of authority. His charisma seemed to fill the front of the room with a certain excitement. The ladies all murmured to each other, now more curious than ever.

Celise recalled her confrontation with the Mad Dog last night in the woods, under the glowing lantern light beneath the twin moons. His scars. The puckered, warped skin along the left side of his face. His half-closed eye. Now she wished she had spent a minute longer looking at him; her memories were all a bit panicky and confusing. Was he handsome beneath his scars, or had she imagined it?

Had she imagined stealing his horse, too?

No, she couldn't imagine that.

I just want this night to be over, she thought miserably.

She listened to the conversations around her with a keen, almost desperate, ear. Had anyone heard about the thieves from the night before or the stolen ghost blades? She had expected the whole castle to know about it, but she didn't hear a peep from the young ladies. Was it possible that word of the burglary hadn't reached the guests?

She felt a sense of relief. Her midnight misadventure would remain a secret.

No catastrophe. Mordwen's prophecy averted. All was well.

Celise ate more than she should have, even though she forgot which fork to use and which hand to hold her goblet. Her stomach pressed painfully against her bodice. She was starving, and the rich food tasted better than anything she had eaten at the Dhastel estate. But she ate too fast, and then she started to feel a bit sick.

As the other guests began to stir, Celise found herself struggling to her feet. She shared a panicked look with Heather.

"Is there . . . a privy or someplace . . . ?"

"The lavatory is in the hallway just outside," Heather whispered, pointing to the Great Hall's entrance. Celise gulped. She would have to traverse a room full of tables where the elite nobility were just finishing their plates. Servants darted back and forth with water jugs in hand and carts laden with plates. She could easily trip over her layered skirts or catch her stiff crinoline on a chair. Before her eyes, the grand banquet hall became a maze of treacherous obstacles.

Suddenly, one of the Bratzian twins stood up next to her. She reached over and took Celise's hand. The girl gave her a cheerful, confident wink.

"I'll go with you," she said. "I was waiting for someone to walk with! I didn't want to go by myself."

Celise felt immediate relief.

Hand in hand, the two girls started through the crowded room. The Bratzian girl wasn't wearing as wide a crinoline under her skirts and had an easier time navigating the tables. She waited patiently as Celise maneuvered past busy servants and wove her way around towering flower arrangements. She passed by Marcella's table, sensing the harsh gaze of her stepmother, but she didn't look back. Finally, she reached the Great Hall's entryway and found herself once again in the corridor of mirrors.

Just next to the Great Hall's entrance, a pristine set of white doors with crystal knobs opened into a powder room. A servant dressed in dark green livery and a white mobcap stood just outside the doors. She bowed as the two girls swept by.

The beautiful bathroom brought Celise to a quick halt. With rose quartz basins, white marble floor tiles, glittering wall sconces and brushed silver piping, she had never seen a room so dainty and feminine. A standing vase full of cherry blossoms stood in the corner of the room, next to a padded white bench. Gilded mirrors lined the walls. The scent of dried rose petals clung to the air.

The Bratzian girl motioned to a pair of stalls at the back of the lavatory. "I'll take the one on the right," she said. "Do you need help with your skirts? I can call for a servant to assist you . . ."

"I'll manage," Celise said weakly. Dasha had explained the whole process to her that morning. Underneath her layers of skirts, Celise wore a special pair of underwear called *pantalons*, which were split at the crotch.

She had never needed to wear such things on the Dhastel ranch, since she had never worn dresses in the stables, but all she needed to do was hoist up her skirts and aim.

With a firm chin, she entered the water closet.

It was perhaps the second bravest moment of her life—the first, of course, being her flight on Tempest through the woods.

Once she entered the privy, Celise hoisted up her skirts and, with some maneuvering, managed to align herself over the pot. The process took longer than she anticipated. Then she very carefully relieved herself.

As Celise hovered over the pot, a swirl of dark thoughts filled her head.

She had survived the banquet, but could she survive the ball?

She was terrified someone might ask her to dance.

She would have to avoid the floor.

By Dust and Moon . . . what if the duke asked her to dance?

No, don't even think about it!

She would make it her special mission to avoid him at all costs.

She heard the door to the restroom open and shut several times as girls came in to check their makeup. Someone knocked on the door to her stall, and with a rustle of skirts, Celise finished up and unlocked the latch. She gave the next girl an awkward smile as they passed each other. Her slippers squeaked slightly on the polished floor tiles as she approached the row of sinks along the wall. Her corset felt suffocating, and her thoughts even more so.

What would happen if she encountered Elias face-to-face?

Celise inspected her reflection in the mirror—her glossy hair, her dove-gray dress, her contoured face—and drew in a deep breath. Lord Elias probably wouldn't recognize her. She looked very different from the little moonflower he had encountered in the dark forest. She didn't need to act so skittish and uncertain of herself. The evening was already halfway over.

As she turned to leave the powder room, a voice reached her from the hallway.

"How dare you mock me!"

Celise paused.

"Please, she did not mean to insult you—"

"What else did she mean, then? How dim must you be to imply I look like *a wild animal!*"

"In Bratzia, we think wild animals are the most beautiful. They are . . . what's the word . . . *untamed*. Pure."

Instead of shrinking away from the angry voices, Celise found herself picking up her skirts and walking into the hallway. Near the entrance to the powder room stood the Bratzian twins, identical except for their elaborate gowns. The one who had escorted her to the washroom wore a dress of deep indigo chiffon and a glittering golden bodice. The second twin wore a burgundy-magenta dress of identical cut, her bodice studded with sparkling onyx stones. Both were trimmed with fox fur along the shoulders, wrist cuffs and neckline. The indigo dress had white fur, while the burgundy dress had black.

Celise thought the Bratzian dresses were perhaps the most unusual and stunning things she had seen at the gala so far.

Soft, silvery curls framed the twins' brown faces, and jeweled tiaras adorned their foreheads. Both young women looked no older than twenty. Both were absolutely stunning. The style and cut of their bodices was notably different from Forsynthian fashion. The glittering fabric encased their necks almost to their jaws and covered their arms down to their wrists. The lack of visible skin made the ladies no less beautiful.

Before the twins, three Forsynthian noblewomen draped in cool blues, teals and periwinkle lace stood with their arms crossed, each looking haughty and defensive. At the fore of the group stood Ambrosia Verabon in her violet-and-lavender ensemble.

"Tell me, do all girls from Bratzia speak with such a thick accent?" Verabon drawled, her lips curled into a sneer of superiority. "In Forsynthia, we're required to learn *three* different languages by the time we complete our schooling."

The twins looked intimidated. One clutched the other's hand.

"My sister can understand you clearly; she just doesn't speak her words well," one of the twins said, a frown clouding her heart-shaped face.

"Well, that remains to be seen." Verabon's eyes raked over the girl's dress. "I'm not sure I understand your fashion sense. These jeweled bodices are so gaudy, and your colors are so . . . *loud*."

"Bratzians dress differently; we prefer heavier fabrics with darker dyes," the outspoken twin said defensively. "Our gowns are made with thicker material for the gray mountains of Rog—"

"And so you wear fox furs in early Hallowsin?" one of Verabon's friends laughed. "You must be sweltering. It's not even harvest time. You should have dressed lighter for the season."

"Why do you care if their dresses are a bit different?" Celise heard her voice cutting through their conversation. She took a step back as the girls all turned to stare at her.

Ambrosia's eyes widened with recognition. She said nothing—but her cheeks paled. If anything, she looked embarrassed to be caught in the act of bullying a foreigner.

"My apologies, I didn't see you standing there," she said.

Perhaps for the first time in her life, Celise felt a twinge of authority, as though perhaps she were a lady after all. She straightened up a notch. She wasn't very tall, and Ambrosia towered over her. But Ambrosia wasn't half as intimidating as Elias's warhorse, Tempest, and that thought gave Celise courage.

"You should show them our Forsynthian hospitality, not mock their dresses," Celise said, her voice stronger than before. For some reason, it was much easier to stand up for the twins than for herself. "Do you plan to insult me next, or have you filled your quota for the evening? If you must criticize someone's dress, you may criticize mine."

A pause. A single scoff. Then Ambrosia wordlessly swept her skirts and walked away, her head held high, with her friends flanking her.

The Bratzian twins stared at Celise with wide eyes.

Celise gazed back, just as shocked at herself. Then she gave them a small, almost sheepish smile. "I feel like I should apologize for Ambrosia's rudeness."

"No matter," the first twin said, the one wearing the indigo chiffon and sparkling, gold-and-crystal-studded bodice. "We've traveled a lot around your kingdom. Not every person in Forsynthia is like Ambrosia."

"Just *some* of them," the second twin said in her thick accent.

"Well, I certainly don't think less of you for speaking another language. I never learned anything other than Forsythian," Celise reassured them.

The first Bratzian twin stuck out her hand. "I'm Ismara, and this is Ilyana. We're from the city of Anvéra in Bratzia."

Celise offered a hand. "A pleasure."

"You should come visit us sometime," Ismara said. "We'll show you the crystal sea and the fur markets—none of this cold smirking and flouncing about."

Ilyana grinned. "Dances in Anvéra are more fun. Less . . . stuffy."

Celise smiled. "I would like that," she said, though in truth, she knew she would likely never see the twins again after the ball. She cleared her throat, a bit awkward, thinking back to the conversation she had overheard between Lord Elias and Meister Barbaros.

"I heard Bratzian artificers make a lot of shined objects," she said. "I heard something called 'dust' can be used to make different ones."

Ismara's eyes widened in delight. "How surprising! I don't often meet a Forsythnian lady who knows about dust. Yes, every Bratzian child knows at least the basics of artificing. My father is the master of the Weaving Hands Guild."

"So then, you know about artificing?" Celise asked, surprised.

"Yes. It would be a disgrace not to, as a guildmaster's daughter." Ismara gave a small curtsy.

Ilyana indicated the gold bracelet on her wrist. "I made this one."

"Oh?" Celise asked curiously, looking at it. "What does it do?"

"It warms your hand."

Ismara cut in. "Do you want to try it?" She reached for her sister's wrist. "Here, let's take it off and let Celise try. It glows a pretty pink color when you channel with it. You only need a small amount of mana; even a child could—"

"Oh, no, that's alright," Celise said quickly. She glanced down the hallway, where guests were walking from the banquet hall to the ballroom. "The dance will begin soon. We should probably head there . . ." In truth, she didn't want to reveal her lack of mana. She didn't know what the twins might think. All of the nobility in Forsynthia were Luminous.

"You're right. Let's go," Ismara agreed.

The three girls started down the long corridor together. Now that Ismara was more comfortable, she chatted about the different guilds in Bratzia, how each one had a different technique and tradition for creating shined artifacts. Celise didn't see Katrina or Heather anywhere, which was a relief. She found herself enjoying the twins' company. They seemed much more friendly than the Forsynthian nobles. Ismara was particularly talkative and walked close to her side.

They started down the hallway to the ballroom.

Outside the tall windows, stars dotted the sky and dusky purple light cast long shadows across the Gravenmere gardens. Cheerful, shined lanterns of different colors illuminated the main corridor to the ballroom. Ismara and Ilyana walked on either side of Celise, sharing stories of their life in Bratzia. As they walked across the west wing of the castle, Celise found herself smiling at the two lively twins. Her heart felt a little lighter, her spine a little straighter.

She thought back to her confrontation with Ambrosia and wondered at herself. Since when had she become so bold? Whatever had sparked her transformation, she was grateful for it, because she had made some new friends.

Chapter 13

The Ball

Twinkling gas-fueled chandeliers hung from the Gravenmere ballroom, casting golden light across a floor of green and white tiles. White marble columns, veined with silver, lined the perimeter of the dance hall. Ladies in fine gowns rustled and shimmered as they moved in little flocks around the room. Gentlemen in tailcoats and cravats clustered at the edges of the dance floor, discreetly searching the crowd for a pleasing dance partner. Laughter filled the air like silver bells, and the music—a graceful waltz played by the Plum Dahlia Quartet—swelled through the glittering chamber. The ensemble sat on a raised dais in the corner of the ballroom, barricaded from the dancers by a wall of standing vases and tables lined with glowing candles.

Two of the musicians' violins were shined. With each stroke, a waft of sparkling mist floated above the quartet, snaking through the air and following the weave of the music. The sight reminded Celise of Heather's harp, which emitted a similar sparkle when she practiced at home. With each stroke of the lead violinist's bow, a gust of silver sparkles showered the air, while the second violin released streams of shimmering green clouds. The crowds gasped and applauded at the sight.

Celise left the Bratzian twins at the entrance to the ballroom and went to join the Dhastel family. As she walked, she couldn't help but gaze upward at the ballroom's painted ceiling, where a heavenly landscape of winged horses and chariots danced around the Goddess of Dust and Moon. In the painting, Valestra held her fabled wand high, conducting the fate of the cosmos like a divine orchestra.

The Dhastels were clustered around one of the tall, circular tables that bordered the dance floor. The tables were meant for standing and not sitting. The only chairs in the room were along the north-facing wall, in a shadowy area beyond the dance floor. The secluded row of short benches and cushioned seats was for dancers to regain their breath. Most of the guests were up and walking about at this early hour of the evening, before the waltz began.

Marcella didn't glance in her direction when Celise arrived at their table. Celise stood slightly behind Katrina and Heather, feeling invisible once again. She wore no extravagant hairpieces, no feathers or sparkling sequins to catch the light. Despite her dress being the finest she had ever worn, she still felt plain next to Katrina and Heather's fashionable skirts. The two sisters shone like polished jewels.

Celise felt herself shrink down a bit as she realized just how simple her dress truly was. The confidence she had gained around the Bratzian twins didn't last very long. Next to her sisters, she felt as out of place as a duck amongst swans. Before long, she found herself wishing to be invisible once again.

As more and more women gathered at the edges of the dance floor, Marcella looked increasingly irritated.

Lord Elias Blackwood still hadn't arrived at the ball.

"Where is he?" Marcella griped. "Old Blackwood *promised* his son would dance with Katrina."

"Now, now, let's not be impatient," Lord Dhastel said into his half-finished whiskey tumbler. "The dance has yet to begin."

"Are you going to drink the night away like a sloth?" Marcella snipped.

"Nothing wrong with enjoying a sip of fine, free liquor," her father muttered. "Relax, my dear; I'm sure His Grace is just adding a few lines to his speech."

"A speech?" Katrina groaned. "But that's so . . . *boring*."

"Why don't you girls stand closer to the dance floor?" Marcella said with a sharp smile. "There's no point to you lurking about in the shadows, hidden away."

Celise knew Marcella's request was not a mere suggestion. Katrina and Heather exchanged a glance, then picked up their skirts and started across the floor with a gentle rustle. Celise felt a knot of anxiety tighten in her stomach—she would very much like to disappear into a shadowy corner of the room, far away from the brilliant dance floor. But she sensed Marcella's mood and followed after her sisters.

The three girls came to stand at the edge of the dance floor, where the other young women were slowly accumulating. Ambrosia stood nearby with her little group of followers. Celise privately thought that Katrina and Ambrosia were the two prettiest girls at the ball. The competitive spark between the two young women wasn't a surprise at all.

Ambrosia fluttered her violet fan as she watched the ballroom. Her luxurious indigo hair was piled atop her head in a towering display, pinned with flowers and jewels. Despite her feigned indifference at the tea party, it seems like she, too, was waiting for Lord Elias to appear.

A bell rang from somewhere in the ballroom, and the music came to a gentle stop.

The old duke, Cornelius Blackwood, approached a raised podium toward the end of the ballroom, not far from where the musicians sat behind a barricade of porcelain vases. The guests all ceased murmuring and turned to look.

Old Blackwood cleared his throat. The bright chandeliers illuminated his graying hair and sharp eyes. His voice, rich with authority, rang through the quiet ballroom, resounding off the painted ceiling.

"Oh ho! Welcome, lords and ladies, to Gravenmere's Grand Ballroom! As old as the castle itself, this ballroom has hosted generations of Blackwood parties and celebrations. The ceiling was commissioned by my great-great-grandfather, a king in his time, His Grace Aberon Blackwood. He was a Luminous king who led the armies of Gravenmere into the Abyss more than two hundred years ago. When he returned, he was named the Hero of the Realm. It was under his guidance that Gravenmere merged with Forsynthia and became one *whole* kingdom."

The guests all gasped in delight and murmured among each other. *"Another Hero of the Realm in the Blackwood bloodline?"*

"I had no idea!"

"I'm not surprised. Their powers are legendary."

The old duke continued his speech, "Tonight, we celebrate our family's legacy and the turning of another year in the life of my son—Elias Blackwood. Many of you have heard the tales of my son's bravery in battle. I say this not as a lord, but as a father: I watched Elias grow from child to soldier, then soldier to commander, and now—he has returned home a man of honor, integrity, and strength. The kingdom owes him a new era of peace. Let me raise a glass for the heir of Gravenmere and, as the bards sing, the slayer of the Daemon King. Let us drink to my son, the Skytouched Duke!"

A thunderous applause swept through the ballroom, accompanied by a few loud whistles. Old Blackwood raised his goblet, and the audience did the same. Celise didn't have a drink in hand, so she nervously clutched at her skirt. Heather and Katrina locked arms and gazed at the old duke in excitement.

Then a tall figure dressed in a dark blue tailcoat, wearing a familiar black mask over the left half of his face, appeared next to the podium where Old Blackwood was standing.

Elias's sudden appearance at the front of the room surprised Celise. She flinched slightly but resisted the urge to hide. The young duke was too far away to recognize her out of the crowd, so she felt relatively safe. She watched from behind a wall of elegant gowns as the young duke bowed to his audience. When he straightened up, he waved a gloved hand in appreciation. The applause continued, and a few people whistled. He didn't seem to resent the attention at all.

Old Blackwood continued above the crowd, "Although my son has won many battles, there is one war I would see him surrender to—marriage!"

Ripples of good-humored laughter joined the applause.

Katrina shared a glance with Heather.

"Let this evening commence under the watchful eye of the Mother of Dust and Moon. May the stars bless us with a fated union. I invite—nay, I *summon*—all noble ladies of marriageable age to stand at the edge of the dance floor, just there. Let my son see the shining stars of our kingdom! By midnight, we shall announce the future duchess of Gravenmere."

Celise heard many gasps and scandalized titters. Then—movement. Katrina gripped Heather's hand and started through the crowd to the front of the room. Skirts of satin, silk, and chiffon began to glide forward. Jewels glinted. Perfumed hair swayed. A procession of young ladies, some flushed with excitement, others pale with nerves, crossed the ballroom floor to stand before the duke.

Celise's eyes darted to the corner of the room, looking for a place to hide. If she could make it to the row of chairs along the back wall, her dress would blend against the silver damask wallpaper, making her all but invisible. She started to sidle in that direction when a young lady scooped up her arm.

With a little gasp, Celise recognized Ismara's light lavender hair and warm hazel eyes.

"Not so fast," the girl said in her clipped accent. "Don't be scared. You should join us. His Lordship summoned *every girl to the front*."

Celise nodded, barely able to breathe. The Bratzian girl gave her hand a warm squeeze and walked with her, arm-in-arm, to the front of the room. There, Ismara stood next to Celise at the end of the row of brightly dressed ladies.

Katrina and Heather stood a few feet away down the row. Katrina looked jittery and excited.

As the old lord left the podium, Elias stepped forward in his mysterious black mask. The duke looked every inch a noble warrior as he descended the stairs, broad-shouldered in a deep navy tailcoat, a row of polished medals decorating his left breast. His black hair was slicked back against his head. The half-mask obscured his scarred face, though Celise's eyes found the patch of shiny white scar tissue at his jaw, which disappeared into his starched collar and silk cravat. He looked arrogant, haughty and far more handsome in the mask than Celise had expected. She felt an odd thump in her chest when his gaze passed over her. His confidence was striking.

He paused at the front of the room for a long moment, gazing at them all, his expression unreadable. Then he approached the line of breathless ladies. Celise found herself trembling alongside every other young woman in the row, her body as tightly wound as a violin string. Every girl in attendance was filled with apprehension: fear of the duke's reputation mingled with the desire to become a duchess.

Celise almost pitied the Mad Dog. None of the young ladies truly wished to court him—they were simply enamored by his title and the mystique of his black mask.

The ballroom hummed with anticipation, and the young ladies all stood a notch taller as the duke walked down their line. Celise shrank back a bit. Elias approached at a leisurely pace, a coy half-smile on his wide lips. His silver eyes, cool as steel, swept down the row, assessing them one by one. Celise wondered what he was looking for. What traits did he prize in a lady?

Would he recognize her?

She swallowed past a lump in her throat.

Her heart began to race as Elias neared her position in line. Now was the moment of truth. Her thoughts tumbled—*He'll remember. He must. The gardens, the woods, the Hellion . . . I stole his jacket . . . how could he forget?*

But when Elias reached her, he did not pause. Not even a second glance. His gaze slid past her, as though she were a cotton handkerchief on a table of silk and lace. No flicker of recognition. No change in his expression. Nothing.

Her fingers tightened on the fabric of her skirt. *Why doesn't he remember me?*

Then Elias halted.

Katrina, radiant in deep red taffeta, tilted her head and beamed up at the duke with a look of triumph.

Elias offered her a gloved hand. "Lady Katrina Dhastel, would you grant me this first dance?"

A gasp escaped someone nearby. Celise didn't know if it came from her own lips.

"He knows her name?" Ismara next to her whispered.

The crowd began to buzz.

"Who did he choose?"

"Is that one of the Dhastel daughters?"

"Do they know each other? He seems familiar with her."

As Elias led Katrina onto the empty dance floor, the orchestra stirred to life. A violin started to play, then a cello, then a viola. The first notes of a lively, romantic waltz drifted through the room.

As though to amplify the magic of the night, little vents in the ceiling of the ballroom opened, and a shower of rose petals drifted down upon the guests. The ladies all gasped and looked upward.

"It's beautiful!" Ismara sighed.

"How romantic!" Celise heard Heather gush.

Elias swept Katrina onto the dance floor and twirled her into a fast, passionate waltz. Katrina floated like a leaf on the wind. She looked perfect.

Celise hung back, confused. She thought of Elias's dismissive eyes as he glanced past her. Did the duke truly not recognize her at all? What about the hairpin? His threat to arrest her? Wasn't he looking for her just that morning?

All of her apprehension had been for nothing.

Lady Ambrosia, standing a bit farther down the line of women, flicked open her violet fan to hide a scowl. Then she whirled on her heel and stalked away from the dance floor.

Celise watched Elias lead Katrina gracefully around the polished marble ballroom. Light on his feet, Elias's dancing was elegant and confident. He turned Katrina in perfect time to the music like a clockwork doll. Katrina looked stunning in her vibrant dress, a perfect match to Elias's navy blue tailcoat and pants.

The young duke appeared to be a skilled dancer, but Celise seemed to recall Old Blackwood criticizing his son's dancing.

She turned to Heather, who had joined her side. She asked, "Didn't the old lord, Cornelius Blackwood, say that Elias couldn't dance? I thought he trampled a lady's lapdog."

"It must have been a joke," Heather mumbled back, then continued to watch the dancing couple with wide, envious eyes.

Celise still felt uneasy. Maybe it was a joke, but . . . something seemed amiss. She pursed her lips. She probably looked different in her gray gown, with her face powdered and her hair pinned up. Elias had encountered her under the cover of darkness in the deep woods. They only got a brief look at each other in the lantern light before she fled upon his horse.

But her unique color of raspberry hair—a shade darker than magenta with violet undertones—was uncommon in Forsynthia. Her features were more like her mother's from Sera'naya. She was also the shortest in attendance. Wouldn't Elias at least notice her?

Perhaps he doesn't remember me at all from yesterday, she thought.

Why did that disappoint her?

Didn't she want to avoid the duke?

She felt conflicted. It was distressing.

As Lord Elias twirled Katrina around the dance floor, more gentlemen approached the row of eligible ladies. Ismara was one of the first girls to be asked, and then more and more couples paired up and began to dance. Celise felt a sense of alarm. *Uh-oh.* She couldn't stay out in the open like this. She didn't know how to waltz. If someone asked her to dance, it would be an utter disaster!

A young man wearing a cream-colored suit bowed to Heather, who blushed happily. The two entered the waltz, and Celise found herself standing alone at the edge of the dance floor. She shrank a few yards back into the crowd of guests, eager to put a barrier between herself and the whirling, gliding couples. She found safety behind one of the marble columns.

Her eyes found Katrina again. She watched her sister dance with Elias for three songs. Then His Grace deposited her gently at the edge of the floor. After a proper bow, he held out his hand to another partner and twirled the next young noblewoman away.

Katrina rejoined Celise's side after collecting a glass of wine from one of the passing servants. She pulled out her fan and began airing her face.

"Did you see us?" Katrina gushed, as though forgetting who Celise was. "Did you see the duke? He danced with me for *three songs!* It means something, don't you think?" With a pleased smile, she added, "He said my dress was stunning!"

Celise nodded. "You're very lucky, dear sister."

"Luck? It's fate!" Katrina gushed. "I'm going to tell Mother all about it. She will be so very pleased! Don't disappear again, Sluggy. If you ruin this for me, you'll regret the day you were born!"

Then Katrina flounced off through the crowd.

Celise sighed. She swayed gently to the music as she watched Lord Elias. He danced with partner after partner. He seemed quite comfortable with a woman in his arms. Very unlike the gloomy recluse she had assumed him to be.

Before long, the musicians took a brief break. Between dances, Elias approached the refreshment table. He stood only a few yards away from Celise's position behind the marble pillar. She watched him with narrowed eyes. The duke wasn't alone for very long. Only a minute passed before he was surrounded by a colorful flock of female admirers. His reputation seemed to have vanished under the spell of wine and dancing. The ladies fluttered about, flirting and giggling, and Elias seemed to enjoy the attention. His booming laugh carried over the music.

Katrina joined them, slipping through the crowd to the duke's side and clinging to his arm. Elias gave her a lopsided grin. He seemed quite charming.

Very *unlike* a mad dog.

This masked marauder also seemed shorter than the man she had met last night, but none of the other ladies would know that.

Was he an imposter?

Nonsense, how was that possible? Elias's scarred jaw proved he was the real thing.

Celise leaned back against the column. It seemed useless to speculate. She knew more about his horse than the man himself. Perhaps Elias was a charming rake, after all.

She watched Ambrosia Verabon enter the crowd of preening ladies around the duke.

Uh-oh.

The women fluttered uneasily as the beautiful heiress entered their ranks. Celise sensed some sort of drama about to start. Katrina was just leaning up to catch Elias's ear, her mouth open, perhaps to suggest another turn on the dance floor, when Elias looked up. His eyes found Ambrosia standing before him with a coy smile on her lovely features.

He seemed captivated. Elias stepped away from Katrina and offered his arm to Ambrosia. The lady fluttered her fan in a cute way, as though flattered by the attention, then dipped into a gentle curtsy.

Katrina froze. She looked livid.

Ambrosia took Elias's arm and swept past Katrina with a calculated little sneer, every movement dripping with a demure sort of triumph.

The quartet launched into a rollicking tune. The next dance began.

Celise watched Katrina grow pale as the duke spun Ambrosia around the dance floor in her violet dress. Another song picked up and still the couple danced under the sparkling chandeliers.

Another song.

Then another.

Still they danced.

Katrina stood alone, a flush of humiliation creeping into her cheeks. A group of young ladies stood nearby, whispering behind their fans. Ambrosia and Elias continued to dance a fourth round. Then a fifth. It seemed like a long time, even to Celise, who knew nothing about ballroom etiquette.

Finally, the musicians took another break. The handsome couple bowed to each other and left the dance floor arm in arm. Ambrosia leaned up to whisper something in Elias's ear, and he laughed. *Laughed.*

Celise watched Katrina's face crumple. With a soft cry, she turned and fled from the hall, ignoring the other well-meaning ladies who called after her.

Celise glanced around for Marcella or Heather but didn't see either of them close by. Then her eyes returned to Katrina, who had already fled halfway across the dance hall and showed no sign of stopping. She appeared to be headed for the balcony at the back of the ballroom, which faced the rose gardens.

"Is she alright?" a familiar voice said by her side. Celise glanced over and caught Ismara's concerned frown. "Someone should comfort her. Verabon is . . . *chitma.*"

"*Cheedma?*" Celise echoed.

"It's not a name a lady would say. But she is . . . no good."

Celise didn't know what the word '*cheedma*' meant, but she could guess. With a sigh, she realized she needed to follow Katrina. She had promised Marcella she wouldn't leave Katrina's side—for different reasons, of course. But Ismara was right. Someone should go and comfort her.

Celise sighed inwardly. *But why does it have to be me?*

Her feet took a slow step forward, even as her spirit recoiled. Her younger sister was a bully and a brute. She deserved to feel the sting of embarrassment.

Except . . . if Katrina failed to win the duke's heart, Marcella's wrath would be unrivaled. Like all of them, Katrina was just a victim of her mother's schemes.

Celise felt her heart twist in unexpected sympathy. For a moment, she hated her own softness. But with a certain sense of inevitability, she knew she would follow her younger sister, if only to make sure she didn't get lost on the grounds.

Imposter or not, he's nothing but trouble, Celise thought, darting a glare at the Mad Dog duke.

Then she ran after Katrina with a groan of resignation.

Chapter 14

The Gift in the Gardens

At the far end of the ballroom, beyond the podium where the quartet played and past the chairs where winded dancers sat, was an exit. A set of double doors stood open beneath a marble archway, which led to an outdoor veranda that spanned the back of the building.

Overhead, the silver light of the Kinder Moon gleamed like a shined coin on the horizon, while the diffused glow of the Maddening Moon filled the grounds with an orange ambiance. The twin moons illuminated the castle grounds better than any lantern or bonfire—so well, in fact, that Celise could see her shadow on the ground as she followed Katrina outside. She passed from the crowded dance hall through a stone archway onto the veranda behind the Gravenmere ballroom.

"Katrina! Wait!" she called, her voice strained.

Her younger sister did not look back.

The red skirts of Katrina's taffeta gown swayed and rippled as she dashed blindly across the raised terrace. The patter of her footsteps echoed off the hard ground. She ran down a sweeping stone staircase, across a flat pavilion, and through the entrance of the garden maze.

As she disappeared behind the hedges, Celise heard a single, broken sob emit from her younger sister's throat.

Oh, Katrina.

Celise wasn't a heartless person. Katrina was obviously upset. She hesitated on the veranda, glancing over her shoulder at the glowing ballroom, wondering if she should go back inside. But she didn't want Katrina to get lost. Somehow, she knew the blame would land on her.

Determined, Celise started down the sweeping steps that led to the garden maze.

The scent of climbing jasmine filled the fragrant night air. A flagstone path, lined with glowing lanterns, cut through rows of boxwood hedges and climbing roses. A sky full of stars glittered overhead like a bucket of spilled diamonds. The dim, purplish glow of skydust rimmed the horizon like a veil.

The walls of the garden maze were almost eight feet high. Celise couldn't see above the hedges. The path twisted left, then right, then left again, following a weaving pattern through the hedgerows. It probably wasn't a very large maze, she reasoned, and the path was well kept. She imagined many guests must have walked through it the day before. She tried not to worry about getting lost as she ran blindly forward.

Celise wove between bushes and under trellises covered in ivy until she found her way to a little garden room within the maze. Katrina had collapsed on a marble bench beneath an arbor of pink clematis at the center of the garden room. A little stream of pale blue water trickled past the arbor, and a footbridge crossed over the stream. It was all very picturesque: the perfect place to find respite from the crowded, noisy ballroom.

Katrina looked up as Celise approached, her eyes puffy and her cheeks streaked with tears.

"Oh no, Sluggy, what are you doing here?" she choked.

"I just wanted to check on you," Celise said, trying to keep her voice neutral. She didn't point out that Marcella would probably beat her to death if she let Katrina get lost. But her reasons were more personal than that. Despite her younger sister's bullying, Celise felt some sympathy for her. She knew what it felt like to be humiliated in front of her peers . . . and she knew the risks of disappointing Marcella. Katrina carried her own burdens as her mother's "favorite."

"Why don't we go back to the Moongazer Tower?" Celise suggested gently. "Dasha can make you a nice cup of tea."

"I don't need comfort from a dunslug," Katrina started to sneer, but a racking sob cut her off. After weeping for another minute, she whined, "He danced with her! That vulture, Verabon. He danced with her twice as long. *And she smirked at me.*"

Celise knelt beside her, placing a comforting hand on her sister's knee. "That doesn't mean anything, Katrina. He danced with you first."

"He ran to her the moment she batted her eyes in his direction."

"You still have your dignity. You won the Teacup Tournament; surely that means something? Your beauty turned heads tonight. The whole ballroom was looking at you."

"It doesn't matter. I can't go back now. My makeup is ruined."

Celise tried not to sigh with impatience—comforting Katrina was proving harder than she first thought. "Well then, perhaps we should retreat to the tower and try again tomorrow?"

"You think I should run off in shame? How pathetic. I can't just leave the ball halfway through. What about the fireworks? The Bratzian twins said there would be fireworks at midnight, when the duke announces his bride. Oh, I just know it will be Ambrosia!"

Celise's patience slipped. "Katrina, get a hold of yourself. Just a few weeks ago, you were mocking the Mad Dog and laughing at every article you could find in *The Lady's Letter*. Perhaps it's a good thing His Grace chose someone else? Do you really want to live with that man? You haven't seen him without his mask."

"And you have?" Katrina scoffed.

Celise bit her lip. The fact that she had seen Elias's face seemed like a pointless piece of trivia at the moment. "What about his past fiancées? They all fled from him. He has a foul temper—"

"Don't pretend like you know the duke better than me. He danced with me *three* times! You don't know what it's like to be held in his arms. He was so . . . *close.*" Katrina sighed with longing.

Celise decided not to point out that the fellow on the dance floor might be an imposter duke. That would probably be a bit far-fetched for Katrina.

"I didn't mean to mock him!" Katrina continued. "All of that was *before* we danced. He's not the man I expected. I think I love him, Celise. I'm *in love* with the duke! I must marry him! How can I live now, knowing I'll never belong to him?"

Celise glanced up at the Kinder Moon. *Oh my.*

She searched her mind for something helpful to say. Obviously Katrina was caught up in the romance of the evening. Her younger sister was only eighteen, her feelings fickle and fleeting but very powerful in the moment.

Summoning every last bit of willpower, Celise patted Katrina's hand again. "You're strong. You'll get through this," she said. "Ambrosia Verabon doesn't hold a candle to your beauty. You would be the perfect duchess. If the duke doesn't marry you, then he's a fool."

"You really think so?"

"Of course."

Katrina sniffled and said nothing, but when Celise caught her eye, she saw a glimmer of gratitude on her tearful face. For a fleeting moment, a fragile thread of sisterhood formed between them.

Then the night darkened.

A cloud passed over the moon, and Celise felt a strange shiver run down her spine.

A sudden pressure thickened the air, and the night seemed to grow colder. A branch snapped somewhere out of sight. All the frogs and crickets in the garden fell silent.

Celise felt a terrible sense of foreboding. She found herself rising to her feet, her eyes darting about the gloomy hedges, searching for . . . *something*.

"What is it?" Katrina asked.

"I think we're being watched," Celise said. "Hello? Is anyone there?"

Then, from the shadows of the garden maze, something grotesque and utterly *strange* slunk forth. At first Celise didn't know what she was looking at. A *being* staggered forward from a gap between the hedges. At first she thought it was a man, but as the moonlight beamed down, she saw a dark, oblong body glistening with an oily sheen. Its limbs were too long, its neck crooked, and its body segmented like a grotesque wasp. Its front two arms appeared to have pincers like a crab. Something protruded from the rear of its oily body like a barbed stinger.

A chittering croak vibrated from the beast: something like a bullfrog crossed with a rattlesnake.

Frozen to the spot, her body paralyzed with fear, Celise forced herself to blink. It was not her imagination. The *thing* was real.

She staggered back a few steps as the monster crawled into the garden pavilion, its gait crooked and uneven.

With a panicked gasp, Katrina leapt to her feet, but her long skirt snagged on the wooden rungs of the trellis. She toppled into Celise's side, who lost her balance and fell back onto the ground. The two girls sprawled beneath the rose-covered gazebo as the horrid nightmare-beast slunk closer.

"What is that . . . that *thing?*" Katrina cried.

Celise struggled back up to her feet, ripping her dress in the process, and grabbed Katrina's hand. "Who cares what it is? Run!"

Having worked with horses all of her life, Celise was much stronger than she looked. She locked Katrina's hand in a steely grip and lunged into the garden maze. She pulled her half-sister along behind her. Terrified, the two women dashed into the hedgerows as the monster croaked and rattled behind them.

Celise's feet pounded on the flagstones. She turned blindly through the maze with no sense of direction: left, right, right, left. The corridor curved at an angle, leading them along a spiraling path. She had no idea which direction might lead back to the ballroom.

Behind them, the many-legged beast crashed through the hedges, ripping a large hole in the maze's wall. With a shrieking roar, it gave chase, its rambling gait like an aggressive wolf spider. The horrible scratching and chittering of its teeth made Celise's hair stand on end. She was running too hard to utter a sound, while Katrina whimpered between panicked breaths.

"Don't look back!" Celise yelled when Katrina started to pull away.

"Do you know where you're going?"

"Of course not!"

"Look there! A gate!"

With a burst of hot mana from the palm of her hand, Katrina forcefully broke Celise's hold on her wrist. Then she darted down an alternative path that cut horizontally through the hedges. Celise yelped, blowing on her burned hand—she thought it might blister. Then she scrambled after Katrina.

Excited by the sound of their voices—and perhaps by the flash of mana—the monster screeched behind them. It crashed through the bushes somewhere out of sight. The sound brought another stab of icy terror to Celise's gut. She followed Katrina down the second corridor through the hedgerows. The path led out of the maze to a part of Gravenmere she didn't recognize. She was utterly lost.

Shined lampposts with curling motifs lined this new corridor. Katrina grabbed one of the metal posts and, channeling her mana into the shined coating, ignited the lantern hanging from its end. The effort made beads of sweat pour down her pale brow.

Celise blinked in the sudden bluish light from the lamppost.

Before them stood the gates to the Zodiac Gardens.

"No!" Celise gasped. How had they managed to run halfway across the grounds? The Zodiac Gardens were a long way from the ballroom, which meant help was even farther away. As Celise's eyes scanned the horizon, she could see the domed shape of the dance hall illuminated with golden light beyond the maze. It looked a lot smaller than it should.

"How . . . How did we come so far?" Celise stuttered.

"Who cares? At least now we know where we are," Katrina snarled, releasing the lamppost. The light flashed and went out, leaving them in deeper darkness than before. "I'm going through the gardens—don't follow me! I order you to lure the monster away! Go now!"

A harsh, ironic laugh ripped from Celise's throat. This was too much. "Lure the monster away? How am I supposed to do that? Where do you find *the audacity,* Katrina?"

"It's what any loyal servant would do! After everything *my father* has done for you, keeping you at the ranch despite your *handicap*, you should show some gratitude—"

"By sacrificing myself?"

"Yes! For *his real family*—"

"I am his *real family!* Ugh, you are so spoiled!"

A terrible, croaking roar issued from the garden maze, silencing both of the girls. Celise whirled around and stared back down the passageway lined with boxwood shrubs. The entrance to the garden maze looked like the mouth of the Abyss itself—ready to swallow her whole.

Leaves shook. Branches trembled. Flower petals fell to the ground.

Something was coming after them—fast.

Katrina lunged into the Zodiac Gardens with Celise following behind her. The two girls entered a large courtyard shaded by black maple trees. The garden beds spread out around them in a circular formation. At the center of the courtyard, bathed in moonlight, stood the fountain of Valestra, the Mother of Dust and Moon.

The two girls took different paths around the fountain. Celise went left while Katrina went right. Celise knew she couldn't outrun the creature in the open like this—by the thrashing sounds from the garden maze, the monster was coming on like a galloping horse.

She flung herself behind the statue of the Lantern.

Katrina, unable to find another statue wide enough to hide her skirts, finally ducked down next to Celise. She awkwardly shoved herself between two bushels of night-blooming jasmine.

"I can't believe you want me to lure the monster away from you!" Celise hissed, her repressed rage boiling to the surface. "You are so delusional, Katrina!"

"Delusional? How dare you!" Katrina hissed back. "I am Luminous, and you're just a *dimlit dunslug!* My life is far more valuable than yours. A good servant would obey me without a second thought."

"I'm not your servant!"

"Well, you're certainly not my sister!"

Celise bit her lip. After their brief moment of connection in the garden, those words stung more than they should.

"If I had my foil with me, I would show that beast what for!" Katrina lamented, though Celise doubted a mere foil meant for sport would do any good against the creature.

"Hush!" Celise hissed. "It's coming!"

The oily, misshapen monster arrived at the gate to the Zodiac Gardens. Celise heard the rustling of bushes and the scrape of clawed feet. A bulky shadow paused just inside the wrought iron gates. The crickets in the garden fell silent. Even the wind seemed to hold its breath.

A slow, terrible clicking sound began in the monster's throat.

Celise bit back a moan of terror. Could it smell them? See them?

She risked a glance around the edge of the statue. The beast's body, illuminated under the cold light of the moon, was a black mass of writhing legs and poking arms. Such a horrific sight was beyond her imagination. It seemed out of place in the world, like nothing she would expect of the flora and fauna of Nilos. No bear, no wolf, no griffon or ogre or water dragon could possibly look so . . . *wrong*.

With a cold chill, she wondered . . . was *this* a daemon?

Was this a hellspawn from the Abyss?

How had it come to Gravenmere Castle? Why was it in the gardens?

Celise wondered how she was going to escape such a creature. She held her breath, her hands fisting her skirt, her forehead pressed to her knees, trying to think of a strategy. How were they supposed to get out of this situation alive?

Then, surprising her, Katrina hissed, "Forget this. I'm not staying here to be eaten!"

Suddenly, her younger sister leapt to her feet, emerging from the bushels of jasmine behind the statue. She grabbed Celise with bruising force and dragged her into the open. Then she flung Celise toward the daemon.

"There, you nasty thing! Take her!"

Katrina's powerful throw sent Celise stumbling through the garden beds. She almost fell to the ground, but she caught herself on a trellis of Abyssal Rose. The spiny, wicked thorns gouged her hands.

"Katrina?" Celise gasped in disbelief, but her sister was already running through the Zodiac Gardens with her taffeta skirts hiked up to her knees. Katrina dashed around the fountain of Valestra. A burst of light followed her through the gardens as the lumenblooms responded to her mana. She was heading for the exit on the opposite side of the courtyard, but to get there, she had to pass frighteningly close to the monster.

The daemon's long neck swiveled around. For a moment, it looked like the creature would chase after the fleeing girl in red.

Celise's heart leapt to her throat.

Let her be eaten! The thought flashed through her mind, but it made her immediately ill. She wasn't like Katrina. She couldn't live with herself, knowing she had sacrificed someone's life for her own safety.

What would a courageous person do?

Feeling foolish and reckless, she waved her arms in the air.

"Hey!" she shouted at the monster. "Hey, ugly! I'm over here!"

The daemon's head swiveled back to her, its neck coiling around like a big python. Past the daemon, beyond its reach, Katrina flew down the garden path and disappeared from sight.

Celise couldn't run after her little sister—the monstrous beast stood between her and Katrina's route of escape. Now its attention was locked on her alone.

She left me here, Celise thought. *That evil, psychotic brat! She truly thinks her life is more valuable than mine.*

It only reaffirmed what she already knew.

Then, with a screech, the daemon flew at her like a tumbling dustweed, all sprawling limbs and dry, clacking claws.

Celise scrambled backward, falling through the bed of Abyssal Roses, long thorns ripping at her dress and catching on her arms. Emerging on the other side of the bed, she fled down an empty path through the Zodiac Gardens. She passed under a trellis of lumenblooms—the flowers did not react to her as they did to Katrina. The garden was swathed in deep shadow. Not even the wind stirred the darkness.

The daemon followed only a few feet behind her, trampling the soft flower beds under its clawed feet. It smashed through the lumenbloom trellis but got several long, spindly legs stuck in the gridded wood. It released a croak of fury.

With a desperate sob lodged in her throat, Celise dashed through the grove of black maple trees, down a weedy, overgrown path to a rusty gate she vaguely recognized. She flew over cracked flagstone and piles of debris. A sign hung above the gate: "No Trespassing." But the entrance was wide open. No locks. No chains.

Celise ran through the ancient archway without slowing her step.

Beyond the crooked garden gate lay an unknown part of the Gravenmere grounds that was off-limits to guests. Celise ran frantically down the dirt path, tripping over rubble and gnarled tree roots. This area of the castle seemed much older than the Zodiac Gardens, and it carried the distinct feeling of abandonment. The grass was high and overgrown, the plants wild and unkempt. A veil of cold mist clung to the moist ground. The walking paths were unmaintained, no more than rabbit trails through the tall grass, and the only buildings she came across were rotted structures full of gaps and holes: concave roofs, missing doors, empty windows, or entire walls fallen to rubble. Servants or gardeners might have lived in the little huts at one time, but they weren't occupied now and hadn't been in many, *many* years.

She had hoped to find a place to hide, but the land beyond the gate was bewildering. Celise stumbled down a short series of steps to the edge of a green pond. She circled around the pool of gleaming water until she reached a dilapidated building on its shore—a shrine to Valestra, by the metal plate that hung above the empty doorway, the ancient symbol of the goddess almost rubbed off. The building wasn't very large, with only enough space for one or two people to pray side by side. The roof was partly shorn off, and the plaster walls were cracked and decayed.

It didn't seem like a promising place to hide—more like a cage to be trapped within.

Celise paused near the shrine to regain her bearings. The shrine was surrounded by a small garden, filled with birthflowers of different kinds. As her eyes probed the darkness, she saw a cluster of Ashfeather Bloom growing around the shrine's front steps and a shimmering bushel of Tideweed in the shallows of the pond. Glowbells sprawled between the cracks in the shrine's walls. It held a haunting, poetic beauty, but she didn't have time to admire the sight.

Schrraaarrgh!!!

The daemon appeared without warning—it was right behind her.

Celise screamed. She turned to run, but with a furious roar, the monster reached out and snagged the back of her dress with a pincered claw. Celise fell down, restrained by her skirts and crinoline. She heard the snap of whalebone as the clumsy cage broke her hard fall. She found herself lying on the ground inside a circle of moonlight.

Above her, a bright white object caught her eye. She looked up. There, just beyond her reach, a stunning, star-shaped dahlia glowed under the stars.

The Starlight Dahlia.

Her zodiac flower.

Celise choked out a half-sob, half-laugh.

So this was her fate.

She closed her eyes, prepared to meet her doom beneath the glowing purity of the starlit flower. The stench of sulfur washed over her as the monster poised above its prey. Its legs trapped her in a living cage. Its neck sloped downward, its mandibled jaws clicking, saliva dripping from its misshapen maw. *Oh Goddess!*

Then, with a sparking, hissing sound, a blade of silver-blue light appeared in the darkness.

Celise gasped.

The daemon recoiled.

From beyond the shrine, a man emerged from the overgrown wilderness. He appeared out of nowhere as though summoned by the Mother Herself.

Flash!—a streak of blue light sliced through the shadows.

The daemon leapt back as the ghost blade arced close to its spindly, long neck. It abandoned Celise to skitter up the shrine's crumbling wall and perch precariously on the half-caved roof.

A low, rattling growl filled the night as the daemon observed the new threat.

A soldier. One of the Daemonguard?

Celise's eyes returned to the ghost sword. Power crackled down the length of the blue rod, sparking fire. She stared at her savior, stunned.

Elias Blackwood's silver eyes met hers—a mere glance, but his confidence was unmistakable.

He wore a double-breasted greatcoat, the collar popped high, his hair loosely swept back from his face in a roguish, careless way. No mask. *This man*—yes—she knew him. Trusted him. But where had he come from?

What was the duke doing in this abandoned area of the castle grounds?

Without warning, the daemon leapt from the roof. It moved fast despite its awkward size. Elias charged to meet it head-on, his sword held before him, prepared to strike. The blade arced upward as the creature flew down, its stinger thrust forward and pincered claws snapping at the air. Celise didn't see whose blow landed, but the daemon released a scream so terrible it made her teeth ache.

Using wide swings of his shined sword, Elias herded the daemon away from Celise's position near the pond. The creature skittered backward on the defensive. It crossed its two pincered front claws before its body to create a shield. Blow by blow, it fended off Elias's weapon with its hard claws.

Elias swung the shined rod expertly, slicing off one of the daemon's pincered arms. The beast took a swipe at his head with its second claw, and he ducked and rolled out of the way. The daemon followed him, hissing, unwilling to give Elias an opening.

Celise could barely follow the battle with her eyes. The daemon was fast and aggressive, whipping its arms about with the speed of a scorpion's tail, but Elias evaded its strikes. He leapt and rolled, dodging behind piles of rubble as the daemon attacked. The pincered arm lashed out again, as long and bulky as a greatsword, but Elias moved with grace and power, dodging the clumsy appendage. The daemon attempted to stab him with its stinger, its body thrusting forward, undulating and wriggling aggressively. Elias evaded by moving closer to his opponent, slipping between the daemon's spindly legs to reach its gooey underbelly.

Celise raised a hand to her mouth in horror, unable to look away.

Inside the daemon's defenses, Elias lunged, cutting deep into its oblong torso just above the stinger. The monster screeched as the magical edge buried itself in its rancid, muddy flesh. Elias hacked and slashed through the daemon's tough hide. Black matter of a kind spattered across the dark clearing.

Celise raised an arm over her face, catching a few drops of the stuff on her forearm. It burned like fire. She gasped and cried out in pain.

The daemon turned toward her, reminded of her presence. It regarded her for a moment before lunging across the grass, its arms and legs scrabbling. The monster bolted toward the easier prey. She heard Elias curse.

Celise screamed, tangled up in her crinoline, unable to run or defend herself.

"Back to dust with you!" Elias yelled.

He lifted his ghost sword. The air crackled. A strange metallic scent filled the garden. With a gasp, Celise's hair suddenly lifted up, floating to either side of her face, charged with static.

The creature's angry snarl was swallowed by a deafening *crack! Boom!*

A fork of lightning split the heavens, blinding white against the black sky. It struck the daemon dead center. The beast exploded in a shower of earth and gummy flesh. The ground shook beneath Celise. A large maple tree behind her groaned and shifted. With a cry, she scrambled out of the way as the tree collapsed to one side, uprooted by the quaking earth.

A thunderous, resounding *boom!* echoed through the wild garden. A flurry of bats rose from the roof of the abandoned shrine, startled by the sound. Shrieking, they dispersed into the night.

The roll of thunder was deafening. Celise crouched on the broken flagstone, trembling with her arms over her head.

Silence fell across the grounds.

When she squinted open her eyes, the garden was in chaos. To one side, a giant maple tree lay like a fallen soldier in the long grass. A few yards away, the daemon's corpse smoked and sizzled. White flames—caused by the lightning bolt—consumed the creature's body. Fire licked up its six limbs, devouring its flesh like dry wood. Celise watched the monster fold up and collapse in a pile of smoldering embers, just like a dead beetle.

She lay crumpled on the ground, not unlike the daemon's fried corpse. Her arm stung and burned where the black gunk had struck her skin. She listened to her own racing heart as blood thrummed in her ears. In the distance, another dull rumble of thunder traveled across the hills surrounding Gravenmere Castle. Clouds gathered in the sky, obscuring the twin moons.

Then it started to rain.

Celise lay on the ground, her ball gown ripped and stained, wet dirt muddying her clothes, trembling from shock.

Boots crunched over wet leaves. Someone knelt before her. A hand touched her arm. She stared at it.

A *scarred* hand.

Just like his burned neck, his ruined ear, and his marred cheek, his left hand was also covered in shiny white scars.

Elias.

Or rather, Lord High Commander Elias Blackwood, the Duke of Gravenmere and Hero of the Realm: the man who had defeated the Daemon King.

"You . . . you summoned lightning!" she stuttered.

"We call them mana-bolts."

"But that's . . . ." She almost said, *"impossible,"* but stopped herself. Of course it was possible, if she had just witnessed it with her own eyes. The immensity of his power struck her. Summoning a bolt out of the blue seemed like a gift reserved for the gods alone. Elias had destroyed the daemon with barely a snap of his fingers.

He knelt by her side, his hand going to her shoulder, his gray eyes sweeping over her for injuries. With a slight *tsk*, he reached down and grabbed a handful of wet leaves, then started wiping the stinging black gunk off her forearm.

"What is that?" she muttered, on the verge of fainting.

"Daemon blood. It's acidic. Best to get it off before it eats right through."

"*What?*"

Her head swooned. She felt a bit sick. Shadows danced across her eyes. Then she collapsed forward against his chest.

Chapter 15

The Proposal

Celise's swoon didn't last very long.

Darkness flickered before her vision, and for a brief moment, oblivion embraced her. Then she started awake. She sucked in a deep gasp of cool night air, like a diver breaking through the surface of a lake.

She was in the arms of the Mad Dog duke.

"Come now, my little moonflower, let's keep our wits about us," Elias's low, raspy voice murmured in her ear as he patted her back. He held her braced against his shoulder as Celise lay limp from shock.

Finally she pushed away, forcing a few inches of space between them. She reclaimed a bit of her independence. Then she gazed into his eyes, unable to hide her trepidation.

Lightless luck.

He recognized her.

So what? A stubborn, petulant voice inside of her shouted. *So what if he recognizes me?* Celise resisted the urge to shrink down. She had just survived the scariest ordeal of her life. Somehow, she couldn't bring herself to fear this man after her encounter with the daemon. She felt a new sense of courage and self-assurance. Elias had saved her life, and she felt with certainty he wouldn't harm her.

The duke considered her with a calculating look in the dim, stormy moonlight. Crouched on the ground, facing each other, silence stretched between them. Celise dared not break eye contact with the Mad Dog. She felt like she was facing down a *real* dog, feral off the leash. *Stay strong.*

Then Elias pushed his hair back from his face and closed his eyes against the rain. She caught sight of his scarred ear. It was truly gruesome. She glanced away too, feeling a bit guilty. He had saved her life. She shouldn't care about his scars.

"Thank you," she murmured, the words inane as they passed her dry lips.

"You're welcome."

"This has been . . . quite an evening," she muttered, moving to stand, but his firm hand encircled her wrist. He kept her by his side in the wet grass.

"What are you doing?" she asked.

"Checking something."

Elias reached into the pocket of his greatcoat and withdrew a small metal object. Then he reached up and pulled a hairpin out of Celise's hair. Her braid tumbled down from her head, falling over her shoulder. He held the two matching hairpins side-by-side in his hands and studied them with an unreadable look.

"Oh," she grunted.

"Yes, oh."

"You've been carrying that around in your pocket?"

"Since you dropped it in the woods, yes," he confirmed. "I recognized you, but I had to be sure. You look much different in a proper dress."

Celise stared at the shiny hairpins with the crystal horseshoes attached at each end. Then she stuttered, "A-Are you going to arrest me?"

"Why would I?"

"You think I'm a spy. . ."

"I think you have a tendency to wander around where you don't belong," he assured her in his rough voice. "But you're certainly not in league with the people threatening my life—nor are you in allegiance with those thieves from last night."

"What makes you say that?"

"Call it a soldier's instinct. You don't seem very . . . skilled."

Celise's mouth opened and then snapped shut. She wasn't sure if that was a compliment or an insult. It seemed Elias found her just as weak as Katrina did. It hurt, but compared to his own powers, she couldn't blame him.

"What is your name?" he asked.

"Celise . . . ah . . . Celise Dhastel."

"Dhastel." He frowned. She saw a glimmer of recognition pass through his intense gray eyes. Beautiful eyes, she realized, framed by long dark lashes. They were wider and slightly slanted at the edges to accommodate his strong cheekbones. She wondered what he would look like if he smiled. In the darkness, the shadows of the garden softened his scars, while the moonlight illuminated the angles of his face. Celise could almost imagine how he once looked, before the wounds that marred his features.

What am I thinking? He is the Mad Dog duke!

But his stormy temper was subdued. He gazed at her, observing her face just as she inspected his own. Was he pleased by what he saw? Why should it matter?

"So, you are a lady after all," Elias said with a bemused twist to his lips. "I thought you might have been a servant."

"I believe you used the word 'chamberflower.'"

"Only to provoke you into giving up your name. It didn't work."

Celise's eyes flickered away from his own. "I am a daughter of the Dhastel house," she admitted, her voice soft. It was the truth, if not the *full* truth.

"That explains how you know so much about my horse."

He reached up and ran a finger along the side of her tender jaw. She raised a hand to cover his own. She had forgotten about her bruise. With a wince, she realized her makeup must have faded during her flight through the gardens, and now with the rain falling, it was bound to come off completely. He inspected her bruise with hooded eyes, his thoughts moving like gray clouds beyond the veil of his expression. He was born in Hallowsin, she reasoned, so his nature would be one of introspection. A man who kept his heart close to his chest. She couldn't guess his thoughts.

"You are . . ." he began, then stopped.

"I am what?"

"You are not what I expected." But his eyes said something else. She could hardly breathe when he looked at her like that.

Interrupting the moment, a gust of cold wind blew through the empty grounds, rustling the leaves of the fallen maple tree. Celise jumped at the sound, turning to face the darkness, suddenly afraid.

"Here," Elias said, as though just remembering the storm that raged around them. He took her hands and helped her back to her feet. Together, they walked to the shrine's entrance. The door had fallen off long ago and lay inside the abandoned shack, taking up half the floor space. The rest of the small, single room was full of cobwebs and old leaves, but at least it was dry.

Once inside the shrine, Elias's eyes flickered down to her muddy bodice, her ripped skirts and her ruined crinoline.

"Let me help you out of this," he said.

Despite her mild protests, she let him reach under her skirts to her waist, where he used a small knife to cut through the straps that supported the broken cage. He wrested it free from her skirts. He worked so quickly, so deftly, that she barely registered how risqué it was for him to place his hands up her dress.

Finished, he tossed the mangled mass of whalebone into the pond, where it disappeared beneath the wavering tideweed.

"Comfortable?" he asked.

"Yes, much better," she admitted. "I'm not used to wearing such constrictive clothes."

His eyes glinted at her. "Then what do you usually wear? A shift?"

Celise blushed. "Just . . . simpler clothes," she mumbled. She felt a strange heat rising in her cheeks. The friction in the air intensified—it seemed Elias felt it as well. He took a half-step closer to her, closing the distance between them. In the dim light of the abandoned shrine, she saw the cut of his strong jaw. She glanced at his lips, which looked wide and soft.

Tha-thump.

Then, not knowing what came over her, Celise raised her head toward him.

Elias searched her eyes for the briefest second, then he leaned down.

The kiss was bold, daring and utterly insane.

A gloved hand went to the back of her head. His lips captured hers. A flare of unexpected passion bloomed between them. Celise wondered if she had lost her mind.

She had never kissed anyone before.

His tongue slid between her lips, exploring her mouth without shyness or hesitancy: a tantalizing taste of something forbidden. Stubble scraped her chin. A wonderful, heady rush swept through her, and she leaned in a bit closer.

Oh, this was *nice.*

She wanted more . . . .

Their kiss began passionately, but after a few seconds, she felt a grin spread across Elias's mouth. His caress became gentle and teasing. Then he pulled back further, lightening his touch, his lips sensual and skilled.

Then he broke away. Holding her by the upper arms, Elias gazed down at her with one eyebrow cocked.

"You're *innocent,*" he said with an amused grin. "Bold, but . . . innocent."

Celise shoved him off, and the man let go with a rough laugh.

"I hope that wasn't your first kiss," he added.

Celise blushed in the darkness. By the stars, was it that obvious?

"Perhaps it was," she said, embarrassed.

"Ah." He regarded her closely. "Why did you grant me your first kiss, Lady Celise?"

"*You* kissed *me,*" she stuttered, mortified. At his look, she continued, "I-I-I don't know! Something came over me. I can't really say . . . ."

"You seem like a woman full of mysteries and contradictions."

"I don't mean to be—"

"I like it. And I intend to discover everything I can about you, Lady Celise Dhastel."

Fear lanced through her at those words, but when Celise met his eyes, she was comforted by their dark humor—and the heat of his gaze. Never in her life had she imagined a duke would look at her like that. Despite her mortification—and their vast difference in status—she wanted to kiss him again. Why? She didn't know. She wasn't behaving like her usual self.

She touched her lips with her tongue. His eyes lowered to her mouth, watching her with a dark, simmering look. The tension built between them until the air seemed about to combust.

Then he heaved a deep, dark sigh.

"I should return you to the ball," he said. "Your family will be worried about you."

Celise nodded, swallowing her words: *they probably haven't noticed I'm gone.*

Then he offered her his arm.

I kissed the Mad Dog duke, Celise thought as she rested her hand in the crook of his elbow. Furthermore, *he* had kissed *her* back. What did it mean?

It seemed too soon—or perhaps too late—to ask.

Together, they stepped out of the old shrine into the rain. Celise looked around the tangled, forgotten flowerbed. For a flash of a moment, she could imagine what this place must have looked like in its prime. It must have been a beautiful little retreat from the world. Someone had loved this shrine—loved it enough to plant a zodiac garden around it.

Perhaps this was the inspiration for the grand Zodiac Gardens above?

Her eyes found the Starlight Dahlia only a few feet away, planted in a stone circle next to the shrine's wall. Weeds, long grass and creeping ivy smothered the plant, though its massive star-shaped flowers sparkled brightly, even in the rain.

She stared at the cluster of white blossoms, unable to look away.

"What is it?" Elias asked, following her gaze.

"It's . . . it's nothing, just . . . that's my birthflower," she mumbled. "I've never seen one before." She sounded like an insane person, considering what had just transpired.

"Ah." With a deft motion, he plucked one of the dahlias off of the dark bush.

"No, wait!" she gasped. "That belongs to Lord Blackwood—"

"It belongs to *me*," Elias said abruptly. "And now it belongs to you." He pressed the Starlight Dahlia into her free hand. She held the long blue stem reverently, almost afraid to touch it.

Arm in arm, Elias walked with her along the path around the pond. As they passed by the location where the daemon's body still smoldered, he stooped down and plucked something out of the grass. The metal object glinted briefly in the moonlight before he tucked it into his pocket. It looked like a large dog tag, perhaps the length and width of Celise's palm, coated with dark green paint.

"What is that?" she asked.

"Something for me to inspect later," he said. "No need to concern yourself."

Then Elias took her arm again and led her up the staircase along the side of the hill. The path continued through the cluster of abandoned buildings. He helped her around fallen tree trunks and piles of rubble. Unlike the brooding soldier she had met last night, he seemed endlessly patient as she struggled to find purchase in her useless slippers. Celise was quietly furious at herself. She wished she were clothed in her usual garb from the Dhastel stables—her reliable boots and coveralls—so she didn't seem so delicate. She truly wasn't a fragile flower—but these clothes made her so clumsy!

Elias guided her through the abandoned grounds with ease as though he had walked them a hundred times. She wasn't surprised—this was his castle, so he must know every inch of it.

"What is this place?" she asked as they approached the gate to the Zodiac Gardens.

"Long ago, before Gravenmere became a territory of Forsynthia, this area housed the servants and shrine maidens that once served our family," Elias explained. "But all that changed during the siege."

"There was a siege?"

"Oh yes. The Blackwoods of old did not give up their royal status willingly. There was a siege on Gravenmere Castle before we joined with Forsynthia, and during that siege, this area of the grounds was destroyed. It's been walled off and abandoned ever since, and the new castle was built beyond it. These lands are off-limits to guests because they're not maintained or patrolled. They house the Blackwood tomb as well."

Celise glanced up at him, wondering at his tone. "Is that why you came here tonight? To visit the tomb?"

"Something like that," Elias said. "Someone sent me a strange riddle. It seemed ominous, so I was investigating the grounds."

"Do you think there are more daemons roaming about?"

"Possibly. I will have to alert the guard when we return to the castle, if my mana bolt didn't do so already."

Celise was appalled. He had mentioned his "enemies" before, but she hadn't realized the gravity of the situation. Who would send a daemon—or multiple daemons—after the Hero of the Realm? How did one transport such monsters from the Abyss? It couldn't be a simple affair. The Abyss was hundreds of miles away.

Could this be the *catastrophe* warned about by Mordwen's cards? She couldn't be sure. The daemon was dead, so how could it change the fate of the kingdom?

"Someone must not like you very much," she pointed out.

Elias smirked. "I am not liked by many—especially my new recruits at the fortress. Thankfully, as a commander, I'm used to it."

Celise fell silent again, reminded that Elias Blackwood lived in a different world than her own—a world of status and authority.

She really had no business kissing him in the gardens.

Perhaps it would remain their little secret—a stolen moment under the cover of darkness.

They reached the Zodiac Gardens and paused before the fountain of Valestra. Celise saw the mangled trellis and toppled garden statues from the daemon's earlier rampage. Her knees felt a bit weak.

Then a horrible thought crossed her mind.

"Wait," she gasped. "What about Katrina?"

"Who is Katrina?"

"My sister. She was with me in the garden maze when the daemon found us. She fled back to the castle. Do you think she's safe? What if another daemon catches her?"

Elias looked grim. "First, let's return you to the ballroom. Then I will send more of my men to look for her."

Celise was not excited to return to the ballroom. She tried to think of an excuse to go to the Moongazer Tower instead, or anywhere she wouldn't create a spectacle. She couldn't imagine the look on Marcella's face when she appeared with her skirts soaked with rain and daemon blood.

"I don't know if I can return to the ballroom like this," Celise began. "I don't want to see my family."

"If you wish to avoid a scandal, I'm afraid it's too late for that."

"No, it's not that, I . . . ."

Elias raised an eyebrow. "Perhaps you are not the real Celise Dhastel, and you're a spy after all?"

"Of course not! Don't be daft!" Celise blustered. "I'm not a spy! Besides, weren't *you* dancing with Lady Ambrosia Varabon earlier?"

"I was not." Elias sounded amused.

Celise felt vindicated. So her hunch was correct—the duke at the ball had been a fake. A convincing stand-in, but not the true Elias.

"Maybe you should avoid the ball, too, if your double is still there?"

"If a daemon wasn't found on my estate, I would agree with you," Elias admitted. "But these are extenuating circumstances."

Then, without asking permission, the Mad Dog reached around her crooked skirts and scooped her up into his arms. "Don't even think about running off, my little moonflower," he said, and started through the garden maze with a sure step. "You've told me your name—now let's see if your story holds."

Hardly able to protest, Celise allowed him to carry her back to the ballroom. The storm increased its ferocity—cold rain poured down on them, falling in torrents from the sky. She was soaked through, her hair plastered to her forehead, her silk dress ruined. She held the dahlia clutched to her bodice and shivered in his arms.

Elias knew his way through the garden maze quite well, even in the dark. As he walked, Celise watched the tall, shadowy hedges with wide eyes. She jumped at every suggestion of movement, but no other monsters appeared along their path.

It felt like an eternity passed, though it was probably more like fifteen minutes, before Celise saw the lights of the ballroom shining against the stormy night sky. As they exited the hedgerows, the glowing windows came into full view. A few strains of violin music teased Celise's ears. As they reached the veranda behind the dance hall, she saw a swarm of people crowding close to the stone balustrade.

Celise overheard some of the hubbub. The same questions were repeated by a hundred different voices.

"A monster in the gardens? But how can that be?"

"Dust and daggers! A monster? Where?"

"It's a prank, is all!"

"Why is it raining? The sky was clear a moment ago. Is it an omen?"

"Was that lightning? I saw a flash."

"Should we call the guard?"

"We should go back inside; my dress will be ruined. . . ."

Celise clung to Elias, wondering when he would set her down on her feet. He didn't intend to carry her around for the rest of the night, did he?

Then her eyes found Katrina.

Her sister stood at the top of the wide, sweeping staircase that led up to the veranda. Katrina's unmistakable red skirts were outlined by the light of the ballroom. Her sister looked perfectly healthy and not at all bothered by Celise's absence. She stood with her back to the gardens, speaking animatedly to a circle of young men who were leaning in close, hanging on her every word. One young man offered Katrina a glass of water, while another held out a handkerchief. By the frowns on their faces, they were all deeply concerned about the pretty young lady.

With a sudden surge of disgust and rage, Celise recalled how Katrina had shoved her in front of the daemon to save herself. For years, Celise had kept her feelings about her family's abuse bottled up inside. She had silenced her pain so completely that she had lost her other feelings as well. Even her joys were subdued. She had survived on the Dhastel ranch only by turning herself invisible, becoming a mere ghost of herself.

But now . . . *now* she really couldn't tolerate this.

Katrina had tried to kill her. How could she forgive that?

She struggled in Elias's arms, overtaken by the urge to march up those steps and slap Katrina silly, but the Mad Dog didn't release her. He was much stronger. She realized she could not overpower him.

"Calm down," he murmured. "You're not leaving my side just yet."

When Elias appeared with Celise at the bottom of the staircase, several people gasped and pointed. Katrina turned to look down at them. Celise watched her little sister's face grow pale and her violet eyes widen. At first she looked horrified and confused. Then she quickly recovered.

"Celise!" she gasped. "My dear sister! You're alive!"

"I am," Celise intoned.

Katrina pointed a gloved hand at her. "But . . . but it was *so courageous* of you, how you sacrificed yourself for my safety! You drew the monster away and gave me a chance to escape. I was just telling everyone . . ."

"I thought you said the monster ate your sister?" a young man asked by Katrina's elbow.

"Well, I thought so!" Katrina said defensively. "I *thought* I saw the beast eat her!"

"Then she saved your life?" another man asked.

"How heroic!" a young lady chimed in. Then, with some irony, "My sister wouldn't do that for *me*, I guarantee it!"

Katrina looked furious as more and more guests took notice of Celise. Murmurs and questions began to spread through the crowd. Celise felt uncomfortable, but all she could do was glare at Katrina in disgust.

"Is that true?" Elias murmured into Celise's ear. "Did you draw the daemon away from your sister?"

"Yes, I suppose I did," Celise said, distracted. "But it wasn't half as noble as all that. I didn't have much of a choice."

Elias glanced between the two women with a discerning frown. More guests arrived on the balcony to look down the staircase at them.

"Who's that? A soldier?" someone called.

"Why, that's High Commander Elias Blackwood," another voice answered.

The gossip started up again.

"But how did he get into the gardens? He was just at the ball!"

"I thought he was dancing with Ambrosia?"

"Who was that man wearing the mask, then?"

Celise watched Old Blackwood, his steward, and the rest of her family—Lord Sebastian Dhastel, Marcella and Heather—break through the sea of guests. Marcella gripped Katrina's arm as she passed by and forcefully escorted her daughter down the stairs. The group traversed the steps and stopped a short distance away, staring at Celise in Elias's arms, looking shocked.

Celise waited for Elias to set her down, but still, he refused.

"*You're* Lord Elias Blackwood?" Katrina demanded.

"I am."

Her red lips parted. "Then who was I dancing with?"

Elias didn't answer but gave a subtle nod to someone on the terrace. Celise's eyes spotted a masked man hanging back near the ballroom doors. As she watched, he slipped over the side of the balustrade with an elegant leap and disappeared into the shadows at the side of the building.

The imposter duke was gone.

Old Blackwood pounded the flagstone with his cane, drawing their attention. "Never mind the ball! What's all this about a *creature* in the gardens?"

“There was a daemon, Father,” Elias confirmed. “I’ve dealt with it, but there might be more. We should alert the guards posted around the grounds, and I will gather Kiran and his soldiers from the south wing."

“How did it get in? Where did it come from?” The old lord blustered.

“Questions for another time. Let's move the guests inside. I will go and assemble a patrol.”

“But it’s almost midnight! You can’t leave now.”

Elias finally placed Celise on her feet. Marcella made a grab for her arm, a snarl on her tight lips, but the High Commander shot the woman a stern look. The duke pulled Celise a step closer to his side as though to protect her. His hand remained firm on her wrist.

“You’re right, Father, it’s almost midnight, but we found a daemon loose on the grounds, and there are likely more wandering about,” Elias said to Old Blackwood. “What would you have me do?”

“Your duty to the crown,” the old duke intoned.

Elias gazed at his father’s furrowed brow, then at the Dhastel family, then down at Celise. She tugged on her wrist, alarmed that he hadn’t released her yet and no one seemed to care. Why wouldn’t he let her go?

Then Elias turned back to the ballroom. Taking control of the situation, he raised his left hand, the one not wrapped around Celise’s wrist, and channeled enough mana to make his arm glow like a beacon. As his mana activated, Celise felt a shiver run down her arm. The air around him crackled with electricity.

“Everyone, please go back inside. For your safety, let’s continue our celebration in the ballroom. I don’t want anyone wandering the grounds. The maze is *off limits.* If you notice someone missing, please report it to a servant, and we will search them out.”

The gathered guests on the landing began slowly and turbulently making their way back into the grand ballroom. The Dhastel family joined the rain-drenched crowd. Old Blackwood remained next to Elias in the rear, herding the guests along while also keeping a firm watch over his son.

"Enough gallivanting around!" Old Blackwood declared. "Midnight is almost upon us, and I've made our guests a promise. Before this wild goose hunt takes off, my boy, you have an announcement to make. Since you're here now, and the dance has ended, you must choose your bride!"

The guests, who were all funneling back into the ballroom, glanced back at Cornelius Blackwood and then began muttering among themselves.

"You heard me!" the old duke roared. "Let everyone know to gather at the front of the ballroom for a special announcement. Dust or daemons, tonight my son will choose his bride!"

Excited murmurs spread through the gathered guests. As Elias entered the ballroom, the finely dressed ladies and gentlemen all assembled at the front of the room, beneath the podium, waiting for his announcement. Celise saw Ambrosia Verabon and her entourage all gathered around the cake table. The ladies looked up in awe as she and Elias walked by. Their eyes flicked up to Elias's face—without the mask. She saw many of them grow pale. Several turned away and raised their fans, unable to look at his scars.

Celise wondered if the young ladies realized they had danced with an imposter. Would they be able to reconcile the charismatic Elias with this brooding, tempestuous man by her side?

She darted a glance at the soldier next to her. Before the scars, she imagined he was the kind of man who could make any woman blush, just like his doppelganger on the dance floor. He had a classically handsome face: dark features, silken hair, angular cheekbones, and a masculine jaw. She could picture him standing in a soiree surrounded by flirtatious young ladies, just as his imposter had done all evening.

But that wasn't the man who walked next to her now. With his grim visage, it was hard to imagine Elias entertaining, let alone flirting with, his guests. He led her through the ballroom at a determined pace, her steps two to his stride. She tried not to look like he was dragging her, but with her hair frazzled and ruined by rain, her dress ripped, and her bodice stained with daemon blood, it all looked a tad barbaric.

The musicians were quiet. The gas lamp chandeliers sparkled overhead. The perfumed air was thick with tension.

Elias climbed the steps of the dais up to the podium, which stood near the stage where the musicians were gathered. Celise followed him up, her shoulders trembling. From above, the gala's guests all looked like a field of flowers. Throughout the room, elegantly dressed women spread out in a rainbow of color. She didn't miss the handful of reporters and photographers setting up a wooden collodion camera on a rickety tripod to one side of the podium. Two reporters were taking frantic notes on little pads of paper. Representatives from several newspapers were in attendance, though how Celise had missed that before, she didn't know.

She clutched the Starlight Dahlia to her breast like a shield. Her heart raced as she gazed out over the assembly. Hundreds of eyes looked up at her. She had never been more scared in her life.

A quiet hush fell over the room, punctuated by the pouring rain against the tall windows.

Celise glanced at Elias's scarred face, just to find him gazing down at her. His gray eyes pierced her own. Then he turned to the crowd.

"You were promised an engagement, so I will announce one," he said clearly. "I give you Lady Celise Dhastel, daughter of Lord Sebastian Dhastel of Windhaven Ranch."

Gasps rippled through the ocean of silk and lace.

"Let the Mother of Dust and Moon bear witness to my words—I let no act of courage go unrewarded. Celise Dhastel stood her ground against a daemon tonight—no easy feat for a young lady. That's when I saw her heart. Although she is small in stature, she is mighty in spirit: a woman of strength, fortitude, and striking intelligence. My lady," Elias took her hand and spun her about as though she were on the ballroom floor. When he finished, they were face-to-face, only a few inches apart. Then he sank elegantly to one knee. His hand never left her own. "Before the stars, by dust and by death—*I choose you.* Will you make your vows before Mother Valestra and join my side as the future duchess of Gravenmere?"

Celise's jaw dropped open. How did such beautiful words spill from such a hardened, unforgiving mouth? She couldn't speak. Her lips moved, but no words came out.

Elias stood up. He twirled her around again, then dipped her in his arms. He planted a chaste kiss on her lips. The crowd gasped and sighed.

When Elias straightened, he held up their joined hands before the assembled guests. The ladies cheered, and the men roared their approval. The cameras flashed and whirred in the front row. Then, at a signal from Old Blackwood, the Plum Dahlia Quartet staggered into a victorious ballad. The whimsical strains of a violin filled the dance hall. The guests all looked pleased and excited and turned to each other to talk about the production.

Celise was stunned.

She hadn't said "yes." She hadn't said anything at all.

What's happening? Am I . . . am I engaged to the duke?

Elias placed her hand on his forearm, and she started down the podium. Celise allowed herself to be led because she didn't know what else to do. She was quite overwhelmed.

This can't be right, she thought, her head spinning. Memories of Mordwen's fortune-telling came to the surface. *No, this is Katrina's fate, not my own!* What about Valestra's wand and the Abyssal Rose? Wasn't Katrina supposed to marry the Mad Dog? At least, that was the story her younger sister had written for herself. The Teacup Tournament was a promising sign—a gold medalist fencing star seemed like the perfect match for the Hero of the Realm.

This night couldn't be any more surreal, she thought.

As they passed through the ballroom, the crowd parted before them. Celise was shocked by the number of smiling ladies who waved at her. *"Congratulations! Congratulations, young lady!"*

Elias leaned down to murmur into her ear, "Breathe."

She sucked in a breath, realizing she hadn't taken one in what felt like minutes.

"At least try to look happy," he whispered

Celise straightened up a notch and forced a smile on her face. She waved back to the crowd. She tried to ignore the little strains of gossip that floated about in every direction.

"Who is she? I've never seen her before."

"I wonder what The Lady's Letter *will say about this?"*

"Just look at her ruined dress. How awful!"

"Another fiancée for the Mad Dog duke?"

"Do you think the daemon was a farce? It seems a bit staged."

The reporters scratched down quick notes. Several of them followed on Celise's heels, hailing down the new couple, a hundred questions spilling from their lips, echoing the gossip already spreading through the ballroom. Elias kept a firm hold on her hand and moved swiftly across the floor, taking advantage of the brief pause after his speech. He seemed bent on making a swift exit before any more guests could approach him.

Celise passed by her father, who stood with Old Blackwood near the ballroom's exit to the rear gardens. Her father's face was flushed with happiness, and his eyes were brimming with tears. Celise didn't think the happiness was for her future—more likely for the business contracts he would acquire through his connection to the Blackwoods.

The rest of the Dhastel family gathered at a table nearby. Heather was eating a piece of cake. Marcella was swooning against Lady Estoria's shoulder while the old duchess fanned her face. Katrina looked angry enough to commit murder.

As Elias and Celise exited the ballroom, the bells of Gravenmere Castle struck twelve. It was perfectly midnight, the hour of fate and prophecy.

The engagement was sealed.

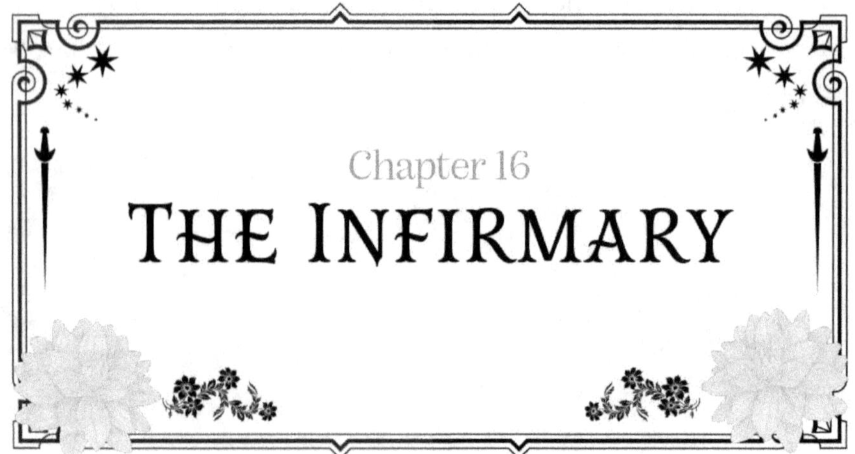

Chapter 16

The Infirmary

Outside the ballroom, rain poured down upon the veranda. Celise found herself once more gazing at the entrance to the garden maze. Her eyes searched the menacing hedgerows for any sign of movement. Her imagination played tricks on her. A conspicuous topiary became a creeping, lumbering monster under the stormy moonlight. She found herself shrinking behind Elias's strong presence. Were more daemons prowling the Gravenmere grounds? The supersoldier seemed to think so.

She glanced up at the war hero next to her.

She still didn't know if his proposal was serious or not.

It all seemed like a grand performance to appease the papers—and perhaps it was.

Elias had charmed the room with his romantic speech, but now, standing next to her, his jaw stiff and brow stern, she only saw a hardened soldier.

A group of people was waiting for them on the terrace near the balustrade that enclosed the space. To her back, warm light spilled through the ballroom's tall windows, casting stripes of gold and indigo blue across the stone landing. A man dressed in a white jacket and wide-legged trousers faced them at the top of the stairs. With a start,

Celise recognized him. It was Kiran Kindale, the same officer who had come to the Moongazer Tower earlier that day.

It seemed he knew the duke quite well.

Two soldiers stood to each side of Kiran. Celise's eyes passed over them curiously. The soldiers wore blackish-blue uniforms with gold insignia on their breasts. Their badges looked like glowing flames. Shined helms covered their foreheads, glowing softly in the darkness from their mana. These soldiers were different from the guards she had seen posted around the estate. Multiple swords and daggers hung from their belts. The weapons were all shined, she was certain.

Was this the Daemonguard?

"Lord High Commander," Kiran Kindale bowed while clasping a fist across his chest. His hand glinted gold in the light from the ballroom. Celise's eyes widened. Where the knuckles should be, she saw intricate rows of gears and knobs. Was it a prosthetic?

"I've assembled a task force to search the grounds," Kiran said in a rich voice. "Where would you like us to start?"

Elias's eyes flickered over the four assembled soldiers. "Is this all the men we have?"

"Yes, Your Grace."

He *tutted* under his breath. "Try to be quick about it. Use horses if you have to, but remember the steeds here are not trained for battle. Begin with the garden maze, then work your way through the different pavilions. Ensure the grounds are safe for our guests."

"Yes, sir. Will you be joining us, Your Grace?"

"I will shortly." His eyes drifted to Celise. "First, I will escort my betrothed to the infirmary. Let's reconvene here in an hour's time. I will join you for the remainder of the hunt. You are dismissed, officers."

Kiran saluted smartly again with his shined hand. Then, with a circle-up motion, he led the four soldiers down the steps. They moved silently, drawing weapons as they entered the maze.

"Well then?" Old Blackwood called from behind them. "What now? Is it safe for the guests to come out?" The old duke, accompanied by Lord Dhastel, hovered by the stone archway that led into the dance hall.

"We should keep the guests inside the ballroom for now," Elias said.

"I can keep them for a bit, but the nobility are not easily handled," Blackwood replied. "They'll want to return to their beds soon. The hour grows late. Your guests are tired, Elias."

"Then they can sleep on the ballroom floor."

"Nonsense! Not at Gravenmere. This isn't a wartime encampment, son. I will arrange escorts for the guests to return safely to their rooms."

"What if they're attacked along the way? How will that look for your publicity?" Elias's voice was thin and icy.

Celise glanced back and forth between the two Blackwoods, shocked. She had never imagined the Mad Dog would address his own father with such disrespect, but there it was.

Old Blackwood firmed up. Then he said, "Can't anyone escort the guests back to the castle? Where is the Daemonguard?"

"Patrolling the grounds, as they should be," Elias snapped. "I am taking Celise to the infirmary for a medic to look at her arm. I suppose, if any guests are staying in the castle proper, I can watch over the flock as we cross the grounds."

"Good, excellent, I will make an announcement. It will take some time to organize everyone—"

"Five minutes."

Old Blackwood stared at Elias. Celise sensed a brief, intense battle of wills. Then, with a grimace, the old lord turned about on his heel and strode back into the ballroom, waving a hand at a group of servants in green livery. Celise watched him walk away.

It seemed his son, the military commander, was now in charge.

"How is your arm?" Elias asked, turning to her.

Celise had been trying to ignore the itching, stinging sensation from her forearm. The daemon's blood was slowly eating little holes through the fabric of her dress.

"It's alright, I think," she said.

With a slight frown, Elias channeled mana into his hand, issuing a soft glow from his scarred palm. Celise gazed at his hand in awe. He inspected her forearm without much concern, as though he had seen hundreds of similar stains before.

"Not bad," he said. "Does it itch?"

"A bit, yes."

"Alright. We should get you to the infirmary before it burns you."

"Why will it burn me?"

"Daemon blood is acidic. Certain kinds are more acidic than others. We call that *toxicity*. We denote it by color. This daemon would be a yellow variety—low acidity. Its many arms and legs we call a *tumbler*."

"So a *yellow tumbler* attacked us, then?"

"Exactly. Some daemons have blood that will melt through solid steel. Those we call *violet* daemons. Violets are the worst to deal with. Their powers are more potent as well."

"I see," Celise said, numb at the thought. Had Elias spent ten years in the Abyss fighting such monsters? How terrible!

Old Blackwood reappeared, leading a large group of sixty guests and servants through the archway from the ballroom onto the balcony. Another hundred guests or so lingered inside the entrance, waiting for an escort back to their pavilions and cottages across the grounds. As Celise watched, a small party of regular nightguards and servants ascended the stairs to escort the next group across the grounds.

She saw her stepmother and sisters huddled by the entrance to the ballroom, gazing nervously out into the night, waiting to return to their guest tower. Marcella's arms were wrapped around Katrina's shoulders to comfort her. Both women looked traumatized.

Her father, Lord Sebastian Dhastel, was accompanying Cornelius Blackwood and a number of other gentlemen back to the castle proper. Perhaps they were retiring to Blackwood's private study for a nightcap and a game of cards?

"This way! This way!" The servants directed the crowd, waving bright lanterns in the air. "Gravenmere Castle is a quick quarter mile this way! Watch your step on the stairs!"

The guests looked happy and jovial, if a bit sleepy, as they crossed the landing to the wide flagstone path that led back to the castle. No one seemed concerned by the daemonic threat with Elias in their company. Celise wondered if the nobility thought it was all a publicity stunt.

"A lovely speech," one of the women said when she passed by Celise and Elias, oblivious to the tension between the young couple.

The gentleman escorting her added, "Very moving! I hope to see your picture in the paper!"

Many other voices chimed in as the guests walked by:

"Such a lovely bride-to-be."

"An adventurous night! Unforgettable!"

"Certainly the event of the year!"

"Thank you for having us, Lord High Commander Blackwood!"

"When is the wedding? I hope to receive an invite!"

Elias waved and nodded to the various socialites as they walked past. The ladies craned their necks to stare curiously at Celise, who bobbed a few awkward curtsies in her muddy dress while clutching the Starlight Dahlia. Then she gave up, too tired to bother. She leaned slightly behind her betrothed, and Elias kept his hand locked steadfast on her own.

Hanging back near the ballroom, Ambrosia Verabon and a group of several young ladies gathered around the stone archway, darting little glances at Celise and chatting among themselves. She wondered what they were saying. Were they talking about her? Or were they discussing Elias's scars? The daemon attack? The ball?

Perhaps they were planning to write to *The Lady's Letter?*

Celise felt her stomach tie itself in knots. What happened after this?

She yearned to be home again, anonymous and safe in her loft above the stables.

After the crowd passed by, Elias escorted her down the sweeping staircase to the flagstone path that led back to the castle, acting very much like a shepherd watching over his flock. They hung back about twenty feet or so behind the last of the revelers so that Elias could keep an eye on the group. As they walked, she stole a little glance up at the side of his face. She walked on his right side, so his scars were hidden from her. His skin was tan like the ranch hands that worked in the Dhastel stables. He was a bit weathered by the sun but still youthful. His strong jawline and high cheekbones gave his face a roguish, masculine appearance. She felt a strange little flutter in her stomach. He was, in fact, a very attractive man.

Then Celise's shoe caught on the hem of her dress. She stumbled forward. Elias caught her. They fumbled with each other for a moment, and Celise found herself once again pressed up against the duke's chest, his arms wrapped around her, leaning back in the overhang of a block wall.

"I'm *so* sorry," she muttered, cursing her shoes, which were a size too large for her feet. Borrowed from Heather's closet, of course.

"This is the second time you've stumbled into my arms. Am I to believe you are simply this clumsy?"

He glanced down at her through dark lashes and caught her gaze. Celise looked away, feeling a slight burn in her cheeks. Was she blushing? Oh no, she hoped not. He didn't kiss her, though for a moment, it seemed like he considered it. Then he set her back on her feet and helped straighten her dress.

Then, surprising her, Elias removed his coat and wrapped it around her shoulders.

"This is the second coat I've given to you," he murmured.

Celise blushed. His greatcoat slouched around her small form, as wide and long as a blanket. It almost reached her ankles. It was made of a finer, newer fabric than the other coat she had stolen from him.

"I have your other coat in my trunk," she mumbled apologetically. "I can return it to you tomorrow. I didn't mean to keep it—"

"That's fine. I shall collect it later," he said.

Celise blinked up at him, surprised that he didn't seem at all upset. He gazed down at her with an unreadable expression on his face, and she wondered at the softening of his eyes.

Then he offered her his arm again.

With a deep breath, Celise accepted it and they followed after the drunken guests. She sensed him slow his pace to match her short strides. He was very tall, and she was unusually short. She felt quite mismatched. She held up her skirts, and, pinching the dahlia between her fingers, she awkwardly navigated the lumpy cobblestone back to the manor house.

All deep in their cups, Old Blackwood, Lord Dhastel and a group of gentlemen sang uproariously into the night. Blackwood's barrel-chested laugh carried like booming thunder. The men stumbled toward the castle in a happy herd. It seemed Lord Dhastel was enjoying himself. Both he and Cornelius Blackwood walked with a cane, and they bumped into each other several times as they wandered across the dark grounds. Each time their canes crossed, the two men guffawed and patted each other on the back like old friends.

In a loud voice, Celise overheard Blackwood promising her father a glass of expensive brandy and a cigar to toast the new engagement.

"I must admit, I forgot you had a third daughter," Celise overheard Blackwood blustering as he walked down the path like a three-legged bulldog. "Somehow, I recall meeting only two. I apologize!"

"Not to worry, Your Grace, my daughter Celise is . . . well, she doesn't leave the house as much as her sisters. She has a fragile constitution."

"If she's caught the eye of my storm-blooded son, she's far from fragile!" Blackwood laughed with good humor.

Lord Dhastel hesitated, and Celise held her breath. Was he going to tell Old Blackwood that she was a dunslug? It would ruin everything. The spell of the night would be broken. The elite Blackwood family wouldn't allow a match with a dunslug. Really, she shouldn't have been at the ball to begin with!

But the moment passed. Lord Dhastel said nothing.

"A fragile constitution?" Elias said quietly. Then, to her silence, "Do you bruise easily, too?"

Celise raised a startled hand to her jaw. She had forgotten all about her swollen cheek.

"I . . . uh . . . ."

Elias's hooded gaze saw too much. He glanced back up at her father with a calculating frown.

Then, startling Celise—or perhaps saving her from a lengthy explanation—a great ruckus disrupted the night sky behind her.

Whoosh! Ziiiing! Boom!

Behind them, fireworks arced across the sky, exploding against a backdrop of storm clouds. The pouring rain only slightly dampened their bright sparks. It seemed the old duke wasn't one to do things by half measure. The crowd of guests stumbled and gazed upward, trying to watch the show as they walked back to the castle.

Elias didn't turn once to look at the colorful sparks filling the sky. His eyes darted instead to the shadows, ever vigilant.

"I suppose the fireworks might distract any daemons on the grounds," he grumbled. "A tactical advantage, if it doesn't distract Kiran's men as well."

"I don't want to encounter another one of those monsters," Celise said with sincerity.

"I'm sure we're safe, my lady."

My lady. She really wasn't used to that. She felt the urge to correct him but held back. How did she explain herself?

When they reached the rear entrance to the castle, the double doors were thrown open wide by a set of staff. More servants appeared with towels and blankets in hand and warm cups of cocoa for the guests.

Old Blackwood and the rest of the gentlemen turned down the hot chocolate in favor of hot brandy. Then disappeared up a set of stairs to the second floor.

Elias entered the castle with Celise's hand still wrapped in his own. The low-lit halls of Gravenmere embraced them. The corridors were dry and cold. Celise heard voices and footsteps echoing from the door above them, then a loud door slam. It sounded like Blackwood's guests were all retreating to their rooms to turn in for the night.

Elias flagged down a passing servant. "Would you wake up Dr. Forrest? It's urgent. We will wait for him in the infirmary."

The servant bowed and headed for a flight of stairs to the second floor.

"The infirmary is just down here, on the left," Elias said, escorting Celise down another hallway. They passed by silver wall sconces lit with low flames.

Easing the silence, Elias said, "The Dhastel estate is in the lower plains across the river, isn't it? From Gravenmere, I believe it's two days by train. You have a long trip ahead of you tomorrow."

Celise cautiously cleared her throat. "I don't mind the train ride. I've never traveled this far from home before."

"Really? Don't you go into the city on occasion?"

"No, not often."

Celise clammed up again. She felt like she was going to say the wrong thing and somehow give herself away. What would Elias think if he knew she spent all of her time with the horses in the pasture or the stables? This was one of the few times she had left Dhastel lands. She sometimes went to the nearby town of Sultan with Mordwen to buy supplies for the house, but those trips were infrequent, and Sultan was no more than an intersection in the road between farms. She had only been as far as Castleberry City two or three times. Gravenmere was the farthest she had ever traveled from home.

At the end of the long hallway, Elias opened a door and ushered Celise inside a large, clean room lit by glowing gas lamps. A long oak table stood before her, scattered with medical ledgers, bottles sealed with colored wax, and slender, shined wands used for mana readings. The mingled scent of dried lavender, clean linens and bitter herbs tickled her nose. She had never visited a mana healer before, but it seemed like the Gravenmere infirmary was equipped with all the latest technology.

She didn't see anyone in attendance.

"Have a seat on that chair over there. I'm sure the doctor will be along shortly. Everyone is fast asleep at this late hour."

Celise nodded and sat down in the nearest wooden chair to wait. A clock ticked away on the wall. Elias stood quietly in the room. The silence was deep and terrible. Celise fiddled with the flower in her hands. The white bloom, so glowy and bright under the stars, was beginning to close. She watched the petals slowly fold inward. According to Heather, it was one of the rarest flowers in the kingdom, and Elias had plucked it from the garden like nothing at all. She wondered if she would be allowed to take it home with her: a token of her fateful night.

Of course, the engagement couldn't last. It didn't feel real at all.

She thought again of Mordwen's fortune, told with dramatic flair in her bedroom above the stables. The final card had been the Abyssal Rose—she wasn't misremembering things. Dasha didn't believe in Mordwen's fortunes, but Celise did, now more than ever before. What did it all mean? Had she somehow managed to steal Katrina's fate? Was such a thing possible? She couldn't imagine her younger sister's fury. Not only had Celise failed to be killed by the daemon, but Elias had chosen her to be his bride. Katrina would not stand for it.

The silence stretched. Celise fidgeted, her thoughts heavy on her mind as her imposter syndrome grew. At least walking across the grounds in her ill-fitting slippers had given her something to focus on. Now, trapped in awkward proximity with the Mad Dog, all she could manage to do was fiddle with the flower in her hands.

Finally, Celise summoned her courage and cleared her throat. "So . . . what happens now?"

Elias raised a dark eyebrow. "What do you mean?"

"I mean, what happens next?"

"Next?"

"The gala, the garden, the proposal . . . it's all very exciting, but . . . this isn't *real*, is it?"

Elias considered her, his hands clasped behind his back, his face unreadable, that of a soldier standing in rank.

"Do you want it to be real?" he asked.

Celise hesitated. Should she tell him she wasn't Luminous?

Now would be the time.

She really should say something before the whole ordeal got out of hand.

"I . . . I don't know," she muttered. She was a coward. She couldn't say it.

"I see." He paused. "We can part ways tonight, if you like. But if you are willing, then we shall play our parts and fulfill our duty."

Celise blinked twice. *Our duty?*

So, it was all an act? It must be. He didn't care for her at all.

Had she imagined all those lingering glances? What about the kiss they had shared in the garden? Oh, how she wished to return to that rainy darkness, where she felt so close to him, without the curtain of propriety falling between them!

Celise gathered up her courage. It was time to reveal her secret. Her lack of mana-channeling would put an abrupt end to this madness, guaranteed.

Chapter 17

The Mana Doctor

Before Celise could tell Elias about her shameful condition, the door to the infirmary opened, making a loud creaking noise. The sound interrupted her thoughts. She jumped and looked up. Elias turned around as well.

A tall, thin man entered the infirmary. His white-blond hair was tied in a healthy ponytail that fell in a thick mane down his back. By his pale, snowy features and tall stature, Celise guessed he was from Dresengard, like Mr. Talisworth, the horsemaster.

This healer was a bit younger than Mr. Talisworth, if she had to guess, despite his silvery locks. He had a long, oval face with a sensitive chin and clear forehead. He looked like he had just rolled out of bed. His face was puffy from sleep. He wore a cream-colored jacket buttoned down the front, though on closer inspection, it seemed the buttons weren't lined up with the right holes, so the whole coat fit a bit crooked. The doctor didn't seem aware of it. Beneath the jacket, he wore gray trousers and a pair of smart black shoes. On his shoulder, he bore the winged symbol of a sanctioned healer of the realm. Around his neck, he wore a long cord strung with a dozen coin-shaped medallions, each one shined a different color, from fiery copper to opalescent blue. The medallions drew Celise's eye. She gazed at their glittering colors, curious.

When the doctor saw Elias, he straightened up, squared his shoulders and saluted.

"Lord High Commander."

"At ease, Forrest," Elias said, his hands still clasped behind his back, his chest wide and shoulders straight. "As I recall, you were discharged a year ago."

"Force of habit, Commander, and one of respect as well," the medic grinned, dropping his rigid posture. He rubbed the back of his neck bashfully. Then he noticed Celise sitting on a chair at the front of the room. He did a double-take, noting the dark stains across the front of her dress. He pushed a pair of glasses up the bridge of his nose.

"I assume that's not *your* blood staining the front of your dress," he said with unexpected humor. "Otherwise, you wouldn't be sitting so calmly in that chair."

"It's not," she said. Despite her composure, she felt far from calm.

"This is Lady Celise Dhastel," Elias interrupted. "My newly betrothed."

The medic blinked twice, the only sign of surprise he gave at the news. Then he turned back to Celise. "Welcome to my infirmary, young lady. My name is Dr. Drandem Forrest. Now, I've heard a strange story circling about the halls at this late hour. The servant who woke me said you were attacked by *a daemon*, of all things."

"That is correct. We were attacked on the grounds," Elias answered for her. "The wound is on her forearm. I wiped off what I could, but it pains her."

"I see," the doctor said. A flash of surprise passed over his face. Then, with an ironic tone, he said to Celise, "That must not have been very pleasant."

"It *really* wasn't. Lord Elias called it a 'yellow tumbler,'" she said helpfully.

"He did, hm?" The healer's eyes flickered to the commander. "Yellow?"

"Seems like it."

"Well, that's good news at least. How a daemon got on the grounds is more concerning."

"A matter I will investigate shortly," Elias said in a foreboding voice. "I've sent Kiran with his squad to search the estate."

"Do you think there might be more?"

"I think we can't take that chance. You might want to keep an assistant on standby for the rest of the night, in case another guest is attacked."

Dr. Forrest nodded, a concerned frown wrinkling his brow.

Then the medic stepped over to Celise's chair. He stood before her, his eyes sweeping over her ruined dress to focus on her arm, where the majority of the acidic blood stained her sleeve. His glasses gleamed, and Celise realized the doctor was using them to inspect her wound. What he saw there, she couldn't guess.

Forrest reached up and tapped the side of his frames twice, a glow of mana encircling his hand as he did so. Then he looked at her arm again.

Celise stared at his glasses curiously. By the vibrant blue and yellow frames, she guessed they were shined.

"Have you ever visited a mana doctor before?" the doctor asked as he looked her over.

"No, I haven't."

"Well, you're in luck, because I happen to be one of the best in the kingdom. I know Elias very well—we served together in the Abyss. I've even consulted with the royal family a few times." Forrest smiled at her, his voice warm and gentle. She realized he was trying to put her at ease.

Admittedly, she was very nervous.

"The royal family? Really?" she asked.

"Yes."

Celise was surprised. She looked at Elias, but he stood stoically with his hands behind his back.

Forrest drew her attention once again.

"Now please, let's move you to the examination table. This won't take long. Will you remove your dress for me and put these clothes on? You can change just over here behind this screen."

Celise felt a little shy. She stood up and hesitated with the flower in her hand. Elias offered to take it from her, and she handed it over reluctantly, certain she wouldn't see the precious bloom again. Then she took the plain white gown offered by the mana doctor and slipped behind a screen at the side of the room. With some amount of struggle, she managed to untie her bodice and unbutton her tattered silk dress. She kicked off Heather's ill-fitting shoes. She would be happy never to see those slippers again.

Celise folded Elias's greatcoat and placed it on a chair behind the changing screen. Then she dropped her gray ballgown in a heap on the floor. Really, it should be burned. She slid on the cotton medical gown in its place. It was several sizes too large, of course, and spilled around her ankles, but she much preferred it to the bloody dress.

When she re-emerged, she caught the flicker of Elias's gaze. But when she looked up, she found him standing at the front of the room with his hands clasped behind his back, bent studiously over a table full of shined tools and instruments. The dahlia rested in one of the buttonholes of his vest.

Perhaps she had imagined his look.

Dr. Drandem Forrest escorted her deeper into the room behind a hanging burlap curtain. There, he revealed a raised metal table. As she watched, he draped a simple sheet of undyed linen cloth over the hard surface.

"I must apologize in advance for the cold metal," he said. "I'll try to be as quick as possible."

She nodded. He offered her a hand and helped her into a sitting position on the table. Then he turned on an overhead lamp and moved it directly above her. She could feel the heat from the gas lamp billowing against her face.

Her heart quickened. She knew nothing could be seriously wrong with her, but she still felt nervous.

Celise waited patiently as Drandem took a special salve from the shelf, wetted a cloth and wiped down the reddish marks on her arm. The stinging, itching feeling eased, then disappeared altogether. It was a relief. Long cuts from the rose garden left bloody trails against her tanned olive skin. He placed a few bandaids over the cuts.

Then Drandem turned her arm over, inspecting the inside of her wrist and elbow. He tapped his glasses over the right lens and looked again.

"I'm just checking your mana channels," he said. "Were you sickly as a child?"

Celise frowned. She stared at the doctor for a beat of silence, unable to comprehend his question.

"Pardon?"

"Were you often ill as a child?"

"No, not that I remember. What do you mean by 'mana channels?'" She held back from stating the obvious—she was a dunslug. She didn't have mana. Her eyes darted to the burlap curtain. Elias was standing at the front of the infirmary, only about twenty feet away. Despite the curtain that separated them, he could overhear their conversation easily.

The doctor didn't seem to notice her trepidation. His eyes passed over Celise's body curiously, his interest purely medical. Then he said, "I only ask because your mana body is damaged. This kind of deterioration is usually caused by extreme conditions, such as famine, childhood illness or malnutrition. In fact, if I didn't know any better, I would think . . . well, it's unlikely, but . . . ."

Drandem hesitated. Celise felt a bit pale.

"What?" she asked, her mouth dry with nerves.

Oblivious to her discomfort, Dr. Forrest continued, "I would like to run more tests, if that's alright. It won't take but a minute. Did you grow up in Sera'naya by any chance? The desert kingdom has extreme climates. Perhaps you survived a famine there?"

"No, I didn't."

"I see. Your coloring is similar to their southern desert tribes."

"I really don't know anything about that. I've never traveled to Sera'naya."

"Really? That's very curious."

Dr. Forrest gazed at her closely, as though trying to peer beneath her skin, and Celise glanced away. She knew the doctor was inspecting her mana body using his glasses, but it felt more like he was inspecting her pores.

"So then . . . I have mana channels?" Celise asked.

"You do, but they are . . . *underdeveloped*. I'll take a closer look once I treat your wound." The doctor gave her a kind smile. "It looks like the daemon left you with a slight infection. I will cleanse your blood and remove the toxins. You're lucky it was only a yellow beastie. They can get a lot meaner."

"Thank you," Celise murmured. She definitely didn't want to run into anything "meaner" than a yellow tumbler!

The doctor selected one of the shined, circular amulets from his lanyard. Celise noticed a curling, spiral design etched into the metal. The lines seemed intentional, as though carved to direct the flow of wind or water.

A pink healing glow surrounded the doctor's hands as he charged up the metal disc with his mana. Then, shocking her, he placed the amulet directly into her palm.

"Hold this for a few minutes," he said.

Celise felt gentle tingles of power massage her skin, like a hundred blunt needles softly tickling her flesh. On the sensitive nerves of her palm, it was almost pleasant. The strange tickle of power moved up her wrist to her elbow, then to her shoulder, where it shot across to her other arm. Her scalp prickled as the sensation grew, and with a small gasp, Celise felt herself *boosted* upward—for lack of a better term. She suddenly experienced a *brightening* sensation within her own body, as though becoming buoyant and full of light. Shivers of skydust-enhanced mana ran over her skin, flowing down her limbs, felt strongest in her injured arm. She almost started to laugh but caught the sound in her throat.

"It tickles," she admitted.

Dr. Forrest noticed her reaction and nodded twice. "Right. Good. Seems like your mana channels aren't completely dead. I'm going to give you a little extra *something*. It might do nothing, but a bit of stimulation might help with your . . . ah, well, we'll see. Stay here for a moment; I'll be right back."

His strange grumbling carried an ominous undertone. Then the doctor straightened up and stepped around the curtain, returning to the front of the room. Although no longer in view, she heard a rustling, clinking sound as Dr. Forrest sorted through his instruments. The amulet in Celise's hand continued to glow with a soft hum.

The warm power of the doctor's mana was very soothing and relaxing. Celise felt herself sinking into a sleepy, trancelike state, but her little bubble of relaxation was interrupted by the murmur of voices. She perked up a bit, focusing on the conversation taking place beyond the burlap curtain.

It sounded like the doctor was discussing her condition with Elias. She leaned forward a bit, trying to catch his words.

"Damaged?" she overheard Elias's voice.

"Clipped. We use the same process to neuter S-rank prisoners."

"S-ranks? But those are murderers and cutthroats, dangers to society who use their mana to harm others—"

"I know. As I said, it's a barbaric process and very risky. It looks like it happened while she was young . . . possibly too young to remember. 'Clipping' is meant to permanently remove a Luminary's ability to channel, but I've never seen it done like this. I pity the girl. It seems her gifts were stolen from her. I'm surprised she doesn't know."

"I see. This is . . . an unfortunate discovery."

Celise caught bits and pieces of Drandem's murmured conversation, her ears straining to hear every word.

Her gifts were stolen from her?

The news hit her like a slap across the face. She felt stunned. For a moment, she couldn't breathe.

Was she born Luminous after all?

She glanced down at the humming, mana-filled coin in her hand. Could it be true? Despite her desires and daydreams, not a tendril of mana had ever stirred in her body. Yet she had always felt like she *should* be able to channel—like some power *should* be there.

If the doctor was right, then it seemed her urges weren't just wishful thinking.

Celise gulped down another breath.

She wasn't just a dunslug—no, her fate was much worse.

She was a . . . *castrated* Luminary.

"Clipped?" she muttered under her breath. Feeling self-conscious, she held the amulet until the glow faded and the vibration died out. She almost wished she hadn't overheard their conversation; she couldn't hide the horror from her face.

Then Dr. Forrest appeared again.

"Sorry for the delay," he said, noticing her raised eyebrows and hollow cheeks. He scratched the back of his neck, a bit awkward. "Well," he cleared his throat, "I suppose you overheard some of that. It's a small room. Do you have any questions about your condition?"

"M-my condition?" she stuttered. After a brief pause, she pushed on. "Is it true, then? I have mana channels? I'm . . . Skytouched?"

"You were born Luminous, but . . . your channels are not active, and to be honest, I don't know if they'll ever be usable. It must be a terrible shock to you to receive this news so late in life."

Celise nodded. A beat of silence passed between them. Dr. Forrest looked strained, like he wanted to say something helpful.

"Did you ever receive a skills assessment?" he asked.

"Skills? No. Not for mana."

"Nobles are typically tested at birth. Almost every person in the kingdom receives some sort of assessment by the age of five, just to rule out mana capability."

"I don't really remember, but . . ." Celise felt her eyes tearing up a bit, though she wasn't sure why. "My mother passed away in childbirth. The midwife told my father I was a dunslug. He never questioned it. I've always been this way. I didn't realize it was possible to have your mana channels . . . 'clipped.' How could this happen?"

The doctor gazed at her solemnly. "I don't know, my dear. I've never encountered a case like yours, not in twenty years of practice. I've performed clippings before, but only on the kingdom's *very worst* undesirables." Dr. Forrest adjusted his glasses. "It's not an easy procedure to perform. It requires precision not to kill the host, especially an infant. Whoever performed it on you was a master. They must have had a purpose, some reason to take such a risk."

Celise stared at the doctor with a blank expression.

"A reason?" she echoed. Who could possibly want to steal her mana ability? A wave of numbness washed over her. "I really don't know why anyone would do that to me. I . . . I'm no one important."

"Give the lady a moment to absorb all this, Forrest," Elias suggested from the front of the room, beyond the burlap curtain. "Why don't you show the girl how it works?"

The duke's dark, rich voice startled Celise. She felt a shiver of apprehension. Then the burlap curtain shifted as Elias pushed it aside, coming to stand next to her on the examining table.

Celise kept her eyes downcast, trying not to think of Elias's disappointment. She couldn't bear to look into his eyes. The newly spoken promise of their engagement was now broken by this discovery. She might not be a dunslug by birth, but she certainly wasn't fit to stand next to him as a duchess.

He's probably thinking of how to eloquently back out of this arrangement, she thought. *Well, he won't have to say much. I never wanted to be married to a duke! We are little more than strangers to each other.*

Celise did her best to look stiff and cold.

Drandem Forrest nodded to the commander and adjusted his white jacket before crossing the room to the back wall. Hanging there, tucked inconspicuously close to the ceiling, Celise noticed a long silk poster rolled up on hinges.

"This is a tool you'll find in every Luminous medic's office," the doctor explained, amused by her curious expression.

Dr. Forrest reached up and snagged a drawstring, then unraveled the silk poster to its full length, a perfect square almost six feet tall and wide. Then he adjusted the knob on an overhead lamp, increasing its brightness so that Celise could see the picture clearly.

The masterfully drawn diagram on the silk sheet revealed the silhouette of an ungendered human. An intricate network of lines mapped the human's body from head to toe. Celise was fascinated. She had seen a few drawings of vascular systems and musculature before, in books on horses a veterinarian had loaned her some time ago. She wasn't a strong reader, so she couldn't understand some of the text, but she knew what a medical drawing looked like. Every line was precisely defined. Scrawled notations indicated entry points and exit points, almost like a complicated water runoff system.

"We don't know everything about the mana body, but we know a few things," Dr. Forrest said helpfully. "I'll do my best to explain how this all works. First, the basics: those who are born Luminous contain mana bodies inside their physical bodies. Mana bodies are only detectable on an energy level—as a *force* or *essence*, a bit like electricity. Yet, mysteriously, they are somewhat intertwined with our physical body, as the use of drugs or malnutrition can impact how they develop."

"I understand," Celise nodded, following along.

"The mana body contains centers of energy called *terminals*. Special pathways move your mana energy throughout your body, called *channels*. If you think of your mana body like a plant, a channel is like the branches, while each terminal would be like the root ball feeding the branches, while the mana itself would be like water feeding the roots. Mana resides throughout the body but is centered or *pooled* at each terminal. Each terminal must remain balanced within the mana body's system; otherwise, diseases can develop."

"Diseases? Like what?" Celise asked, never having heard of such things before.

Dr. Forrest tapped on his head. "Mostly psychological," he said. Then he touched his stomach. "Sometimes digestive issues or back pain."

"Oh."

"What we call the axis terminal is here—" he pointed to a large mass of blue at the heart of the human figure. Then he pointed down below the drawing's navel to the base of the spine. "This is the root terminal, sometimes called the *terminal bud*. Proceeding up the spine, this is the earth terminal, the wood terminal, and then the water, wind and fire terminals. And here in each hand you have the star terminals."

Celise subconsciously flexed her hands, thinking of the Starlight Dahlia, then of the many times she had imagined holding power in her balled fists.

"Here at the base of your spine, this main branch extending upward from your *terminal bud* has been clipped." Dr. Forrest made a cutting motion across a thick silver vein that connected the root terminal to the rest of her energy centers up the spine. "Without power from your root, the rest of your mana body has remained undeveloped."

"So it's like having a broken spine," she murmured.

"In the mana-casting sense, sure. But try not to catastrophize it. You've lived a happy life so far without knowing about your condition. Please don't think less of yourself, Lady Celise."

Celise realized she was holding her hands over her abdomen, pressing against her belly as though she were in pain. She rearranged her hands and clasped them in her lap. Catastrophize? Well, perhaps she wouldn't go that far, but she certainly wasn't unaffected by the news. In all honesty, she didn't know how to feel. She had always assumed she was a dunslug. She had daydreamed at times about being a hidden Luminary, with some delayed power and *specialness* waiting to be unveiled within her bones. But this? She hadn't expected *this*.

Celise gnawed on her bottom lip as the room remained quiet.

Faced with this new knowledge of her crippled mana body, Celise felt a strange sense of loss, as though a precious gift had been handed to her and stolen away in an instant.

If her powers had manifested in her youth, as they should have, her life would have been very different.

Marcella and Katrina would not have bullied her—at least, not so brutally.

Why was she clipped?

Celise tried not to let her devastation show as she struggled to accept this new knowledge about herself.

Elias leaned in close to her. She was ashamed to meet his eyes.

"Do you know why someone might have clipped your mana channels at such a young age?" he asked, his voice rough and low. "Would anyone in your family have knowledge of this? Would they hide it from you?"

Celise blinked to clear her thoughts, then she shook her head. "No! No, I don't think so. My father, Lord Sebastian Dhastel, would have celebrated a Luminous daughter. When he found out I was a dunslug, he . . . ." Celise swallowed, refusing to admit to her father's discard. "Why would he believe anything else?"

Celise's voice trailed off under Elias's suspicious gaze. She couldn't think of anyone who might have wished to harm her in such a way. Even Marcella seemed beyond such cruelty. Her stepmother had married into the family when Celise was four years old, many years after the midwife had announced her a dunslug. The timing didn't make sense.

"What about the midwife?" Dr. Forrest asked. "Would she have any reason to do this?"

"I don't think so. I'm not sure. She was my mother's handmaid, but she was sent home after my mother's death."

"To Sera'naya?"

"Yes, I think so. I really can't say. I don't know much more than that." Celise struggled to make sense of it all. "I can't think of anyone who would do this on purpose. Is there any way to . . . fix it?"

Dr. Forrest hesitated, sharing a look with Elias. Then the doctor came to kneel down in front of Celise. He pulled something shiny out of the pocket of his long robes.

"We call this a *lens*," he said, holding up a large metal disc. It was slightly dome-shaped like a cymbal. "It helps convert mana energy into different frequencies to stimulate your body's natural healing." The healer's hand started to glow a soft pink color. "As my mana strikes the lens, the shined material emits a sound—not a sound we can hear—and activates your own body's ability to heal."

"I see," Celise said, trying to follow, but her mind was filled with strange sorrow.

"This lens is shined with a special dust we call 'Bluelight,' because it stimulates your *blue* channels. Those are the main arterials running through your mana body up and down the length of your spine, which vibrate to a specific frequency. You have red and green channels as well, and some people even have yellow channels, which extend outside the body in a sort of aura. Every mana body is somewhat unique from the next—"

Elias cleared his throat, and Dr. Forrest noticed the glazed look on Celise's face. At another time, she would have found this information fascinating, but after her hectic evening, she had reached her limit.

"I'll have to give you a full tutorial another time," the doctor said with a sheepish grin. "To put it simply, if we can stimulate your terminal bud to grow, we might be able to restore some functioning to your mana channels, but . . . well, let's just see."

Celise felt a tendril of hope stir in her heart.

"Do you think there's a chance, then?" she asked.

The doctor sighed. He exchanged another solemn look with Elias. Then to her, he said kindly, "There's always a chance, my lady. But I don't wish to mislead you. Restoring a mana body after this kind of damage would be similar to rescuing a jade plant from a hard frost. It will likely prove unsuccessful."

Celise could still see the hope in the healer's eyes despite his caution. She glanced up at Elias. The duke's face was unreadable, a grim frown marking his scarred features.

"You don't have to undergo a procedure if you don't want to," Elias reminded her.

"I feel like I owe it to myself to try. It's not painful, is it?"

The doctor shook his head. "No, my lady. I will make sure to sedate you. If it works, you might feel some discomforting sensations during the days to come, but . . . I have to be honest, the damage is extensive. It's worse than, well . . . ." The doctor cast another look at Elias. "Worse than piecing this raggedy tin soldier back together."

Celise blinked up at Elias, noticing the bond between the two men. It finally clicked. "Did you help His Grace recover after the war?"

Dr. Forrest nodded. "Yes, my lady, I was one of the surgeons who had the honor of saving his life. I assisted Dr. Maeve Shelley, a genius medic and scientist far ahead of her time." He noticed how Celise's eyes traveled to Elias's scars. "Unfortunately, we could not make him more beautiful."

Celise stifled a laugh. Sharing a hesitant smile with Drandem Forrest, she felt a bit better. She nodded. "I trust you. I'm willing to try."

"Then lie down on your back and get comfortable. This will take a few minutes."

Celise nodded and rearranged herself on the table, pulling up her legs and lying down on her back. The cold metal radiated up through the thin linen sheet. Celise waited, holding her breath, as Dr. Forrest rubbed the amulet again between his hands, focusing his power into it, and then rested the shined disc on her abdomen, just below her bellybutton.

"Don't worry," Elias said from her side. "Forrest is one of the best healers in the kingdom."

"Kingdom?" the healer joked. "Try the whole continent of Agea!"

"You always did have a big head."

"I've more than earned it, bringing you back from the dead. Speaking of which, I saw Kiran earlier today. He looked distraught. Mentioned something about you skipping your medications?"

"I can't fathom why he would say that."

"How are you sleeping?"

"Better than a corpse."

Celise listened as the men's conversation became more and more muddled. The soft vibrating sensations were making her sleepy. Her thoughts felt cloudy and far away. She yawned, her eyes dropping closed.

The metal disc was warm through the fabric of her medical gown. Dr. Forrest secured it with a leather strap. Then he began charging up a second disc.

"Don't worry, my lady," he said, noticing her look. "You'll be asleep soon enough, and then all of this will pass like a dream. You'll wake up tomorrow right as rain."

"Thank you," Celise said softly. She was beginning to feel very drowsy, an effect of the healing mana seeping up through her belly like a tranquilizer.

Elias leaned over her. He removed the Starlight Dahlia from the buttonhole in his vest and placed it beside her on the table. "I'm leaving now to join Officer Kindale on the grounds. Do you need anything?"

"No, I'm alright," Celise murmured. Then, softly, she added, "I meant to tell you sooner, but everything happened so fast."

"Tell me what?"

"That I'm a dunslug. I don't have mana."

Elias was quiet.

"So?" she asked, barely conscious. "I suppose that makes the betrothal impossible. You must call it off to save face."

"Is that what you want?"

Celise squinted at Elias, her thoughts growing fuzzy, her head light. "I don't deserve to wed a duke."

Her words slurred. She wondered if he understood what she meant. She felt drunk.

"Please rest, my lady," he said.

Celise hovered on the verge of sleep, thinking back over the evening, trying to understand the unpredictable series of events. The soothing, humming mana energy washed over her, triggering strange sensations in her body. She felt little flashes of intense heat, then cold chills. Little tickly sensations in her armpits, then down her spine. Without the sedating effect of the amulets, it would have been quite maddening. But mostly, she felt the urge to fall asleep.

Celise closed her eyes. She didn't dare to hope. Dr. Forrest had told her outright the operation wouldn't work. The damage was too severe.

So then, she gained nothing and she lost nothing. She would wake up tomorrow still a dunslug, with her farce of a betrothal already over. She felt a little wistful, but she knew she had done the right thing, telling Elias to call things off and save face. He had picked the wrong bride. But now he knew better.

She wondered if she would wake up tomorrow in her bed above the Dhastel stables and discover the whole weekend had been a dream.

Chapter 18

The Daemonguard

Elias watched Celise's face soften and the lines smooth from her brow as she fell asleep on the examining table. Wearing a plain cotton hospital gown with her hair a mess of reddish-pinkish knots, her beauty still entranced him. Her face was narrower than some, her nose pointed and pronounced in a way that spoke of the desert tribes. Her skin was not powder-pale like the Forsynthian upper class, but carried an undertone of copper. Her full lips reminded him of a mischievous cat, resting in a natural, bemused expression. She seemed like a haunted little thing, a shy oddity with bursts of unexpected assertiveness. When he slid his arms beneath her small body, he caught a slightly grassy aroma that reminded him of, well, *horses.* But only in the most calming, pleasant way.

He lifted her easily into the air and moved her to a cot near the window.

Dr. Forrest followed him. The doctor rearranged the mana-infused discs over her stomach, adjusting their placement so they correlated to her mana terminals.

Elias's eyes roved over Celise's face. A smudge of purple bruising underscored each eye. Her lashes were long and delicate. She looked younger in her sleep, more peaceful and less wary.

Outside the tall window next to her bed, rain spattered against the glass in sporadic bursts. It seemed the midnight storm was slowing. He needed to rejoin Kiran and the rest of the Daemonguard on the grounds, but he couldn't bring himself to leave Celise's side just yet.

Her soft words rang in his mind: *"I don't deserve to wed a duke."*

She didn't have mana.

Now he understood why she shrank down to make herself invisible. She believed herself to be inferior to those around her. Elias felt some amount of compassion for her situation. As the daughter of an elite household, she must have struggled to hide her handicap from the other Luminous families. The abuse of a lightless child in a noble house wasn't unheard of. Her father must have hidden her disability out of shame. She might have been punished for it. He thought again of the bruise on Celise's jaw. A frown pursed Elias's lips. He was growing more and more curious about his future wife's family.

"She brings up a good point, if you don't mind me saying so," Drandem spoke up at Elias's shoulder. "It's . . . *unconventional* for a man of your station to wed someone without mana. I'm sure Celise is a nice girl, but she's used to a simple existence. Have you considered the challenges she might face as your spouse? You both come from different worlds. Your job is to train Luminous soldiers at Firehelm Fortress. For her, even unlocking a shined doorknob will prove a challenge. She will struggle to fit into your world."

"Her condition is not her fault," Elias said, his words accompanied by a surge of protective feelings. "I intend to have her, come what may."

Forrest's pale eyebrows flicked upward. He searched Elias's face. "You're already attached, I see."

"I am."

"Obsession is not love, Elias, and . . . you have a tendency to ruminate. Don't make this girl one of your *preoccupations.* I would caution you to continue taking your medications."

"*I am,*" Elias snapped.

"That's not what Kiran told me."

"Kiran doesn't know a medicine bottle from a whiskey flask," Elias snarled. "As for Celise, I have no intention of *dehumanizing* her with my affections. My feelings for her are sincere."

Drandem gave him a piercing look but said nothing.

Elias continued, "I would ask you to keep her condition private. I will handle my parents in due time."

"Of course. I won't tell them anything."

The more Elias thought about Celise's damaged mana body, the more his temper flared. In a clipped tone, he asked, "What is the punishment for performing an illegal surgery on a newborn infant?"

"It would fall under the most grievous misuse of a medical license—a charge of sordid malpractice," Drandem agreed. "I don't know of any prior cases like this, but I imagine a doctor would face lifelong imprisonment, if not execution."

"Can you compile a list of all of the mana healers capable of performing such a surgery?"

Dr. Forrest sighed as he stroked his smooth chin. "I suppose," he mused. "I can attempt to compile a list of top-tier medics and midwives in Forsynthia, but as for the other kingdoms, I'm not so sure. . . ."

"Ask around. After compiling a list, we can begin narrowing it down to midwives who were practicing near Windhaven Ranch twenty-three years ago. Whoever did this must be brought to justice."

"Yes, Your Grace."

Without another word, Elias turned on his heel and strode across the room, his anger obvious in his quick movements. He paused just long enough to don his coat, which Celise had left folded on a chair. Then he stalked to the door. Forrest bowed as the commander glided past him into the hallway.

After leaving the infirmary, Elias made his way back through the castle, traversing several flights of stairs, two different courtyards and a labyrinth of hallways to reach his family's treasury in the castle's north wing.

With Celise safely abed, he needed to prepare for the battle to come.

He forced his mind to turn away from his newly betrothed and focus on his next challenge—the hunt.

He needed two things: weapons and armor.

Not all of the weapons in the Blackwood trophy room were relics. Some of the shined weapons were extremely powerful and well-kept for their age. The rest of his arsenal was split between Firehelm Fortress and his home at Summervale Cottage, where he kept a personal armory. He carried Thunderbreak at his hip, the shined sword he had used to protect Celise in the gardens. It was one of his favorites.

From the treasury, he collected Blacklight, which the thieves had attempted to steal from him the night before. It was another rare and powerful ghost sword he would use on the hunt.

After equipping his two swords, he threw open the wardrobe. He found a tactical vest tucked behind an array of old military greatcoats and wool jackets.

He pulled out the vest, which was made of leather-encased metal plates, and slid it on over his white silk shirt. This was a vintage design popular in the previous war. New flak vests were made of lighter material with shined threading to enhance a Luminary soldier's mana power. When this older piece was made, shined thread had not yet been developed.

Two steel backstraps ran down each side of his spine on the vintage armor's design. The straps were segmented to allow for some mobility, though the stiff leather kept the vest from bending too much. The front of the vest sported two plates across his chest and four along his abdomen, each sewn between thick pads of leather. The full ensemble was a bulky fit—more than twenty pounds of material—but worth the protection.

He tightened the buckles around his waist until the vest encased his torso like a glove. Then he donned his greatcoat over the vest.

He had one last weapon to collect before joining Kiran and the Daemonguard on the grounds.

Moving at a jog, he left the treasury and ran down the empty corridor to his office. He blew through the door and crossed the dreary room to his desk, where he reclaimed the Starcaster Cannon. He located the case of shined bullets—Dust #210 Bloodglass—and loaded the gun's chamber. Clicked it shut.

He gazed down the length of the cannon, feeling its considerable weight in his hand. He couldn't imagine a better opportunity to put Meister Barbaros's prototype to the test.

Elias didn't have a holster that would fit the anti-mana pistol, so he held it down at his side with the thick muzzle pointed to the ground.

Then he left the room, his greatcoat sweeping around him in a cool wind.

As he traversed the midnight halls of Gravenmere Castle, he realized he was smiling. His scars stretched in an unfamiliar way along his left cheek. A sense of adrenaline coursed through his veins, and excitement coiled in his stomach.

A daemon hunt.

An unexpected gift.

He might actually enjoy his birthday after all.

As he left Gravenmere Castle behind and started across the dark, silent grounds toward the ballroom and the garden maze, his mind returned to the girl with the raspberry hair—Celise. His newly betrothed.

What anomaly had put her in his path not once, not twice, but three times?

It seemed like fate.

Elias felt like some part of him was awakening after a deep slumber. He found himself lingering on the taste of her mouth and the warmth of her touch. Genuine. Authentic. The memory of their stolen kiss remained imprinted on his mouth. The intensity of that moment left his spine tingling and his mana crackling in his bones.

He couldn't remember the last time a woman had kissed him with real desire. The difference was electric. He didn't keep a casual mistress on hand, as men in power often did. Since returning from the war, he had spent most of his time in physical therapy. He was only just getting back on his feet. He was inexperienced in romance or courtship. He barely believed in friendship these days.

Yet Celise's kiss left him with a strange and unexpected . . . *yearning.*

He wanted to kiss her again.

They were engaged, and yet . . . they were strangers to each other, barely acquainted.

Her mystery, her subtle strangeness, made his mind burn with curiosity. He kept going back to her story, over and over again. Who had clipped her mana body? Who would carry out such a heinous crime on an innocent child? The Dhastel family had always been loyal to Forsynthia, yet this discovery cast a shroud over their family name. If Celise was their daughter, then she was no spy, no villainess, and no threat to anyone. Who would want to hurt her—as a mere baby, no less?

He had never felt anything as powerful as his need to protect her.

Why? She was no one, just a slip of a thing without mana.

Yet her gentleness soothed something deep in his heart, something he couldn't name. When he touched her hand, his aching muscles eased, and his turbulent thoughts became settled and still. He felt like he could breathe again. Like he had some chance of finding the man he had lost—the one who had lived before the war.

A shout from ahead of him drew Elias's attention, interrupting his thoughts. He saw movement on the terrace at the back of the dance hall. He recognized Kiran's white jacket from a distance. Celise faded from his thoughts as Elias raised his hand. A flash of mana ignited his palm so the men on the terrace could see his approach. *Flash hands.* Kiran signaled in return, his red mana answering Elias's blue.

The hunt was on.

Elias felt another grim sense of anticipation. He had missed this; his skills had become obsolete over the past two years of political functions, speeches and parades. The night brought back a flood of memories from the Abyss: destroying nests of daemons; soldiers culling their way to the heart of the monsters' domain. Reaching the depths of the crater, where the remnants of the ancient meteor pulsed with alien life, was the goal of their campaign. Only at the very heart of the Abyss could they locate and kill the Daemon King.

Those memories were still fresh in his mind.

He was a warrior first, a duke second, and on this night, he was in his element.

With his half-plate armor donned, gun in hand and two shined swords sheathed at his belt, Elias joined Kiran Kindale and the four soldiers of the Daemonguard on the veranda outside the ballroom. In the early morning hours, a thin veil of mist pooled in the lower parts of the grounds, obscuring his father's daft idea for a maze. The misty gardens lay before him, macabre and haunting, and utterly silent.

"I see you've brought your new toy," Kiran barked as he approached Elias on the terrace. He indicated the gun in Elias's hand. "Do you plan to test it tonight?"

"Seems like a perfect opportunity."

"I agree. If it gets too heavy for you, I'll gladly carry it—"

"Not until I've tested it first. It could . . . *backfire.*"

Kiran looked amused by his choice of wording. He raised a reproachful eyebrow. "If it blows off a hand, it might as well be my prosthetic," he pointed out.

Elias hesitated. He glanced down at his own hands, thinking of the months of surgery and immense amount of mana it had taken for the doctors to attach his new limb. Kiran's donation to his new body couldn't be overlooked. After struggling for a moment, he released a long sigh.

"I suppose you have a point," Elias conceded, and handed the cannon to Kiran, who looked ecstatic. He twirled the gun around in his shined hand, the dainty gears of his knuckles clicking mechanically, his bronze fingers only slightly stiffer than their organic counterparts. Then Kiran slid the gun into the deep inner pocket of his white coat. It created a noticeable outline at the side of his breast.

Elias made a mental note to request a custom holster from Meister Barbaros.

"May I be the first to congratulate you on your engagement?" Kiran continued. "Have you set a date for the wedding?"

"Let's not get ahead of ourselves," Elias growled. "The girl is unconscious in the infirmary. She might come to her senses in the morning and flee the noose."

"Oh please, you're too self-deprecating. The girl was lucky to come across you in the gardens. It must have been terrifying for her to encounter a daemon alone like that."

"I imagine it was," Elias said quietly, his mind returning again to his moment of passion with Celise in the shrine. Somehow, he wouldn't choose *"terrifying"* to describe the evening.

Kiran slapped him on the back. "I'm glad it all worked out, because I was having a difficult time choosing a bride for you. The obvious one was the fencing champion, Katrina Dhastel, but after she fled—"

"Katrina," Elias murmured, frowning as he recalled the name. "She was the girl in red who met us on the steps."

"Yes, that one. Why? Did you take special notice of her?"

"No, not like that." Elias thought of Celise's expression when her sister appeared on the staircase: a look of fear mingled with disgust and loathing. It contained no familial love or tenderness. He wondered about that. The two girls didn't look related, but they obviously belonged to the same family. Sibling rivalries were common in aristocratic families, but Celise didn't seem like the type of girl to hate someone without reason.

Damnable dust, I must get her off my mind.

"I'm not interested in Katrina," Elias snapped. "I simply proposed to the girl I held in my arms; that is all."

"Which is why you turned out half the archives looking for her family name." Kiran smirked at him in a knowing way that set Elias's teeth on edge. He glared at his adopted brother, but the man only smiled. Kiran looked delighted by his discomfort.

"*Alas*," Kiran continued, "My evening was much less eventful. After the Dhastel girl fled the ball, I thought I would swoop up the lovely Ambrosia Verabon. I found her to be a fine dance partner, but she reminded me of your first fiancée. What was her name? Raelia? Very charming, yet somehow sinister."

"Raelia Riverton," Elias sighed, "and I don't appreciate you reminding me of her name. I am trying to forget it."

"Right. Sorry, old chap."

"Enough talk of brides and ballrooms," Elias grumbled, noticing the rest of the Daemonguard milling around nearby, obviously eavesdropping. "Let's get back to business. Attention! To rank!"

"Sir!" The guards saluted and formed a neat line, standing at attention near the balustrade. Kiran fell into place at the end of the row. Elias's eyes traveled over the members of the Daemonguard at his disposal. He recognized the four officers—he had promoted them personally: Ravenna, Fenrick, Riordan and Cherry. They formed a special task force for high-risk missions around the kingdom. All of them had served in the Abyss, though Cherry, the youngest, only caught the tail end of the campaign. She had spent six weeks in the pit before the Daemon King was defeated, but her talents were extraordinary.

Ravenna and Fenrick were married, he recalled. Riordan was Fenrick's older brother, and both were mixed blood from Dresengard. The brothers were tall, lanky and golden-haired, while Ravenna was as dark and dramatic as her name.

Cherry had short auburn hair and indigo mana. She specialized in defensive tactics. She was young, perhaps the same age as Celise, but he had never seen a daemon break through her barriers. She had the rare ability to see shadowhide daemons, which made her indispensable as an operative.

Elias addressed the soldiers in a formal tone: "As you all know, a group of daemons has infiltrated Gravenmere Castle. Who brought them and how they came to be here has yet to be seen. I found tracks in the ruins of the old castle, in the mud near the lake shrine. That's where I engaged and defeated the first daemon, a yellow tumbler, beside the pond, but I suspect there are more. Consider this a traditional hunt, just like we would execute on the tertiary levels of the Abyss. We shall embark at once."

The soldiers all saluted as one.

"Follow me," Elias commanded in a clipped tone. Then he started down the staircase, crossed the flagstone pavilion, and bolted into the garden maze, the squad jogging behind him in single file.

As he walked, he recited low under his breath:

"Hidden behind the moonlit veil,
Eagle, fawn and otters dance.
Your gift awaits the midnight hour,
A dark reminder of your past.
Tonight, the scales shall be righted.
A visit of abyssal doom
to seal the grave you should have entered.
More awaits within the tomb."

"That sounds familiar," Kiran said by his side, overhearing Elias's somber chant. "Is that not the ominous riddle you received in the mail yesterday?"

"It is." Elias repeated the riddle one more time, a bit louder for Kiran's sake. His brother-in-arms looked thoughtful.

"Whoever wrote that letter put a lot of effort into arranging all of this. They must have a strong personal vendetta against you. It's not easy to transport a daemon—or several daemons—so far from the Abyss. It's more than a hundred miles away. Whoever planned this must have had a lot of help. Do you have the riddle on you, by chance?"

"No. Berrybean spilled tea on it."

"That rascal." Kiran winced. "Did I hear that right—'*More awaits within the tomb*'?"

"Yes."

"There's only one tomb on Gravenmere grounds."

"I know. Let's head there directly."

"Yes, sir."

Elias prowled like a wolf ahead of the small group. He drew Blacklight, carrying it before him like a torch through the hedgerows of the empty maze. Certain daemons could camouflage themselves, becoming invisible in the darkness, but Blacklight's illumination could reveal them. The length of the rod was matte black and shimmered with a dull purple color from his mana.

Thunderbreak was the second ghost sword that hung from his belt. It was not an everyday weapon; it required immense mana to activate the sword, more than the average Luminary soldier could channel. Elias had had it custom shined for his remarkable talents. Its thunderous strikes were deadly to the most towering behemoths of the Abyss. He had demonstrated only a small flick of the sword's power to Celise. Thunderbreak could take out a horde of daemons by summoning a storm of mana bolts from the sky. But he didn't expect to find that many monsters around the castle grounds—at least, he hoped not.

The soldiers of the Daemonguard, clad in black-blue leathers with gold insignia, drew their weapons as well, following his lead. They walked behind Kiran with their swords drawn, their blades glimmering with mana.

They entered the Zodiac Gardens without incident and continued past the ruined trellis and trampled garden beds. If the soldiers took note of the chaos, they didn't react except by shared glances. They moved in complete silence, mere shadows across the ground.

On the other side of the courtyard, they passed through a grove of black maple trees and a rusted gate into the forbidden ruins of the old castle.

With Elias in the lead, they took a different route that skirted around the pond and the old shrine. They traveled uphill for a ways, then through a grove of manawood trees and tangled hawthorn bushes. Celise hadn't traveled this deep into the abandoned grounds—she hadn't seen the proper ruins of the old fortress, just what remained of the gardens.

Buried within those ruins was the Blackwood family tomb.

The soldiers passed through a labyrinth of crumbling stone archways and broken statuary, weathered smooth by rain and neglect. The walls of the old castle looked like a dream left to rot. Touches of beauty still existed amidst the crumbling stone. Pale flowers—lumenblooms and Ironclad Aster—glowed faintly in the silver light of the twin moons. Glowbells grew in mossy clusters between the cracked stone walls, like little pockets of earthbound stars.

The soldiers passed by overturned benches and collapsed gazebos. Their feet crossed over ancient foyers and trod through rooms overtaken by ivy.

Senior Officer Kiran Kindale followed closely behind Elias with an amulet in hand. Not dissimilar in size and shape to Dr. Forrest's medical discs—which the doctor used to treat Celise's mana body—Kiran's amulet was created for a different purpose. The circle of shined metal was meant to detect daemonic dust, similar to mold spores or dandruff, that constantly shed from the monsters' bodies. The residue was harmless in small amounts, but walking through a cloud of it could damage the lungs.

Elias had encountered such conditions on the deepest levels of the Abyss. Special breathing masks with filters had been developed to protect against the daemonic residue, similar to plague masks, but many soldiers lost their lives to infection.

Technically, the daemons themselves were like spores cast off by the Daemon King. The comparison had come to Elias's mind often while campaigning in the depths of the Abyss. Although called the "Daemon King" due to ancient superstition and folklore, the beast of ancient lore was more like a mother plant spawning endless copies of itself to infest the world. It governed no city, it declared no law, and daemons themselves were far from sentient beings with a culture or society. From what he could tell, they were mindless mutations driven by incessant hunger, with no more sense of self than a mosquito.

Modern scientists had autopsied thousands of daemon corpses over the last two centuries. Until recently, researchers hadn't been able to locate anything like a brain or traditional nervous system within the creatures. Their anatomy was far from human. Each monster was spawned individually from the Daemon King's flesh, so each daemon was unique—although they seemed to follow certain patterns. The acidity of their blood seemed to exist on a scale that correlated to the intensity of their power. This also seemed to relate to the depth of the Abyss they chose to haunt, with stronger daemons lurking farther inside, while the weaker specimens remained closer to the surface.

As for the Daemon King itself—only a handful of warriors over the years had come anywhere close to observing it. Elias was one of those few. Since returning home from the war, he had been interviewed dozens of times by the realm's leading researchers, yet besides a few flashes of chaos and violence, his memories of the final battle were tragically absent. What did the Daemon King look like? Could he draw a picture? What was its size, shape and color? He only remembered the creature's fire and rage.

Just breaching the monster's chamber had cost the lives of a hundred men.

He thought of those men's sacrifice each morning as he donned his uniform.

Kiran's eyes remained on the shined amulet in his hand as various different colors moved across its surface. As the group of soldiers traveled deeper into the abandoned ruins, the amulet's colors began to glow with a definitive strength: a sure sign that Elias's hunch was correct.

"Commander," murmured Kiran, as the amulet flashed from green to purple. "Something ahead."

Elias held up a gloved hand. His squadron slowed down, boots muffled by moss and wild grass. Between swaying vines and overgrown laurels, a low gate appeared—iron, ornate, half-swallowed by creeping lumen-blooms. The rusted chains that once secured it were broken. He knelt down and picked up a length from the ground. The old iron looked melted and distorted in some areas.

Acid.

He and Kiran exchanged a glance.

He dropped the chain on the ground and motioned to the Daemonguard with an open-palmed gesture: a warning to stay alert.

In single file, they entered the Blackwood tomb.

Chapter 19

The Blackwood Tomb

Elias pushed open the gate, which groaned on its hinges. The violet glow of Blacklight's blade revealed a narrow path buried in clumps of dark green moss. Fireflies hovered low to the ground where a thin veil of moisture gathered above the grass. They bobbed and glimmered gently in the mist.

As the Daemonguard passed through the old gate into the Blackwood tomb, lumenblooms stirred faintly around their feet, responding to their mana. The small, trumpet-shaped flowers awakened and unfurled their white petals as the soldiers slipped by, turning their pale blooms toward the group of mana channelers.

The center of the hidden courtyard came into view. Carved of dark granite stone, a solemn pyramid stood amid a bed of glowing flowers. The ornate door to the tomb was closed. It didn't appear to be disturbed in any way. The sigil of a dragonfly was etched into a plate that hung above the tomb's entrance.

Elias's boots slowed to a halt, reluctant to trample the glowing flowers that surrounded the grave.

"It's been a long time since I visited this place," muttered Kiran. "Not since your grandfather became ill."

"We were children when he passed," Elias said in a soft voice. The tomb held several generations of Blackwood warriors. He assumed his own body would lie there some day, and he had visited the tomb often since his return from the war. It had become a sanctuary where he could be alone with his thoughts. Somehow, that made the letter's ominous quality more personal. Was the mention of the tomb merely a coincidence? Or had someone been spying on him since his return to the castle?

At his signal, the soldiers spread out, two flanking him on each side. "Stay vigilant. Someone entered the premises recently."

"Ugh. Do you smell something?" Cherry asked. "It's rank . . . like rotten flesh."

A breeze stirred, and Elias sucked in a breath. Yes, he smelled it too. Cautiously, the squad started to circle the tomb, their eyes searching the grass and lilies for the source of the smell.

"Look there," Fenrick whispered, coming to stand by Ravenna's side and pointing at a tangle of ferns beyond the tomb, at the edge of the woods. "I see something on the ground."

The soldiers raised their weapons and remained on high alert. Elias crossed the dense underbrush and pushed it back with his sword. A mound of gnawed-on bones lay on the loamy forest floor. The pile was impressively large—it obviously contained the remains of more than one animal. By the sweet, pungent stench of decayed flesh, the bones were fresh.

Elias's eyes flickered from the mess of gore and blood to the surrounding woods. He saw several ropes, frayed at the ends, dangling from a manawood tree.

"What do you think they were?" Kiran asked in a low voice. "Deer?"

"Pigs."

Elias's face was grim. It looked like he had found the cook's missing delivery of pork for the banquet. He ran a hand through his sleek black hair, a troubled frown on his lips. Where was the pig farmer who was supposed to deliver the sows? He didn't see any human bones amid the pig carcasses, but the farmer's remains could still be present. There was a lot to sift through.

He would have to initiate a search for the pig farmer when he got back to the castle. If the man couldn't be located, then he had to assume the worst. The thought left him simmering with rage. If an innocent farmer had met his death due to a madman's gruesome birthday prank, there would be hell to pay.

"This must be where your well-wishers kept the daemons before releasing them into the gardens," Kiran said, looking about the clearing once more. *"More awaits within the tomb. . . ."*

"Yes. And the monsters needed to be fed."

"Where are the daemons now?" Riordan asked in a deep, booming baritone. He was a large man who seemed incapable of speaking at a low volume—so he rarely spoke at all.

"What does the focus say?" Elias asked.

Kiran answered, "The amulet's color is strong. The air is thick with daemon dust. Definitely more than one creature, and still present by the look of it."

The soldiers all shifted, raising their weapons and looking around the forest again. Elias's eyes flickered to the disc in Kiran's hand. Sure enough, it glowed bright purple, a sign of high dust density in this area.

"They're close," Elias agreed.

A bit of movement flickered in the corner of his eye. A tremor passed through the trees surrounding the tomb, faint as a breath. Somewhere beyond the wild overgrowth, an unnatural whine carried through the darkness.

The wind shifted, and he caught the sharp stench of sulfur.

"Break!" Elias ordered.

The Daemonguard scattered expertly, creating a star-shaped formation with their backs to each other, each one facing a different section of the forest. They were prepared to meet the threat head-on from any direction.

With a shriek like steel on glass, a massive body dropped down from the thick branches of an ancient manawood tree. Blacklight flashed in Elias's hand, revealing the threat under a beam of eerie violet light. Dropping its camouflage, the monster climbed onto the roof of the tomb and snarled at the soldiers. Its reptilian body seemed unnaturally thin and tall. Its skin was cracked like tree bark, oozing thick purple sap that smelled of rotten eggs. A flap of skin encircled its neck, which flared outward like a flower's blossom. The head rolled and bobbed from side to side like a demented daisy. Where the monster's eyes should be, Elias saw four slits like nostrils and a great, sucking mouth. From its shoulders sprouted spine-like protrusions similar to branches, each dripping with poisonous sap.

The daemon appeared to be part lizard, part poisonous plant, and altogether foul.

"A violet climber," Kiran confirmed.

Then, as though the nightmare was just beginning, two more lumbering shapes appeared through the trees.

Emerging from the woods, the second daemon was slow and awkward. Red saliva dripped to the ground, sizzling where it struck the stones, from an alligator-shaped monstrosity with giant fins along its back.

The final daemon was so large, it pushed over two sapling trees to force itself into the clearing. It resembled a mammoth-sized slug: a fat, limbless body covered in slime, a lime-green belly dripping with acid, and eyes on two stalks that swiveled above its head.

"Kiran, you take the violet climber," Elias said, indicating the aggressive one on the tomb's roof. "Use the Starcaster."

"With pleasure," Kiran grinned.

Then Elias motioned to the rest of his soldiers. "Riordan and Cherry, take the red one. It looks like a crimson crawler, so be careful of those spines! Fenrick and Ravenna shall deal with the worm."

"He's kind of cute," Ravenna said with a bold smile. "Do you think it's yellow?"

"I think it's a nice middling green," Fenrick shouted back.

Elias unsheathed Thunderbreak while Kiran reached for the Starcaster Cannon in the pocket of his greatcoat. He withdrew the bulky, heavy gun and clicked off the safety.

"We'll see if these bullets do as they're promised," Kiran grinned. Then he turned to face the violet climber. "Come at me, you ugly bastard!"

With a keening, high-pitched howl, the daemon leapt off the roof and landed on the ground just yards away from Kiran's position. It swung its branchlike tail with destructive force. Kiran threw himself to one side, dodging the long tail. The daemon followed him, moving with fierce aggression. It opened its mouth, its skin flaps quivering, and shot out a long stream of acid. Kiran dodged again. The stream of acid struck a tree behind him, burning through the trunk.

"Watch out!" he yelled as the tree began to topple.

"Shrrriiieeeee!" the monster screamed.

Wham! The tree fell over, blocking off half the clearing with a shower of silver leaves.

As Elias watched, Kiran took shelter behind the fallen tree and raised the mana cannon, taking aim down the blunt barrel. Channeling hot mana through the palm of his prosthetic hand, Kiran charged up the shined gun. The second chamber on the cannon began to glow and spin, absorbing the excess mana so it didn't overheat and "backfire." Soon, Kiran's shined prosthetic was also glowing red with the force of his mana.

"Cheerio!" Kiran yelled as he fired off two shots. *Bam! Bam!* The cannon roared in the night. Each flash from the gun's barrel was blinding, and the kick was strong enough to send Kiran flying backward with a whoop. He landed somewhere in the forest's underbrush.

"Holy Mother of Dust!" Riordan yelled.

A shockwave rippled off the cannon with each blast. Elias felt the wind of it ruffle his hair. Ravenna and Fenrick turned to gasp in amazement at the sight.

The bullets struck the daemon's side. The monster screamed and shuddered. Dust #210 Bloodglass was brutally efficient. Veins of silver and gold ran across the creature's hide, which then began to crumble and cave inward as all the moisture evaporated from its body. Its flesh took on a fragile, glass-like appearance. Within a minute, the lizard's bones disintegrated, and it collapsed with a choked cry, unraveling into ash that evaporated on the wind.

Elias felt a surge of satisfaction at the sight. A smile stretched across his face. Yes—*that* was a gift.

Any concern for Kiran vanished from Elias's mind as his brother's wild laughter filled the clearing. Kiran was cackling like a proper maniac as he climbed back to his feet, brushing bits of leaves and grass from his coat. Elias remembered that laugh from the battlefield.

"By the Maddening Moon, that's a sight to behold!" Kiran cheered. "I'm keeping this new pet, Elias. You'll have to order another one for yourself."

"How was the kick?" Elias called.

"My shoulder isn't broken, and the gun didn't explode—so that's something," Kiran yelled back, still laughing like a mad hatter.

"I expect a full report on my desk in the morning," Elias said. "I'll hand it off to Meister Barbaros before he leaves back to his atelier in Gigas."

"It's always about work for you, isn't it?" Kiran shouted, though his complaint wasn't serious. "Fine, fine, I'll have the report on your desk before noon."

"At dawn would be preferable."

Another daemonic howl captured Elias's attention. Across the clearing, Cherry and Riordan were tackling the crimson crawler. Elias didn't feel the need to interfere—his soldiers had faced a lot worse during the war.

Using a pair of shined bracers on her wrists, Cherry projected her mana into a broad field of indigo light. The powerful mana barrier shielded Riordan as he stabbed repeatedly into the monster's flesh with a pair of shined daggers. The monster tried to whip its powerful tail about, but the barrier held it at bay.

As Elias watched, the daemon collapsed to the ground, bleeding from a dozen wounds.

Meanwhile, engaged in a separate battle, Ravenna and Fenrick charged at the big green worm. Fenrick stabbed into the daemon with a double-handed blow. With a burst of mana power, he ignited his ghost sword—Dust #361 Firefly—searing through the daemon's thick hide with yellow light. Flesh sizzled. The blade cut deep, yet the massive slug barely seemed to feel the wound. When Fenrick withdrew the blade, it was dripping with slime.

Infuriated, the wounded beast curled up into a ball and rolled across the mossy ground.

"Watch out!" Fenrick yelled as Ravenna ducked out of the way. The slug smashed through another manawood tree on its way into the forest. It barreled through the underbrush, plowing through bush and briar patch to escape the soldiers.

"Stay on him!" Ravenna roared, leaping back to her feet.

The married couple chased the giant slug into the woods, eager to put an end to the threat. Elias could have sworn he saw them holding hands, as though they were on a date. He glanced skyward. He supposed he should let the soldiers enjoy themselves. They were used to going up against hordes of daemons—not just three or four at a time. Kiran's squad could probably take on a few dozen before breaking a sweat.

As the daemonic threat passed and the night grew calm again, Elias's mind turned to other matters. His brow furrowed. Something kept nagging at him. Something Kiran had said: *"Whoever wrote the letter . . . must have a strong personal vendetta against you."*

A strong personal vendetta.

Someone had chosen the Blackwood tomb to stage this attack. The tomb itself was a message. Someone hated the Blackwood bloodline enough to orchestrate this elaborate scheme. But who? It must be someone close to his family—someone with access to the grounds.

He didn't think the villain would be content to remain at a distance. This plan was too complicated to leave in the hands of a few hired hoodlums. No—the mastermind would want a front-row seat. He or she wouldn't leave anything to chance.

Was his enemy watching now?

Elias's eyes swept over the tomb again, probing every shadow, every strange shape he could discern in the darkness under the trees. He felt a slight pressure on his neck, like he was being watched, but he couldn't say by whom.

Then, abruptly, his eyes found what he was looking for. A human shape stood—bold, confident, visible—atop the crumbling tower of the castle ruins. The figure was fully illuminated in the orange light of the Maddening Moon.

Ah.

With certainty, he knew this must be the author of the riddle.

Elias started to run.

Without a word to Kiran or the rest of his men, he took off at a sprint down the dirt path that led into the ruins of the old fortress. Elias traversed the chaotic landscape, his jaw clenched with determination. His leather boots crunched on the gravel-strewn ground. He navigated around hills of rubble and climbed over fallen pillars. Cold sweat beaded his brow, and urgency coiled in his stomach. He couldn't let the mysterious figure get away! But how did he reach the top of the tower?

He climbed up a pile of crumbled stone to a collapsed archway, which he crossed like a bridge to the top of the eastern wall. There, atop the wall, he ran along the length of the ruins, his feet dislodging loose bricks and mortar as he went. A sheer drop into a gully on his left side forced him to remain cautious. He stumbled but did not fall. The Hallowsin wind howled through the skeletal remains of the old castle, carrying the woodsy scent of pine and a metallic hint of skydust.

His eyes raised up to the tower, outlined by the light of the moon, where the mysterious figure was still present, waiting for him at the highest point of the ruins. The hollow tower leaned slightly to the side like a dead tree, its outer stones covered in a garment of ferns and vines. He reached the tower's entrance, but at a glance, he could see the spiral staircase had collapsed long ago. He would have to scale the exterior wall. His hands scrabbled for purchase, his muscles straining with the effort as he pushed on relentlessly. The burn of obsession consumed his mind. He had to know—had to *see*. Who was the enemy atop the tower? Who had penned the riddle? Who had sent the daemons?

He would arrest the villain happily and lay this nonsense to rest.

Sweat dripping from his brow, muscles straining in his arms, Elias pulled himself up the final few bricks to the top of the tower. There, he found himself teetering on a mere lip of stone with hardly room to stand up. The tower's roof had collapsed. The figure had vanished from the top of the turret into a circular chamber beneath the concave roof.

Elias dropped down into the room, landing gingerly on the ancient wooden beams that crisscrossed the tower's interior. The thick beams might have once supported a proper floor, but most of the boards had long ago rotted out. Only about half remained, with plenty of generous gaps in between them. He kept to the edge of the room, remaining close to the stone wall where the beams were firmly bolted into the tower's structure.

Across from him, a figure stood in the darkness, his hunched back turned to Elias. He could hear the fellow breathing—a heavy, unnatural sound, as though he suffered from some sort of asthma or lung damage.

"You," Elias panted, seething, mana glowing around his clenched fists. "Who are you?"

The figure shifted, proving it was real, not a ghost. A person stood across from him dressed in a shabby greatcoat of frayed, stained leather and scuffed boots. Elias couldn't tell if a stout man or a tall woman was hidden under the heavy coat. The figure's back remained turned.

"Face me! Show yourself!" Elias repeated in a commanding voice, his words echoing off the stone walls of the tower. *"Who are you?"*

"Commander Blackwood," the person spoke in a raspy voice that was somehow familiar. "Did you enjoy your birthday gift?"

A chill passed down Elias's spine. "As duke of Gravenmere, I have authority to arrest you and prosecute you to the full extent of the king's law. Surrender at once!"

The stranger laughed. Then he or she turned around to face him. Moonlight reflected off a mask of polished obsidian. Elias's breath caught in his throat. He recognized the mask instantly. Beneath it, the criminal's features were identical to his own, as if he were staring into a mirror.

Himself—the enemy.

The poetry of the moment struck him but did not last. Elias dismissed his discomfort with a flick of his hand. The criminal was wearing the shined mask he had loaned to Kiran for the duration of the ball.

"Give that back," Elias said, his mouth suddenly dry with unexpected fear. The shined object was not registered with the Department of Deviant Artifacts. No one in the kingdom knew of its existence except for him, Kiran and Meister Barbaros. Possessing such an item was illegal without registering it, but currently, that was the least of his concerns.

If the mask were to fall into the wrong hands . . . the hands of a violent terrorist, for instance . . . it could lead to catastrophic results.

"Give *what* back?" his reflection grinned. "I *am* you, Elias: both a warrior and a defender of the realm."

"You're an imposter."

"How so? I, too, sacrificed my life in the Abyss. Like you, I was resurrected and returned to this meaningless existence against my will. No one awarded me medals or named me a hero, but I suppose some sweet justice shall come of it nonetheless. Now I shall use your face to fight for my cause."

"Which is?"

"Utter annihilation of the Daemonguard and all that it stands for."

Elias was shocked. "That's absurd," he said.

"Is it?" his own voice mocked him. "The Daemonguard is a farce, a means of sending young men and women to their deaths. Tell me, the royal family is Luminous, yes? But do they *ever* send their own blood into the pit?"

"They are royals."

"They are corrupt," his reflection snarled. "King Valienthe sends his rivals' heirs into the pit, destroying any noble bloodline he wishes. Every time the Daemon King respawns, Luminary men and women are forced into the military, forced to endure the horrors of the Abyss, while the Valienthe family and all of their friends sit safely behind the throne. I will not stand for it any longer. You are a coward if you support this regime. At the king's command, you brainwash new recruits at Firehelm Fortress, convincing children to throw away their lives for an impossible cause. Why? The Daemon King is never defeated; it only respawns! Do you really think King Valienthe doesn't know how to kill it for good? His family has been sitting on the secret for generations!"

"That's a lie!" Elias snarled.

His shadow laughed mockingly. "I won't let them send more innocents to their death. I will force the Valienthe family to reveal their secrets. Peace shall be restored to the Kingdom of Forsynthia once and for all—then we shall see who is the true Hero of the Realm!"

"You're insane. The Valienthe family harbors no secrets. As for the Daemonguard—we are the only shield that stands between the daemons and the lightless commoners of this kingdom. We must be prepared for the Daemon King's resurgence at any time."

His reflection scoffed. "Do you really believe your job is that important?" The man before him crossed his arms, his jaw tilting upward, a defiant look in his eye.

Am I really this cocky and insufferable? Elias wondered.

"They put you at Firehelm to retire you. You'll never lead another campaign. Your mind is broken," his enemy sneered. "I know it. You know it. You hide it, thinking no one understands the horror you carry inside. But I know it, Elias. *I know it.* I lived it with you. Deep down, if you really thought about it, you would agree with me. Disband the Daemonguard! Don't send another innocent life into the pit."

"Who are you?" Elias demanded again.

"I am your shadow."

Elias glared. "You're a coward hiding behind riddles!"

"So what? You're just an animated corpse, fueled by survivor's guilt and self-loathing. Tell me, do you ever think about the men who died under your command? King Valienthe decorated you with *so many* medals, *Hero of the Realm.* If only the people knew the truth—how you sacrificed *thousands of lives* for your glory. You're no better than the Valienthe family—all of you, *murderers!* You left your men to be buried in the Abyss, their lives and families forgotten. How can you call yourself a hero?"

Elias found himself shaking and his head throbbing. His balance wavered. A hole in the floor behind him looked dark and inviting. The villain's words were powerful, like echoes of his own thoughts in his darkest moments.

But this man was not his reflection—nor was he some mystic embodiment of his shadow self.

This man—his enemy—had fed a pig farmer to a daemon.

"I never called myself a hero," Elias said, dismissing the villain's words from his mind. "But . . . I *am* a man of honor and duty."

Elias drew Blacklight from its sheath. He held the violet-flaming ghost sword high, fueling it with a burst of mana from his left hand. The blade flickered to life along the shined rod, burning bright purple.

Blacklight could unveil the presence of shadowhide daemons.

It seemed to work on the mask as well.

The illusion before him flickered, revealing another face beneath: a person who looked very different from himself. Under the heavy trench coat, he still couldn't discern if his enemy was a man or woman. He saw lengths of matted, oily hair and a dramatic widow's peak. Whatever they were, they were not beautiful.

The spell was broken.

Realizing their disguise had slipped, the criminal threw their arm up over their face, cringing away from Elias. They hunched down like a rodent and scurried deeper into the shadows.

"Running so soon?" Elias called after the villain, swinging Blacklight tauntingly through the air. "Come back and face me, coward!"

"I shall—when the time is right. We shall meet again, Commander Blackwood!" the person yelled in a hoarse, gasping voice.

With a decisive motion, the criminal leapt through the hole in the floor, vanishing into the depths of the crumbling tower. Elias ran to the edge of the pit but dared not follow. To plunge in blindly might lead to certain death, or at best, a broken ankle.

The criminal plummeted downward, the obsidian mask catching the light of Elias's ghost sword one last time before disappearing into the darkness below.

Elias stood alone at the top of the tower, breathing heavily, a headache pulsing behind his eyes.

The mirror was shattered, the illusion passed, but the confrontation still haunted him.

"Your mind is broken . . . You hide it, thinking no one understands the horror you carry inside. But I know it, Elias. I know it. I lived it with you."

Elias sheathed his sword, those words ringing in his ears.

Who was the masked soldier who taunted him?

He left the tower the same way he had come. Climbing down the tower's exterior wall, using sturdy vines to support his weight, was a lot easier than traversing the dark and treacherous interior. When he reached the bottom of the ruined tower, he searched the ground. He found two deep footprints in the mud just outside a gaping hole at the tower's base, where the criminal must have climbed outside before fleeing into the night. Mid-sized boots. Still no definitive sign if it was a man or a woman.

He searched the area around the tower, but his enemy had vanished. With a frustrated sigh, he finally gave up. In his mind, he recalled the flicker of a face he had discerned in the shadows when he first drew Blacklight from its sheath. Long, oily hair. Angular features. Still, he wasn't sure he could pick out the person in a crowd.

The sound of footsteps drew his attention. When he looked up, he saw Kiran and his squad approaching him through the ruins. Kiran raised his hand and flashed his red mana, signaling to him. Elias flashed his blue mana in return.

Cherry came to stand by his side. "We were worried about you, Commander. Did you see another daemon?"

"I thought I did . . . but it seems I was mistaken," Elias said.

"Was there something on top of the tower?" Fenrick inquired, squinting upward. "I thought I saw a shadow."

"So did I," Elias sighed. "There was no one."

Kiran watched him closely. Elias met his gaze. He would speak to Kiran about the shined mask in private; the other soldiers of the squad didn't know about it.

"Are you finished with the creatures in the Blackwood tomb?" Elias asked.

"Yes, the threat has been neutralized," Kiran answered him.

"Good job, soldiers. Good to see we haven't lost our edge."

Cherry tried to hide the grin from her face. Riordan came to stand nearby, tall and silent as usual. Fenrick and Ravenna smiled at each other. They looked flushed but exuberant from the brief battle.

"And I thought life after the war would be boring," Fenrick said with a grin.

"They should send more daemons," Ravenna agreed. "We'll be ready!"

"It's nice to feel useful again," Kiran said.

The members of the Daemonguard fell into rank out of habit as they waited for their commander's next orders.

Elias took a step closer to Ravenna and met the woman's dark eyes. "Ravenna, take Kiran's amulet," he said. "Do a quick search of the ruins. This is probably all of the monsters, but we should check the terrain to be certain. *Don't stray too far.* Remain close to the tomb."

Ravenna frowned, searching his expression, then she nodded curtly. The four soldiers of the Daemonguard saluted. Kiran tossed his amulet to Ravenna, who took it with a fierce grin. Then, as one, the four soldiers melted into the ruins.

Then Elias clasped his hands behind his back and faced Kiran with a scowl. "Come with me, Kiran. There's something at the Blackwood tomb I need to check."

Without further explanation, Elias started back down the path toward the tomb. His brother-in-arms fell into step by his side. As they walked, Elias asked, "Where is the shined mask, Kiran? The one I loaned you for the ball?"

His officer looked blank. "I returned it to your office."

"Where did you put it?"

"On your desk."

"Kiran—I told you the mask was a secret. It should have been secured."

"It was!"

"How?"

"I put a folder over it."

Elias groaned and pinched his nose, trying to dampen the headache that was growing behind his eyes. He would need one of Dr. Forrest's tinctures after this night.

"Why?" Kiran asked. "Did something happen to the mask?"

"Someone got their hands on it, and they're not our friend. The person who wrote that letter is a proper maniac, not your garden variety. They lured me to the top of the tower, and we had a small confrontation."

Kiran's eyes widened. "Did you get a good look at them?"

"I didn't, because they *have the mask.*"

Understanding dawned. Kiran looked pale. "The person who wrote that riddle has your shined mask? He can disguise himself to look like you whenever he wants?"

"I'm not entirely sure it's a man," Elias said, "but yes. That's the gist of it."

"Blinding stars, Elias, I'm sorry—"

"What's done is done."

"Should we report it stolen?"

Elias paused just outside the gates to the Blackwood tomb. He gathered his thoughts. "I'm not sure. It wasn't registered with the Department of Deviant Artifacts, which could look bad in the eyes of King Valienthe.

Our families are not on easy terms right now." He hesitated, thinking of the secret his enemy had taunted him with. Did the Valienthe family truly know how to kill the Daemon King? It sounded like a bald-faced lie or a groundless rumor at best. But if it were true, how did he go about proving it? Putting an end to the Daemon King once and for all took precedence before anything else. What if such knowledge existed?

"Let's not speak of this to anyone for now, until I decide what to do," Elias said. "That's an order, Kiran."

"Yes, High Commander," his officer bowed.

"Now, for our next order of business, come with me." Elias entered the courtyard around the tomb and began searching the grass. He drew Blacklight for the extra illumination as he searched the ground around each of the fallen corpses.

"What are you looking for?" Kiran asked.

Elias's hand slipped into the pocket of his jacket, where his fingers found the cool, hard edge of the metal tag he had plucked from the grass earlier that evening. He had found the tag in the grass just after rescuing Celise near the lake shrine. The square of metal was similar in size and shape to a cattle tag, though heavier, made of a strip of hammered iron.

He knew what it was, but how had it come to be at Gravenmere Castle?

Elias took the metal tag out of his pocket and tossed it to his brother-in-arms. "What do you think this looks like?" he asked.

He didn't need to see Kiran's face pale over his shoulder to know his officer's reaction. He could hear the quiver in Kiran's voice as he gasped, "This is from Firehelm's secret stock."

"Indeed." Elias found what he was looking for amidst the ashes of the violet crawler. He fished out another metal tag from between the scorched bones. He pocketed it. Then he continued toward the corpse of the green worm, looking for the next tag.

"We keep a handful of daemons in underground containment units for demonstrations for our recruits," Elias mused as he circled around the tomb. "I started the program last year. It's better that Luminous soldiers encounter a live daemon before heading into the trench."

"Yes, I know. I supported it, remember? I recall the trouble you had getting it approved by Admiral Voch."

"Well, it would seem our enemy didn't have far to transport the daemons if he got them from Firehelm Fortress. But only a few individuals know about our secret underground menagerie. Therefore, this enemy must be someone well-trusted and knowledgeable about our military base and operations to access the underground vaults."

"I could speak to the zookeeper, if you wish," Kiran offered.

"Unfortunately, Kiran, I don't think I'll be able to trust you with this investigation." Elias turned to look his officer in the eye. *"Arrest him."*

"What?" Kiran looked shocked.

Without warning, Ravenna and Fenrick emerged from the shadowy woods that surrounded the tomb. Kiran didn't struggle as each soldier took hold of one of his arms. Using shined cuffs, they locked his wrists behind his back, activating the special qualities of the metal so Kiran couldn't break free. The cuffs glowed with a soft blue light.

"What are you doing?" Kiran demanded. "Elias! This is absurd!"

Elias calmly approached his adopted brother. He reached into Kiran's white jacket and withdrew the Starcaster Cannon from his breast pocket. He transferred the gun to his own coat. Then he looked Kiran in the eye, searching his face, trying to discern if he could trust his oldest friend or if the man had turned against him.

His heart told him it couldn't be true—but his intellect argued otherwise.

"I know of six Luminous soldiers who have access to the underground vaults. Only one of them would know about the Blackwood tomb or my frequenting the area. As for my missing *artifact*, it was last in your hands. Unfortunately, Kiran, I must detain you for questioning."

His adopted brother stared at Elias with a shocked expression. "But the maniac in the tower—it couldn't be me! I was with Ravenna and Fenrick this whole time! Why would I plot against you, Elias? I am your brother and your biggest supporter. *I gave you my hand.*"

Elias didn't flinch, despite the sincerity of Kiran's words and the pleading look in his amber eyes. The Mad Dog wore the face of a military commander: stoic, emotionless, authoritative. Ravenna and Fenrick looked less certain, but neither one balked at their duty.

"Lock him up," Elias repeated. "I will question him in due time. Perhaps you are innocent, Kiran, but I must know for certain before I let you go."

"This is absurd!" Kiran repeated, a skittish laugh ripping from his throat. "Balderdash! Nonsense! *Ridiculous!*" He continued to laugh in a strained fashion as Ravenna and Fenrick escorted him about-face. Side by side, the three soldiers started the long walk back to Gravenmere Castle.

Elias turned to face his last two soldiers: Cherry and Riordan. The two stood side-by-side, polar opposites of each other. Cherry, short and fierce, barely kept her lips pressed closed; Riordan, tall, pale and somber, looked begrudgingly reproachful.

"Sir, with all due respect, I don't think Officer Kindale—" Cherry started to say, but Riordan shifted, touching his arm against hers, which was enough to silence her.

Elias pretended not to notice the lapse in protocol. Instead, he bent down and picked up another metal tag off the ground. Three tags. One more to go.

A soft clatter echoed through the shadows, interrupting the quiet night. Elias glanced up. It sounded like boots slipping over loose stones, followed by a loud splashing, sloshing sound.

Was there a pond or a lake nearby? He didn't think so.

Elias shared a look with the two remaining soldiers. Then he nodded.

Cherry took off at a sprint, eager to work out some of her frustration over Kiran's arrest. Riordan followed at a slower, more methodical pace, drawing his daggers from his belt. Elias took up the rear, his eyes roving over the ground in search of the last of the metal tags. The first three clinked softly in his pocket.

The splashing continued in the distance. The three soldiers traveled through the dense grove of manawood trees, thrusting aside large ferns and stepping around moss-covered boulders.

Then a frightened voice reached them through the shadows: *"Help! Hello? Hello? Help me!"*

Elias felt a chill run down his neck. He moved faster through the woods.

Before long, he joined Cherry and Riordan at the edge of a deep pit. The large, square hole was hidden between several crumbling cabins. It must have been a cellar or basement at one time, perhaps a servants' quarters or undercroft. All four sides of the cellar were walled in with heavy stone blocks. Whether the floor was paved or not was irrelevant, as the bottom of the ancient cellar was submerged in a deep puddle. The muddy water had yet to drain out from the recent rainstorm.

A man stood in the pit, submerged up to his calves in the fresh rainwater.

"Hello! Oh, thank the Goddess you found me! I thought I would die here! Please, get me out of this place!"

Elias came to stand at the edge of the hole. He drew his ghost sword from his hip and held Blacklight high, casting a violet glow throughout the cellar below him. There, a squat man with a round, sunburned face in muddy overalls stared up at them. The fellow was middle-aged with a white handlebar mustache and a tweed cap that had seen better days. He looked at once drenched by rain and scorched by the sun—his meaty forearms and nose were blistered red.

Elias could take a guess at the man's identity. Leaning over his knee at the edge of the pit, he called down, "You wouldn't happen to be a pig farmer by any chance?"

"I am, Your Grace!" the farmer called back. Elias recognized his rolling, lilting accent; it was common to the northern villages of his father's estate. "I was delivering a wagon of pork to the banquet for Elias Blackwood's birthday! Alas, I never made it. Bandits attacked me on the road. They took me here and fed my stock to . . . to . . . Well, you rightly won't believe me, but they fed my pigs to a pack of monsters!"

"We believe you!" Cherry called down into the pit. "Not to worry—the monsters are gone now. We've dealt with them."

"Righto! I thought my luck had changed when I heard the explosions," the farmer agreed. Despite his ordeal, he seemed to be in high spirits. "I've been hiding down here for days! I was scared to make a peep before now, in case the monsters came after me. I think the bandits assumed I would be eaten. Luckily, those creatures didn't find me. Oh, but the Goddess answered my prayers! Thank you all for saving me!"

Riordan left the side of the hole and returned with a couple of long branches. With Cherry's help, in a brief amount of time, the two soldiers fashioned a ladder to help the farmer out of the pit. Elias leapt down into the hole to help the farmer up the first half of the ladder. Despite his cheerful attitude, shallow cuts and bruises ran along the man's arms and neck. With a lot of help, the farmer was able to climb out of the muddy hole. Riordan's strong hands assisted him the final few feet to solid ground. Elias followed him up.

Once safely above ground, Cherry offered the farmer her flask of water while the old man leaned up against the side of a manawood tree.

"Do you remember any names or details about the men who kidnapped you?" Elias asked. "Do you think you would be able to recognize them?"

"They didn't use normal names, just nicknames like 'Kitty,' 'Hawk,' and 'Bucket.' I got a good look at one or two of them when they first attacked my wagon, but they kept a bag over my head the rest of the time," the farmer admitted. "I think I would be able to recognize their voices before I saw their faces."

"Well, that's something," Elias murmured. "Even if they used nicknames, we should gather as much information as possible."

"I *do* remember one name," the farmer suddenly said, his bloodshot eyes growing wide. "It was 'Dead Jackal' . . . or maybe '*Dread* Jackal?' They mentioned that name several times."

Dread Jackal? Elias was reminded of the thieves who had stolen from his treasury. He had yet to find the time to interrogate them, but he remembered the name falling from their lips several times in the forest. Was their ringleader, the "Dread Jackal," also responsible for the daemons at the Blackwood tomb? Or perhaps this jackal was working with a wide network of other criminals?

Perhaps he was the man behind the shined mask in the tower?

"Very good," Elias said, clasping his hands behind his back. He would remember the name—it gave him a place to start investigating. "That's very helpful. Once we get back to the castle, I will make sure the staff assigns you a comfortable room with a bath and a hot meal. On the morrow, once you are rested, I'll have you meet with Riordan to draw a portrait of the men who attacked you. He is a skilled artist—handy with charcoals. Try to remember every small detail you can. You'll be well compensated, I can assure you."

"Of course, my lord!" the farmer said eagerly. "I will help you in any way I can. Though I must admit, a hot meal sounds lovely. I haven't eaten in days."

Elias left Cherry and Riordan to assist the farmer while he started back to the castle at a faster pace.

As he passed through the Blackwood tomb, Elias's eye caught on a square shape in the grass, and he collected the last of the metal tags from the daemon corpses. He slipped the metal square into his pocket. Then he continued on his way through the ruins of the old castle, his thoughts burning up his head in a feverish frenzy. Much had happened in the last few hours—he would have to write it all down, or else risk forgetting the smaller details. Who was the man in the shined mask? Were the daemons transported from Firehelm Fortress? Was the mysterious riddle written by the Dread Jackal? How was it all connected?

Was Officer Kiran Kindale—his adopted brother, closest friend and confidante—in league with his enemies?

As Elias walked, he ruminated on the events of the evening, turning each small detail over and over again in his mind. *Someone* had delivered a pack of daemons to his castle. *Someone* had threatened his guests, endangered his family, and stolen from his office. Someone had attacked *his betrothed.*

He would find the culprit—by whatever means necessary.

Chapter 20

After the Ball

After a night spent in the Gravenmere infirmary, Celise woke up to the patter of rainwater dripping from the slanted roof outside her window.

Drip. Drip. Drip.

She cracked open her eyes and looked toward the gentle sound. Next to her cot, a tall window revealed a dim, gray morning outside the infirmary. Her eyes were met by a wall of swirling mist. She couldn't see the castle's grounds below or the distant gardens—it seemed Gravenmere was enveloped in a fogbank.

On the other side of the infirmary, a cheery fire battled against the moist air of the castle. The flames did little to warm the room. Celise shivered under her blanket. It seemed the cold weather of Hallowsin had finally arrived. She already craved a cup of Mordwen's apple-cinnamon tea.

Celise lay still for a moment in her bed, gazing at the white, featureless fog outside the window. She felt . . . calm. Serene. Empty. Her mind was like the placid waters of a lake.

Then, finally, after several minutes, a bit of memory stirred. With a terrible lurch, she recalled Lord Elias Blackwood dropping to one knee before her in the ballroom to propose. The flash of cameras. The gasp of the crowd.

"Before the stars, by dust and by death—I choose you."

Celise felt her stomach twist, a strange flutter in her heart.

Lord Elias had proposed to her in front of the Forsynthian elite. The papers had been there—a photo was taken.

Was she to be the next duchess of Gravenmere?

No, she told herself. *I won't fall under the same spell as Katrina! I don't want to be betrothed to a duke!*

Yet, in the old shrine next to the pond, she had kissed him.

—his lips warm and teasing, his skilled mouth summoning an addictive heat to her body, his hands cupping her jaw. Her first taste of passion.

She had kissed the Mad Dog duke.

No, no, no, she thought. No, it was a mistake. The night was more of a fever dream than a reality.

But her troublesome heart quickened again, rising into her throat, as a pleasant warmth tickled her stomach.

What was this vulnerable feeling?

The sharp cadence of a female voice interrupted her revelry.

Oh no.

"I didn't realize Gravenmere had an infirmary wing! I suppose that fits, considering the castle's history. Bit of a maze in this place, isn't it? Oh, here's the door. We must collect her before our train leaves. I'm sure you understand our urgency, doctor."

"Please lower your voice, Lady Dhastel. Your daughter might still be sleeping."

"Lazeabout that she is, I hope she's awake!"

Celise sat up in bed as the door blew open. The mana doctor, Drandem Forrest, entered with Marcella on his heels. Her stepsisters weren't far behind. Her stepmother swooped into the room like a furious hawk, her eyes scanning the empty beds until they alighted on Celise. The fine ladies were all dressed in modest daywear: square-cut necklines and fluffed-out petticoats beneath their pastel skirts. Padded bustles lent form to the back of their dresses. Their leisure clothes, fit for traveling on the train, were not as grand as their ballgowns from the night before.

Oh no, the train!

Celise watched her family approach with a sense of dread. They were supposed to depart from Gravenmere Castle today and begin the long journey back to Windhaven Estate. The fog outside the window made it difficult to gauge the time. She wasn't sure when their train was supposed to depart.

Marcella bustled through the room to Celise's bedside, her two daughters in tow. She didn't see Lord Dhastel with Marcella. If Celise had to guess, her father had spent the night gaming with other members of Old Blackwood's inner circle. Wherever he was now, he likely had a roaring hangover.

"There you are, Celise!" Marcella gasped and leaned over her bed, dragging back the covers from Celise's body. Thankfully, she still wore a medical gown, though she didn't think Marcella would have cared if she were naked and humiliated in front of the room. "There's much yet to do this morning, and the train leaves this afternoon! Do you know where your father has gone?"

"I don't. Maybe the Gravenmere servants know?" Celise said groggily.

Marcella raised an arched eyebrow as though Celise had said something insulting. Then she turned to Dr. Forrest, who remained hovering by the door.

"Medic, did my husband not accompany Celise to the infirmary last night?"

"He did not," Forrest's tired voice reached them. "Lord Elias escorted her."

"I see. So then, where is my husband?"

"I do not know, my lady."

"Well, can't you call for the steward and ask?"

"I'm afraid the steward is busy assisting His Grace with all the guests in attendance," Forrest said politely. "But I can ring for a hall boy. They're quite clever. I'm sure someone must know of your husband's whereabouts."

"A hall boy? No, I demand a valet!" Marcella began fussing with Forrest, insisting he call for a higher-ranking servant to find her husband, while Forrest tried to convince her that none were available.

Celise tried to ignore her stepmother's high-pitched, grating voice. She was still a bit groggy from the long night. She glanced down at her arm, noticing that someone had removed the shined circlet from her wrist. Her forearm was wrapped in soft linen bandages where the daemon's poison had burned her. She stretched it out experimentally. It felt alright, though a bit sore.

Then more shocking memories of the night before struck her like tiny lightning bolts. Forrest's words echoed in her mind: *"I've never encountered a case like yours, not in twenty years of practice."*

Celise sucked in a quick gasp.

She was born a Luminary.

A wave of strange grief mingled with repressed hope swelled through her heart. Part of her floatiness, she was sure, came from the influence of the mana-infused discs she had slept with the night before. She searched the bed for them, but it seemed the discs had been removed and put away. Then she ran her hands down her torso, inspecting her body. She glanced over her arms and legs but saw no visible difference. She tried not to feel disappointed. Dr. Forrest had said her mana channels likely wouldn't recover.

With a frown of concentration on her face, she tried to sense anything different about her body—some spark of latent energy—but she felt the same as always. Just a normal, unspectacular dunslug.

Her eyes returned to Marcella's face. She watched the scowl form on her stepmother's features as she argued with Dr. Forrest about her husband's whereabouts. Celise felt a growing sense of suspicion. Did Marcella know about her clipped channels? Would her stepmother do such a thing on purpose? She caught her lower lip between her teeth and bit down softly in thought. No, despite Marcella's abuse, she didn't think her stepmother knew anything about her condition. According to Forrest, her channels had been clipped during infancy, which implicated the midwife, or . . . her father.

Would her father do such a thing? Why?

Her brow darkened further.

Why would he turn her into a dunslug on purpose? Or was it a terrible accident? A taste of uncertainty entered her thoughts. Was that the reason for her father's feigned indifference toward her? Perhaps he felt so guilty he couldn't even look her in the eye.

Was it a conspiracy? A cover-up? An assassination attempt gone wrong?

Celise shook her head at herself. No, that seemed like far too much intrigue for her boring, sad life.

Other than her father, Mordwen was the only person on the manor staff who would remember the midwife and the days that followed Celise's disastrous birth. Most of the staff had turned over since then, especially with Marcella's pickiness. Only Mordwen would remember what might have happened, and perhaps Mr. Talisworth, though he was hired on a few years later. She had never thought to ask him about his history at the ranch—he seemed like a fixture around the property, although he was not very old yet.

Interrupting her thoughts, Marcella threw up her arms. "I suppose I'll have to go look for my husband myself!" she exclaimed, casting a glare at Dr. Forrest. "Since you refuse to be of any help, I'll go fetch my own servant, Dasha, and waste even more time crossing the grounds back and forth from the Moongazer Tower. Ridiculous. I will most certainly mention this to Cornelius when I see him."

Celise noticed how her stepmother used Old Blackwood's first name as though they were good friends. But the doctor didn't seem concerned. Forrest tilted his head, a sign of modest respect, or perhaps a mocking sort of apology.

"Please be sure to express any complaints you might have, my lady," he said.

"I will!" Marcella snapped. Then over her shoulder, she said, "You girls stay here. I'll be back as soon as I find your father."

Lady Dhastel bustled out of the room with her nose in the air and cheeks flushed with anger. Celise wondered if she would slam the door behind her—as she would have at the manor—but Marcella restrained herself. At least at the castle, she was still attempting to comport herself with some class.

After her dramatic exit, Dr. Forrest quietly crossed the room to stand at the foot of Celise's bed. The doctor was dressed in the same white jacket as the night before, though his crooked buttons were fixed. The only marking on his jacket denoting his station was a blue medical insignia on his shoulder. He looked tired, and a bit of redness tinged his eyes.

Despite his obvious exhaustion, he gave her a kindly look that put her at ease.

"Good morning, Lady Celise. How are you feeling today?"

"Much better, thank you."

He adjusted his glasses and glanced over her again. By the intensity of his eyes, he was peering into her mana body. It made her feel a bit self-conscious.

"I'm afraid to say nothing has changed after our treatment last night. I'm referring to what we talked about. You know . . . your condition." Dr. Forrest glanced over at Celise's two sisters, who were wandering about the room, curiously looking at the shined tools and equipment. They seemed a bit lost and uncomfortable without Marcella's domineering presence. Katrina glanced over at Drandem twice, trying to hide the fact that she was eavesdropping.

Celise appreciated Dr. Forrest's instinct to keep her diagnosis private.

"I understand," she whispered.

"It's to be expected. The damage is extensive, so as I explained last night, it's likely not recoverable." Forrest gave her a sympathetic look. "We've done what we can for now, with the tools we have on hand."

"Is there anything more I can do?" Celise tried to keep her disappointment hidden, but her voice cracked anyway.

Dr. Forrest pushed his glasses up the bridge of his nose. He cleared his throat. "Not at Gravenmere Castle, no. But . . . some larger hospitals in the royal city of Astravelle are equipped to do more extensive procedures. There is high risk involved. I wouldn't suggest it for someone like yourself."

"I see." Celise nodded, casting her eyes down. *There's nothing to be done about it,* she told herself, trying to push her disappointed feelings away. *It's not like I've lost anything. My life is just as it's always been.*

Dr. Forrest continued in a soft voice, "Lord Elias asked me to prepare a tincture for you to alleviate any discomfort you might feel while you travel. It will help you sleep as well. I expect you'll be a bit under the weather for the next few days, as the daemon's toxicity works its way out of your body."

The doctor set down a stoppered glass bottle on the bedside table next to her. That's when Celise noticed the Starlight Dahlia sitting in a vase on the tableside. She reached for the flower and picked it up, lightly touching the white petals, which were almost completely closed. She set it down next to her on the bed.

Dr. Forrest continued, "Lord Elias asked me to apologize on his behalf—he can't attend to you this morning. His patrol found more daemons on the grounds last night, and Senior Officer Kiran Kindale has been taken into custody. They're arranging to transport him back to Firehelm Fortress. It's serious business, as I'm sure you can imagine, my lady."

Celise paled. "I hope everyone is alright."

"Of course. They're trained for this sort of thing, unlike you or me." Dr. Forrest gave her a reassuring smile. "Not to worry, I'm sure he will reach out to you soon. And I should add—congratulations on your engagement."

Celise nodded with wide eyes. "You mean, he hasn't called it off yet?"

"Yet?" Dr. Forrest frowned. "Why would he do that?"

"My . . . my condition . . . I don't have mana."

"Ah." Dr. Forrest patted her shoulder reassuringly. "I wouldn't overthink it, my dear. Elias is a tactical man. He doesn't make decisions on a whim. I don't think he would announce an engagement to the kingdom's elite and then disregard it the next day."

Celise swallowed past the lump in her throat. Perhaps that was true, but Elias didn't have all the facts last night when he proposed to her in the ballroom.

"Please pass along my gratitude to His Grace," she said politely, her voice soft.

The doctor bowed. "Once you are ready to leave, my lady, if you'll just sign your name in the book at the front counter and the time you left, that would be most helpful. We keep a record of all of our patients."

"I can do that," Celise agreed.

The doctor left her side, crossing back through the room. As he walked away, Celise felt a stab of disappointment. The strength of the emotion surprised her, and she had a difficult time pushing it down. Lord Elias's absence from her bedside confirmed her worst fears—he was simply fulfilling his duty to the crown. Their engagement wasn't as important as his military work. He didn't harbor any true feelings for her. She doubted he wanted to see her again before she left the castle.

"I'll be back in about an hour," Dr. Forrest said as he gathered a stack of papers on his desk. "Please ring the bell at your bedside if you need anything. It will summon a servant." Then he left the infirmary and closed the door behind him.

No sooner had the door clicked shut than Katrina and Heather came to huddle at the foot of Celise's bed. Heather's eyes were wide and a little sparkly. She leaned in close and whispered, "Oh my, but the doctor is handsome, isn't he? He seemed so kind and caring! You're so lucky, Celise, to have all these men doting on you!"

"*Harrumph!* He's just doing his job," Katrina snapped, her lips curled in disgust. "Why are you lying around in bed, Sluggy? You don't seem injured to me."

Celise stiffened. She thought of the night before, when her younger sister had shoved her in front of the daemon. She caught Katrina's eye.

"Are you disappointed?" Celise asked, finally letting her anger show. "You meant for the daemon to *eat me* when you pushed me in front of it!"

Katrina's smirk wavered on her face.

Heather looked shocked. "Katrina, what does she mean?"

"Nothing," Katrina snapped. "She's misremembering."

"I'm not misremembering!" Celise exclaimed, sitting up straighter. Anger strengthened her voice. "You told me to lure the daemon away from you! You told me it's what *any good servant* would do. Then you threw me in front of the monster to make your escape! You left me to die!"

"Oh please, don't act like such a victim. Obviously you turned out fine. The duke proposed—your scheme worked—you're the hero of the hour."

Heather glanced between her two sisters with troubled eyes. Her gaze lingered on Katrina in a distrustful, apprehensive way. Katrina saw Heather's expression and crossed her arms before her voluptuous chest.

"What?" she snapped. "Stop staring at me. What's wrong with you?"

Heather sighed. "I'm just happy you both survived a terrible ordeal unscathed. It's been a long night, so let's not argue."

Katrina snarled, "I'm not arguing—Celise is *wrong,* and that's a fact!"

Ignoring her sister, Heather came to stand close to Celise's bedside and continued, "I'm very glad a daemon *didn't* eat you in the gardens. I couldn't sleep last night; I was so frightened. I made Dasha check under my bed twice for monsters. I haven't done that since I was little. It's good to see you safe and sound!"

"Thank you, Heather."

The youngest Dhastel sister gave her a shy smile, then sent a guilty glance at Katrina, as though she were doing something she shouldn't. Celise returned her smile just as hesitantly. Heather wasn't mean-spirited like Katrina or Marcella. Her worst trait was her spinelessness. She had a bad habit of "going along to get along," even when Celise was being bullied. But Heather never seemed to wish her harm. She couldn't imagine Heather pushing her in front of a rampaging monster, for instance.

Uncomfortable with the peaceful silence, Katrina sneered and said, "I'm disappointed in the duke. He must have a soft spot for damsels in distress. It's so *traditional,* it makes my skin crawl. Ugh."

"I think it's kind of sweet," Heather muttered, but her words were lost in Katrina's tirade.

"Now I see my mistake," the dark-haired beauty continued her rant. "I should have stood around like a fool waiting to be eaten! Then I would have caught the duke's eye! Instead, I had the good sense to run for my life, and this is how I'm repaid." Katrina shot Celise a look of pure loathing.

"Why are you *really* upset, Katrina?" Celise asked in a weary voice.

Katrina looked furious. Then her truth came pouring out in an emotional flood: "You knew about my feelings for the duke! I confided in you! Then you *pretended* to comfort me last night in the gardens, all while plotting to steal Elias away from me. *How could you?* You're worse than that vulture, Ambrosia! You're a scheming wench. You had your eye on him all along, and you acted *so* innocent. I hate you! I hate your ugly face, your bastard blood, and your common, dimlit bones! You're an imposter! *You stole my fate!*"

Those words rang out in the room, and a brief silence followed.

Celise paled a bit. *"You stole my fate!"*

Did Katrina know about Mordwen's fortune telling? No, she couldn't possibly have heard about the Abyssal Rose and Valestra's Wand. Katrina's accusation was a heartfelt feeling and a brutal coincidence.

"I-I didn't!" Celise stuttered. "It just happened that way."

"You can't even take responsibility. How *common* of you."

Katrina's fists were bunched at her sides as though she wanted to punch the wall. Celise saw a glow of mana around her hands. She cringed backward, her heart quickening. She wondered if Katrina would attack her in the infirmary.

"I did not steal him away from you," Celise repeated. "Elias is a man with his own thoughts and feelings. The duke made his choice."

"You're right—he simply chose the *easiest* option. You seduced him in the gardens, didn't you? You must have spread your legs *to thank him* for his heroism—"

At that moment, the door to the infirmary blew open. Celise turned toward it with a gasp, while Katrina stopped mid-sentence, a pink tinge to her cheeks.

The short, choppy cadence of two Bratzian accents filled the room.

"She's in here? Is this correct?" Ismara said.

"This looks good," Ilyana agreed.

The Bratzian twins entered the medical room at a quick pace. Ismara held a bouquet of flowers in hand. When she saw Celise, a smile alighted on her full lips.

"Celise! At last, we found you!"

The two ladies crossed the room. Unlike Heather and Katrina, they didn't wear any bustle or crinoline to support their skirts. Instead, their soft robes were cinched at the waist with sashes of bright satin, and their dresses were woven of rich cloth that resembled peacock feathers.

Katrina and Heather were forced to step back as the twins approached Celise's bedside. Ismara thrust the bouquet of flowers into Celise's hands. The cluster of white roses and yellow daisies smelled divine.

Celise felt a bit confused by the sudden interruption. It took her a moment to clear her head of Katrina's venting. She took a deep breath to settle herself, then she focused on the Bratzian twins and ignored her sisters.

"The proposal was all anyone would talk about this morning at brunch!" Ismara gushed. "It was a shock for everyone. The duke didn't even dance with you at the ball! In fact, some of the ladies say there might have been *two dukes* attending the gala. Can you imagine? It's all so mysterious!"

"Much speculation," Ilyana said in her thick accent.

"But we are so happy for you!" Ismara quickly added.

"Yes, so happy, *supramin'ka!*"

"That means 'congratulations,'" Ismara laughed.

Katrina turned away to look out the window, hiding her scowl.

The twins seemed oblivious to the tense atmosphere in the room. Heather looked relieved by their interruption. Celise felt the same way; she smiled brightly at the two women. At least, as brightly as she could while her body felt like a heavy sandbag. "Thank you; truly, it means a lot."

"We heard you were too sick to come down for breakfast," Ismara said. "We were worried for you! But I'm glad to see you are doing well. It must have been terrifying to face down a daemon!"

"It was pretty frightening," Celise agreed.

"The castle is crawling with reporters," Ismara added, her hazel eyes growing wide. "Everyone is getting interviewed. You're lucky not to be outside. They would jump on you!"

"Oh yes, they would tackle you to the ground!" Ilyana laughed.

"Nobody believes the proposal is real. They all think it's staged," Katrina sneered from her place near the window, unable to help herself. "Everyone wants to know about the 'great Sluggy,' future duchess of Gravenmere! I'm so sick of hearing your name. It's not like you're *a royal*."

Ismara and Ilyana both looked up, shocked by Katrina's sarcasm. Then the twins glanced at each other with unreadable expressions, perhaps confused by her animosity.

"But she is your sister," Ismara said. "Aren't you happy for her?"

"Forsynthian families are strange," Ilyana muttered.

Catching the girls' reproachful looks, Katrina switched to gloating. "Of course I'm happy for our family. I've already been approached by *three* reporters about the daemon in the gardens last night," she bragged. "That's the real story—not the engagement. One of the journalists from *The Lady's Letter* gave me her card. Oh, she was wonderfully witty! She asked me to give a personal interview, a bit of a 'tell-all.' I promised to send her *every last detail* I can remember."

Katrina's eyes glinted with wicked glee.

Celise tried to appear indifferent, but she felt the blood drain from her cheeks. She had a terrible suspicion her sister would exaggerate the night's events. *The Lady's Letter* was a gossip column, so they wouldn't care if some of the details were fabricated.

Celise shared an apprehensive look with the twins.

Misunderstanding the full extent of her fear, Ismara patted her hand and tried to reassure her, "Don't worry about all the reports. Enjoy your moment! It's an exciting day. The guests are happy to have something to talk about; that's all."

Celise nodded. She tried to absorb Ismara's comforting words, but she still felt nervous. She had never been the center of attention like this before. She hoped the gossip would pass quickly and soon be forgotten.

"We have to go now, but we wanted to give this to you," Ismara said. She pressed a small letter into Celise's hand. "This is an invitation to our townhome. We are staying for a month in Castleberry City. Old Blackwood has provided our father, Meister Barbaros, with a house in the city for the next few weeks. I heard Castleberry is not far from Windhaven Ranch. Please come visit us. Here is the address. You may write to us as well!"

"Yes, please write," Ilyana nodded, her hazel eyes sparkling. "I'll practice my Forsynthian letters."

"Thank you," Celise said with sincere feeling. The twins couldn't possibly know how rare and wonderful she found their invitation. She struggled for a moment, feeling sentimental tears sting her eyes. Then she leaned forward and gave the two girls a hug, squishing the bouquet of flowers between them.

"I will make sure to write," she promised.

As the Bratzian twins turned to leave, the infirmary's door opened again. Marcella reappeared with Dasha and Lord Dhastel in tow. Dasha was carrying a carpetbag in hand. Lord Dhastel was still dressed in his vestments from the night before, his tailored coat rumpled and his cravat undone. He looked *very* hungover. Celise was not surprised.

The twins bowed to both Lord and Lady Dhastel as they left the room. The girls shut the door softly behind them.

Celise's father wobbled for a moment on his feet. He reached out and pressed his hand against the wall. After teetering for a moment, he slouched down on one of the cots with a groan and lay back, resting his head on a pillow.

"Sebastian, pull yourself together! We must get ready for the train!" Marcella cried.

Her husband waved off Marcella with a weary hand. "There will be time for that later."

"There is no time!"

As Marcella dealt with her sloshed husband, Dasha rushed to Celise's bedside. She looked flustered. The young maid set down her carpetbag at the foot of the bed and opened it. She pulled out a mossy dress of sprigged green cotton and a long white shift.

"Come along, my lady, we must get you ready for the train!" Dasha said. "I'm so relieved to see you made it safely through the night. The servants are telling wondrous stories about how Lord Elias saved you from the daemon in the gardens. I've heard at least fifteen different versions this morning. Come now, let's get you groomed and dressed for the day. We don't have much time. Have you eaten?"

"I will eat on the train," Celise said. "I don't wish to make us any later than we already are."

"I'll ask the kitchen to pack a lunch basket for us to take on the carriage. It's the least they can do for the future duchess," Dasha said with a wink.

Marcella snorted at those words. Celise glanced over at her stepmother, but the woman was turned away, tending to her husband.

When Celise looked back at Dasha, the maid was biting her lower lip in a mischievous way. "*Oops*," Dasha mouthed. Then the cheerful maid helped her up from the bed and led Celise behind the dressing screen at the corner of the room.

As Dasha helped her out of her medical gown and into her day clothes, she leaned in close and asked in a soft voice, "So, should I assume Lord Elias is the owner of that mysterious frock coat in your trunk?"

Celise's mouth gaped open like a caught fish. She had completely forgotten about the coat!

"I checked it again this morning just out of curiosity, and I couldn't help but notice the initials E. B. sewn into the neckline of the collar," Dasha whispered. "Soldiers always sew their initials into their uniforms.

I could tell from the cut it's a military jacket. Anyway, it's in your trunk. A nice souvenir of the weekend, don't you think?"

Celise was horrified. So, her maid had put it all together, just like that?

"Dasha, please, you can't tell anyone about the coat!" Celise hissed, her voice soft. "I was going to have you return it to him—

"Don't worry, I won't tell anyone. You should give the coat back to him when you see him next." With a smile, the maid added, "I'm happy for you. Truly, I am."

"Thank you, Dasha . . . but I don't think this betrothal is going to last."

"Why do you say that?"

"Because Elias knows the truth—I have no mana. He would never marry someone like me. He's the Hero of the Realm . . . it would disgrace his family name."

"Oh." Dasha sucked on her bottom lip. Finished with the buttons on Celise's dress, the helpful maid undid her braid and started brushing out her hair. "Well, my lady, let's not go fishing for trouble. These are modern times—women can own businesses, join the military and inherit land. Love matches are in vogue. Perhaps the duke isn't all that worried about his family's reputation." Dasha gave her shoulders a small squeeze. "We'll just have to wait and find out."

Chapter 21

The Train Home

As morning turned into afternoon, the fog lifted and the tepid sun of Hallowsin appeared in the rugged blue sky. The afterglow of the ball clung to Gravenmere Castle like a dream that refused to fade. The servants were lively, and laughter filled the halls. Outside, in front of the castle, noble families from across the realm boarded their carriages, assisted by footmen and drivers, to return home.

Considering her new engagement, Celise expected Old Blackwood to see them off in lieu of his son, but the steward met them instead at the front door. Mr. Bernard Friza apologized profusely for the old duke, who had yet to recover from the night's revelries. Lord Dhastel shared a knowing laugh with the steward while Marcella fumed quietly in the background. Celise buried her smile behind her bouquet.

"Don't look so smug, you little chit," Marcella snapped when she caught Celise's smirk. "If you were a proper match for Lord Elias, the whole Blackwood tribe would be seeing you off. This is a huge disrespect to our family!"

"Now, now, Marcella, Old Blackwood is getting on in years, and we aren't the only guests in attendance—" her father began.

"You're the worst of *all of them*, Sebastian. I won't deign to mention how I found you this morning. I am utterly disgusted."

Her father flushed red and dropped his eyes, looking suitably cowed. Heather and Katrina's ears perked. Celise kept her eyes focused on the wallpaper, schooling her face to be utterly blank of expression. Celise wondered what her father had gotten up to the night before and where Marcella had found him.

Then Marcella sailed past her like a battleship. The irate noblewoman passed by the butler, who was holding the door open for them, and down the front steps of the castle.

Luckily, no reporters stopped them on the brief walk from the castle's front door to their carriages. Dasha handed up their luggage to the drivers. Her stepsisters climbed into the first carriage while her father and stepmother boarded a second one.

Celise lingered for a moment before climbing into the coach after her sisters. Her eyes scanned the castle doors, the fountains and the hedgerows. Several other families were settling into similar carriages up and down the drive. She waited longer than necessary, hoping to catch sight of a familiar black-haired soldier in a decorated military jacket.

But Elias did not appear.

She tried to quell the creeping sense of dread within her. Marcella's words were harsh, but something about them rang true. Did the Blackwood family truly not care about the engagement at all? She didn't know what to think.

"What are you waiting for, Sluggy?" Katrina called to her. "You'll make us late for the train."

With a sigh, Celise pulled herself up into the polished wooden coach. The driver whistled to his team of horses and cracked his whip. Then the Dhastel family started on their way.

The two carriages would carry them from Gravenmere Castle down a long country road to the train station at Bloomheather Crossing, where a train would transport them to Castleberry City. From there, they would switch trains to Sultan, then arrange a second coach to carry them to

Windhaven Estate. It would be a long and boring journey. Celise was not looking forward to sitting on hard wooden benches for the next two days. She felt a bit out of sorts since leaving the infirmary: some weakness in her legs and a bit lightheaded, just as Dr. Forrest had warned. Dasha was carrying her medicine in her carpetbag, and Celise would probably take it on the train.

Her bouquet resting in her lap, Celise gazed out the window as the carriage passed through the iron gates of Gravenmere Castle, which slowly disappeared behind a screen of tall maple trees. She wondered if she would ever visit the Blackwood estate again. The Starlight Dahlia was neatly hidden among the white roses in her bouquet; none of her sisters had mentioned it. She hoped to get it safely home without their notice. Dasha had wrapped the bouquet in a wet rag to keep the stems moist.

As the carriage rolled on, Katrina sulked while Heather reveled in memories of the ball. Dasha worked on a bit of sewing in her lap. Celise settled back against the hard wooden bench and prepared for a long and ponderous ride.

She was just drifting off to sleep when the carriage began to slow down. It seemed far too soon to have reached Bloomheather Crossing. She heard the driver call out and click to the horses. "Whoa now! *Ease up, boys!*"

"What's going on?" Heather asked, confused, and turned to look out the window. Katrina also craned her neck, trying to see outside.

A patrol of mounted soldiers—each grim-faced in dark indigo uniforms—pulled up behind the carriage. Celise craned her neck to see who it was. The soldiers sat atop four brown steeds. She counted two women and two men. With a start, she remembered them from the night before, gathered on the veranda with Kiran Kindale.

In the lead, mounted atop his stormy black stallion, Tempest, was a man she didn't expect to see.

Celise's breath caught.

In an instant, all of Marcella's scathing words and Katrina's jealous sneers vanished from her mind.

Lord Elias Blackwood was dressed in a long black greatcoat buttoned up to his neck in a conservative fashion. His military medals flashed in the midafternoon sun. His black hair fell across his brow in a careless tousle, as though he hadn't bothered to comb it yet that morning. A half-mask hid part of his face and the worst of his scars. The high collar of his coat hid some of the damage along his neck, but when the wind blew, his malformed ear was impossible to ignore.

Elias's eyes locked on hers through the window. Celise stared at him, frozen in her seat, unable to comprehend what was happening.

"My lady," Dasha admonished. "Open the window; he wishes to speak to you!"

Hands shaking and fingers numb, Celise fumbled with the window's latch on the coach door. It was stuck, and her grip strength suddenly seemed to be lacking. With a groan, Dasha reached past her and forced the window open with a firm shove.

Celise peeked outside like a guilty child.

"My lady," Elias said. "An escort has been arranged for your family's safe passage to the train station."

"An escort?" Celise stuttered. "Is that necessary?"

"No less than four daemons were found on Gravenmere grounds last night," Elias said, his gray eyes unreadable behind his mask. "I wish to ensure the safety of our guests—especially you, Lady Celise."

"Oooh!" Heather cooed, as though the duke had just recited a love poem.

Katrina jabbed her younger sister with a pointed elbow.

Elias ignored the other girls in the carriage. His gaze remained fixed on Celise, stern and intense. *Th-thump.* She found her eyes sliding to his lips, remembering their brief embrace from the night before. She nodded and hiccuped, her cheeks flushing red with embarrassment.

Then she shrank back against her seat, her heart pounding, wondering at her reaction to his softly spoken words.

Katrina leaned toward the window, a wide smile on her face, and clapped her hands primly. "How very gallant! We are honored to have *the hero who defeated the Daemon King* escort our carriage back to the train station. We will feel very safe along the way! Aren't we *so lucky,* Celise? Really, you should thank His Grace." Katrina darted a little sneer at Celise across the box. "Where are your manners?"

Dasha looked horrified. Heather giggled into the back of her hand.

"Yes, thank you," Celise managed. "That's very thoughtful of you, Your Grace."

Elias raised an eyebrow, his stern gaze falling upon Katrina, who smiled up at him brazenly. Then he looked at the bouquet of flowers in Celise's lap. His eyes picked out the Starlight Dahlia. When his gaze returned to Celise's own, a quiet smile hovered about his lips. She didn't imagine it.

"Very good," Elias said. "Let us continue on our way." Then he tapped the side of the carriage, indicating the driver should continue down the road.

As the carriage pulled forward, Dasha closed the window with some difficulty. Then she sat back with a huff.

"Well, that was exciting!" the maid said, shooting a smile at Celise.

"He's just . . . fulfilling his duty," she replied, trying to deflect Katrina's bitter scowl. "It doesn't mean anything."

"You're so modest," Dasha teased.

Celise glanced down at her bouquet and refused to look up again.

Outside, the team of horses snorted, and their harnesses jingled in anticipation of the long ride. With a low cry, the driver's whip cracked, and the carriages creaked forward again. With a gentle rocking motion, the Dhastel caravan continued its journey away from Gravenmere Castle through the acres of untamed countryside.

Celise kept her back pressed against the wooden bench, her heart thudding erratically in her chest. Her eyes met Katrina's again, and she saw the open look of disgust on her sister's face. No need to hide her loathing now that they were alone.

"Really, Sluggy, I can't imagine you as a duchess," her younger sister sneered. "You can't even thank your betrothed for an escort of soldiers?"

Celise felt ashamed. She couldn't argue with Katrina—she, too, was frustrated at her shyness. Elias deserved better.

She turned to stare resolutely out the window at the scenery, hoping to catch a glimpse of the soldiers riding next to their small procession.

Before long, the turrets of Gravenmere Castle faded behind them, becoming no more than a distant silhouette at the foot of the Grapevine Mountains.

The carriage bumped along a dirt country road toward Bloomheather Crossing, where the rail line would carry them eastward to the Dhastel estate.

Despite the possible threat of daemons, the ride to the train station was uneventful. To one side of Celise's carriage, rolling hills interrupted by pockets of forest moved slowly past the window. On the other side, a wide expanse of wild grass and meandering vineyards stretched across the valley. Little brown swallows darted back and forth across the road, chasing after the carriage and twittering at the horses. Butterflies fluttered through the wildflowers amidst fields of tall grass, frolicking from dainty bluebells to yellow buttercups to patches of white clover. Lazy dragonflies hovered in the shadows beneath the oak trees that grew sporadically along the road. In early Duskwane, just before the leaves changed color and harvest began, the warm afternoons were languid and peaceful.

Celise pressed her fingers gently to the glass window.

Outside, riding alongside the carriage at a steady pace, was Elias.

At times his majestic horse, Tempest, trotted parallel to her window. At times Tempest dropped back or strode forward. But Elias remained close to her carriage the entire way.

Golden afternoon sunlight softened the hard angles of the duke's face: sharp cheekbones, a firm chin and a wide mouth pressed into a solemn line. Dark hair fell elegantly to the side of his face. On horseback, he looked more rugged and less princely than he had the night before; his clothes were plain and unadorned, the garb of a military man, not a rich noble. It suited him. His gaze remained trained on their surroundings, scanning the fields and hills for any sign of trouble. Performing his duty. A concerned soldier, nothing more.

Then he glanced toward her window.

Their eyes met. Just a flicker.

Celise flushed and sat back, hoping her sisters hadn't noticed. Katrina's solemn silence was like a gray cloud over the whole carriage. The inside of the cab was tense and quiet, despite the beautiful day outside.

Dasha unpacked their lunch basket provided by Gravenmere's kitchens: a cold buffet of soft cheese, crackers, fruit and generous slices of smoked sausage. Celise ate quietly while Heather pointed to landmarks outside the window, sharing what she knew of the geography.

Their meal finished, Dasha dozed beside Celise, her head cushioned by a soft shawl. Heather gave up her geography lesson and cracked open a book of poetry. Katrina stewed as she nibbled on the last few grapes from the basket and picked at her nails.

Celise chanced another look outside the window, admiring the pale dun markings on Tempest's powerful flanks. The dun gene was more apparent in the afternoon light. Under the cover of darkness, the large stallion had appeared perfectly black with only the slightest shimmer of a dun pattern beneath his coat. Now she saw how Tempest's legs were a deeper black—as though dipped in ink—than his smoky body. The opaque, almost cheetah-patterned dun markings along his flanks and hips lent a silvery buff to the stallion's coat, like faded charcoal against black ink. She had never seen anything quite like it. The stallion was remarkably beautiful, stocky and muscular like a draft horse, though of smaller build overall, making it more manageable for a single rider.

She could imagine the stallion fighting a daemon—its thick legs and sharp hooves looked capable of crushing bones.

Elias handled the large horse with skill, one hand holding the reins, the other propped up on his leg, completely at ease, as though he were born in the saddle. Against his hip, she saw a long, narrow sheath.

It must be a ghost blade, she reasoned.

She wondered what it would be like to go on a ride with the duke. The thought filled her with a burst of exhilaration. She recalled her brief flight through the forest on Tempest's back. The Hellion was utterly fearless—and impossible to control, unless he went along with you. She had barely managed to stay in the saddle.

She wondered if she would ever ride Tempest again—if she had the courage to win over such a horse.

She thought, perhaps, she did.

She wondered what would happen after she returned home. The duke hadn't given any indication that he meant to court her like a proper lady. Marcella wouldn't allow it; she already knew. Her stepmother would do anything to stop this marriage from taking place. Katrina was her favorite—only Katrina deserved to become a duchess.

Once they returned to the Dhastel estate, it wouldn't take long for Marcella to punish her for stealing away Katrina's destiny.

Celise's gaze out the window became decidedly less happy. Elias had no idea about her life. She supposed she was grateful for his protection, as impersonal as it seemed.

Then Elias dropped back out of sight, responding to one of the voices of his men.

Celise's gaze returned to the empty fields at the side of the road, watching white butterflies flit about the wildflowers. Her fingers curled around the edge of her seat as her mind traveled back to the night before. She could still see the glow of Elias's ghost sword, crackling with silver and blue power, as he battled the daemon. Could still feel the brush of stubble against her cheek as his lips met hers in the darkness.

She wondered what the next leg of their journey might entail.

Bloomheather Crossing was a quiet jewel of a town nestled among three different vineyards. Neat rows of twisting grapevines covered the hills around the town like a woven basket. Harvest had just begun, and Celise saw ox-drawn wagons filled with crates and tools parked along the rows of espaliered grapes. The sun was setting, and the farmhands were just finishing their work for the day.

Although Bloomheather Crossing was merely a small burg—no more than a few intersections of cobbled streets and gabled rooftops—it thrived with a self-assured charm. Ditches next to the road overflowed with blue-petaled bloomheather, the town's namesake. Its crisp, clean scent lingered in the air.

As the sun began its descent across the deep, cool sky, the streets remained crowded with people. Celise's carriage struggled to make it through the handful of intersections to reach the train platform, where they would continue their journey to Castleberry City. Elias and his soldiers intervened several times, forcing pedestrians to wait for their carriages to pass.

The train platform was a slate-stone affair with ornate lanterns and a modest, wrought-iron clock tower that struck the hours of the day with a deep, melodic chime. Heavy burlap canvases covered the platform where passengers could wait in the shade. It was more crowded than Celise expected, and she saw a dozen carriages lining the street across from the train tracks. She recognized a crowd of upper-class passengers already gathered beneath the awnings, dressed in bright silks and tailored finery. It looked like the Dhastel family weren't the only Blackwood guests with first-class tickets on the train.

Perhaps because of this, Elias directed their carriage to the very end of the platform, which was more private, and sent off his men to wait at a tavern across the street.

The clock began to chime, marking five o'clock in the evening, as Celise's carriage came to a halt. Their train would be arriving in just a few minutes. As the driver untied their luggage and placed it on the ground, she battled her way out of the cramped carriage box. She pushed past her sisters to take a bit of space and fresh air. The last hour of their journey had been stiflingly dull, the carriage humid and unpleasant, and Katrina's mood increasingly foul. Celise didn't know how she was going to endure another two days of forced proximity with her siblings. She yearned for the comfort of the Dhastel stables. Even the smell of horse dung seemed preferable to another two days of choking on Katrina's perfume.

Celise spotted her stepmother and father climbing out of the carriage behind them. Marcella's high-pitched voice was already carrying across the train platform: "Do you have our tickets? Why can't you answer me? I told you to keep them on hand. Didn't you put them in your wallet?"

Celise watched her father check the pockets of his vest and coat. "I recall placing them just here. . . ."

Celise walked in the opposite direction, away from Marcella, before her stepmother could notice her. She scanned the platform for Elias, trying to quell the desperate squeeze in her stomach. She told herself she needed a few minutes of peace and quiet before enduring the next leg of her journey, but she yearned to stand in his presence again.

For the moment, she didn't see him anywhere nearby.

"A basket of moonberries or a jar of lemon preserves, my lady?" a merchant called to her from the edge of the platform. The young man stood before a wooden stall filled with fruit baskets, baked goods, and crates of mason jars full of preserves. "May I interest you in a sweet treat for your train ride? Or perhaps a gift for a lover back home?"

"Oh . . . I . . . ." Celise's cheeks turned pink.

"She won't be sending home any gifts to a lover," a deep, raspy voice came from her side. "But I will send her off with a basket of moonberries and a bag of honeyed biscuits."

The merchant ducked into a deep bow, almost hitting his head on the table.

"Yes, of course, Your Grace! Thank you for your patronage."

Celise turned to gaze at Elias Blackwood. It was a long way to look up. He stood at ease in his dark blue greatcoat, his hands clasped behind him, his hair mussed from the long ride, and his boots smudged with dust from the road. He looked a bit weary and ruffled, but none the worse for wear.

He glanced down at her, meeting her gaze. "Is there anything else you would like?"

Celise didn't know what to say. She couldn't ask the Duke of Gravenmere to buy her biscuits at a farmer's stall—could she?

"No, thank you, this is more than enough, Your Grace," she stuttered, slipping into servile speech, a force of habit.

She winced.

Elias raised an eyebrow.

The merchant handed them a basket laden with treats. Celise thought she saw quite a few extra bags of biscuits and a small jar of honey hidden amid the plump, pebble-sized moonberries.

"Here you are, my lady," the young man said.

"Oh, thank you," Celise murmured. She reached to take the bag, but Elias grabbed it first, his arms longer than hers. He handed the boy a few coins. As she watched the copper chips exchange hands, she felt a bit self-conscious.

"Really, Your Grace, this is too much. . . ."

"Is it?" Elias asked. "It's just a handful of biscuits and a few berries."

"I mean to say, you don't need to trouble yourself—"

"It's no trouble." He gazed at her with a piercing quality that made her tremble. In the bright sunlight, her veil of nobility began to slip, and she cast her eyes down, hunching her shoulders. The spell of Gravenmere broken, she was suddenly returned to her lowly status as a stable-hand, standing before one of the highest lords in the realm.

Surely, he could see that?

"I believe you still have my coat," he pointed out in a dry voice.

"Oh! I do. Um, I'm sorry, it's in my trunk. I was going to return it to you, but we left the castle before I could. . . ." Celise glanced around, wondering where their bags had gotten to. Then, down the platform, she spotted a familiar-looking gray trunk being loaded onto the train. She gulped.

"I can fetch it if you'll wait for a moment—"

"No need, you may keep it," Elias said, a glint of amusement in his eyes.

"Keep it?"

"Yes. To remember me by."

"Oh."

"Wear it, should you wish. It's good luck."

"I . . . I couldn't do that . . . ."

"Whyever not?" His smile widened. "It suits you."

Celise didn't know what to say. Her jaw hung open. She imagined she looked as stupid as she felt.

"I also wanted to give you this."

He held out his hand, offering her a leather-bound book. She took it curiously. The black cover was worn with age. The sides of the pages were dusted in gold leaf. It looked valuable, perhaps a first edition of a classic.

"What's this?"

"It's a novel about horses. The story of a horse's life, actually. It's written from the horse's perspective."

"Really? Then I will be sure to enjoy it."

"There are a few chapters of political commentary in the middle. You can skip those. I always do."

Celise gazed at the title along the binding. The cursive script was hard to decipher. She wasn't a very strong reader, and she hadn't tackled a full novel in a long while. Reluctant to reveal her ignorance, she pretended to open the book and glance over one of the pages. Then she closed it, once again shy. She didn't know what to make of the gift. Did it mean he wanted to see her again?

She looked up at him. Their eyes met, his gaze glinting, a half-smile curling about his lips. The hiss of steam from the train and the platform's hubbub faded into the background. She knew people recognized him—she had seen several groups pause to look in their direction—but at that moment, she didn't care. His features became her sole focus.

He reached out a hand. He pinched her chin between his thumb and forefinger, effectively capturing her head and holding her still. He searched her gaze, not quite asking for permission, though giving her a chance to pull away if she wished. She didn't.

Then, with hooded eyes full of unnameable heat, he dipped his head down and placed a kiss on her mouth.

Celise's heart thundered in her chest. The softness of his mouth startled her. It was only her second kiss, and she didn't really know what to do. At first her lips were stiff and awkward. He sensed her shyness and took control, gently nibbling at her bottom lip, teasing her until her jaw relaxed. Then he went deeper.

Her breath caught. His tongue slid against hers, not deep enough to drown her, but enough to express his need. His hand cupped her jaw: possessive, firm. *Mine.*

If anyone on the train platform doubted who she was—who she belonged to—now they knew.

Celise melted forward. She moaned softly, greedily, startling herself.

Encouraged by that small, breathy sound, Elias angled her head farther back, deepening the kiss, effectively stealing her wits and silencing her thoughts. Celise's head went completely empty. A beautiful heat curled through her belly. A flush grew in her cheeks. The sweet sensations he drew from her mouth overwhelmed her senses. Her ears were burning, the top of her head tingling, her fingers going numb. She could feel his mana. It tickled her nose, spilling into her through their shared breath, heating her blood. Was it possible for him to share his mana with her? The flicker of thought opened up a new world she had never before considered.

What happened to a Luminary's mana when they fell in love?

Was it shared? Gifted to one another as she breathed in his oxygen?

Her hands curled into the lapels of his jacket. How could he express so much through a simple touch? No longer did he seem cold and unapproachable. She curled closer against his powerful body, seeking the shelter of his arms.

In status and rank they were worlds apart—yet in this, they fully connected.

Seconds passed by, stacking up to an inappropriate amount of time for a public embrace. But she held on. When he began to straighten, she leaned forward, stubborn, her hand clutching the lapel of his jacket.

She sensed his smile.

Please . . . she felt the words pass through their joined lips. *Please don't let me go.* She didn't want to return to the Dhastel ranch. She wanted to remain in his embrace forever.

Then she realized—the engagement wasn't a farce. Whether by fate, chance, or accident—*this* was real. The duke had chosen her to be his bride. She didn't know why. It didn't make sense. But if he wanted her, she didn't think she could refuse him.

She didn't *want* to refuse him.

Except she needed to breathe—needed to take a breath.

She finally pulled away with a soft, reluctant gasp. Elias's hand went to her face, gently brushing a strand of raspberry hair behind her ear. His thumb stroked across her cheek as he cupped her face. "Better?" he murmured.

"Yes."

"Let's not be strangers to each other."

"Alright."

"Take your medicine on the train. Don't put it off."

"I will."

"Good."

She found herself gazing up into the duke's secretive silver eyes. Eyes that she recognized; eyes that she trusted. She thought of the thieves outside of Gravenmere Castle and her abduction. How she stole his horse and ran off with his coat. How he mistook her for a spy. His knowing gaze met her own, sharing those secrets, and a complete conversation passed between them in a single glance.

I don't know you well, but I know I was meant to meet you.

Despite herself, Celise subconsciously raised a hand to her mouth, pressing her fingers against her lips in memory of their kiss.

Elias watched her movements, a spark of fire igniting his gaze.

Then the train whistle shrieked across the platform, shattering the moment.

Lady Marcella's voice was the next sound to interrupt them: "Come, Celise! It's time to board. We've made it this far; let's not miss the train." She bustled up to Celise's side and grabbed her by the upper arm, interrupting her brief, intense moment with the duke. "Decorum and decency! We are *in public.* Don't make such a spectacle of yourself, girl. It's improper for a young lady!" Then Marcella beamed at the duke, showing the whites of her teeth. "My goodness, did His Grace buy you all of this? What a kind gesture! Katrina and Heather just love honeyed biscuits! This will make the train ride much more enjoyable. You really shouldn't have, Elias. Thank you for your generosity."

Marcella reached for the bag in the duke's hands, but Elias jerked it away.

She stopped cold.

Celise flinched as well, sensing Marcella's indignation.

Instead, Elias motioned to Dasha, who stood a tactful distance away on the platform. The dark-haired maid quickly approached them and took the heavy paper bag out of Elias's hands, bowing as she did so.

"Please ensure my betrothed is provided for on her ride home," Elias instructed Dasha, who nodded with wide eyes. "I entrust you with her care."

"Yes, Your Grace," Dasha bowed again.

Then Elias turned back to Marcella, who still looked pale. "I will have to visit your estate presently, Lady Dhastel, to discuss the terms of the engagement with your husband."

"The terms . . . of the engagement . . . of course," Marcella said with a crooked, utterly false smile. "We will look forward to it. Please pass along our gratitude to your father. It was a charming weekend. Very . . . *eventful.* I mean, *wonderful.* We are *so happy* for our girl." Marcella seemed incapable of looking at Celise directly, so she smiled at the hedges that bordered the train platform.

Elias raised an eyebrow. Then he turned back to Celise.

"I suppose this is goodbye for now," he said.

"Yes," she agreed. She couldn't think of a single thing to say—no charming joke or witty remark. He seemed to sense her insecurity and took her hand.

"Read the book. We can discuss it when we next meet. I will write to you."

"Yes," Celise repeated, feeling more stupid than ever before.

Then the train whistle blew a second time. "Last call for boarding!" the conductor yelled.

Marcella rushed off to find Lord Dhastel, with Dasha following close behind. Elias caught Celise by the elbow and placed her arm in his. Then he strolled with her across the platform, escorting her down the long line of passenger cars to the first-class carriage. Celise tried to ignore the gawking passengers staring at them from the public cars down the platform. Elias was easily recognizable due to his black mask, and news had probably traveled across the countryside by now of their engagement. Bloomheather Crossing was not far from Gravenmere Castle, and guests had been arriving all day to catch the train.

"Until next we meet, Lady Celise," Elias said as he helped her onto the steps of the first-class car. He pressed the back of her hand to his lips and held her eyes for several seconds too long. Then he turned and retreated across the platform to where the other members of the Daemonguard were watering their horses across the road.

Celise watched him go, her gaze lingering on his broad shoulders, his tousled hair, and his long coat flapping in the wind. That strange, fluttering warmth filled her chest again. She wanted to leap off the train and run after him, but she forced herself to watch him from a distance. Some part of her feared this might be the last time she saw the duke. But the heavy weight of the book in her hand reassured her of his intentions. It was tangible proof of his promise to see her again.

She clutched the book to her chest, her gaze still locked on his retreating silhouette. He was aloof and brash, moody and tempestuous, and yet . . . did she *like* the Mad Dog duke?

"Come, Celise, stop gaping after His Grace like a randy scullery maid; you're embarrassing yourself," Marcella snapped, emerging from the depths of the car with a bundle of train tickets in hand. "Our cabin is this way. Pick up your feet."

The attendant took their tickets and escorted them to a private booth: a little pocket-sized room near the front of the train with cushioned seats that folded out into sleeping cots for the evening. It was cramped but more comfortable than the wooden coach seats, and most importantly, it was private. Dasha was not present. She had been sent off to the cheaper cars where the servants traveled, forced to leave the bag of moonberries and honey biscuits unattended. As Celise entered the cabin, she saw that Heather and Katrina were already snacking on the sugary treats. Marcella reached for a biscuit before taking her place next to her husband.

Celise was not offered any.

She sighed. It looked like her family had already stolen Elias's gift right out of her hands.

In either case, she would not give up her bouquet of flowers with its hidden Starlight Dahlia. She planned to put the rare dahlia in a vase on her windowsill, where it could bloom under the stars. She held the bouquet protectively in her lap as she squeezed into a seat next to the window.

"You should throw that away, Celise. It takes up too much room, and it will rot before we get home," Marcella said, indicating the flowers.

Celise felt her heart plummet—she thought she might be sick.

Unexpectedly, her father came to her defense. “Let the girl have her roses, Marcella,” he grumbled. “What would His Grace think if he discovered you made her throw them out?”

Marcella’s jaw clicked shut. Celise gazed at her father in shock. Lord Dhastel didn’t look at her. He almost seemed uncomfortable with his own intervention. He adjusted his jacket and picked up his newspaper, ignoring the ladies just as he did at the dinner table back home. He opened the paper wide and disappeared behind the printed page.

With a pale face, Celise found herself confronted with the newspaper’s front-page headline: **"The Mad Dog Bites Again: New Engagement Announced to Windhaven Heiress."**

Beneath the title was a fuzzy, black-and-white photo of Celise standing before the ballroom in her tattered dress, the blood stains on her bodice softened by the bloom of the camera’s lens, while the duke stood irreproachable by her side.

She hiccuped.

Marcella didn’t bring up the bouquet again.

Celise was startled by the picture on the paper's front page. *The Mad Dog bites again?* Even the paper's headline sounded skeptical of their engagement—like she was the victim of a wild dog attack! How terrible! She didn't want to read the article—didn't want to know the reporter's take on the evening. There was no way to stop the rumors and speculation from spreading. By tomorrow morning, the story of her engagement to Elias would be the talk of the kingdom.

Her mind flew ahead to the Dhastel manor. What would the servants at Windhaven Ranch think? The manor would be in an uproar of excitement. She could already imagine Mordwen's gleeful smile as the housekeeper bragged about the outcome of the weekend. The old bitty's oracle deck would be given full credit for Celise's engagement; many other servants would probably ask her for readings. Steffie would point to her skills as a seamstress, claiming her design for the silk dress caught the duke's eye. Mr. Talisworth would shed a tear of pride.

Dasha would be in her element—she wouldn't tire of telling the story of the gala over and over, even if half the details changed with each retelling.

It was enough to make Celise smile, and she buried her little grin in her bouquet. She missed her friends—and she couldn't wait to be back in her cozy bedroom above the stables.

The train's whistle blew, and with a gasp of steam, the cars rolled forward.

Celise settled back in her seat. Outside the window, a single crow took off from the platform and followed along next to the train, wings flapping, racing against the wind.

She watched the crow fly with furious wing flaps as rows of grapevines passed by outside the window. Although Gravenmere Castle had long since disappeared from view, her eyes flickered to the distant horizon, where she imagined those high curtain walls standing in the distance. In her mind, she walked through the decadent halls of the Blackwood estate. She thought of the Zodiac Gardens, the ballroom, the Brazian twins and the many new faces she had met. As she reflected on her adventures at Gravenmere Castle, it was hard to believe so much had happened in such a short weekend.

Truly, the gala had been a clandestine event.

Although she was returning home to Windhaven Ranch, she had a feeling her life would be far different now than it was before. But she wasn't afraid. Instead, a buoyant sense of hope remained in her heart.

Her eyes followed the crow alongside the train, who so arduously tried to keep pace with the thundering steam engine. Despite its struggles, the crow continued to fall farther and farther behind, until it banked its wings and soared out across the rows of vineyards, heading toward the sunset.

Fin . . . for now.

VIMSPRING

Brightspell—Days 65-96

Constellation: The Fawn
Attributes: Hope and New Beginnings
Zodiac Flower: Glowbell
Tradition: *Vision Fasting* – priestesses, daemonguard and channelers renew mana gifts.
Characters: Heather Dhastel's birthday.

Description of the Fawn

The eternal optimist, children born in the month of Brightspell are notoriously bright-eyed and bushy-tailed. The Fawn is the perfect season to begin new projects with hope for the future. People under the "Fawn" zodiac are considered pleasant, innocent, and prefer peacemaking to arguing or fighting. Sometimes this means they are too easygoing and appear to have no backbone or personal values, but really, they just want everyone to get along.

Description of the Glowbell

A small, dainty flower shaped like a little bell that glows in the late evening or early morning, this sprawling perennial prefers shady spots like the crooks of stone walls and gaps beneath tree roots. It's rare to find in the wild, as its delicate stems are easily crushed underfoot, so it tends to grow in hidden areas with little traffic. It's considered good luck for travelers.

Budreach—Days 97-129

Constellation: The Eagle
Attributes: The Seeker, The Observer
Zodiac Flower: Bloodroot Iris
Tradition: *Valestra's Rebirth*—spring parades, planting season begins.

Description of the Eagle

The Eagle is the messenger of the zodiac, bringing tidings of things to come. Children born in Budreach are often more focused on the future rather than the present. Sometimes this can lead them to have almost prophetic intuitions. However, it can be difficult to stay grounded. Characterized by an adventurous spirit, the eagle often experiences wanderlust and enjoys traveling to new places.

Description of Bloodroot Iris

Bloodroot Iris has a rich red color; even its stems and roots are red, which is where it gets its name. A popular medicinal plant in Forsynthian medicine, the roots are used as a cure-all for the people of Forsynthia. Its dried petals, when ground into tea, can lower fevers. Rich in iron and dust, it strengthens the blood while cleansing mana channels. It's also seen as a symbol of virility.

Greencall—Days 130-161

Constellation: The Cat
Attributes: Mischief, Creativity
Zodiac Flower: Crested Thistle
Tradition: Shrine maidens bless fields.

Description of The Cat

Children born under the constellation of The Cat are curious and mischievous by nature. Playful, spontaneous, and intelligent, they can sometimes come off as flaky or self-interested. As romantic partners, they only prefer closeness on their own terms and can withdraw when stressed out. The Cat zodiac relates to a popular children's tale in the Kingdom of Forsynthia. Legend has it that the first king often consulted his pet cat about matters of the kingdom. If the cat brought him a dead bird or a dead mouse the next day, he knew an enemy at court was plotting against him.

Description of Crested Thistle

With a long stem and bristling, orb-shaped flowers, crested thistle is a silver plant with a dainty, whimsical appearance. It grows to about three feet tall. Popular in gardens for its unique shape, this spurious puffball leaves small prickers in the hand if touched directly. The orb-like blossoms, although similar in appearance to dandelion puffs, are deceptively sharp and unpleasant. The Crested Thistle is one of the most recognizable flowers in Forsynthia and a common symbol of springtime.

ARDOURSOL

Sungilt—Days 162-192

Constellation: The Wolf
Attributes: Confidence, Energy
Zodiac Flower: The Abyssal Rose
Tradition: *Valestra's Hunt*—a great hunt in the Grapevine Mountains that celebrates Valestra.
Characters: *Katrina Dhastel's birthday.*

Description of The Wolf

One of the most coveted signs of the zodiac, children born under the sign of The Wolf are natural leaders and warriors. Bold, confident and aggressive, this zodiac can have difficulty managing its energy, sometimes burning "too hot" and collapsing in the summer heat. Children of The Wolf are notorious for their strong emotions and zealous convictions. Heastrong and passionate, Wolves often become the unofficial heads of their respective families or communities despite birth order or gender.

Description of The Abyssal Rose

The first month of Ardoursol is drenched in sunlight and marked by long, languid days. The Abyssal Rose is a stunning perennial that blooms from early Ardoursol to Hallowsin. A tenacious grower similar to blackberry vines, this powerful rose bush needs to be cut back each year. It can grow almost three feet over the course of a single season. It is the only flower to survive on the craggy cliffs close to the Abyss. Stubborn and strong-willed, it's believed that those born with the flower of the Abyssal Rose are meant to stand out from their peers. Due to its resilient nature, the Abyssal Rose is used as a sigil by some factions of the Daemonguard.

Solmere—Days 193-223

Constellation: The Hourglass
Attributes: Patience, Good Timing
Zodiac Flower: Gilded Lupin
Tradition: *Skyglow*—midsummer nights glow like days due to skydust.
Characters: Mordwen's birthday.

Description of The Hourglass

People born under the constellation of The Hourglass are seen to embody saintly characteristics such as patience, discernment, and tactfulness. By nature more contemplative than other signs in Ardoursol, the character of The Hourglass is one of long walks through languid golden evenings, late-night gatherings, and reading a good book by the beach. Although known for their patience and ability to see "all sides" of an argument, children of The Hourglass can become obstinate and moralizing if they feel their values are compromised.

Description of Gilded Lupin

A flower symbolizing royalty, wealth and success, Gilded Lupin stands at a striking height of six feet tall. With long stems and giant, cone-shaped flowers of bright gold or deep indigo blue, it creates a stunning addition to any garden. Popular at weddings and official ceremonies, people born with this birthflower are thought to be noble, upright, trustworthy and righteous. Gilded Lupin is also thought to bring good fortune, especially in finances. Some people plant Gilded Lupin in front of their business or home to attract wealth.

Amberfen—Days 224-255

Constellation: The Twin Otters
Attributes: Friendship
Zodiac Flower: Tideweed
Tradition: *Kingdom Day*—bonfires and fireworks to celebrate the founding of Forsynthia.
Characters: Dasha's birthday.

Description of The Twin Otters

The Twin Otters is the only zodiac featuring two distinct figures joined as one. The two otters are usually shown floating on their backs holding hands. The zodiac symbolizes friendship, brotherhood, sisterhood, deep family bonds or business relationships. People born under the constellation of The Twin Otters are loyal to their family and community, tend to make warm and loving friends, and benefit from lifelong friendships. On the other hand, children born under The Twin Otters can struggle when they are alone. They do not like solitude and prefer to spend their time around people or pets.

Description of Tideweed

This tall reed grows on the banks of the Blush River. It symbolizes an easygoing, calm and relaxed character. Simple, straightforward and untroubled, it bends whichever way the river flows. Tideweed has a slightly sweet, mellow flavor similar to a mild onion, and it's used in soups, pancakes and curries around the Kingdom of Forsynthia.

HALLOWSIN

Duskwane—Days 256-287

Constellation: The Lantern
Attributes: Illumination, Giftedness
Zodiac Flower: Ashfeather Bloom
Tradition: During the month, shrine maidens offer fortunes for alms.
Character: Elias Blackwood's birthday.

Description of The Lantern

During the first month of Hallowsin, the days grow shorter and colder, and summer activities are set aside for quieter pursuits. Duskwane is the month that harvest begins. Children born under the constellation of The Lantern are thought to carry special spiritual illumination and giftedness. This zodiac sign is associated with strong mana channelers. Thoughtful and introspective by nature, people of The Lantern tend to be night owls, artists, dreamers and philosophers.

Description of Ashfeather Bloom

Commonly seen at funerals, Ashfeather Bloom symbolizes grief and spirituality. A tall flower with lacy, floating plumes at the end of each stalk, it's found in swamps and marshes around Gravenmere province. Despite its delicate appearance, this birthflower has a morbid reputation. For reasons unknown, Ashfeathers tends to grow in clusters over graves. Finding a large mound in the middle of the woods indicates a corpse might be buried nearby.

Fallowmere—Days 228-319

Constellation: The Veil
Attributes: Madness, Funerals
Zodiac Flower: Lumenbloom
Tradition: *Daemon Night*—a night of chaotic revelry against the Daemon King. Meant to honor the dead.

Description of The Veil

Mist rolls in from the ocean to shroud the royal city of Astravelle during Fallowmere. This month is considered more ominous and sinister than Duskwane. Dedicated to the Daemonguard, the Abyss, and the ongoing battle against the Daemon King, Fallowmere is a time of madness, funerals, midnight vigils and chaotic revelry. Children of The Veil are thought to be "a little strange." Secretive about their inner worlds, they are slow to make friends and prefer to spend time in libraries or solo walks through the woods.

Description of Lumenbloom

Pale blue with a faint inner glow, this trumpet-shaped, vining flower glows when mana channelers are near, responding to the mana in their Luminous bodies. Thought to be "the flower of the Skytouched," it's commonly seen growing on trellises near a noble manorhouse. Considered a medicinal plant, a tincture distilled from its petals stimulates the mana body and helps it heal. It's also used to identify Luminous newborns. The flowers glow when placed on a baby's forehead above their Sky terminal.

Hearthbrim—Days 224-255

Constellation: The Guardian
Attributes: Duty, Protection
Zodiac Flower: Shadethistle
Tradition: *Darkwell:* a night when the Maddening Moon is alone in the sky and ghosts are thought to walk the land. Darkwell marks the end of harvest season and the beginning of winter. Tournaments in the royal city of Astravelle celebrate a successful harvest.

Description of The Guardian

Hearthbrim signals the end of harvest, when most farmers quit working in the fields and gather around the fire with their families. Often depicted as a man wearing archaic armor holding a long shield, The Guardian zodiac symbolizes strength, fortitude and protection. Children born under The Guardian are often the first to stand up for a cause. Fueled by a strong sense of duty, they protect those closest to them. They make loving fathers, strong mothers, and reliable warriors.

Description of Shadethistle

The only birthflower of the zodiac that is poisonous, Shadethistle grows in open fields and pastureland around the Kingdom of Forsynthia. Its acidic leaves, once ingested, cause numbness or tingling in the hands and feet. Too large a dose can cause seizures, hallucinations or respiratory problems. Its bitter flavor symbolizes envy or repressed anger. According to Forsynthian lore, Shadethistle was historically used by spurned lovers to poison their rivals. This plant is often associated with the darker side of romance: obsession and jealousy.

Brumadir

Stargrave—Days 352-384

Constellation: The Star
Attributes: Destiny, Fate
Zodiac Flower: Starlight Dahlia
Tradition: *The Last Spark* – a celestial event where shooting stars fill the sky over the Kingdom of Forsynthia, thought to be a sign of the mother goddess, Valestra.
Dimsleep – the longest night of the year.
**Celise Dhastel's birthday.*

Description of The Star

Stargrave contains the longest night of the year, Dimsleep, which is a night usually spent around the fire telling stories and eating sweets. A time of darkness and intense cold, children born in Stargrave are thought to be "bad luck" due to high infant mortality rates. The constellation of The Star carries an aura of mystique. At once bright and shining yet also cold and mysterious, children born under The Star are whimsical, thoughtful, creative and often gifted in some way. They are thought to be "people of destiny."

Description of The Starlight Dahlia

Symbolizing fate and destiny, the starlight dahlia is the rarest flower in all of Forsynthia and perhaps all of Agea. It only blooms under starlight and its white flowers are only visible at night. When gifted to a new bride-to-be, the Starlight Dahlia is thought to symbolize soulmates and a fated love that will survive the test of time, even carrying over from one life to the next.

Frostfall—Days 1-32

Constellation: The Phoenix
Attributes: Wisdom, Resurrection **The New Year!*
Zodiac Flower: Solaris Lily
Tradition: *Valestra's Light* – New Year's celebration! Paper lanterns are lit for the new year and sent into the air with prayers and wishes, believed to be carried to the stars where Valestra lives.

Description of The Phoenix

The solar new year lands in Frostfall towards the middle of the month. Although the middle of winter, this makes Frostfall *both the first month and the last month* of the solar year on Nilos. The constellation of The Phoenix is a symbol of resurrection. Children born under The Phoenix are thought to be wise, discerning and serious. Favoring tradition, they are seen as "old souls" who lead by example. They bring honor to their families and assist their parents in old age.

Description of the Solaris Lily

A symbol of grace and balance, the Solaris Lily is a boon in the winter months when most flowers fade. Its large purple flowers fill the air with fragrant, calming perfume. Elegant and refined, those with the Solaris Lily birthflower are thought to have good taste. Forsynthia's queen loves Solaris Lily so much that she dedicated an entire courtyard to them at the royal palace.

Thawmere—Days 33-64

Constellation: The River
Attributes: Awakening, Inspiration
Zodiac Flower: Ironstem Aster
Tradition: Skydust Vigil – citizens wear dark blue to honor the Daemonguard.

Description of The River

Thought to be a month of awakening, Thawmere is usually a time when snow begins to melt in the Grapevine Mountains and rivers swell to bursting around the Kingdom of Forsynthia. Whether surging forward or going with the flow, children born under the constellation of The River are quick-witted and silver-tongued. A zodiac associated with famous actors and orators, The River can symbolize a person who has a gift for inspiring people to action.

Description of Ironstem Aster

Perhaps the strongest plant in Forsynthia, Ironstem Aster cannot be cut by everyday knives and tools. Only special blades developed by artificers can slice through their "iron" stalks. Popular for walking sticks, poles and crutches, the Ironstem Aster symbolizes sturdiness, dependability, and "backbone." People born with this zodiac symbol are not easily swayed.

Glossary

- **Artificing**—the art of developing, refining and applying different mixtures of "dust" to different objects to create items used by mana channelers.

- **Astravelle**—the royal city and capital of Forsynthia.

- **Castleberry City**—a major city and popular tourist location close to Windhaven Ranch.

- **Chip**—the lowest unit of Forsynthian currency. In Castleberry City, servants take their raw dough to the market square where, for six chips or a half-dhram, a baker will cook the rounds in a communal oven. 10 lbs of flour is equal to 12 loaves (4 to 5 days of food for the average laborer), which is equal to 1 dhram, which is roughly 1 chip per loaf. The average laborer has to make a half-dhram a day to eat, so "minimum wage" would be 6 chips or a half-dhram for a day's labor. (◔◡◔)

- **Dhram**—a form of currency equal to twelve chips. Minimum wage remains at a half-dhram for a day's labor (or six chips.)

- **Dimlit**—an adjective used to describe a person who is "stupid" or "dull." For example, "You *dimlit* fool!"

- **Dresengard**—a kingdom located to the north of Forsynthia. Despite Dresengard's vast landmass, it is not very populated because of the harsh winters. Most of its people live in small fortress towns spaced days apart from each other. Although Dresengard claims territory up to the Northern Pole, most of the land is uninhabitable for humans and occupied by land whales, mammoths and ice dragons. The people of Dresengard value sportsmanship above all else: fairness, honor and amiability between rivals. Famous for their war machines called "Dreads," the people of Dresengard are known to be powerful mana casters. With the advent of Bratzian dust and Dresengard's access to machine oil, they've created massive mechanical walking suits, with early models appearing as cauldron-bodied spiders or burrowing centipedes.

- **Dullspark**—a derogatory noun like "dimwit." A name used for a stupid or thoughtless person.

- **Dunslug**—a noun, similar sounding to "dunce." This is the everyday term for commoners who do not have mana. Although not meant as an insult, it carries a context of "useless" or "low skill."

- **Dust**—similar to "frit" used by potters, "dust" is a special mixture of Skydust and other elements that, when applied to metals or ceramics, gives the item a special magical quality. Artificers in Gigas develop different mixtures of "dust" to create different kinds of shined items and weapons.

- **Galleon**—a form of currency equal to four dhrams (or forty-eight chips.)

- **Goldlark**—a form of currency equal to three galleons (twelve dhrams or 576 chips.) A goldlark is a store of national or sovereign wealth primarily used as a means of transaction for infrastructure improvements.
- **Gravenmere**—a province of Forsynthia overseen by the Blackwood family.
- **Gravenmere Castle**—the ancestral home of the Blackwood family.
- **Griffix**—small, domesticated griffons kept as pets by the Forsynthian nobility. Cute, fluffy and mischievous, their intelligence is debatable.
- **Hellion**—a special breed of horse used by the Daemonguard that is specifically bred by the Dhastel family on Windhaven Ranch. Hellions have notoriously stormy temperaments. The breed is inspired by Warlander stallions or Belgian-Quarterhorse crosses.
- **Illysea**—an island kingdom off the coast of Forsynthia roughly the size of Japan. The small island nation is in negotiations with Forsynthia to become a province rather than an independent kingdom, and their princess is betrothed to the Forsynthian prince. Some of the islands are friendly, while others are suspicious of outsiders. Illysea's "Red Island" is home to a fierce but small cult believing in the End Times since the meteor hit. Their people worship the Three-Headed Goddess of Birth, Life and Death. They subsist mostly off of fish, seaweed and grains.
- **Kinder Moon**—the smaller of Nilos's twin moons, it appears as a friendly silver orb in the sky. *Stylistic choice:* the word "Kinder" was used to both indicate the sweetness of the little moon's

appearance and its "childlike" quality being the smaller moon. *("Kinder" in German meaning "children.")*

- **Lady's Walker**—a specialty breed of horse bred for fine ladies on Windhaven Ranch, walkers have a smooth gait and calm temperament. Most Lady's Walkers are around thirteen to fourteen hands high, with thirteen hands being the most desirable height. They come in colors ranging from white to cream.

- **Lightless**—a neutral adjective indicating a person without mana. Can be insulting in certain contexts.

- **Luminous / Luminary**—the upper-class name for those born with mana-channeling, especially from elite families.

- **Maddening Moon**—the "Maddening Moon" is the second of Nilos's two moons. It appears as a large golden orb in the sky, not unlike a harvest moon, with a certain ominous quality. When the Maddening Moon is alone in the sky and the Kinder Moon has set, it's believed to trigger madness and delusion in susceptible people. A common Forsynthian phrase is, *"I can't be blamed—it happened under the Maddening Moon!"*

- **Mana**—a mysterious power that infuses living beings on Nilos.

- **Mana body**—a network of special channels that exist as an "energy body" within the physical body.

- **Sera'naya**—A kingdom bordering the Abyss, Sera'naya (The Jeweled Land) is a mysterious place of sultans, veiled princesses and lost cities. Their main exports are spices, salt and rare jewels, and their people are known to be gifted horsemasters, musicians and dancers, with a natural penchant for rhythm and rhyme. Although modern living exists in the cities, desert tribes still wander the land, each with their own unique way of life. Earning trust in Sera'naya is difficult, but once gained, foreigners are invited into a vibrant culture filled with warmth and beauty.

- **Shined**—an adjective used to describe an object that's been enhanced by skydust. "Shined" objects are used by mana channelers to enhance and magnify their power.
- **Skydust**—ancient dust from a meteor that struck the planet Nilos ten thousand years ago. Skydust permeates the atmosphere of Nilos and has a profound effect upon its flora and fauna, changing the evolution of almost every species on the planet.
- **Skytouched**—the everyday common name for those born with mana-channeling.
- **Terminals**—nodes of the mana body where mana is pooled. Terminals exist up the spine to the crown of the head and in the palms of the hands. (This is modeled after Vedic medicine.)
- **Valestra**—the Mother Goddess of Dust and Moon, Valestra is a divine feminine energy that oversees the fates of the people on Nilos. Her grand temple in the royal city of Astravelle houses the priestess class. Shrine maidens are more common in the countryside, with smaller temples or shrines serving most communities.
- **Windhaven Ranch**—the ancestral home of the Dhastel family. Their family's color is pale blue.

Letter from the Author

Writing a Victorian Fantasy Novel

Hello there, wayfarers! Greetings from the other side of the page.

I *really* must commend you for finishing *The Skydust Duke*. This novel has seen many different drafts since its inception in August 2023 (*yes, I went back to check the original file!*) Inspired by *My Happy Marriage* and other Cinderella retellings, I think Celise and Elias's adventure at Gravenmere Castle landed exactly where it needed to be.

I did not set out to write a Victorian Fantasy novel. Rather, I had an image in my mind of Elias driving Celise through the countryside in an old-school automobile, perhaps to a county fair (which did not make it into this first book in the series). This spark of creativity led to research into the history of the automobile, which led to women's fashion (such as the advent of printed cottons), military uniforms, forage caps, plague masks, and graveyard luncheons. That's when I landed at Gaslamp Fantasy. For those who are unfamiliar with the genre (as I was), Gaslamp Fantasy is the more whimsical, magical cousin of Steampunk. From there, I landed on Victorian Fantasy due to the "high fantasy" feeling of some plot elements—however, the two subgenres overlap quite a bit.

For those of you who are familiar with my previous work, *The Cat's Eye Chronicles,* you know I write almost exclusively high fantasy. Some of my biggest inspirations are Terry Goodkind, Terry Brooks, Brian Jacques, Juliet Marillier and Robin Hobb. So, writing in a different century with different technology was quite a challenge!

Once I knew I was writing a Victorian Fantasy novel, I absolutely wanted to add in some Victorian-era Easter eggs! I really wanted to find ways to "ground" Celise's story in a relatable century, since there is so much about the world of Nilos that is *new,* such as the seasons, the months in the year, the Abyss, skydust, and so forth.

Here are a few Victorian-era Easter eggs that I have hidden in the book for you to enjoy:

1. A subtle reference to the classic novel *Black Beauty* appears at the end of the book: not that Elias *gives* Celise a copy of *Black Beauty* to read, but it's implied that it *might* be a book *similar* to *Black Beauty*. I thought it would be a fun little wink for those who are in the know! (*Black Beauty* was a beloved book my father used to read to me as a child.)

2. Fencing was considered a fashionable sport among ladies of the upper class in the late 19th century, a nod to the progress of women's status in the later Victorian era (Women's Suffrage began in the 1850's.)

3. Although published in the pre-Victorian era in 1818, Mary Shelly's famous *Frankenstein* is foundational to Gothic literature. Since Elias was resurrected from the dead, I thought it would be fun to sprinkle in a bit of that Gothic flavor. Not only is Elias's body one of borrowed parts (ie. Kiran's arm and possibly more we have yet to see), but the genius doctor who restored Elias to life is named Maeve Shelley, who intentionally shares the same initials as *Frankenstein*'s author.

4. Leaning a bit forward outside of the Victorian era, the idea of a masked war hero was inspired by the compassionate work of Anna Coleman Ladd, an American sculptor working in France, who created lifelike masks for soldiers whose faces were mutilated in WWI. Her lifelike masks allowed disfigured soldiers to enjoy public life without fear of ridicule or rejection. If you haven't looked up her work, it's definitely worth checking out.

5. Although tarot cards were invented in the Renaissance as a casual game, they were heavily rebranded and occultized in the 19th century, which is when they became popular for mysticism. Mordwen tells Celise's fortune using a deck of oracle cards, which was very trendy in Victorian England. Other occult curiosities such as seances, astrology and zodiacs were popular among the Victorians.

I'm sure if I dug around a bit more through my notes, I would find a half dozen more little Easter eggs to entertain you with. For me, the fun of worldbuilding a new series is researching history and reworking it into a fantasy setting. Otherwise, my imagination would be introducing sundials and harpsichords into an era meant for clocks and grand pianos! I truly believe these little details add an unquantifiable depth to a story.

Thank you for reading *The Skydust Duke* and I hope you will continue to follow the series. If you haven't read my high fantasy series, *The Cat's Eye Chronicles,* the first book *Sora's Quest* is permafree on Amazon and other major ebook retailers. If you enjoy strong heroines, treacherous journeys through magical lands, exciting battles and brooding assassins, you should give it a try. It might just become a new escape!

Thank you for reading my work, and it's been a pleasure to write for you!

The kindest regards,

T. L. Shreffler

Book 2: The Starlight Dahlia

Celise and Elias's story continues in the next book, The Starlight Dahlia, with a release date of June 2027.

With word of their engagement swiftly spreading around the kingdom, Celise and Elias find themselves faced with a new challenge: *courtship*. Celise doesn't know the first thing about *being courted by a duke*—and Elias is much more comfortable as a military commander than a paramour.

To complicate matters, Marcella and Katrina are bent on disrupting Celise's engagement, and the Dread Jackal is still on the loose. Elias has a lot of obstacles to overcome before he can claim his newly betrothed.

Join the author's mailing list to stay updated!

www.skydustkingdoms.com

Book Club Questions

I hope you enjoy discussing these questions with your reading group!

1. Did Celise find her courage?

2. What might the story be like reimagined from Katrina's perspective, with Katrina as the main heroine?

3. Was Mordwen's prophecy true or false?

4. Dasha is skeptical of Mordwen's fortune-telling, while Celise begins to believe in it by the end of the book. Do you consider yourself more like Dasha, or more like Mordwen? How do ideas like "fate" or "destiny" influence our daily lives?

5. Does Elias show signs of "toxic masculinity," or is he more of a brooding hero?

6. Why does Marcella dislike Celise so much?

7. Did Celise steal Katrina's fate?

8. Do you think Kiran is guilty of aiding the Dread Jackal? Or is he innocent?

Meet the Author

T. L. Shreffler grew up only a few blocks away from Warner Bros. and Disney studios in Burbank, CA, where she attended John Burroughs High School (class of 2006) and pursued an English degree from Cal State Northridge. Inspired by a creative community of friends, family and neighbors, she has dedicated herself to her creative goals since her teen years. She has been writing *The Cat's Eye Chronicles* and other works since she was 12 years old.

In 2020, she moved to Washington State and currently lives in Snohomish County with her family. She loves diversity, travel, and experiencing different cultures. She especially loves good coffee, rainstorms, small towns, big trees, and uncovering strange and eclectic artifacts while thrifting.

She holds a BA in Eloquence (English) and her poetry has been published in *Eclipse: A Literary Journal* and *The Northridge Review*. She is author of *The Cat's Eye Chronicles* (YA/Epic Fantasy), *The White* (a dragon-hunting YA adventure currently being reworked,) and her latest project, *Skydust Kingdoms.*

Keep in touch!

@catseyeauthor

Instagram – https://www.instagram.com/catseyeauthor
Facebook – https://www.facebook.com/tlshreffler/
Tiktok – https://www.tiktok.com/@catseyeauthor

SIGNED COPIES!
Tarot decks!
VISIT
T. L. SHREFFLER'S
AUTHOR STORE
BOOKISH STUFF!
Gifts & Things
authortlshreffler.etsy.com

T. L. Shreffler's Youtube Channel

https://www.youtube.com/@authortlshreffler

Other Books by T. L. Shreffler

Don't miss out on *The Cat's Eye Chronicles* by T. L. Shreffler! Published in 2012, her debut series has been beloved by fans and readers for over fifteen years. **Sora's Quest is permafree on Amazon!**

Winner of the SKOW Best Fantasy Award! *Perfect for fans of Sarah J. Maas, Cassandra Clare, and Tamora Pierce, this award-winning Fantasy adventure follows the journey of Sora Fallcrest on an action-packed quest to find her mother. She is joined by a party of intriguing characters: a thief, a mercenary, and a mysterious assassin. If you love high fantasy quests, enemies-to-lovers romance, plucky heroines, snarky side characters, and complex villains, this series is for you!*

Synopsis

Sora Fallcrest always dreamed of adventure, but as a member of the nobility, she learned the ways of a lady instead. Now seventeen, she is expected to choose a husband and marry. She plots to run away, but just as she is stepping out the door, she is kidnapped by a mysterious stranger!

Plunged into a world of magical races and forgotten lore, she finds herself at the mercy of a dangerous assassin: a man of few words haunted by a dark past. A powerful bloodmage pursues the assassin on a quest for revenge, and Sora is now caught in the middle. Her Cat's-Eye necklace is the only thing that can save the assassin's life, and he won't let her go until the bloodmage is defeated.

The Cat's-Eye necklace was given to Sora by her mother, who vanished shortly after Sora's birth. She always thought of it as a family heirloom. In truth, the Cat's-Eye necklace is an ancient weapon from the long-forgotten War of the Races, and its magic has the ability to steal souls. Can Sora learn to wield its power, or will the power wield her?

List of Fantasy Tropes

Coming-of-age adventure

enemies to lovers
slow-burn romance
kidnapping
strong female lead
brooding assassin hero
snarky sidekicks
traveling through dangerous lands
sword and sorcery
fantasy worldbuilding
magic systems
magical races & fantasy creatures
deep lore
action-adventure
sword fights
damsel in distress
emotionally complex villain

The Cat's Eye Chronicles Complete Series (In Order)

Sora's Quest (Book 1)
Viper's Creed (Book 2)
Volcrian's Hunt (Book 3)
Ferran's Map (Book 4)
Krait's Redemption (Book 5)
Cerastes' Curse (Book 6)
The Wanderer's Fate (Book 7) – coming November 2026!

www.ingramcontent.com/pod-product-compliance
Lightning Source LLC
LaVergne TN
LVHW010632110826
845149LV00014B/2834